CAGED ROYAL

THE KNIGHTS OF ECHOES COVE #3

LILY WILDHART

Caged Royal
The Knights of Echoes Cove #3
Copyright © 2022 Lily Wildhart

Editor: Encompass Press, LLC
Proofreader: Sassi's Editing Services
Interior Design: Wild Elegance Formatting

Caged Royal - Alternate Cover ed
ISBN-13 - 978-1-915473-04-2

It doesn't interest me who you know
or how you came to be here.
I want to know if you will stand in the center of the fire with me and
not shrink back.

PLAYLIST

Burn It All Down - PVRIS
Favourite Place - All Time Low
Strangers - Yours Truly
Heavenly - Broadside
Orchestra - Drew Ryn
That Way - Tate McRae
Foolish Believer - Broadside
When The Sky Falls Down - Yours Truly
Stitch Me Up - Point North
Nothing Left to Lose - Point North
CWJBHN - Jake Scott
I Wanted You - McKenna Breinholt
When You're Around - Jutes
Figure You Out - VOILA
Someone Else - Loveless
Lock Me Up - Paloma
Left You Instead - Taylor Acorn
Teardrops - Bring Me The Horizon

ONE

LINCOLN

"She's not here."

Three words is all it takes to shatter my already-spinning-out-of-control mind.

"Then where the fuck is she?" I growl down the line.

"I don't know, man. We're going back to her house to deal with that and check the security feed to see if there's anything on there we can use." Finley sounds like he's holding it together as well as I am.

Fuck.

I run a hand through my hair, tugging on it, hoping that the pain helps me ground myself. "Okay, keep me updated."

The sounds of doors slamming filter through the call, followed by an engine starting. I want to be with them, searching for her, but there's no way I can leave East.

I've never felt so torn in my entire fucking existence.

"Any updates on East?" Finn asks, sounding hollow as he puts me on loudspeaker.

"Not a fucking one. I'm just sitting here on my hands like a fucking idiot waiting for news."

I hate feeling this helpless. This isn't who I am. I'm the guy that fixes shit but this time as my world burns around me, I have nothing.

"Okay, let us know when you know anything, brother. And we'll keep you up to date too. They're both going to be okay."

I nod at his reassurances, even though he can't see me. "What if it wasn't the Knights that took her?"

"It doesn't matter who took her, we're going to get her back."

I can't help but wonder if this was her stalker. If whoever is behind all of that is involved with the Knights, then it makes sense that they'd have a team to call on. The Knights have made it more than clear that they want her in, so it's definitely the most obvious explanation.

"Check the bodies for the mark. Then we'll know where to start at least."

"Consider it done."

"I should call Harrison." I sigh, the idea about as appealing as pulling my own teeth.

The approaching squeak of sneakers on the shiny floor draws my gaze up. Seconds later, a nurse bustles through the door.

"I need to go."

I hang up, knowing he'll forgive it, and focus on the blonde nurse heading toward me. "What's wrong?"

"Nothing, Mr. Saint. I just wanted to let you know your brother has gone into surgery, and the surgeon will update you when we have any more news." She smiles tightly at me, and I drop back down into the chair I just vacated.

Twiddling my fucking thumbs like a useless asshole.

I knew we shouldn't have gotten close to her, that we should have just made her leave.

If I'd stayed strong, done what I fucking said I was going to, she'd be safe elsewhere and East wouldn't be fucking dying.

My self-loathing reaches a new all-time high.

I should've known better than to think I could grasp any kind of happiness. I don't deserve it, not with the amount of blood on my hands. It was foolish to think that just maybe, she could be the exception to all of the darkness.

I look down at the blood crusted on my hands and head to the bathroom. Scrubbing at my hands and my arms until the water runs clear. The guy staring back at me in the mirror is a fucking mess. I try to clean up as best I can, removing the blood from my face and neck, but there's nothing I can do about the blood crusted into my clothes.

It's not important enough to pull one of the guys away from looking into the shit with Octavia. Even if it does make my skin fucking crawl. I'm not a stranger to blood... but this is East's.

It's just fucking wrong.

I look at my phone, contemplating calling Harrison. East is his son, and he might die, but I'm not sure that Harrison will even care, and fuck me if that isn't depressing as hell. I have no idea what happened between the two of them, because neither of them will fucking tell me, but it's bullshit.

Harrison should be here.

Hell, Fiona should fucking be here.

Not leaving me to shoulder everything, like always.

I take a deep breath as I clench my hands into fists.

Wallowing in self-pity isn't going to fix a fucking thing, Lincoln. Pull your head out of your ass.

Sucking down the out-of-control feeling and shutting it away, I let the cold, killing calm take over. It's the only way I'm going to get through this and get Octavia back.

Right now, she needs my monster, not the man that controls it.

I can't do much of anything to help East beyond what I've already done. But her... I can do something about that. I might not be able to leave the hospital right now, but that doesn't make me powerless.

So I head back to the waiting room, scrolling through my

contact list, and make a call. Calling in the last person I wanted to drag into this fucking mess.

"Lincoln, son, what's happening?" My uncle's voice is almost soothing, he's always been more like a dad than Harrison ever was, but the two of them are estranged so I haven't seen him in a long time. I'm just hoping he's actually in the country, not in a foxhole somewhere.

"I need your help, Uncle Luc."

"What's wrong?" His voice is somber but sharp. I can almost see him in my mind's eye, turning into the Lieutenant Colonel he's spent his life being.

"East is in the hospital, and I'm not sure he's going to make it. And Octavia... she's been taken."

"Well shit, kid, that's a lot to unpack. I didn't even realize she was back in town. Start from the beginning and I'll see what I can do."

I let out a deep breath, relieved to have someone I can trust to help. It's not often I'll go outside of the guys, but we might just be out of our depth.

So I briefly explain everything to him. From Stone's death, to Octavia coming back, and everything that's happened since then.

"Shit, kid. You should've called earlier. And you think this stalker is a Knight?"

"Pretty much. It's kind of why I didn't call sooner."

He barks out a laugh. "I get it. Your dad isn't exactly the helpful kind, and he likes me about as much as he likes your mom. Okay. I'm on my way. I'll be at the hospital in a few hours. Stay there, do not call your father yet."

"Sure thing, Uncle Luc."

"I'll see you soon, chin up." The line goes dead and I feel a little lighter. Lucas might not be part of the Conclave, but he's still a Knight. The difference between him and my dad, is that he doesn't really buy into the bullshit. He joined the forces as soon as he was old enough and dedicated his life to that instead. He's been in the special forces for as long as I can remember, so he's not really been around much. It's been occasionally useful to the Knights, but for some reason, they've left him to it for the most part.

He's really fucking good at what he does, so if there's anyone who can help me stop this ship from sinking, it's him.

I just hate dragging him into the center of it all when he has the luxury of living on the outskirts. No one should be pulled into this shit if they don't *need* to be, but I'm desperate.

Helpless isn't a good look on me.

Unable to sit still in the silence, with nothing more than the tick of the clock to keep me company, I end up pacing around in the small six by twelve room.

Time seems to stretch out forever, and each second feels like an hour.

Waiting for Uncle Luc to arrive might take more strength of will than I have.

My phone buzzes in my hand, and when I see a message from Octavia on the screen, my heart stutters in my chest. I swipe the message and a video starts playing.

The screen is so dark that I almost don't see her... strapped to a fucking table, bound at her ankles, wrists, and throat.

Rage tears through me as laughter crackles out of the speaker and the camera zooms in on her.

"I told you, you couldn't protect her."

"Is there a way to trace the video?"

I've tried to stay calm, listening to Finn tap away on his computer while I'm still stuck in this godforsaken waiting room, but my calm is in short supply and quickly running out.

"We knew this guy was good, but it's been bounced off a ton of proxy servers, which I didn't expect. Pretty sure she isn't in Novosibirsk. It also wasn't sent from her phone, despite coming from her number. A dozen apps can do that, so that's a dead end too, but I'm trying. Doesn't help that the voice was filtered. It doesn't give us much to go on."

I grip my phone tightly, staring up at the ceiling for a second before bringing it back to my ear. "Okay so what *do* we have?"

"We know that the bodies dropped here aren't branded. So either her stalker isn't a Knight, or he hired privately. We also have a plateless black SUV."

"So we have nothing," I hiss, "maybe Luc will think of something we haven't."

"Luc is coming? How much longer till he arrives?"

"Not sure. Few hours, he said."

I look up at the squeak of shoes on the floor and see the same blonde nurse from earlier, who looks at me like she's carrying a fucking IED. "I've got to go. I'll call when Lucas arrives."

"Laters."

For the second time today, I look at her and ask, "What's wrong?" She shifts from foot to foot, looking like I might slit her throat. I do not have the time or patience for this right now. "Spit it out."

"Your brother, he has a very rare blood type. We have some, but not enough. Are you willing to be tested to donate? As his brother, you could hopefully be a match."

I nod once. "Whatever he needs."

"Okay, please come with me." She turns on her heel and rushes down the hall. It's so empty that the click of my boots bounces off the walls and echoes down the empty space. Its only accompaniment the squeak of her sneakers.

I follow her into another room and sit on the bed, rolling up the sleeve of my shirt. I make a fist as she smiles at me, tightening the tourniquet before sliding the needle into my vein. It doesn't take her more than a few moments to collect the blood. "I'm going to put a rush on this, but to speed up the process, I'll hook you up for a donation now anyway, just in case."

"Yeah, whatever," I grumble and lie back on the bed at her instruction. I don't care if I'm treated like nothing more than a pincushion. I just need to know he's going to survive so I can start searching for Octavia.

The very blood she's taking feels like fire under my skin. Everything about this day is wildly out of my control, and it seems like nothing I do will put it back on track.

Except this. This I can do.

This is needed.

So I lie here, my blood draining from my arm, hoping it's enough to save my brother.

At least I can do something to save one of them.

I fucking hate being this whiny lost asshole. It's not who I am, but I'm barely holding my shit together right now.

I stare at the ceiling as another nurse monitors the blood donation, running through a checklist of questions longer than my arm to make sure I'm eligible to donate, which I'd laugh at if I had it in me right now, considering I'm already donating.

The blonde nurse reappears about thirty minutes later, looking fucking terrified again. "Mr. Saint, I'm, uhm, not quite sure how to tell you this but your blood type is A positive. Your brother is AB negative so we won't be able to use your donation for him, but we have a call in with all other nearby hospitals to see if they have any O negative available that they can send us."

I take a deep breath, trying not to let my rage overwhelm me. "I'll call my father."

Luc might've said not to bother, but I don't have any other choice.

"That might be wise, Mr. Saint. We've not been able to reach him."

I clench my fists, trying to rein in the anger. Of course they haven't. I let out a growl, and she squeaks before literally running away from me.

The other nurse removes the needle from my arm, and everything spins when I sit up too quickly. "Careful, Mr. Saint. You just lost a substantial amount of blood. Let me grab you some juice and a cookie."

I nod, grunting because that's about all I have right now as I fight off the dizziness.

This is such fucking bullshit.

I dial Harrison's number, but it rings out. Fucking asshole. So I try again. This time, he answers on the third ring.

"Two calls, Lincoln. It must be important."

I grind my teeth together at his haughty tone. "East was shot. He needs blood and I'm not a match. I need you to come down here."

I finish speaking and he laughs.

He fucking laughs.

"You really don't know, do you? I didn't think he'd actually keep it from you." He laughs again, and I hear the sound of a door closing before the background voices disappear. "I won't be a match either, Lincoln. I'm not his father. Call Fiona."

He ends the call and I blink down at the phone.

Say fucking what now?

This day can get fucked.

When I get my hands on whoever the fuck it is that took Octavia and shot East... I'm going to bathe in their fucking blood.

It's been a few hours since East went into surgery and I still haven't heard anything beyond they managed to source more blood. While that makes me feel a little better, it's not enough to erase my need to break things. People.

"Lincoln!" I look up as Uncle Luc saunters into the room and wraps his arms around me. I stiffen at the touch, and he backs up. "You doing okay?"

I deadpan, "I've been better."

"Yeah I guess you have. Do we know anything new?"

"Nothing yet, just a whole lot of waiting. Oh and finding out that East isn't Harrison's. And the fact that there is exactly zero anything leading us to whoever the fuck took my girlfriend. So yeah, fuck all."

He nods stoically, his brown eyes softening. "It'll be okay. I'll help where I can." He takes a seat next to the one I was just in. "Why don't you tell me everything you *do* know. This is one of your hospitals, right? So anything you say here is safe enough."

I let out a sigh, nodding as I sit. "Yeah, it's one of ours..." I trail off, trying to get everything lined up in my head after this fuck fest of a day and try to explain everything to him again, in more detail this time.

"Fucking hell, you definitely know how to wade into the really shitty waters, don't you, kid?" He scrubs a hand down his face as he processes.

"So your girl is wanted by the Knights, but we don't know why. We suspect they killed her dad and that's somehow tied into all of this. A secondary crazy has her held hostage somewhere, and we don't know why, and East is fighting for his life. That sum it up?"

"Yeah that's about it."

The squeak of sneakers on the floor echoes out again, and I stand, coming face-to-face with a woman I haven't seen before. "Mr. Saint?"

"Yes?"

"I'm Dr. Stanton. Your brother is out of surgery. It took longer than expected because they had to do a sternotomy in order to remove the bullet that damaged the right ventricle. Your brother had to be placed on bypass in order to repair the right ventricle."

Luc shakes his head as I try to work out what the fuck she just said. Pretty sure most doctors learn in med school not to use bullshit technical language when talking to civilians, but if the hatred she looks at me with is anything to go by, she knows exactly who I am and isn't a fan.

"What does that mean in normal people terms, lady?" Luc asks, and I roll my eyes but keep my mouth shut.

"Sorry, yes of course, Mr. Saint," she says, disdain dripping from the word Saint as she rolls her eyes at him. Fucking hell. "What I meant was the bullet entered the chest just below the fifth rib near the sternum and damaged part of the heart. We had to open his chest to fix it. In order to repair the right side of his heart, we had to put him on an ECMO machine since his heart stopped and his body continued to need oxygen. We were able to repair the hole in his heart and get it to start beating again. We then closed his chest. He's lost a lot of blood, so the next twenty-four to forty-eight hours are critical. If we can find the blood, he *might* make it through the next forty-eight hours. If he makes it through the next forty eight-hours, his chances of survival increase, but if we don't find a donor in the next couple of hours, he won't survive the night."

Pain rips through my chest at the thought of losing him. East not surviving isn't acceptable. "I don't care what it costs to do it, but you get that fucking blood."

She quirks a brow at me before she nods.

"Can I see him?"

She looks me over like I'm nothing more than a hindrance, and at any other time I'd want her head on a fucking pike, but East isn't out of the woods yet, so I need her alive for now. "He's still on a ventilator and in critical condition, so you're welcome in the room but…"

"I get it," I growl, and she leaves the room without another word.

I can't just do nothing. Uncle Luc claps a hand on my shoulder. "You head back to the house, kid, see what your friends have found out. Eat, shower, take care of yourself. I'll stay here with East."

I nod, thankful that I don't have to once again choose between the two of them, and head outside, dropping a message in our group chat to let them know I'm coming home. I stride through the hospital and everyone gets the fuck out of my way. One of the few upsides of my surname today. Though if I didn't have it, this wouldn't be my life and I wouldn't have been here in the first place.

I exit the front doors and take a deep breath, filling my lungs with the brisk air and taking a second to compose myself after this fucking day.

"Sainty!"

I look up and find a smirking Maverick behind the wheel of my Porsche.

"Need a ride?"

Usually I'd argue about being the one to drive, but today? Today I have other battles to fight, so I climb in the car and lean my head against the rest.

"We're going to find her, right?" he asks as he pulls away from the curb.

"We'll find her," I say. I just wish I knew for certain we'll find her in time.

TWO

FINLEY

I don't know how this day went from bad to worse, but the punches just keep coming. The drive back from The Cage is tense and silent. Usually, I'm not one for being alone, but between the fury flooding my system and Mav's nervous energy... it's suffocating as fuck in this car.

My knuckles are white as I grip the steering wheel, trying to hold it together. Control is something I've craved most of my life. Lincoln and I are the same in that. He's one of the few people I feel comfortable enough with to trust him with shit, but this... spiral, it's too much. None of us are in control right now, and I feel so unfocused. Like there's an elephant sitting on my chest, and no matter what I do, I can't fucking move it.

Except, letting myself spiral isn't going to help anyone. And it sure as fuck isn't going to help V.

If she's hurt...

Nope, not the rabbit hole to go down. Not today. At least not right now.

We're going to find out who took her, who shot East, and then fucking deal with it.

Whoever it is might be a Knight, but we're the fucking legacy *and* junior Conclave. Never in my life did I think I'd be thankful for that, but right now... right now it means we have the might of the Knights at our fingertips if we decide to use it.

I know Lincoln will want to leave them out of it if we can, especially because we don't know who this sick fuck is, but I'm not averse to using the monsters we have in our closets if it means she's okay.

I'm willing to unleash hell on fucking Earth if it means we get her back unscathed.

The drive back takes too fucking long, even with my lead foot.

We need to clear the house, check the bodies, *dispose* of the fucking bodies, clean up as best we can, and see if there are any traces of whoever the fuck took her left behind.

Even just listing it out in my head slows my heart rate.

I have shit to do.

That's what I need to focus on.

That's what's going to bring her back.

I just keep seeing her face as he grabbed her. The way she tried to fight him off. The way he dragged her by her fucking hair after he drugged her.

I let out a deep breath, trying not to let my anger boil over and take control.

That's not going to end well for anyone, and I don't have time —V doesn't have time—for me to lose it.

By the time we pull back up at the house and get the gate closed, Maverick is so restless I think he's going to burst out of his goddamn skin.

"I need something to do, Finn. Someone to question, someone to bleed. I can't just keep sitting doing nothing." He looks at me, and all the raging emotions that simmer under my skin are written clear as day on his face. I'm envious of his ability to just feel everything and channel it, even if he does channel it into making people bleed.

"There will be plenty of time to make people bleed. We need to clean up the house, call Smithy, see if we know the bodies. I'll leave the heavy lifting to you. Maybe some manual labor will keep you distracted." I smirk and he punches my arm. Asshole. "Yeah, I probably deserved that, but still. We've got shit to do. Suck it up for now, and we'll make this dickhead bleed when we find him."

He nods, looking more than a little lost. It's almost unnerving. I haven't seen him look like this since the day Stone left with V. "Okay. You guys have a plan, right? How to find her?"

"We have a plan. We're going to get her back." I say it with way more bravado than I feel, but I have to believe the words as much as I need him to believe them. We can't all come undone at the seams, otherwise she is as good as dead.

Her stalker might've said that no one could protect her like him, but that doesn't mean she isn't in danger.

I climb from the car; the front door of the Royal home is still hanging from its hinges, and as I push it open, the metallic stench of blood and the heavy, putrid scent of death hits me. My stomach doesn't even roll anymore. It's just another smell, like grass after a rain or burning wood. It's just there—a normal part of my day.

Pretty sure that's really fucked up, but if I puked at every dead body I saw, I'd never fucking eat.

"We really made a mess," Mav comments as he pushes past me to the first body on the floor and rips off the guy's ski mask. "You recognize him?"

I shake my head, moving toward them. "We need to check them to see if they're branded." I absentmindedly rub the scar on my wrist, my own reminder that I'll never escape. Mav pulls up the guy's sleeves but there's no brand. "Nothing on show... but it could be somewhere else."

"Nah, the Knights are fucking ritualistic with that shit. It'd be in the same place as ours if he had one. Let's check the others just in case, but if this one isn't branded, I'd put money on the rest of them being clean. Which means they're private hires, and we have another fucking dead end."

"I'm going to check anyway. Are we calling in a cleanup?" he asks, looking at me like I have all the answers.

I scrub a hand down my face and stand back up. "No, this one's on us." I toss him my keys as I try to work shit out in my head. "Go grab the work truck from my place and bring it back here. We'll deal with it. I'll start looking at the security footage while you're gone. Bring me my laptop from the trunk before you take off."

"Sounds good, man. I won't be long."

He jogs back out of the house, and I feel a little better that he's busy at least. No fucking idea what we'll do with the bodies if we're not calling on the Knights, but I'll think of something. Or Lincoln will. We always figure it out in the end.

For now, I need to check the footage from V's security system and see if there's anything on there. I'm not that hopeful. Whoever this is has done a fantastic job of covering their tracks up to this point. I doubt they'd be stupid enough to leave us any breadcrumbs now, but I have to hope 'cause it's all I've fucking got.

"Laptop!" Mav calls out as he re-enters and slides my bag across to me. "I'll be back!"

He disappears again as I grab the sliding bag and pull my laptop from it. Once I'm in the security room, I get it connected and fire it up. The firewalls on this thing are a fucking joke; it's not a surprise someone hacked in. When we get V back, I'm going to personally revamp this bullshit.

First things first.

As I tap in, I notice a code path that leads to another server. Different. I set up a trace for all things tagged or mentioning Octavia or Stone then get back to the task at hand.

I run through the footage, and like I figured, there's fucking diddly-squat The guy, who is easily 6'4, throws V in the back of a plateless black SUV and peels off like a bat out of hell.

Just fucking awesome.

I hack into the local police surveillance, hoping beyond fucking hope, but there's nothing. Of course there isn't. I take a deep breath and go over the footage again. That's when I notice it's been looped.

How the fuck do people who are trained to find this shit *not* notice cams have been looped?

This is why the police force around here is in fucking shambles. I know the Knights prefer it that way, but fuck my actual life right now.

My phone pings with a message from Linc.

Linc:
<video>

What the fuck?

I press play and I swear to fucking God my heart stops. Indistinct shadows flicker on the screen for a few moments. Then I see her.

Clenching my fists, I take a deep breath and count back from ten, trying to keep my shit in check. I dial his number and he answers before the first ring even finishes.

"You saw it?"

"Of course I fucking saw it."

This day can go straight the fuck to hell.

I email the video to myself and start checking the tags on it. If I didn't hate this motherfucker, I'd be impressed with his skill set, but right now, all I want to do is gouge his eyes out with my fingers.

"Is there a way to trace the video?"

I sigh and try to track V's phone. Naturally, that's a dead end

—because that'd be way too fucking simple—so I start a trace on the video.

"We knew this guy is good, but it's been bounced off a ton of proxy servers. Pretty sure she isn't in Novosibirsk. It also wasn't sent from her phone, despite coming from her number. A dozen apps can do that, so that's a dead end too, but I'm trying. Doesn't help that the voice was filtered. It doesn't give us much to go on."

Silence filters down the line, and I know Linc is as frustrated as I am. We're not used to running into so many brick walls. That said, we've never gone directly up against one of the Knights before. We've had no real reason to. This has to be someone high up the chain though. There's no way someone has this kind of skill and ability to fuck with stuff without being at the top of that particular food chain.

"Okay, so what *do* we have?"

"We know that the bodies dropped here aren't branded. So either her stalker isn't a Knight, or he hired privately. We also have a plateless black SUV."

"So we have nothing. Maybe Luc will think of something we haven't."

"Luc is coming? How much longer till he shows?" I ask, feeling a sliver of relief. Luc might be a Knight, but he's about as willing as we are. I know he hates that Linc effectively stepped into his shoes, but that's the way the Knights work. Seats on the Conclave are almost always passed down from father to son, so when one brother vacated his seat, the eldest son of the eldest brother filled the vacancy. Not that I think Luc hates his relative freedom from the Conclave... just that Linc had to step up into the position.

"Yeah, he said a few hours." He pauses and before I get the chance to ask him what he wants our next steps to be, he says, "I've got to go. I'll call when Lucas arrives."

He sounds fucked up, so I just say, "Laters," and rack my brain for another option. There has to be *something* on this video.

"Honey, I'm home!" Mav's voice echoes through the house. I poke my head around the security door and he's grinning as he drags a body out of the foyer. Only that crazy bastard could smile while moving dead bodies. I'm thankful for it though. If he's willing to take care of them, it means I don't have to and I can focus on the task at hand without worrying that he'll miss something. He might be a crazy sonofabitch but he's not stupid. He'll clean the house as well as any cleaning team would. Even if it's just because this is V's house.

"Fuck," I utter, remembering that Smithy is going to be home at some point soon. Pulling my phone from my pocket, I pull up a message thread with him.

Me:

It's not safe at the house, you should stay in the city. We're handling it.

I should probably tell him that V is missing, but I'm not sure what there is that he can do to help, and I don't want to be the reason the old guy's heart gives out. V will kick my ass from here to fucking Taiwan if anything happens to him.

My phone rings and I groan at Smithy's name on the screen.

This is going to go well.

Pasting a smile on my face, I answer the phone. "Smithy!"

"Don't you Smithy me, Master Knight. What in the blue blazes have you boys gotten yourselves into now?"

Officially dressed down in the politest way, I let out a sigh. "Octavia's been taken. We're working on it."

I wince at the shouting that comes through my phone, half of which I can't even make out.

"Smithy! We're handling it. We think her stalker is a Knight, which means he won't kill her."

"You better hope not," he chastises. "I left her in your care. You all promised me she would be okay. I'm coming back."

"There's nothing you can do here. Luc is coming into town to help. If we're forced to get the Conclave involved, I will let you know. But if you come back, it's just going to put a target on your back, so I'd really prefer it if you stayed put."

The image of him blustering at my words is crystal clear in my head. "You keep me updated, Master Knight. Because if any harm comes to her..."

"I know, I know."

"Do not let me down." His voice is more harsh than I've ever heard it. "More importantly, do not let her down."

By the time Maverick arrives with Lincoln in tow, we've managed to photograph and take prints from each of the bodies, clear the house, and take the bodies to the crematorium.

Thank God for friends in weird places.

The house still looks like something out of a horror movie, but the smell isn't quite so bad anymore. I send the pictures and prints to Smithy to forward to his friend with the feds to see if we can get a hit on any of them. They might be private hires, but if we know who they are, maybe that will help us. There's no way these guys aren't in the system somewhere.

My only worry is that if this guy is a Knight, then it's likely he's already wiped them from any database. He's always three steps ahead of us, and I am sick of chasing our fucking tails trying to catch up.

I'm in a thundercloud of a mood by the time I finally step

away from my laptop, but if *my* mood is foul, Lincoln's is downright tempestuous.

"How is East?"

"In critical condition. They need blood, rare fucking blood. Luc is handling it," he snaps at me, but I don't hold it against him. Shit might be bad for us all right now, but he's carrying more than we are. "What do we have on Octavia?"

"We need help with this." I sigh, yet again. At least this might be the distraction he needs to bury himself in. "I know you don't want to involve the Knights, but we need help from someone. Luc has connections, but he doesn't have the pull that someone on the Conclave does."

"I will not ask my father for help. He's made his stance on East and Octavia quite clear," he grinds out. I can hear his teeth grinding together like gravel in a cement mixer.

"What does that even mean?" Mav asks as he sits on the sofa. He's about as tense as Lincoln is, and without East here to be the cool, calm, and collected one, that leaves me trying to be level-headed about it all.

Which is far easier said than done.

"It means," Lincoln starts, "that Harrison just told me East isn't his kid, and he couldn't give less of a fuck whether he lives or dies. And he's been telling me for months not to bother with Octavia."

"Holy shit, what?" I blink in shock at that little bombshell. "East isn't his? Well fuck. That explains a lot."

"No shit," he grunts. "I guess I need to apologize to him if he survives."

"So who is his dad?" Mav asks, brow furrowed.

"No fucking clue. I've called Fiona, but shocker: she's not answering." He pinches the bridge of his nose as he leans forward. "I was hoping Luc would have more information, but while he knew that East wasn't Harrison's, he doesn't know who his dad is either."

We sit in silence for a minute while I try to process this new information.

I wonder if his dad is a Knight?

More importantly: if he is, would he be willing to help us?

"But that doesn't help us find Octavia. I feel like we're just sitting here with our fucking dicks in our hands. We need to *do* something." Lincoln's frustration bleeds all over us all, while I rack my mind for options. Seeing him like this is jarring as fuck.

"We could talk to Ryker?" I offer. "The Kings have people on every corner of the city. Someone might have seen something."

He nods, even though I can see the conflict in his eyes over asking the Kings for help. "That means we'd owe them one…"

"We can give him Diego," Maverick offers, and I nod in agreement. "The Conclave are done with him. I heard my dad bragging about it."

For a guy who says he isn't the one to come up with a plan, he's full of good ideas today.

"I like it. Where is he?" I ask.

"He's in one of the cells at The Cage." Lincoln rubs a hand over his face before adding, "We don't have any other options, so let's do it. I can't sit around doing nothing anymore. We can stock up while we're there too. Whoever has her might not want to hurt her, but I'm sure as hell going to fuck him up anyway."

He stands, his face like thunder as he walks out of the house, dodging the drying pools of blood still dotting the floors. I grab my phone and send a message to a friend who is used to cleaning up after the Knights and call in a favor. The last thing I want is for the floor to stain and V be reminded of this day every time she sets foot in her living room.

"Let's go," I say, and Mav stands with me. "If we let him go alone, we'll probably end up with another war on our hands."

Mav just grins at me and shrugs. "I could use a fight."

"I think we've fought enough for one day." I shake my head as my phone buzzes with confirmation of the cleanup.

I just hope we get some answers, because the whole ghost routine this fucker has going on is getting on my last nerve. Just once, I'd like to get ahead.

Maybe then we'd feel closer to finding her.

Getting Diego from The Cage was the easy part. Getting him to shut the fuck up on the drive back to Echoes Cove was a whole other story. As we pull up at the Donovan residence, the tension in the car is thick enough to cut with a knife.

"You guys can't tell them where I was," Diego says, looking a little panicked. "They'll kill me if they know I made a deal…"

"They're your brothers. They won't kill you," Mav snorts.

"You don't know my brothers." He gulps, eyes wide. "But I was talking about the Kings as a whole."

"Fine by us. We'll say we tracked you down and in return, the Kings are going to help us," Lincoln commands, and Diego nods. I don't know what they did to him, or what deal was struck, but he looks fucking terrified.

At least he knows to be afraid of the Knights I guess.

I climb from the front of the car, opening the door for Diego and pulling him out. "If you betray us…"

"I won't," he squeaks, but I don't trust him. He's a fucking coward, and they always take the easy way out. Even if it means betraying the people closest to them.

And he doesn't give two fucks about us.

Lincoln walks toward the house and I push Diego to walk behind him while Mav takes my six. A very pissed off Ryker swings the front door open before we're even halfway up the walk.

"I fucking *knew* you had him."

"We didn't," Lincoln states, squaring off with him. "But we found him, and we're returning him."

They stare each other down, neither one of them willing to back down.

"He's telling the truth," Diego says quietly, and I can't help but wonder how this guy created the Kings. He's a fucking pussy. It's working in our favor for now, but fuck knows how long that will last. It might've been better for Ryker if his brother had stayed away.

Ryker glares at his brother, not exactly the warm welcome I was expecting, but steps back to let us in. I follow Diego in and head down to the basement where Ellis, Dylan, and Indi are all sitting playing Xbox.

Indi's head whips around first, and her gasp draws the attention of the others.

"What's wrong?" she asks, her brow furrowed as she stands, her gaze bouncing between us all.

"They brought Diego back," Ryker says, pushing past me. "Nothing's wrong."

"Yes it is," she stresses. "Look at them. What is wrong?"

I'll be fucked if I know how she knows. Especially since reading any of us is usually impossible, but I guess she's hung around with V long enough to work some shit out.

"V was taken. East is in the hospital," Linc confirms, and her eyes go wide. He shifts his focus over to Ryker, and I can practically see how hard it is to say the next words that come out of his mouth. "We need your help."

Ryker smirks, letting out a sharp laugh before Indi elbows him in the stomach and he winces.

"What do you need?" she asks, and I am thankful once again that V found a friend like her. Fuck knows she deserves one.

"The guy who took her left in a black, plateless SUV. He put the surveillance on loop, so there's no trace of him," I start so Lincoln doesn't have to. He's having a shit enough day as it is. "We know you guys have people on every goddamn corner of the Cove, we just need to know if anyone saw the SUV so we can work out where she is."

"You mean it wasn't the Knights?" Ellis asks, scratching the back of his neck. "I thought that's who wanted her?"

"It is, and it's a long story. But it's not the Knights. Not as a whole, anyway."

"The stalker?" Dylan asks, and I nod.

"Yeah, except we think he is a Knight—he's just working unsanctioned."

"Well isn't this just a right fucking shit storm you boys have walked into," Ryker says with a smirk while Diego disappears into a different room. "I suppose since you brought Diego back, we can help."

"We will help because it's my best fucking friend," Indi snaps at him. The smile drops from his face and he nods.

"We'll help however we can." He looks at Dylan, who nods and takes his phone from his pocket, dialing as he leaves the room, motioning for Maverick to join him. "Why don't you tell us everything you've got so far and we'll see if there's anything we can do to help you guys out?"

Lincoln looks like he chewed a fucking wasp's nest, but this was a good idea. Whether he likes it or not. He knows it too, otherwise we wouldn't be here.

We sit with the three of them and lay out *almost* everything, leaving out some of the finer Knight-related details that aren't vital; Indi looks like she's going to have a freaking heart attack. "Why didn't she tell me it was this bad?"

"She probably didn't want to scare you," Ellis says softly, hugging her.

"That or she thought you guys would sort it before it got out of hand," Ryker snarls, and Lincoln clenches his fists so hard I wonder if I'm going to have to restrain him before we're done here.

It feels like hours pass as we wait in that fucking room. Linc makes a dozen calls trying to call in favors to help trace the car, Mav stays busy helping Dylan, while Indi flits around like her ass is on fire, trying to distract herself from the wait.

Me, I sit with my laptop trying to trawl through some of what I found while I was searching for Octavia. There isn't much more I can do to help with the hunt for the car right now, but if something is hidden in these files, something that might help her, then I'm going to fucking find it.

"We have a lead on the car," Dylan says as he and Mav enter the room. "And we think we have a potential location. You guys want help going in?"

Ryker looks like he might take Dylan's head off his shoulders, but I nod. Lincoln and Ryker might have a tenuous truce going on for the moment, but we need their help, and I'm not one to cut my nose off to spite my face. Especially when it comes to Octavia.

"We can use all the help we can get," I say, and he grins wide.

"I was hoping you'd say that."

My phone buzzes in my pocket as the Kings start to gear up. My eyes go wide when I see what my ping trace reports are showing. I flick to the document the trace has pulled up on my laptop and start to read.

Holy fucking fuck.

"Linc, I think I know how we can get her back and away from the Knights. For good."

THREE

OCTAVIA

I have no idea how much time has passed. The drugs he's giving me through the IV in my arm have me in and out so fucking much that I could've been here an hour or a week and I wouldn't know the fucking difference. My mind is so fuzzy, so patchy, it's all I can do to focus right now.

And I need to focus so I can get myself out of whatever this fucking is.

I blink against the blindfold that feels like silk against my skin. Confused, I frown. I wasn't wearing it earlier. Was I? Was that a drug fueled hallucination? Or just a dream?

The bindings around my neck, wrists, and ankles are icy cold, but there's a little bit of give to them. I think they're leather.

"Oh look, my little dove is awake. Are you feeling better? I gave you a drip to make sure you're not dehydrated, though you might still be a little woozy."

His voice makes my heart race, and by the sound of the beeping in the room, he knows it too.

Nope. Definitely wasn't a dream.

Fuck.

This is bad.

Never in a million fucking years would I have thought it would've been him.

I trusted him.

My heart aches at the betrayal as I try to wrap my head around my reality.

"No need to be afraid. I'm not going to hurt you, not unless you make me. I'm trying to protect you."

I gulp and my throat is so fucking dry, like I haven't drank anything for days. "Protect me from what?" My voice is scratchy and I jump when I feel the straw at my lips.

"It's just water."

I take a tentative sip. As soon as it's clear that ice-cold water is the only thing hitting my tongue, I take a few more. It might be stupid to accept anything from him, but he says he wants to protect me, so I'm hoping he isn't going to hurt me any more than he already has.

"There's a good girl, little dove." I flinch as he brushes back some of my hair and takes off the blindfold. I blink against the light, my eyes slow to adjust, but at least it's not as bright in here as it was before. Once my eyes focus, all I see is him.

This can't be happening.

"You need to sleep some more."

He lifts the syringe to the IV bag beside me, and I whimper as the drug burns through my veins before my vision blurs and fades to black once more.

"Sleep well."

FOUR

MAVERICK

The Kings' arms room is enough to make anyone smile. I get the feeling that Diego having been gone was good for them. Ryker is definitely the bigger, better beast. He has the same sort of smarts as Linc, which makes him a worthy rival. I'm just glad that he's on our side this time.

We need all the monsters we can get on our side to get V back.

Finley and Linc have been muttering in a corner for the last five minutes while I've been gearing up.

"You are not leaving me behind!" Indi argues with Ryker, and I'm not going to lie, as much as I bicker with her, it's almost as much fun to watch her argue with them. She's grown a lot since V blew back into town. Last year she took a lot of shit, and I feel massively guilty about it now. "She is my best friend. I'm not just going to sit on the fucking sidelines. I can help."

"Baby, I love you, but I'm not going to be the one to watch you march into whatever hell we're about to see."

She screams in frustration, and I smirk as I check over the gun Dylan gave me again.

"I'm going to get V to teach me how to shoot after all this, maybe then you'll stop treating me like I'm made of fucking glass. I can drive, so I'm driving. Whether with you or behind you. You pick." She juts out her chin, and I have to press my lips together to keep from laughing. Yeah, her and V are way too similar.

I leave Ryker to deal with his wildcat and head over to my boys. "So, what's the deal?"

They both look at me, and I know something's wrong. "What?"

"It doesn't matter until we get V back, but we worked out why the Knights haven't just inducted her. And if it is one of the Knights that has her, this changes *everything*." Lincoln's words send a rush of adrenaline through me.

"Okay, we'll talk it out, but later. First, let's go get our fucking girl." I don't need to know the details and they know it as well as I do. I bounce on the balls of my feet, anticipation at the thought of getting her back—and fucking up whoever took her and put East in the hospital—has me all kinds of giddy.

I might not have started the fight for once, but I'm sure as fuck happy to finish it.

I crack my fingers and curl them into fists before stretching my neck from side to side in an effort to try and calm the raging inferno inside of me that just wants to burn it all down. Linc and Finn gear up quickly and we're heading out of the Donovans' basement to the cars in a matter of minutes.

I didn't even ask where we're going. The finer details are Linc's thing. Me? I'm ready to be pointed in a direction and go nuclear. She's only been gone a few hours, but that's a few hours too fucking long.

Ten seconds away from us with this sick fuck is too long.

Whoever it is, Knight or not, is about to discover that you don't fuck with what is mine. I am not a patient man with most things, but with punishment? I have all the patience in the world.

I jump in the back of Finn's Range Rover and triple check my knives. I've used them a lot already today, so I give them another wipe down, making sure they're the way I like them.

We convoy through town and pull up to a townhouse near the middle of the Cove.

"Well fuck," is all Lincoln says as we climb from the car. It's late enough that we're shrouded in darkness, but since this place is residential, it restricts some of what we can get away with. Even in *this* neighborhood.

"You take the back, we'll go in the front," Linc says to Ryker, who nods, glancing back to where Indi sits in the front of his car with Thomas, who looks about as happy to be sidelined as Indi does.

"Make sure she doesn't get hurt," Ryker grumbles at Thomas before heading to the back of the house with Ellis. I nod, even though he can't see it. If anyone is in here, they're not getting out with the ability to hurt anyone ever again.

That much I can promise.

"You really think she's here?" I ask Linc as we climb the stairs to the front door.

He glances at me, and I already know he doesn't. It's in the stoop of his shoulders. "Even if she's not, we might pick up a fresh trail here."

My stomach churns at the thought of her not being here. It was too easy. I should've known, but I take a deep breath and prepare myself for a fight anyway.

Finley moves up to the door and tests the handle. The door swings open without resistance. We're greeted by darkness and silence. Finn signals for us to go in quiet and start a sweep. He points to the stairs and I nod, my heart racing as I draw my gun and flick off the safety.

We move into the house as a single unit before we split up and

I head to the stairs. Keeping my steps light, I climb them as quickly as I can while staying quiet. It's a typical townhouse, tall and narrow, and apparently not the biggest. I clear the first few rooms as Dylan approaches from the back. I nod when I see him. Nice to get an extra set of eyes. He helps me clear the rest of the level before we head back downstairs, finding the others holstering their firearms. "It's basically a shell. Not even a mattress on the floor."

"That's because whoever was here was set up down here," Ryker says as he appears from a door that I'm assuming leads to the basement. He flicks on a switch and heads back down, the rest of us following behind him.

I'm trying not to be too fucking twitchy about the fact that she isn't here; that I feel like we're failing her.

Again.

We were supposed to keep her safe. We're her Supermen and I'm sick of being bested by whoever the fuck this prick is.

My heart stutters in my chest as my feet touch the concrete floor of the basement. People might think I'm a little unhinged, but what in the actual fuck is this? The walls are papered with photos of V. The most recent of them was taken last night, hours before she was taken. The oldest, as far as I can tell, is from the day she arrived back in The Cove. There are even pictures of all of us and a few other Knights scattered throughout. Red string loops around push pins, drawing haphazard and mostly wildly inaccurate connections between us like a fucking crime board.

None of it makes any sense to me.

"What the fuck is this?"

"It's his nest," Lincoln growls, studying the walls. "He watched her, but there's obvious gaps. This was her at Nate's, I'd say before school started, but then there's nothing for a few weeks, because this was in September," he says pointing to a picture of him with V.

I lean in to study the photos more closely and realize he's right. There are gaps. Tons of them. Though fewer and fewer the last few months. It's almost like constant surveillance.

"Could all of this have been done by just one person?" I ask, fucking stunned stupid from the sheer number of photos.

"It could," Finn says, "but if he's a Knight like we think, he could've had help. Or just paid a private PI. It's easy enough to do."

"Whoever it is followed her on both trips she took with Indi," Ellis says from his spot on the far side of the room. "That picture over there is from the bar they went to when Octavia went viral for singing. Indi told me all about it... and this one is from the spa retreat they went on. I recognize the building." His finger taps one of the pictures in front of him.

"This is seriously fucked up. Who the fuck is after your girl?" Dylan mutters, and Lincoln glares at him.

If looks could kill, Dylan would be in a body bag already. "If we knew that, we wouldn't be standing here, dick in fucking hand, like idiots."

I rake a hand down my face. The last thing we need is for those two to start fighting. And coming from me, that's saying something. Because I really, really want to see someone bleed right now. My monster is scratching the inside of my skull, beating against the walls of his cage. Someone has what's ours and all he wants to do is make the streets run red until we have her back.

"We're going to need to go to the Conclave," Finn says, and Lincoln curses. My heart races in my chest. Why the fuck would we ask them for anything? "With the information we have now, they'll help us. They won't want her hurt by a Knight. Your dad will have a fucking conniption and I don't want to ask them for help any more than you do, but we're in over our heads."

I guess whatever I need to catch up on is fucking vital if they think this is a good idea.

"If you need us, you know where to find us," Ryker says, nodding at Finn. "But our girl is sitting outside and we've been in here too long already."

"Thanks," Lincoln responds. "We should head out too. If we're going to ask the Conclave for help, we should leave this as it is for the sake of preserving evidence."

Not our usual M.O., but okay...

The fire in me burns red-hot as we leave the basement. How the fuck are we going to find her? This was our only lead. Even if the Conclave *does* help us, we have nowhere to even start.

"Fuck!" Ryker's shout has my feet moving faster as we run out of the house.

Holy shit.

Thomas is on the ground bleeding, both cars are fucked, and Indi is gone.

Ellis crouches down to assess his friend and lets out a sharp breath. "He's still breathing." Rolling him over, Thomas groans and I move to help Ellis while the others secure the rest of the area. Noticing the gaping wound in his gut, I apply pressure to try and stop the bleeding.

"Indi," Thomas coughs, blood trickling from his mouth. "Rebels."

He passes out again and Ellis curses before calling for his brother. "We need to get him to Doc, and quick. Rebels were here, they took Indi."

"Motherfuckers!" Ryker shouts, pulling his phone from his pocket. He yells at whoever picks up the other end, giving them our location. He finishes the call and curses again. A few lights go on in the house we're sitting in front of and the front door opens, but when the guy sees Ryker, he closes the door and turns the lights back off.

Clever man.

A car screeches to a stop in front of us and I help Ellis get Thomas in the back, Dylan taking over the application of pressure.

"Let us know if you need anything," Linc says to Ryker as he climbs into the front of the car. He just nods and slams the door shut before they tear the fuck away.

I stand there, the blood on my hands dripping onto the concrete, wondering how the fuck all of our worlds imploded in one fucking day.

"We should get back to the house," Lincoln says, pulling me from my thoughts. "It's nearly two in the morning. Much as I hate to say it, we're not going to find her tonight."

I grind my teeth together at the thought of trying to sleep while she's with this sick fuck. Much as I know I need sleep to function, and I can't find her if I can't function, I still hate it. But I nod regardless.

Finley checks over the Range Rover before deciding it's okay to get us home at least. We have to kick out the windshield to be able to actually see, but we get it done and make the drive back in silence.

I just have to tell myself we'll find her tomorrow, because nothing else is acceptable. I might have blood on my hands, but it isn't the blood I wanted and my monster isn't sated.

But he will be, and God help whoever has her, because no one else can save them from me.

The sound of my phone wakes me, and I groan groggily as the chiming just gets louder. I roll over and pull my phone from the nightstand, trying to shut off my alarm for school. I've barely slept an hour because my mind would not shut down and I felt antsy as fuck. After spending an hour in Linc's gym, I managed to wear myself down to a point where I could sleep, but by then, the sun was already coming up.

School can get fucked today. I'm not exactly a genius, but I have more important shit on my agenda today. Like finding V and checking in on East.

Linc called Luc on the drive back here last night to find out there's been no change with him, and he still hasn't woken up. I still have no idea what the fuck Finn found yesterday, because I wasn't in any mood to listen to more Knight bullshit last night, but today... today I want to know what the fuck is going on.

Throwing off the duvet, I climb to my feet and stagger into the bathroom. Switching on the shower and twisting the water to its coldest setting, I jump beneath the cold spray, the icy water pummeling my back as it helps me wake up and clears the fog from my mind.

Once I'm shivering, I turn the heat up and shower quickly. I don't want to waste any time fucking around when V is God knows fucking where, with this psychopath that has her. I'm the only psycho she needs in her life.

I'd sell my soul to the devil if I thought it'd help get her back... though I'm pretty sure that ship sailed a long time ago.

By the time I've sorted my shit out and get downstairs, Finley is already set up on the kitchen table, laptop out. "There're eggs if you want some. Or there are bagels."

"Thanks." I grab some eggs and put a slice of bread in the toaster. Culinary whizz I am not. Ramen and toast is about as far as my skills go. When it's done, I sit down opposite Finn and try to eat. "What's going on?"

"I've been trying to see if there's any footage on the cameras around the house we went to last night. I found the black SUV that took her pulling up and taking her into the house. The SUV leaves shortly after, but there's no sign of her or anyone else leaving." He turns the laptop around and shows me the sped up footage, right up until we arrived last night.

"How is that possible? You think they took her out the back?"

"Must have, but of course, that's a dead spot and there's absolutely zero fucking footage on the back street. Which is probably why he took her that way." He pinches the bridge of his nose and shakes his head. "This guy is a ghost. It confirms my suspicions that the people who came to get her were hired guns, rather than her stalker himself. Why risk being caught? Which means he's not stupid, even if he is fucking insane."

"Well fuck. Any way to trace the guy who actually took her?"

He nods, and for the first time since yesterday afternoon, I feel a glimmer of hope. "I've been running the details of the bodies we dropped. They all work for a private military company headquartered on the East Coast called *Dranas*. I'm hoping I can find out who hired them, or at least which of the team made it out alive. I've put a call in already, just waiting for someone to call me back."

"At fucking last." I look up and find Linc entering the room. "If you don't hear back in an hour, call them back and cause merry fucking hell."

"With pleasure." Finn grins. "What are the other plans for today? I hate feeling like we're doing nothing while she's gone."

Linc pours himself a cup of coffee and joins us at the table. "Since we're waiting on Dranas, I'm going to head to the hospital to see if there's been any change, and then I'm going to call a Conclave meeting. The two of you need to stay on Dranas. Any news on Thomas or Indi?"

"Nothing," Finn answers. "I dropped Dylan a message this morning, but he hasn't responded."

"Thomas said the Rebels took her," I tell them. "Either of you have any idea who they are?"

Linc frowns as he nods. "They're the Kings' rivals, but from the city. I didn't realize things had gotten that bad between the two gangs. If it was the Rebels… I'm going to make a call, because if something happens to Indi while V is gone, she's going to have our balls when we get her back."

He's not wrong. I'm just glad he knows who they are and that they're not someone we need to worry about. We've got too many balls in the air already at the moment, I'm not sure how much more we can juggle. At least not until we get V back and we know East is going to make it.

My phone buzzes in my pocket, and I pull it out, secretly hoping that it's Octavia's phone. That we can trace it. But my hopes are dashed when I see my mom's name on the screen instead. "Gimme two minutes," I say, and leave the kitchen before swiping the screen and answering the call.

"Maverick, I need you to come home." Her voice wobbles, and my heart sinks.

"What's wrong, Mom?"

She sniffles and I clench my free hand. I already know what's coming. "I need to go to the doctor."

"What did he do now?" I ask through clenched teeth.

"He didn't mean to… he just came home a little angry, he went down to the basement but that didn't make him feel any better and, well, I pushed his buttons."

"Don't make excuses for him, Mom," I growl. Taking a deep breath, I look up at the gray clouds in the sky. Fitting. "You need to leave."

"I can't do that, Mavvy. You know I can't." She sniffles again. I hate hearing her cry, but I'm not sure what else I can do. "I'm as trapped as you are."

"That's not true. Fiona got out, she's in the Caribbean. Erica is in rehab, though she probably doesn't need to be. You have options, Mom."

"Please just come help me. I can't drive. My eye…" she trails off, and it takes every ounce of patience and control I have not to launch my fucking phone.

"I'll head out now, but Mom, if you don't leave this time, I'm done helping." I hate saying the words, but I can't keep protecting her if she won't save herself. It breaks me every time, when she says she'll leave, and then just comes back for more of his bullshit.

"Thank you, Mavvy." I end the call and head back inside, dropping back into the seat I had vacated.

"Everything okay?" Finn asks as I shovel what's left of my cold breakfast into my mouth.

I shrug. "Need to take Mom to the hospital."

"Your dad?" Linc asks and I nod. "Well, I'm going to visit East, so I can drive if you want? Or you can take one of the cars in the garage."

"Thanks, man. She'll probably freak out if you're with me, so I'll just take one of the cars."

"Sure thing." He nods. "You know where the keys are. I'm going to go call Alexander, see if I can get some info on Indi and what's going on. Then I'm heading out. Let me know if you need anything, and I'll call once I've talked to Harrison."

"Alexander? As in, your cousin?"

He nods as he stands. "The one and only. He's affiliated with both the Rebels and the Knights. Go figure. Apparently my cousin likes to live dangerously."

I laugh, because only Alexander Saint would be crazy enough to play that game.

"I'll catch you in a bit," he says as he leaves, refilling his coffee cup on his way out.

"You sure you're good going on your own?" Finn asks as I finish eating.

"I don't think he's home. She probably wouldn't have called me if he was." I get up and rinse off my plate, putting it in the dishwasher before grabbing a bottle of water from the refrigerator. "If I need help, I'll call. Thanks."

It doesn't matter how many times we save each other, or how much we know about each other's shitty home situations, it doesn't stop the shame that crawls up my throat over the fact that I can't save my mom from my dad. It might just be my biggest failure... that I can't make her leave him. Not for me, not for her. Not for fucking anything.

I feel so fucking sick with the shame of it I can barely look at Finn. "I'll check in in a bit. Let me know if you get anything from Dranas."

"Will do," he calls out as I leave the room and grab the keys to one of the cars in Lincoln's garage. I don't pay attention to which ones, 'cause it doesn't matter. On autopilot, I slip on my boots, grab my hoodie, and head out to the garage.

I hit the button on the key fob, and the lights flash on the Mercedes. I slide behind the wheel of the midnight blue SUV and hit start along with the clicker for the garage door.

The drive over to my house doesn't take long, and as I suspected, my dad's car isn't here. I leave the Mercedes idling as I hop out and open the front door. "Mom?" I call out, but realize I didn't need to, she's sitting on the stairs waiting for me.

"What the actual fuck?" I hiss when I take in the sight of her. It's not a surprise she couldn't drive, both her eyes are almost completely swollen shut, her nose looks broken, and her lip is split. God knows what's hidden beneath her clothes.

"Maverick, language," she scolds, and I roll my eyes.

"Fuck that, Mom. Look at you."

"I know perfectly well what I look like, now are you going to stand there and judge me, or are you going to help me into the car."

It hits me. She probably can't stand. Which means he beat the living fuck out of her.

I move forward and help her stand, practically carrying her out to the car. One day I'll free her. Free myself.

Even if it means killing him.

FIVE

LINCOLN

I wish I could say I didn't know when my life became so complicated, that I couldn't pin it down to the reappearance of a single human. Somehow it seems like that would make all of this feel less... chaotic. Chaos is not something I accept in my world. Not since initiation. I work fucking hard to ensure that my ducks stay in a row, that I have control of the shit in my life. But somehow, since Octavia came back into my life, my ducks have morphed into fucking rabid squirrels.

I have no idea what I'm going to do about my father pushing Georgia on me. He keeps hinting at me taking it further with her to secure his deal with her father. That's on top of the whole 'East isn't a Saint' bullshit, Octavia's stalker, and the documents Finley found. And because I need another fucking squirrel in this circus, Indi has been taken by the Rebels and if anything happens to her, Octavia will likely take my balls.

Which is how I find myself dialing Alexander's number before I do anything else this morning. I lean forward, resting my elbows on my desk, and pinch the bridge of my nose, hoping it helps the headache that's forming. It's too early in the day to feel this shitty.

"Lincoln! Cuz! How you doing? It's been a minute." Alex's

cheery voice filters through and I smirk a little at how alike he and Indi are.

"I'd be better if my balls weren't about to be in a vise because your guys took my girl's ride or die."

His laughter on the other end of the phone is about the response I expected. Life has always been a game to Alex. He's a Knight, but he's not Conclave, so his initiation was substantially different from mine. Though I always thought he'd be better suited to life on the Conclave than I am. He lives for the darker side of life. Which is hilarious considering his sunshine demeanor.

"And here was me thinking I was the dramatic one in the family. I assume you're talking about the fiesty, purple-haired demon the boys brought in last night?"

"The one and only."

"Well shit, Linc." He pauses as voices sound in the background. He murmurs something to whoever it is before continuing. "What do you need?"

I roll my eyes, unsure how I can be more clear about what I need. "I need her back."

"That's not going to work. Wish it could, but the Donovans owe a debt and until we get what's owed, the girl is collateral." He actually does sound apologetic, but that doesn't help me right now. "But, since it's you... I can make sure nothing happens to her. She'll be treated as my guest rather than a prisoner."

I laugh dryly, because of course that's his offer. "Sounds like you've taken a few steps up the food chain."

"You could say that. The city is mine, Cousin."

I lean back, eyes wide. Well that could work in my favor at some point, I tuck the information away for later and get back to the task at hand. "Congratulations, I guess?"

"You know I'm a sucker for positions of power." I can practically hear his grin.

"That I do. So I have your word Indi will be okay and returned in the same condition you received her? Which, last I checked, was in one, *unharmed*, disturbingly sunshiney piece. I like my balls where they are and Octavia will take them if anything happens to her."

"Oh shit, V's back? And this is her best friend? Well, life just got a little more interesting. Unfortunately, she's not quite in one piece, but I'll make sure to patch her up."

I groan. What the fuck does that mean? With him, it could be anything from a skinned knee to missing digits...

Alexander always did like games.

Though he sounds far more interested in Octavia than I'd like. "Yes she is, and yes, that's her best friend. Don't fuck me over, Alexander. I'll owe you one."

"And I'll likely come calling. I'll keep you updated, gotta run." He hangs up the phone before I get a chance to say another word and I take a deep breath. This is either going to end really well, or really fucking badly.

Ryker *has* to know that Alex is my cousin. He's not stupid, it's not a secret, and that would definitely explain some of the extra hostility coming from him lately. As if the Knight bullshit wasn't enough.

Fuck my life.

Why is nothing ever simple?

I drop Luc a message to check in on East, letting him know I'll be there soon, before making my next bullshit call of the day.

Fiona.

What fun this should be. I press her name on the screen and put the call on loudspeaker. My headache can't take her usual screeching directly into my ear today. It goes through to voicemail, as usual, so I leave her a message telling her to call me and leave it at that.

Luc still hasn't responded, so I decide to just head to the

hospital. There's no point in reaching out to Harrison to call a meeting with the Conclave this early in the day because he won't answer the phone. Instead, I wrestle my limbs out of my sweats and hoodie and grab a quick shower, trying not to think about the girl who haunts every waking—and sleeping—moment of my day.

She's the end game for me, so I need to get her back, and in one piece. Today is fucking Valentine's Day, and she's not even here. We had surprise plans for her last night and everything. That, quite literally, got shot to shit.

I've been trying not to focus on what could be happening to her, especially since I'm convinced that she's with a Knight and most of them are sick fucks. I've been going through everything in my head, trying to come up with a suspect list. While Edward Riley is near the top of that list, because he's had a weird obsession with her since she got back, I'm pretty sure he would've already boasted to Mav about having her. He's a twisted bastard who would derive a sick sense of pleasure just from taking her, but he'd tell Mav about it as a means of torture. He enjoys hurting people more than anyone I've ever met, but the amount of satisfaction he gets from fucking with his son is on a different level.

It's pretty much the only reason he isn't at the top of my list.

My other worry is that there are plenty of Knights I don't know. I'm just not sure how they could've come into contact with V. Especially in the time since she got back. I know she had a stalker before, but Evan dealt with him. The dead don't usually come back to stalk you again.

And while I don't *want* Evan to be on my list, he is. As is Mac. I'm not positive that guy is a Knight, but he seems like the perfect watch dog for my father. Especially knowing what we know now. Panda might've been there to keep an eye on V, but I have zero doubts someone else was there to keep an eye on Stone. Who better than his head of security? But it's not like the Knights keep a database of members that I can just have Finn sift through.

At least not that I know of.

There are limitations to being a junior.

My frustration only grows with each dead end I remind myself of, so I rush through the rest of my shower and dress quickly. I want to check on East and run my idea past Luc. He knows my dad better than anyone, he's probably the best person to help me hash it out before I make the call later.

I grab the keys to the Cayenne and head out to the garage. The guys know I'm going out, so I don't bother tracking them down again.

I need to zen my shit and realign my focus.

Chaos isn't going to get her back and I'm sick and tired of chasing my fucking tail.

By the time I make it to the hospital and park, there's still no response from Luc. That alone is enough to make me suspicious, but I head into the hospital anyway. He could've fallen asleep or put his phone on silent.

My brain continues to churn and lands on the fact that he didn't mention Alex's new position with the Rebels. I know the two of them aren't exactly on the best terms and we had a lot going on, but that's the sort of shit he'd usually mention.

Unless he doesn't know.

There are too many balls in the air right now, and if I don't sort some stuff quickly, I'm going to drop everything. Which is not an option.

I am Lincoln Saint. Failure is unacceptable.

Especially where Octavia Royal is concerned.

Even if it means letting everything else burn down around me,

I'm going to make sure she makes it out of this alive and unharmed. The only things keeping me reasonable right now are the knowledge it's been less than twenty-four hours, that her stalker claims to want to protect her, and that we have proof-of-life in the form of that damn video.

I cling to those threads of hope like my life depends on them.

But really, it's her life that depends on them, and that's worse. I'd happily sacrifice myself if it meant saving her.

If only that were an option.

The walk to East's room is quiet. The advantage of the small, Knight-owned hospital is that no one stops me and no one questions me. I pause at the door to his room, taking a deep breath to center myself. As far as I know, there haven't been any complications, and my brother—because he is still my brother, regardless of what Harrison might think—should still be alive, breathing and healing.

I'm not sure what I'll do if he doesn't pull through.

I step up to the door and before I put my hand on the handle, it swings open, bringing me face to face with Luc. "I was wondering how long you'd stand out there for."

"Just taking a minute." I enter the room, avoiding his judgmental look. The room is quiet except for the beep of the monitor and the whooshing of the ventilator. "How is he doing? I tried to text…"

"He's fine. No change since you left here last night, though you look like you've been through the wringer. Thought I told you to go rest." He quirks a brow at me as I drop into the chair beside East's bed.

"No rest for the wicked," I say with a shrug. "There's too much to do right now anyway."

"Lincoln, you're only eighteen. You shouldn't be this stressed." He frowns as his gaze roams over me.

"Yeah well, Knights don't tend to live that long. I guess stress is a part of it."

"You want to tell me what happened after you left here?"

I run a hand through my hair, wondering how much more to tell him. I need his help, but it's been a minute since he was around. I know I need him, but I can't help question how much help he'll be with anything beyond dealing with my dad.

Being this cynical and distrusting doesn't exactly make life easy, but when you've lived through and experienced what I have... it's kind of impossible to be any other way. Letting out a deep breath, I make the decision to just tell him everything. I called him here for a reason, I just have to hope he doesn't fuck me over to curry favor with Harrison.

I tell him everything that's happened since I left the hospital, trying to ignore the steady rhythm of the machines surrounding East. He doesn't interrupt or react, he just listens while I lay it all out. He speculates on a few points as I go but, for the most part, he just lets me work through it out loud.

The only information I keep to myself is what Finn found on Octavia's computer system.

I don't want anyone to know what we know until I get a meeting with the Conclave; an ace up my sleeve, as it were. God knows I need as many of those as I can get.

"So Alexander stepped up with the Rebels and had your girl's best friend kidnapped... on top of you thinking you found your girl, but instead of finding her you found that she was taken by a team from Dranas and delivered to whoever's been stalking her. Is that an accurate summary? Just so I know I'm not missing anything."

I nod as he leans back against the wall, folding his arms across his chest. "I know some of the Dranas boys. I can reach out to them, see if I can get any information on that for you. I might be able to get details Finley can't."

"Thank you."

Groans from East steal my attention, and when his eyes flutter open it's like the crushing weight around my chest loosens a little.

"I'm going to go get the doctor," Luc says before hightailing it from the room.

East raises a hand to the tube in his mouth, but I intercept and squeeze it. "Welcome back, Brother. Don't touch it, Luc's gone to get the doctor."

His eyes are a little glassy and unfocused, but he's awake. It's like I can almost take a full breath, and once we have Octavia back, I'll be able to breathe properly again.

It's not more than a minute before Luc returns with a nurse on his heels.

"Welcome back to the world of the living, Mr. Saint." She smiles at him before she shoos me out of the way so she can tend to him. "This is going to be a little uncomfortable."

I look away, because I know I wouldn't want anyone witnessing me like that, and I'm not about to steal any of my brother's dignity by not. When the nurse announces that she's done, and that the doctor will be by soon, I move back to East's side. His eyes are closed again, but they already told us to expect him to be in and out.

"He'll probably be thirsty, but we need to limit his intake for the time being. I'll go grab some ice chips for him," she says before she leaves the room.

I take my seat again and drop a text to Finley and Maverick to let them know he's awake.

Finn:
Glad to hear it. Still no call from Dranas, but I'll keep on it.

Me:
Luc knows some people at Dranas. I'll drop you his number so you can coordinate.

Finn:
Sounds good.

Mav:
Glad he's awake. Mom's getting seen now. I'll take her home and then come by to see him.

I put my phone away and focus back on East. The other monitors are still steady and his eyes flutter open again. He opens his mouth and rasps, "Octavia."

I smile, because of course it is, then grimace because he's going to be pissed. I shake my head, deciding not to tell him yet. "Once we've talked to the doctor, I'll catch you up."

The nurse reappears and helps him sit up properly, walking him through what he can and can't drink right now. He looks like he just chewed on a wasp, but he nods along as she goes through her spiel.

The doctor comes in just before she's finished. The same one I spoke to yesterday. She shakes East's hand before picking up his chart and looking over it as Luc slips back into the room. "You, Mr. Saint, are one very lucky man. I've seen injuries like yours before and the survival rate isn't great. Thanks to your brother acting quickly and getting you here as fast as he did, things went a lot better than expected." East looks at me, but I don't let on that I know about him and Harrison. "The bullet entered the chest just below your fifth rib near the sternum. We had to open your chest to repair the damage to the right side of your heart. In order to do that, we had to put you on a bypass machine. We were able to repair the hole in your heart and get it to start beating again, obviously. All of this to say you are very lucky, but the road to recovery is only just beginning."

"What does that mean?" I ask, a little tired of having to ask that in this place.

She looks over to me, arrogance coming from her in waves. I drop all emotion from my face, and she gulps. Fucking good. I am not in the mood to be fucked with right now.

"It means that your brother will be able to get out of bed in a few days and try to walk around. He'll be here a week, at least, so we can ensure there's no infection or complications before we discharge him." She looks back to East, who nods even though he still looks a little spaced out. "Then he'll be allowed to go home and will need to start cardiac rehabilitation as an outpatient."

"Cardiac Rehab?" Luc asks, and the doc jumps as if she forgot he was there.

"Yes. Basically, that is where they'll give him an exercise regime to help strengthen the heart after the damage it sustained both before and during surgery. He'll need to go twice a week to begin with, which may drop to once a week depending on how well he responds."

"And how do we arrange that?" I ask, thankful that it doesn't seem too restrictive.

"We'll have the referral put in and his first appointment will be scheduled before he's discharged," she says, nodding.

East croaks, drawing everyone's attention as he tries to speak. He looks like he's struggling, so I hand him my phone. "Type it out."

He takes the phone, his hands a little shaky. It takes him a minute, and he keeps blinking and shaking his head, but eventually hands the phone to the doctor, who laughs. "Mr. Saint, you're lucky to be alive. Sex can wait." I smirk and Luc barks out a laugh at the doc's words. She just glares at me before continuing. "You're looking at at least two months before your ribs and lungs are in good enough shape for that sort of activity. Anything like that before then could push your recovery back. You're officially on light duty until further notice. Five pounds, Mr. Saint. I assure you, you will regret lifting anything heavier than that."

East rolls his eyes as the doc hands me my phone back, and it takes everything I have not to laugh. Of course that was his first question. He doesn't even know about Octavia yet and that's what he asks. I guess the drugs really do have him feeling all the good things.

"If that's all…" the doctor says, and I nod. She leaves with Luc on her heels.

"V…" he croaks, and I sigh as I drop back into the chair beside his bed.

Shaking my head, I run a hand through my hair. "She's gone. We're still looking for her, but whoever took her is a fucking pro. We have leads we're working on, but I need you to focus on healing, because *when* I get her back she's going to kill us both if anything happens to you."

He laughs softly and nods before putting another ice chip in his mouth. "Not wrong."

"Oh I know." I scrub a hand down my face, his eyes flutter shut, and the pain meds drag him back to sleep.

I check my phone once he's fully out and decide it's time to call Harrison.

He's not going to be happy, but he can choke on a dick. I'm getting Octavia back, and if that means a deal with the devil, then so be it.

East stirs again, as if fighting the sedation. "I need to tell you something."

I straighten my tie, feeling all kinds of fucked up, but I pull on the monster inside of me and let that cold, stoic demeanor wash over me. I need my monster close to the surface when dealing with the Conclave. "You guys ready?"

"About as ready as I'm going to be." Mav laughs from the back seat, while Finn just nods beside me.

"Then let's get this show on the road shall we?" I climb out of the Porsche and look up at the office block the Conclave uses for meetings. I'm pretty impressed everyone convened as quickly as they did, but I've never called a meeting before and Harrison seemed pretty on edge.

Time to lay our cards on the table I guess.

We head into the building, the two of them flanking me. They wear suits as well, as expected by the Conclave. When you want to get shit done where they're concerned, there are some rules you play by no matter how trivial they may seem. Especially when you're about to fuck shit up in the way we are about to.

No one stops us as we walk through the lobby to the bank of elevators and head straight to the private one that requires a keycard to use. I swipe my card and push the button. It only takes a few seconds until it dings and the doors open. We enter the car and make the ride up to the forty-fifth floor in silence.

I gave Mav a quick breakdown on the way here so he doesn't look shocked when we get in there. He has one of the best poker faces I've seen, but still. Better to be safe than sorry.

When the car comes to a stop and the doors open, we walk into the reception area. This place looks like a swanky law office, but really, it's just a place for dealings and meetings with prospects and the Conclave. Or the Board, on the exceedingly rare occasion they deign to grace us with their presence.

The sound of our shoes on the marble floor echoes around the space as we head toward the main conference room. Voices filter down the hall and I'm pretty sure we're the last to arrive, which was the plan.

I push the door open and the room falls silent as we enter. Harrison sits at the head of the table, the other senior Conclave members flanking the seats to his left and right, so I head to stand opposite Harrison. Finn and Mav stay flanking me, and none of us bother to sit.

"Lincoln, good of you to finally grace us with your presence, considering you requested this meeting." My father glares at me as if we're late, but the clock literally just hit nine as we entered the room, which was the time he gave me.

"I like to be prompt," I tell him. "If you're ready, I'll begin."

A challenge flashes in his eyes at my defiant tone, but he nods while the rest of the Conclave remain silent. Except for Edward, who snorts a laugh, stifling it when Harrison glares at him.

"Perfect. So as I'm sure you are all aware, Octavia Royal is back in Echoes Cove after the... untimely death of our old Regent." I pull the folded document from my pocket and drop the copy on the table in front of me. "As I'm sure you're all also aware, Stone put several failsafes in place for Octavia, so that she remained free of the Knights. The document on the table is the contract he made with you all."

I push the paper across the table to Finn's dad, who opens the envelope and nods at Harrison after he confirms what I've said. If looks could kill, I'd be dead and cold on the ground from the look Harrison gives me.

"That contract clearly states that in the instance of his death, Octavia is to be protected by the Knights, but that her freedom is still granted. Her freedom is for life, and the rest of Stone's line will remain free but be granted the benefits of the Knights, unless they choose to join the Knights under their own volition *without* active influence from *any* member." I pause for effect, letting everything sink in before continuing. "It also states that, should Octavia be approached, hurt by, or initiated into the Knights, she instantly takes the Regency."

Murmurs go up around the room and it occurs to me that maybe not everyone was privy to the details of the deal Stone made when he stepped down. And considering the fact that my father looks like he's going to implode, I'm guessing he wasn't aware either.

"What is the point here, Lincoln?" Harrison asks through clenched teeth, and it takes a lot of strength not to just laugh at him.

"My point, Father," I spit, "is that Octavia has been taken, we think, by a Knight. It means that if any harm comes to her by his hand, she will be the rightful Regent of this Sect."

SIX

OCTAVIA

My eyes flutter open for a moment, but my head pounds like a jackhammer with each heartbeat, forcing them closed again. My mouth is so dry I have to peel my tongue from the roof of my mouth. Everything feels so heavy.

Then I feel his breath on my skin and I flinch, opening my eyes again, the blindfold having slipped down enough that I can see a little, and find him watching me...

Standing way too fucking close.

I have to be imagining this. There's no way...

"Oh good, you're awake." His voice sends a shiver down my spine. It feels like he knows it when he smiles, looking crazier than I've ever seen him. He leans in closer, too close. His warm breath on my cheek makes my stomach flip-flop.

I try to speak, but my throat is so dry I can't form words. *How long was I out?* Where the hell am I?

What does he want from me?

This can't be happening to me right now. I close my eyes for a second, trying to calm the rising panic inside of me. How did I not see this? He wasn't even on the *second* list of people possibly stalking me. How did he get away from the tour?

How is this real?

I jump as something bangs, and I open my eyes again. I'm not sure what's worse. Seeing and knowing, or closing my eyes to this insanity.

He walks away from me, over to the darker side of the room. I realize the overhead lights are off, a dim lamp on a short table beside me the only source of light. I can't see much else, but my eyes are grateful for the break from the harsh glare of the fluorescent lights from earlier.

I need to be smart about this. I have no idea where the fuck I am, why I'm here, what time it is, or if my guys are still alive and on their way to save me. All I know is that it's cold and dark.

"Evan..."

He grins at me again, stroking a finger down my cheek and laughing when I flinch at his touch. "You should call me Panda. You always call me Panda."

I cringe at his touch. He looks at me like I'm his prize and it makes me feel sick. There's something sinister in his look that I've never seen there before.

"Why am I here?" I ask quietly, hoping not to push him too hard. He's never hurt me before... but I mean, he took me, drugged me... who knows what else he's capable of?

"Because those stupid boys don't deserve you. They just get in the way. You were always meant to be mine. I'm the only one who can protect you. Even your father knew it."

Bile rises in my throat at his words as they trigger my memories.

Oh God.

Lincoln.

East.

The vision of them lying in a pool of blood fills my mind, and I choke back a sob.

Please let them be okay.

"You don't get to speak about my father." The words come out as more of a croak than forceful, as intended. "You don't know anything about him."

His eyes narrow before his smile widens. "I think, little bird, you might be the one that didn't know him. Trust me. I knew your father pretty well..." His manic laughter causes bile to rise in my throat. "He promised you to me a long time ago, but he reneged on his deal, stole you away, and sent you here. Away from me and the protection *only I* can give you."

The sound of metal on metal screeches out, followed by a clatter. He leaves momentarily in the direction of the sound then moves back toward me. "I told you. I'm trying to protect you."

I blink up at him, trying to work this all out. "Protect me from what?"

"From them. From all of it. From me."

None of this makes any sense.

"You don't understand. Your father was a coward. He wasn't protecting you either. You were just left out in the cold. Clueless, defenseless. But you were meant for more. And the only way to *be* more, is if I help you."

I shake my head, more confused than I was when he started talking.

"Evan... Panda. P. None of this makes any sense. What do you mean more? And why am I tied up? I thought we were friends." I can't work out if I'm more angry or hurt right now.

He was supposed to be my friend.

He glares at me briefly then softens again, running a finger down my cheek.

"That's exactly why you're here. I need to deprogram you. They all made you believe their lies. I'm going to make everything better. Then you'll realize the truth. They infected you. Messed with your mind. It's the only reason why you'd let them do to you what they did; the only reason you'd forgive them. But I knew...

when I saw you had forgiven them, I knew you'd forgive me too."
He pauses and steps back, tilting his head as he looks at me.
"You'll forgive me right, little dove? All I ever wanted to do was
protect you. I saved you before, and that's all I'm doing now.
Protecting you, mending your broken wings."

"The only one trying to break me is you," I hiss. This is such
utter bullshit. "I will never forgive you, and I will never let you
win. You can't keep me locked up here forever."

His smile turns into a glare and he stomps back toward me,
moving so close his lips practically whisper against my skin. "You
have no idea what I can do."

I take a deep breath and try to calm myself, because I think
the only way I'm going to get myself out of this shit is if I play
along with him. I'm not sure what happened to him. When did he
stop being the guy I trusted and become this monster? Or has this
always been him and I just didn't see it?

"My head is still a bit fuzzy, P," I say, forcing a smile on my
face, wincing as my head pounds at the movement. "I just want to
understand what you're protecting me from."

"The Knights," he hisses. "Don't you understand? No one else
is trying to protect you, they're just preparing you to take over
where your dad left off. It's all just a show, to lull you into a false
sense of security."

"I want to believe you, P. But it's kind of hard to trust you
when you have me tied up like this."

He frowns at me, then shakes his head as he mutters to
himself. "You have to stay tied up for now. It's the only way. I'm
doing this for you."

"P, are you okay?" He seems like he's lost his goddamn mind
and when he looks at me, he almost looks like a lost little boy.
"Maybe if you untie me, we can talk this all out?"

"I am not untying you! Stop trying to trick me!" he yells, and I
startle. He starts to pace back and forth in front of me, tugging on

his hair. Fear floods me, I've never seen him like this. "You're still under their influence. We need to break you free of it first."

I bite my lip, sad for my friend, because something is very obviously wrong with him. I can't help but wonder if this is because of his initiation, or if something else happened after I left the tour. He wasn't like this before. He was chill and stable, funny even. He was someone I could depend on, but the guy in front of me right now is a world away from the P I used to chill with.

I rack my mind, trying to think back to the Midnight Blue gig I took Indi to. He seemed okay then, just like the old P... had the flowers started arriving by then? Or was that trip what started his spiral?

He was quiet at Thanksgiving, sure, and I know he spoke to the guys, but he wasn't like this.

"What happened, P?" I ask, trying to keep my voice even and steady. I am very much at a disadvantage right now, but I don't think he wants to hurt me. Maybe if I can reach the guy I used to know, this won't end in tears. Or worse.

He looks at me, confused. "What do you mean?"

I take a deep breath and hope to fuck I can reach him. "I mean, what happened after I left the tour? Why did you think you needed to protect me?"

"I knew what would happen when you went back... I knew it. But I had to stay on tour. It was where they wanted me, and I didn't hate it. Then you came back, but we were there—at that venue—and I saw what it did to you. I knew I'd been right, that I was the only one that could protect you. I just need to put the final pieces in place. I think you should sleep some more."

He grabs a syringe and a knife from the metal table beside me, and fear spikes in my heart. "No, P. Please. I don't need to sleep."

I try to move, to get free of my binding, but the thick leather buckles don't move. He puts the knife against my throat to stop me from moving before using the drip already in my arm to administer whatever the fuck it is he's giving me, and the world spins.

"Sleep for now, V. We'll talk more when you wake up. Maybe then you'll be ready."

Please, someone, find me.

I wake up, my head pounding again, except this time there's no blindfold. Just darkness. I stay quiet, attempting to even my breathing despite my heart beating out of my chest. I can't hear anything but the rushing of my blood in my ears.

Trying to calm myself takes longer than I'd like, though that could be the brain fog.

I still can't believe it's him.

None of this makes any fucking sense to me. I've barely been in contact with him since Thanksgiving.

I shake my head, there's no way. But as I rack my mind, I can't think of what would push him to this. I have to focus on this, rather than the last thing I remember before coming here, because that was Lincoln and East in a pool of blood. If I focus on that, I'm never getting out of here. If either of them didn't make it... because of me...

I don't know what I'll do.

The overhead light flickers on and I blink against the harshness of the yellow light.

"You're awake," he says as he comes down the stairs, which is when I realize I'm in a basement. It's as if that knowledge turns my senses up, and I take in the stone walls and wrinkle my nose at the damp smell down here.

"Where are we?" I ask, my eyes watering against the harsh lighting.

"That doesn't matter. We won't be here long," he says, running a hand through his hair. "We need to get you away from them before they get you too."

"Before who gets me?" I ask softly, trying to remain calm. Pretty sure no one expected the guy who saved me from my last stalker to be the one to put me through this again, but I listen to my dad's voice in my memory, telling me to stay calm and collected, and it helps.

Only a little, but I cling to it like it's my only lifeline.

For all I know, it might be.

"The Knights." He spins to face me. "The Regent will send his guard dog for you. It's what he does. He came for everyone else in your line. He'll come for you too if I don't get you out."

My eyes go wide and my heart rate increases, but there's no beeping this time. I guess he took the monitor away. I shake my head, trying to clear the fog clouding my mind. It's useless, but I have to try.

"What does that even mean, P?"

"It means you're in danger, and I'm the only one who's trying to help you. Those four, the four you trust so willingly? They're in on it. Why else would they keep you so close? Covet you? They tricked you into thinking they wanted to keep you safe, but really, they want to gift you to the Knights." He pauses his pacing and scrubs a hand down his face, looking at me as if he's pleading with me to trust him. I've always trusted him, trusted him with my life... but he has to be wrong. There's no way they'd do that to me. "The final step of initiation. Losing something or someone you love. They just want power. I thought you'd be safe, but no. I've been watching. They don't want you to be safe. They want to sacrifice you for their own gain. The only potentially innocent one is East. He doesn't know everything, but they don't care. They'll sacrifice him too if that's what it takes to secure their seats in the Conclave."

I blink at him. He has to be wrong.

He has to be.

"They wouldn't do that to me, P," I spit. Listening to that voice in my head that says to remain calm and collected is a lot easier said than freaking done.

He glares at me, angry that I don't believe him. "Did they tell you about how your dad really died? 'Cause they know. They know the guard dog came for him."

I choke on the lump that forms in my throat. I try to swallow but it doesn't clear. He has to be lying. "I don't know what that means, P."

"It *means* that the Knights want you. I didn't tell your stupid boyfriends, because I didn't want them to know I knew anything. And I couldn't tell you. How could I? I knew the guard dog was coming and I didn't do anything. I didn't think he'd kill Stone. I didn't. And then you found him and I panicked. I don't want you to hate me, but I didn't want them to kill me."

"Who is the guard dog, Panda? Who killed my dad?"

He looks at me like I'm insane, like I should know.

"Riley... Riley is the guard dog."

My heart beats so fast I think I might have a heart attack. He can't mean Maverick. "Riley?"

"Yeah, Riley. Edward. The Regent's guard dog... he took your mom, then he came for your dad."

"My mom?" My mind spins, trying to filter through all of this. I'm half glad I'm strapped in, because I'm not sure I'd be able to stay standing right now. "Why?"

"I don't know. If I knew, I'd tell you. I swear it. I just know that he wants you now, and they're going to give you to him. So I had to get you away from them. Only I can protect you, V. You have to believe me."

A tear slips down my face and I try not to flinch as he wipes it away. "Don't cry, V. I didn't want to make you cry."

Rage bubbles up inside of me, and I snap. "You didn't want to make me cry? Are you fucking kidding me? You stalk me, threaten me and my friends. My boyfriends. Then you fucking kidnap me, shoot at us—they could be dead for all I fucking know —and now I'm tied up while you tell me that Maverick's dad took my mom and killed my dad. What the fuck did you think I was going to do? Laugh? Thank you? This is fucked up, Evan."

He steps back, looking like I slapped him when I called him Evan, but I'm all out of fucks right now.

This is so messed up.

I scream out into the nothingness as tears stream down my face and allow myself to break. There's no point in trying to shove it down this time. It's not going to save me.

Nothing is going to save me. Either I die here with Panda, or I die at the hands of the Knights apparently.

I'm not usually one for woe is me moments but right now, I'm going to woe the fuck out.

"V..."

"You don't get to call me that," I hiss. "My friends call me V, and you, Evan, are *not* my friend. Friends don't kidnap each other and tie them up, or fucking shoot at each other. This is bullshit." I struggle in my restraints, hoping that something comes loose. But even if it doesn't, I get to at least *try* to do something.

He presses his lips into a thin line. It's like a switch inside of him flips and that darker side of him comes back to the surface.

He just laughs in response as he moves toward me. "I'm assuming you need to use the bathroom. Are you going to behave, or do I need my gun?"

As if triggered by his words, my bladder makes itself known. Apparently being hooked up to an IV will do that to you, and I'd really rather not pee myself. Though the thought of being even close to submissive to him raises my hackles.

I shake my head. "You don't need your gun."

He moves closer, unhooking the IV from my arm before

releasing one of my ankles from its binding, but then shackles it to my other leg with a length of rope. He does the same to my wrists, binding them in front of me. "If you do anything stupid, I will teach you a lesson about disobeying me. Do you understand, little dove?"

I ignore him while trying to make sure I don't fall. I have no idea how long I've been here, but my body is weak as fuck. As much as I'd love to fight him right now, I'm not sure my body could do it.

"Little dove?" The new nickname is gross. Like I'm something small and fragile to be protected and coveted. Fuck this, and fuck him.

I snap my gaze back up to meet his. "My name is Octavia."

"There's that fire. I'll break you down soon enough, then you can rise. Like my very own phoenix from the ashes."

I don't respond, because it's useless and I need to save my energy to move. I also have no idea how to deal with this version of him. "Where is the bathroom?"

"Up the stairs." He grins. I waddle toward the stairs as best as I can, but I'm out of breath and dizzy by the time I reach the bottom step. I try a few times to lift one foot up high enough to climb them, but the bindings make it impossible.

"I've got you, little dove," he says and steps up behind me, lifting me into his arms bridal style. He looks down at me with a twisted sort of affection in his eyes. My stomach rolls from being so close to him.

He buries his nose in my hair and sucks in a breath, and it's all I can do not to swing both hands up and hit him in the face.

Goddamn my body for betraying me, leaving me so weak.

He carries me up the stairs and across a dilapidated kitchen, down a hall, to a half bath. "Do you need help in there?"

"I'll be fine," I say through gritted teeth. There is no way I'm letting him in the bathroom with me. I'm all too aware that he could easily make me, but he seems to want to keep his façade of protector up, so I've just got to hope that stays in place. He puts me down, holding me until I'm steady. My skin crawls under his touch, but my head spins at the sudden movement, so I can't even pull away from him as quickly as I want to.

He hands me a fresh pair of pants and a tank. I consider ignoring them, the idea of accepting anything from him almost as disgusting as this imaginary relationship he seems to think we have, but I'm fucking gross right now.

As soon as I'm sure I'm not going to face-plant, I scoot toward the door and nearly fall on my face.

I turn back to face him, trying to look as broken as I can. "Can you untie me, please? I can't clean up if I'm tied up. I can barely walk."

He watches me closely, tapping the gun on his hip. "If you try to run, or do anything else just as stupid, I will use this."

My heart pounds in my chest at the possibility that he might actually untie me, but also the thought of getting shot. I really want to get out of here, but I really don't want to get shot. He steps forward and unties the bindings at my wrists before stepping back and pulling the gun. "Untie your ankles and head inside."

I do as he says, trying not to freak out about the gun pointed at my head. Usually I wouldn't think he'd pull the trigger, but he's a little unhinged right now. I pull at the bindings on my ankles, freeing them before shooting into the bathroom and locking the door behind me. It's a flimsy as fuck lock, but it's something. Pretty sure it'd be useless if he really tried to break it open, but it makes me feel a little better at least.

I look around the room at the broken tiles, the flickering light, and the window that's been bricked closed. Awesome. Definitely no way out of here except for the door then.

Feeling resigned, I undress, washing as best I can, trying not to look at my reflection in the dirty, grainy mirror. It's impossible to miss the dark purple streaks under my eyes, and my hair is matted and gross.

How long have I been here?

I get redressed and splash my face with water, taking a few mouthfuls as I do. The cool, refreshing sips do more for my mood than I expect, so I take a couple more, savoring the small boost of serotonin.

"Are you nearly done, little dove?"

Happy feeling's gone.

He sounds kind, patient even, but I'm not stupid enough to believe him.

One day I'll work all of this out, I just need to survive this very real hell I've been thrust into. Panda never would've raised a finger against me, but I have no idea what this new Evan is capable of.

So I take a deep breath and undo the lock, pushing the door open.

"Feel better?"

I nod, glaring at him as he steps forward with new bindings, handing them to me. "Tie your ankles, and don't make them loose. I don't want to hurt you but I will."

The gun trained on me once more, I take a deep breath and tie my ankles together, not as tight as he had them, but tight enough that I'm not going to be able to slip them without breaking my ankle.

I fucking hate this.

With my ankles bound, he ties my wrists and picks me back up, taking me back down to the basement. He doesn't seem to notice the daggers I'm staring at him. If he does, he doesn't say anything. When we reach the bottom of the stairs, I realize why he'd been so quiet while I was in the bathroom. The table I'd been tied to is gone, and in its place against the back wall is a cot with a thin mattress.

"I thought this might be more comfortable until we're done. I doubt it'll take me long to get you to see the truth and become my phoenix. I'm a determined man. You'll be mine eventually." He drops me onto the cot and I clench my jaw as the water I swallowed threatens to resurface at the jolting movements.

He unties my hands first, binding me to the bed, and then my ankles, before moving to get the IV.

"I think you need to sleep. Everything will be better if you sleep."

"Do not fucking drug me again, Evan," I growl, but he isn't listening to me anymore, he's muttering to himself.

I hiss as he pushes the needle into my arm and tapes it in place before hooking up the tubes.

He brushes my hair behind my ear, and grasps my chin in his thumb and forefinger. "I need to go out, so you need to sleep again."

I whimper as whatever he put in the IV bag burns in my vein and the room fades away.

"Sleep well, little dove. Soon you'll be mine, and there's nothing anyone can do to save you."

The edges of my mind go fuzzy, but in this moment of helplessness, I make myself a promise.

If I survive this, I won't ever be this helpless again.

Ever. Fucking. Again.

SEVEN

EAST

L ying in this hospital bed is killing me slowly. I feel like a giant waste of space, unable to help the guys search for V.

That might be what ends me, not the whole, bullet-to-the-heart-with potential-catastrophic-complications thing.

I'm losing my goddamn mind. She's been gone for over a week. A whole eleven fucking days of not knowing who has her, or what's happening to her... of knowing that the others had to ask the Knights for help.

None of it feels right.

Or good.

It's all very much bad, but I'm practically tied to this stupid fucking hospital bed, unable to even walk the length of the fucking hall yet because, apparently, a bullet to the heart will fuck with your ability to do just about anything.

I hide behind a brave face when the boys come to visit because I need them focused on V rather than my shit right now

The last I heard from Luc was that they thought they had a location. But that was late last night and none of us have heard anything since. The ticking of the clock in this room is so loud that I want to throw it across the damn room, but that would require moving, which technically I'm not allowed to do alone yet.

Stupid fucking bullet wound.

I don't regret taking the bullet for Lincoln. I'd take it again a thousand times over if it keeps him safe, but that doesn't mean I have to enjoy the recovery.

It's only ten in the morning. It feels like eons have passed since my meds at seven, but that's the joy of three hours alone in a room with nothing to do and no one to talk to.

As if summoning someone with my very thoughts, the door to my room opens, and a guy I don't recognize stands in the doorway.

"Hello?" It comes out as more of a question, and I grab my phone to dial Luc just in case. Living around the Knights has taught me to be safe rather than sorry, and suspicion is my go-to with people I don't know.

"Easton?" he asks, almost warily as he steps into the room, letting the door close behind him. He looks very at odds with how unsure he seems. His at least five-thousand-dollar suit, shiny shoes, and styled hair scream money, confidence. He looks like a man who is typically sure of himself.

But he says my name like a bomb is about to detonate and my suspicion grows. So I nod, the weird tension in the room growing. There's a pit in my stomach as I take in his appearance, but it doesn't stop me from asking, "Who are you?"

He inches closer to the bed and motions toward the chair. "May I?"

I quirk a brow and say nothing, so he sits down and takes a deep breath. "My name is Chase Armstrong. I received a call from Fiona after she got a message from your brother."

My ears heat and tingle at his words. I can't breathe.

Holy fuck.

This isn't how I expected this to go down.

"You're my father?"

He nods in response and I let out a deep breath. "I haven't heard from your mother in just over twenty years. I never knew…"

The air is thick, and it's like I can't breathe. My chest tightens, like a weight sits on it as I watch him struggle to think of what to say. What excuses to make. Who to blame. I already know the answers to all of that, but it doesn't make any of this feel less stifling.

"You never knew she had your kid," I finish, because he's looking at the floor. Why am I not surprised that Fiona said nothing? Though, it's very likely that was Harrison's doing. He's a giant fucking prick like that.

My stomach churns as he sits in silence, his eyes searching my face as if looking for the answers to the universe. He lets out a sigh and his shoulders drop a little. He takes a deep breath and straightens up again, squaring his shoulders and calling on that confidence I'd expected of him. "Exactly. She only called yesterday, otherwise I'd have been here sooner."

"That sounds about right," I mutter. Of course I nearly die, and she can't be bothered to respond to Linc's message for over a week. Typical Fiona.

I feel awkward as hell sitting across from the man who is essentially my sperm donor. What exactly am I supposed to say here? What does he want from me?

"Why are you here?" I ask, folding my arms across my chest carefully, trying to construct barriers between us. If he thinks he can just walk in here and everything's going to be a love fest, he has another thing coming. He also has that air about him, the one that comes from a lifetime of being tangled up with the Knights, and my hackles are raised.

I am done with being a pawn for those fucking people.

"I don't have any other children, and I'm aware that you are fully grown, your own man, but I'd like to get to know you, if you'd give me a chance." He looks earnest, but the jaded asshole that I am struggles to believe there isn't some ulterior motive here, no matter what he says. Knights always want *something*. "I know you don't know me, where I'm from, the kind of man I am, but if I'd have known about you…"

I shrug, and cut him off. "There is no way Harrison would've let you know the truth, so don't feel too guilty. And if you had, he wouldn't have let you live. Not back then."

"Harrison Saint doesn't scare me." There's a fire in his eyes that makes me question if this guy is a Knight. There *are* three families that sit on the Conclave that I know next to nothing about. "He might be the Regent, but after what Lincoln brought to the table this week, that might not be the case for long."

"So you *are* a Knight." I sigh, rolling my eyes.

Just awesome. Any thoughts of maybe seeing what he wanted just disappeared. I'm not getting any deeper in with the Knights than I am. The idea was to escape, not become one of them.

"I am, only because my family have been since the founding of the Cove. I'm not like the others. I have no need for their particular brand of… ethics. I abhor everything about the organization and if it wasn't for my own initiation, I wouldn't still be with them, but you know as well I do. Blood in, blood out."

I nod. He's not wrong, I know that all too well. He seems earnest, but I don't trust him and he seems to know that. He lets out a deep sigh, and runs a hand down his face.

"I don't expect you to trust me, Easton. Hell, I didn't expect you to let me get this far, I just… I don't know what I wanted, but I needed to explain myself to you. To give you options other than whatever your current situation is." He lets out a deep breath before continuing. "The Knights are the reason I chose never to marry or have children. I didn't want to drag anyone else into the madness. I'd rather see the institution burn to the ground than help it continue. It's why I struggled with coming here to see you and why I helped Stone the way I did when he wanted to leave."

His revelation piques my interest, but I remain guarded, reminding myself that stringing together pretty words, telling you what you want to hear, is what the Knights thrive at. Yet, I still find myself asking him the question on the tip of my tongue. "What do you mean?"

His phone sounds in his pocket. He pulls it out, glances at the screen and silences it before giving me all of his attention once more. He pauses, as if weighing his words, and the air in the room grows thicker.

Fuck this is weird.

I'm not sure if I'd be happier if he never came, or if he'd just say what he came to say. "I mean, that I was the one who helped him craft a way to get Octavia out. I am not your enemy, Easton. And if you'll let me, I could be a very good ally."

My mind spins at all of this new information. This guy is my dad, and he turns up, hating the Knights, offering to help us all. It seems too good to be true. And when something seems that way, it usually is. Yet my heart still races at the possibilities. I'm not about to tell him my every fucking secret, but I might be more willing to hear him out.

I run a hand through my hair, trying to work out what to say, how not to give everything away with just a few words. How desperate I am to find a way to get them all out. Especially when, for all I know, Harrison put him up to this.

I wouldn't put it past him.

"You wouldn't be very good at poker," he laughs. "Your every thought broadcasts clearly. I understand you have no reason to trust me, but I'm going to show you that you can. If you'll let me."

I quirk a brow and fold my arms over my chest, wincing a little at the pressure on my healing incision as I move too quickly. "What do you mean exactly?"

"I mean, that I found your girl, and your brother and his friends are gearing up as we speak to go and get her."

EIGHT

OCTAVIA

I've been awake for what feels like hours, but Panda isn't here. It feels like I've been here for days, but I have no idea how long it's been. What I do know is I'm fucking covered in grime and dirt. It's so fucking gross. I've been unbound every time he has let me go to the bathroom, but I haven't been able to escape. He's got the IV in my arm again, but I still haven't eaten and I'm getting even weaker. The dizziness is almost unbearable.

Wherever I am has been dark and silent since I woke up. Not even the lamp in the corner is on. My eyes adjusted a little while ago, but that doesn't help the fact that I really need to fucking pee.

He apparently moved me while I was out. I'm still cuffed, but I have some movement at least. Enough to scratch my nose, thank God, because that was a fucking nightmare earlier.

I keep going over everything in my mind, trying to distract myself from the fact that I need a bathroom, and trying to work through how the hell we ended up here. Panda's behavior is completely out of character for the guy I knew. It's almost as if he's come unraveled. To my knowledge, he doesn't have any history of mental illness, but this sudden and drastic change in him can't be anything else.

It just doesn't make sense.

But the fact that I'm kidnapped and tied to a bed tells me that something obviously happened.

Knowing that he's a Knight explains some things, but he's been a Knight the entire time I've known him. So it doesn't make sense why everything would just change over the last eight or so months.

I can't even remember when all of this started. That's how fucked up my world has been since Dad died. I'm trying not to focus on what P told me about Dad being killed, because well, I've been so angry at him for leaving me, and if he didn't leave me, then the guilt is going to cripple me.

I can't afford to be overwhelmed by that right now.

So I'm focusing on everything else he's told me.

Another thing that doesn't make sense to me is why the Knights sent him to watch me in the first place. He joined the tour about two years in. I can't pinpoint anything that happened around then that would've sparked their interest, but then, I don't know why they killed my dad either.

The creaking of the wooden boards above my head makes my heart race.

Is Panda here? Is it someone else?

As much as I don't want it to be someone else, maybe if it's not P, they'll let me go.

I can hope anyway, right?

I slow my breathing to try and pay attention to the footsteps, kicking myself mentally for not doing more training with Maverick, for not going back to my self-defense lessons, for everything I could've done to not end up here.

The steps move away from me, leaving me to scramble, and as I wave my right hand around, trying to grab the other handcuff, it's like a see-saw effect; the tension on the rope allowing me to move one arm at a time, but only if I sacrifice the motion of the other. If I want to scratch my nose with my right hand, the left one has to be stretched above my head in order to have enough range of motion to reach.

Refusing to get frustrated about how helpless I am, I go still again and close my eyes, focusing on the sounds from upstairs.

It's gone quiet.

Shit. Fuck. Tits. Wank.

Silence has never felt more dangerous.

I try to steady my breathing, but it's all I can hear and that just makes my heart pound harder. It feels like it's too loud amid the quiet, like the beat of a drum. The footsteps start again and I hold my breath, trying to focus on them, when I realize there's more than one person upstairs.

He's working with someone else!

The murmur of voices reaches me as the steps grow louder, and it becomes apparent that whoever is here is coming down the stairs. Adrenaline rushes through me, my previously non-existent fight or flight response finally kicking in, but struggle as I might, I can't get free of these stupid fucking cuffs.

I want to cry in anger and frustration.

I hate being this helpless. Weak. Being at someone else's mercy.

It just feels wrong.

The door at the top of the stairs creaks as it opens a moment before the crack of wood echoes around me as one of the stairs breaks, followed by a fuck-ton of cursing.

I pretend to be asleep, but only one set of feet comes down the stairs.

"Little dove?" Panda's voice is loud and direct. The most coherent he's sounded since he's had me here. My eyes flutter open, and I blink a few times, feigning adjusting to the brightness.

"You're awake, good. I need you not to fight me."

He steps toward me and I flinch, jerking my body backward. Not that it gets me anywhere, but he pauses, frowning.

"What does that mean?"

"It means I need you to not fight me," he says, stepping toward me again and pulling a blindfold from his back pocket. "I'm not going to hurt you if you do what I say. I promise."

"Why?" I croak, my eyes wide, my gaze not leaving the blindfold as he advances across the room.

"Because the person who has been helping me wants to make sure you're okay with their own eyes, but they want to remain anonymous."

"But why? If they're helping and you don't want to hurt me, why remain anonymous?"

"That's just how they want it. Once they see you're not hurt. We'll move to the next phase: getting us out of here."

"I can't just leave here, P. Please don't make me." I hate begging, but I can't leave my life here. Panic floods my system and I'm officially too weak to try and fight it off. I hadn't wanted to come back to Echoes Cove at first, but now... now there's too much for me to leave behind.

He shakes his head, anger washing over his features as he closes the last bit of distance between us. "You're still brainwashed. I'll fix that too, don't worry. I'll help you realize the truth of it all."

Before I can respond, his hands dart forward and he wraps the soft material around my head, covering my eyes and plunging my world into darkness. "Panda, please. Don't do this."

My voice is thick with uncried tears. Not being able to see anything makes all of this so much worse. I was not raised to be helpless. "You were supposed to help me. Protect me. But this... this isn't that, P. Please see that."

"I see everything. Far more clearly than you. Just trust me." I feel the warmth of him disappear and choke back a sob. I swore I wouldn't cry, but fuck my life, this is too much. I've managed to survive until now, but this might be the thing that finally breaks me.

"You can come down now!" Panda's voice echoes around the bare room, followed quickly by the creak of the wooden stairs. The smell of peppermint, wood, and spice fills the space. It's so thick it makes my nose itch. "I told you. She's fine. Are you satisfied now?

A beat passes, and Panda says, "Good."

Whoever is standing there keeps their mouth shut as the blindfold soaks up my tears, all while my heart pounds so loud in my chest, I'm sure they can hear it. It feels like eons pass in the silence before the creaking starts again when whoever it is leaves again. At least I assume so. I guess it could've been Panda, but I didn't hear him walk across the room.

When the door slams, my blindfold is ripped away. "We'll be leaving here soon. Our lives are going to be so much better. Just the two of us, far from here, where the Knights can't reach us."

"I will never forgive you for this, P. You're going to have to hold me captive my entire life."

He shakes his head, looking at me like *I'm* the crazy one. "No I won't, not once we de-program you. You'll see." He trails off into a mumble and turns off the lights, flicking on a projector which lights up the wall in front of me, images flickering brightly. I guess this is part of his deprogramming bullshit. I struggle against the restraints as he heads back up the stairs.

I need to find a way out of these fucking bindings, because if he gets me away from here, the only outcomes are that I'm going to end up dead or killing him.

———

I wake up to the flashing of images on the wall in front of me. It's so bright that my eyes water and it takes me a moment to actually see what the images are.

Pictures of my guys, of Indi, of me with them...

I'm strapped back to the table I had been on when I first got here, tilted upright so it's like I'm standing, except there's an extra brace around my neck and forehead so I can't look anywhere but at the images.

Then the pain begins. "They are no good for you. They just want to hurt you," Evan whispers in my ear, and the burning on my forearm intensifies. "They will only bring you pain."

I try not to scream out, try not to play into whatever sick game this is, but it's impossible. I don't think I've ever felt pain like this before. I can't even work out why it hurts so much because I can't see it.

"This isn't going to work, Evan. The only one hurting me is you."

The pain recedes a little before he appears in front of me. "I'm not hurting you. They are!"

He disappears again, the images continuing, and then I hear voices. Their voices. Our conversations playing around the room. I feel the cold sting of metal on the inside of my thigh, before the pain starts again as he slices my skin, blood running down my leg to the sound of Lincoln's voice telling me how useless and pathetic I am.

I will not let this break me.

Even if I thought it might. I won't let it. I have too much to live for outside of this hellhole.

The metal around my ankle heats as images of me from Homecoming flash on the screen, and a tear slips down my cheek as I take in the jubilance on my face, dancing with Indi before her guys arrived. The heat grows and I see a flicker of orange out of the corner of my eye.

Flame.

I scream as it licks against my skin, all while trying to hold onto my mental walls. I can survive this. It's just pain.

"Our initiation…" Lincoln's voice starts, and another tear trickles down my face.

"Panda, please," I croak. "Stop."

The heat reduces and he moves to stand in front of me, running a finger down my cheek, wiping away my tears. "We've only just started," he says quietly. "I know it hurts, but this is the only way. I'm doing this for you. Once you're all better, free from their control, then we can stop. Then we can be free."

"I'm already free."

He frowns at me before shaking his head. "You're lying. They made you a liar. I'll bring you back."

He drags his blade from the top of my bicep down to my wrist. "You just need to remember how bad they are for you. All of this is their fault."

I close my eyes and try to shut everything out. The pain, the sounds… that Panda is the one doing this to me.

"Open your eyes!" he yells in my face as the flames lick at my ankle again. I try to clamp down on my lips, to stop the screams that threaten to burst from me at the searing pain. "You need to see that they did this to you. That this is their fault!"

He moves to the other side of the room, returning with a dark pole in his hand. "You need to be reborn in fire, only then will you see the truth. There is no other way."

He uses his knife to cut away part of my tank top, exposing my stomach before placing the tip of the pole against the very bottom of my stomach. It's cold at first, but then electricity rips through my body, and pain like I've never known grips me as I convulse against the table. The voltage comes in bursts as he starts and stops the pain.

Tears run down my face. From the pain, yes, but also for the guy who was once my friend. Whoever this person is, it isn't my Panda. This person is beyond unhinged, and my heart sinks as I wonder just how far this version of him will take all of this.

"How long have we been here?" I ask Panda as he walks me back to the basement, my arms bound behind my back and my ankles shackled together. The cuffs rub on the gauze from where he tried to patch me up after his multiple attempts at breaking me. It hurts a bit, but at this point, everything hurts.

I've spent the last day or so—I think—trying to seem more compliant. Hoping I can make him believe I'm coming around to what he wants. After the last time I was taken, my dad and Mac did months of training with me in case I got taken again. Stay calm, don't antagonize, and try to get out. Send up a signal if I can. If only they'd told me how much harder it would be in reality as opposed to my lessons with them. I'm trying now, I just have to hope it isn't too late. If I can get him to trust that I believe him, then maybe he'll unshackle me and I can get the fuck out of here.

That sinister side of him hasn't come back out since his last attempt to 'deprogram' me, and I'm thankful because my entire body still hurts from what he did. It feels like days I've been trying to play on that softer side of him and I think it's working, but I'm still so weak and dizzy that I'm not exactly firing on all cylinders.

"Just over a week," he mumbles as he walks beside me, tapping away on his phone. "We'll be here another few days. The final arrangements are just being made."

I try to look as doe-eyed as I can, all while trying to smother the rage and fear inside of me. "Where are we going?"

He pauses to look at me, almost confused like he expected me to fight him or argue. I can't tell if he's suspicious of my compliance or just shocked. I keep the innocent, doe-eyed look on my face, as if just waiting for the answer while he watches me.

His mouth opens, then closes, like he doesn't know what to say before shaking his head. "We're going far from here. That's all you need to know."

"Okay," I say, shrugging my shoulders and continuing to waddle toward the basement door, looking down at the floor. Being this submissive is not in my nature, it goes against everything I've ever been taught and every part of who I am, but I tried fighting him and it got me nowhere. This is the next option on my list.

I can't wait for someone to save me.

I am not a princess in a tower.

I can save myself.

But first, I need out of these goddamn bindings. He opens the door for me, and I pause at the top step. There is no way I can make it down with my ankles bound, so I wait for him to lift me, the same way I got up here. Inky darkness presses against the windows, the light of the moon the only thing illuminating the kitchen of the dilapidated house.

Thanks to a high fence surrounding the property, I haven't been able to get a sense of our surroundings, so I have no idea if we're even still in the Cove or not.

Panda lifts me bridal style down the stairs yet again, which is more than a little uncomfortable considering my injuries and that my hands are behind my back, but I don't complain. I just use the pain as a reminder of who I am, that I can survive this. That I've survived worse.

This is not the end of my story.

I wince as he takes the last step down onto the concrete, jolting me, and he frowns down at me. "What's wrong?"

"My shoulder jarred, it's okay. My wrists are a little raw too. I hurt all over." I keep my eyes down, not looking at him as he places me on my feet.

He pauses, like he's trying to make a decision, but then walks me back over to the cot I've been tied to the last few days. It's better than the table I was on, so I'm not about to complain, but also, I am sick to fucking death of being bound.

"Let me redress your wounds. We don't want them getting infected. I think the deprogramming is working. I don't want to hurt you anymore, but it's for your own good. Just a little more and I think I'll have you back. My little phoenix." My heart races at the thought of going through that again. I barely survived it the first time.

"You don't have to hurt me again. Or have to tie me back up. I won't go anywhere. You're just trying to help me, I see that now," I whimper, and I sound fucking pathetic. I hate it, but it's exactly what I was going for.

"I don't know..." he trails off, turning me back to face him. "You could be trying to trick me."

"I wouldn't do that," I say softly, glancing up to meet his gaze before looking back down. "You're my friend. You're trying to help me. Why would I trick you?"

He looks away, but then shakes his head. "I don't believe you."

"Okay." I sigh and stay compliant as he binds my wrists back to the bed, though he leaves my ankles free, even if they're still tied together. I get to actually sit up, so I'm not going to complain too loudly. It's a step in the right direction.

He moves back to the IV bag and my heart races. I really do hate fucking needles. "Can I have something to eat though? Maybe a drink? I don't like needles. You know that."

He glances at the crate of water bottles in the corner of the room, and I swear my mouth waters. I never thought I'd miss water, but I'd do a lot right now to get my hands on one of those bottles. My stomach grumbles so loudly at the thought of food that it almost startles me. I've only eaten a cheese sandwich and a handful of pretzels twice since being here. It's a wonder I'm not so light-headed that I can't stand. I guess that's the one upside of the IV.

"Please, P," I whimper, one arm clutching at my stomach as much as I can with these stupid fucking cuffs. I'm just glad he seems to be at least hesitating, which means he wants to believe that I'm coming around. He's had that projector flickering images at me for too long at this point. I just close my eyes when he leaves, because some of that shit is horrific.

"Yeah okay, we can do that. I'll give you some painkillers too, just to help." He pushes the IV stand back into the corner, and I let out a deep sigh of relief. One win. I'll take it and clutch onto it with everything I have, because maybe, just maybe, I can do this. I can get myself out of here, and find out what happened to the others.

God, I hope they're okay.

They *have* to be.

I won't accept anything else.

P brings me a bottle of water and opens it before passing it to me, along with a couple of pills. I try to sip it down, knowing that if I chug it, I'll probably be sick. The urge to slam it down is almost too strong to resist though. He watches me closely as I swallow the pills and drink the water down, letting me take a few mouthfuls before taking the bottle away. I swear I could scream as he does, but instead I paste a thankful smile onto my face. One advantage to growing up how I did: faking a smile is something I learned how to do real early on.

He seems to accept it and heads back toward the stairs. "I'll go make you a sandwich and then we can talk some more if you like?"

I widen my smile and nod. "That'll be nice."

My eagerness makes him smile and I do a mental fist pump

that he seems to believe me. He disappears up the stairs, and I adjust myself to a more comfortable position. Testing the wrist cuffs now that I'm sitting. I still can't bring my hands together, but it's a damn sight closer than it was before.

You can do this, Octavia. Just a few more steps and he'll free you.

I take a deep breath, trying to refocus and steel myself to what I have to do. I don't want to kill Panda, but if I have to do it to get free then it becomes do or die. I don't think he'd want to kill me, but if he's backed into a corner… he's still a Knight.

I guess this makes me more my father's daughter than I realized, but right now, I don't give a fuck. The burning anger inside of me is all that keeps me focused. Focused on surviving. I'll deal with everything else when I'm free from here.

If I find out this was the Knights' doing, I'll do whatever I can to burn their entire empire to the ground. Everything I know about them tells me they're rotten to the very core. I'm not one for killing everyone in my path, but if my guys are hurt—if the Knights are responsible—I already know that the darkest parts of who I am will come to the surface, and the part of me that gives a fuck is going to disappear.

Panda reappears with a sandwich on a paper plate. I never thought a slice of cheese between two plain slices of white bread would be so appealing, but here we are. I never thought I'd be tied to a bed in a creepy basement and tortured by one of my closest friends either.

He holds the plate out toward me before seeming to realize that, bound as I am, I'm not going to be able to eat. "Sorry," he says with a shrug before picking up the sandwich and offering me a bite. I take a small one, not wanting to torture my stomach with too much food.

He holds the sandwich until I'm done, then offers me the bottle of water again. "I need to go out for a little bit, but I have the cameras and security up, so you'll be fine here till I get back."

"Where are you going?"

"We need supplies for where we're going, and you'd probably like some fresh clothes... and a shower. I'm going to get what we need, and then we only have another day or two until we start our new lives. Evan and Octavia will die, and we can be whoever we want to be." He sounds so passionate, so rooted in his belief, it's shocking. I just nod and smile.

"A shower would be divine," I gush, smiling wider, not having to fake it this time. Though showering with these bandages is going to be interesting.

He nods before taking back the water. "That's what I thought. I'll be back soon, and then we'll get you sorted. I've missed you, V."

I swallow the bile that rises in my throat as he looks at me like he's loved me a thousand lifetimes, and force out the words I know he wants to hear. "I missed you too, P."

He turns and leaves, shutting off the main lights and leaving me with just the lamp again.

Panic rises at the thought that I only have a day or so to get myself out of this mess. But I have no choice. There is no way I'm being taken away from the people I love.

The only way he's getting me out of here is dead and cold.

Evan has been gone for so long that I'm starting to think something happened to him. I can't decide if that's a good or bad thing. The food has perked me up a fair amount and I no longer feel like I'm going to pass out at any given minute, but the burn on my ankle is beyond itchy.

I've been working on trying to slip these cuffs, but I'm at the point where I've realized I'm not getting out of them without dislocating something unless he releases me. My wrists and ankles are already raw from being burned and bound, but the pain is one of the few things keeping me coherent.

He has been softening the closer we get to 'leaving,' and the more submissive to his bullshit I get, the more he seems to let his guard down. I'm just glad he hasn't put me through his deprogramming again yet. Now all I have to do is make him believe I'm entirely on board and with him. I'm not sure how that's going to go, but I am all in and committed to it.

Whatever it takes to get free and get back to my guys.

If they survived everything.

I shake away that thought and refocus on my plan. If it means hurting Evan, then that's what it takes. I've come to the realization since he's held me here that survival for me might mean doing shit I'm not happy about, but I'm not letting him win.

Not this time.

I am sick of being on the back foot with everything in my life. Starting now, I'm being proactive rather than reactive. I'm not just going to let shit happen *to* me. I might've had my head in the sand regarding a lot of stuff after my dad's death, and I've tried to be more with it the last few months, but I am done with *trying*.

From here on out, I'm *doing*.

Starting with getting myself out of here. I can't rely on the possibility that someone *might* come save me. My dad taught me better than that, and I'm not about to dishonor his memory by being *that* girl.

The sound of footsteps overhead makes me pause. It's just one set this time, and I'm hoping that means it's just Evan. Something heavy thuds above me and I jump at the sound.

Goddamn being so on edge.

My hands tremble from the exertion of trying to free myself when I have so little energy. I just have to hope he doesn't question it.

I steel myself as the door at the top of the stairs opens and his heavy footsteps clamber down the stairs. "Oh good, you're still awake. It's nearly time for us to go."

I smile softly, biting down on the rage and panic that simmers beneath the surface. "Okay, that sounds good. Can I clean up before we go?"

He watches me closely, as if looking for any sign of deception, but my poker face has always been better than that. "Please don't make me hurt you."

It's all he says as he moves toward me. I eye the gun on his hip, gulping, because if he unties me, this could be my only chance, but the gun puts me at a major disadvantage. If that darker side of him shows itself, I have very little doubt he'll hurt me and convince himself it was to help me.

"I won't," I say, looking down at the ground, but he cups my chin and lifts my gaze to his before kissing me tentatively. My entire body screams at how wrong this is, but I force myself to kiss him back softly. His groans turn my stomach, but I force myself to lean into him.

He pulls back and unties my ankles, then my wrists. I fall forward onto him, and he wraps his arms around me. I pause for a moment, sad for what our friendship has become as I wrap my arms around him, then do what I know I have to.

I wrap my hand around the grip of the gun and pull it from the holster as I step back and dart around him. Pulling the gun up so he's looking down the barrel, adrenaline floods me and I feel like I could do anything.

"Do not make me hurt you," I parrot back at him as his eyes narrow at me. Taking a tentative step backwards toward the stairs, I keep the gun raised, flicking the safety off. "I don't want to hurt you, but I will."

He rushes at me, and in my broken and bruised state I'm not quick enough to get a shot off before I feel the burning pain in my ribs as he tackles me to the ground. I drop the gun, staring at the bloody knife in his hand. He looks shocked and sad as he stares at me.

"Why would you make me hurt you?"

I try not to cry, but the pain is bad. Almost as bad as the burning he put me through, but I can breathe, so I don't think he did any major damage. It just fucking hurts. "Panda, I need—"

My words aren't even fully formed when a loud bang sounds upstairs moments before footsteps clamber down the stairs behind me. I risk a glance at whoever is there and almost cry when I see Lincoln's very pissed off face, with Maverick and Finley right behind him.

Despite them being here, I keep my eyes on a now very angry Evan.

I'm just glad he didn't have time to pick up the gun I dropped, and I use this moment to scurry over and retrieve it.

"You three ruin fucking everything!" he shouts, pulling at his hair. He raises the knife, brandishing it in front of him.

Maverick saunters forward, putting himself between Evan and I, smiling that crazy smirk of his, pulling a blade of his own. "Now you're talking my language," he says, bouncing on the balls of his feet.

Lincoln moves toward me, putting his hand over mine on the gun, taking it from me and passing it to Finn who keeps his own gun trained on Panda. "I got you," he murmurs as he pulls me into his arms. I hiss as I sag against him.

"You're bleeding." His gaze rushes over me, taking in all of the injuries and the bandages before he applies pressure to my ribs. "I got you. You're going to be okay."

"She is supposed to be mine! You don't deserve her!" Evan shouts. "Especially you, after your father killed hers. You're monsters! All of you!"

Lincoln stiffens beneath me at his words as I hold my hand against the wound in my side, but Maverick doesn't respond.

Whether he knew, or whether he believes it, I can't tell, he just remains poised to attack should Evan make the wrong move. True or not, I wouldn't hold Maverick responsible for his father's actions. Holding someone accountable for the actions of others is just abhorrent.

"Evan, please." I sigh, pulling back from Lincoln. "I don't know how you saw this ending, but it was never going to end the way you wanted it to."

He looks over at me, almost deflated at my words. "I just wanted to rescue you. That's all I was ever good at." He raises his blade to his throat and my heart stops. "I failed at even that. I'm sorry. I won't let them take me too."

He drags the blade across his throat as a scream tears from me. Lincoln's arms wrap around me as I dive forward. Maverick and Finn rush to him. Maverick, covered in the spray of blood, presses his hands over the insanely deep wound, blood rushing between his fingers as the artery spurts blood. Evan's gasping breaths in these moments will haunt me forever. The seconds tick by, lasting eons as Lincoln holds me against him. Evan's grip of the knife loosens and he stills. Finn shakes his head before looking back at us.

"He's gone."

NINE

OCTAVIA

I tremble in Linc's arms as the pool of blood spreads on the basement floor.

What the fuck just happened?

Is this it? Is this the moment I break? How the fuck is one person supposed to survive all of this and come out of it in one piece? I might've been ready to kill him to survive, but watching him die like that...

"Octavia," Lincoln murmurs in my ear, while he holds me tight enough to keep me tethered to reality. "We should get you out of here. You need a doctor."

I can't say anything—do anything—but stare at Panda's pale body on the ground. Finn moves toward me, but Maverick just watches me from a distance, not able to meet my gaze.

Finn puts a finger under my chin, taking my focus from the blood so that I'm looking him in the eye. His jaw ticks as he looks me over, spotting the bruising around my wrists, but in a blink it's gone and he looks at me like I'm the most precious thing in the world. "Hey, pretty girl. We've got you, but we need to get you out of here and to a hospital."

I nod, but look back over his shoulder at Maverick who still won't look at me. "Mav?"

"He'll be okay, V. Just let us look after you before you worry about us, okay?" Finn's voice is low and soothing. He could almost convince me everything is going to be okay, but nothing about any of this is okay. "We'll sort this out. Just go with Lincoln, pretty girl."

He strokes his thumb down my cheek as a sob rips from me. Should I cry for the man who stalked and kidnapped me? Probably not, but P was more than that. He deserved better than this.

"He wasn't working alone," I croak as tears run down my face. My mind is running at a million miles a minute with everything. There are so many things I want to ask them that I can't focus properly, so it takes me a second to realize that East isn't here. "Where is East?"

Finn's face barely moves, but his jaw twitches, and I know that something is wrong.

Lincoln turns me in his arms to face him, a murderous calm about him, though I'm pretty sure it's not directed at me right now. "Just come with me, Octavia. Let's get you checked out, and then I'll tell you everything."

I shake my head, ignoring the pain as Lincoln uses one of the spare bandages to wrap my ribs. I don't think he slashed deep enough to do any major damage, it just hurts like a fucker. I wipe the tears from my face as my heart races at the memory of the night I was taken. That image is all I can see. "Where is East?"

"I'll take you to him. Come on." Lincoln's words don't set me at ease, not even a little, but I let him lead me up the stairs and out of the run-down house. It's dark outside, the moon is high in the sky, and I shiver as the cool night air hits me and my sock-covered feet hit the cold ground.

Lincoln curses and opens the back door of the Cayenne. He

reappears and pulls his hoodie over my head, which is much better than the now-bloody tank top. My leggings might not be in the best condition, but they are at least warm. He rubs his hands up and down my arms before opening the passenger door and bundling me into the car. Pulling my seatbelt over me, he buckles me in, all without a word.

I open my mouth to say thank you, but the lump in my throat makes it too hard to speak. Trying to process everything is proving too much for right now, so I wipe my mind and focus on getting warm, on the smell of Lincoln on his hoodie, on the soft, supple seat beneath me.

Anything to keep my emotions at bay, because if I let myself feel everything right now, I'm not sure how long it'll take to get myself back from that tsunami.

Lincoln climbs into the car and starts the engine, turning the heaters up to max before pulling away from the house. I have no idea where we are. The house is in the middle of nowhere and there's nothing but flat, open space as far as the eye can see.

"How hurt are you?"

I shrug. "I'm okay," I say, playing down the pain because I know we're already on our way to the hospital. I just need to keep myself conscious until then.

"How did you find me?" I ask, my mind wandering to P and how he even found this place.

His hands clench on the steering wheel, his entire body taut, shoulders stiff as he speeds down the dirt road. "We asked the Conclave for help."

A shiver runs down my spine at his words.

No.

What had they traded for help to find me?

Guilt slams through me at what finding me must have cost them.

"I'm sorry," I choke out. He slams on the brakes and I fly

forward, only held in place by the belt he put around me, the sharp pain in my ribs causing my vision to swim.

He turns to look at me, his gray eyes a full thunderstorm. "You don't apologize. Not for anything. None of this is your fault. Do you understand me, Octavia?" A tear slips down my cheek, and he reaches over, wiping it away with his thumb. "There isn't anything in this world any of us wouldn't give for you. We did what was needed, and I'd do it a thousand times over."

I nod at his words, unable to say anything at the angry passion radiating from him. He nods once in return and puts his hand back on the steering wheel, moving us forward again. I pull my knees up to my chest, clinging to them as I make myself smaller in the silence, even though it hurts. It's nothing compared to what I've felt the last however long I was with Panda.

I lose track of time as we drive, it's only once I spot the city in the distance I realize we've been driving for over an hour. I should probably ask how Finn and Mav are going to get out of that house, what we're going to do about Panda, what has happened while I've been gone... but I have nothing right now. It's like I've used every reserve I've ever built up while I've been trapped in that basement.

I know I'm supposed to be strong, at least stronger than this, but I know I'm safe with Lincoln, so I don't have to hold my shit together right now.

We keep driving until I spot buildings I recognize as part of Echoes Cove, and before long we're pulling up to the hospital. Linc pulls the car into a vacant spot and shuts off the engine before looking over at me, scanning me as I sit here shaking.

"Are you okay to walk?" he asks softly, and I don't answer straight away, taking a second to take stock of my body. The trembling isn't something I can control, and all of the adrenaline I felt earlier is long gone. In its wake, I'm just exhausted, dehydrated, in pain, and weak. That being said, I'm pretty sure I can walk into this hospital.

I nod at him and unbuckle myself before opening the car door. Before I've even climbed out, he's out by my side, offering me an arm to lean on, like he knows I'm running on fumes. I'm just glad he doesn't try to take this from me.

I won't let this bring me to my knees. This Royal doesn't crawl.

He walks me into the hospital, and the staff jump to attention, swarming around us like they'd been waiting. Someone appears with a wheelchair and Linc guides me into it, not leaving my side as I'm taken to a private room. One of the male nurses reaches for me and I flinch from his touch. I don't want anyone else touching me right now. The only person in this room I trust is Lincoln, and I'm pretty sure he won't agree to stitch me up.

I look up at Linc, and he must see my unease. He points at the female doctor in the room. "Everyone out of the room but you." His voice gives no room for argument and people scurry at his command. Once they're gone, Linc lifts me from the chair and places me on the bed. "Better?"

I nod, hating how small I feel right now. I'm a fucking mess and I hate it.

"Miss Royal, I just need to run some tests so we can make sure you're okay," the woman says softly. "I need to take some blood and get you some fluids, but if you would like to clean up first..."

She trails off and I nod. "Yes, please."

"Your ribs," Linc interjects. "She was bleeding."

I glare at him, but she moves to me and insists I lift my clothing. She inspects the wound and frowns. "It's not too deep, mostly a flesh wound, but it's going to need some stitches. Once I've done that, you can clean up and we can look at everything else." She glances at the other bandages on my body, and I nod, knowing that between the two of them, I'm not going to win this fight.

I lie on my other side, giving her access to the torn skin, wincing as she cleans the wound, and injects a local anesthetic before stitching me up and dressing it.

"I've covered it in a waterproof seal so you can clean up. Are you sure you don't want me to look at your other injuries first?"

I nod, realizing this must be a Knight hospital. There's no other way Lincoln would be able to overrule the staff the way he had. But I'm going to take the upside, because I really just want to shower. "They'll keep until after I shower."

She looks at Linc, who nods once, and she leaves the room too. I fight the urge to snap at him over pretending like he has the final say in what I do and how I'm treated.

"Did he...?" Linc starts but I cut him off.

"He didn't touch me. Not like that. I'd just really like to shower and get clean." His eyes soften and he steps back.

"Okay, but I'm going to be in there with you. Letting you out of my sight isn't going to happen anytime soon."

I chew on my lip, but relent. I'm not positive I'm going to be all that stable on my feet anyway and I don't have it in me to argue with him. Not when I know his gruffness comes from a place of fear. I take his offered hand and walk to the private bathroom attached to the room; it's not huge, but it has a shower. That's all I need right now.

I twist the handle to turn it on and take off Lincoln's hoodie, shivering instantly at the loss of heat. A wave of self-consciousness washes over me at how gross I am right now, and the fact that his eyes won't leave me. I might've been kidnapped, and I should probably give no fucks, but the way he looks at me is so intense it's hard not to waver.

"You're beautiful, always. Now get undressed and get in the shower before I have to undress you myself." He smirks at me and I feel lighter instantly.

"You're such an ass." I smile, but pull off my tank top and push down my leggings before stepping under the spray of water. I lean against the wall as the hot water cascades over me, letting out a bone-deep sigh as the grime swirls down the drain and the warmth chases away the chill that seems to have taken up residence in my bones. My cuts and burns sting under the water, but the need to be clean outweighs the pain.

"Smithy is bringing you some clothes," Linc says from where he's leaning against the far wall. "Do you want anything in particular?"

"Just some fresh underwear, and something comfortable," I respond, knowing that I'm going to steal his hoodie again once I'm done. If he thinks he's getting that back anytime soon, well, sucks to be him. "Are you going to tell me about East yet?"

"I will, as long as you promise to let the doctor look at the rest of your wounds and run whatever tests she needs when you're done."

A knot forms in the pit of my stomach. "That's not exactly encouraging."

"Promise me, Octavia."

I chew on my lip as I lather myself with the body wash from the pump attached to the wall. I use it to wash my hair too, it might be shit for my hair, but it's matted and gross, so anything is better than nothing.

"I promise," I say finally. He already would've told me if it was anything *really* bad. At least I hope so.

I look over at him, watching as he takes in all of the damage to my body, his jaw ticking as his brow furrows. He doesn't speak again until I shut the water off. He steps toward me, towel in hand, and wraps me up. He grabs a second one and wraps it around my hair before pulling me back into his chest. "I thought I'd lost you again."

The words are almost inaudible, but he's holding me so tight I hear them loud and clear. I don't fight him, letting him take the solace before leading me back to the main room. "There's a robe here for you, or you can put my hoodie back on. It somehow doesn't have any blood on it and it comes down to your knees, so you'll be covered at least."

"Hoodie, please," I say, and he passes it to me. It doesn't take me long to dry off and slip it over my head before he helps me back onto the bed. "Now stop stalling and tell me about East."

He wipes a hand down his face and sits on the bed with me. "He's in the hospital. *This* hospital, down the hall actually. He's okay, all things considered. He was shot, but he had surgery, and he's going to be fine. He just needs a few months of rehab and recovery."

My eyes go wide. "Rehab and recovery? Where was he shot? What sort of rehab?" My mind races through the possibilities, but he's saved from answering as Smithy bursts through the door.

"Oh, Miss Octavia, thank goodness you're okay. I was worried out of my goddamn mind!" I chuckle a little because I don't think I've ever heard him curse before, but lean into the hug he wraps me in. He smells like home and I swear I could cry. He pulls back, looking me over. "I brought clothes for you as requested, along with a few comforts. I've only been allowed back in the house today." He glares at Lincoln for a second, which makes me smirk, before looking back to me. "I hope everything is to your liking. Now, are you really okay? What on earth happened?"

"I'm fine, Smithy. Thank you for the clothes. I'll explain everything shortly, but can I get dressed first?"

"Oh, yes! Of course," he says, flustered. "I'll just step outside. I need to make sure Matthew found his way to your room, I just kind of bolted from the car as he pulled up to the doors."

I raise an eyebrow at him. "Matthew?"

"Get dressed, Miss Octavia. We'll speak in a moment," is all he says before dropping the bag in his hand on the bed and leaving the room. I look at Lincoln who is checking his phone. "Everything okay?"

"Yeah, fine. The others are on their way here now."

"Do I want to know what's happening with Panda?" I ask, and the grim set of his lips tells me I don't. "Okay, I'm just going to get dressed." I point to the bathroom and he rolls his eyes.

"Octavia, I just watched you shower, you can get dressed in front of me."

I'm glad to see that Lincoln is still in there under this softer version of him that's been here since we arrived at the hospital. I open the bag Smithy placed on the bed and pull out a pair of fuzzy socks, some soft leggings, a pair of comfortable undies, and a long sleeved t-shirt. I've said it before and I'll say it again: that man is a godsend.

I wiggle into the underwear and leggings, pulling the socks onto my battered feet before shrugging out of the hoodie to put on the long-sleeved shirt. The hoodie goes back over my head before he can get any ideas about changing his mind and taking it back.

"Better?" he asks. I nod as I snuggle into the neck of the hoodie. "Good, I'll go get the doctor."

"Then I can see East?" I ask, biting my lip. "I just need to see he's okay with my own eyes." Guilt runs through my veins like ice. I *need* to see him.

"Then we can go and see East," he says, seeming to understand that I need to focus on that rather than how shitty I feel, or anything else that's going on. Once I've seen him and I know he's okay, then I'll probably crumble. Until then, I cling to it like it's my last tether to reality.

He steps outside the door and returns with the doctor on his heels. I suffer through the blood tests and another IV being attached to me. I try not to freak out and Linc takes my shaking hands in his, holding my gaze until the doctor is done. She asks me a ton of questions that I answer as best I can. She puts a salve on my burns and cleans and wraps the other cuts on my body. It all passes in a sort of blur.

When she's finished, she turns to Linc. "She needs to rest. She's malnourished, dehydrated, and she's been tortured and drugged. She needs to sleep."

"I need to see East," I say, leaning back against the pillow and murmuring as exhaustion slams into me now that I'm warm and comfortable.

"I've given her a sedative to help her relax. I'm a little worried about her blood pressure, but once she's slept and has some fluids, I'm hopeful it'll right itself. I'd like to keep an eye on her for at least twenty-four hours."

"Understood," Linc responds, as my eyes flutter closed. I hear the door close, and the bed shifts as he climbs in beside me and moves me so I'm lying more on him than the bed. "Sleep, V. I've got you now."

He strokes my hair, and as much as I want to be pissed about the sedative, the beat of his heart under my ear is like a lullaby.

Just this once, I'll forgive him for letting her sedate me.

He saved me. Again. I still don't know what it cost him, but as sleep pulls me under, I promise myself that he won't suffer anymore because of me.

I wake up to the sound of hospital machines beeping and I panic for a split second, thinking that me getting out was just a dream, that I'm back in that basement hooked up to the machines Panda had in there.

But then the smell of Lincoln filters into my senses and I feel him wrapped around me. I relax again. The pain drifts around the edges of my consciousness and I groan at the aches in my body.

I open my eyes and find him watching me in the dimly lit room. Leaning down, he kisses me on the top of my head. "Morning."

His voice is scratchy and quiet, like he's not been awake long.

"Hi," I murmur before looking around the room and finding Finley and Maverick asleep in the two chairs that were apparently brought in here while I was sleeping. "What time is it?"

"Early. You should go back to sleep."

I shake my head before snuggling back down on his chest. "When did they get here?"

"About ten minutes after you passed out."

I frown, sad that I missed them. "Is everything okay? What happened with Panda?"

"They dealt with it. Smithy went back to the house to make sure everything is okay for when we head back later on. Though that took more than a little convincing. The old guy is stubborn as hell."

I chuckle softly, nodding. Smithy is a big protective papa bear when he wants to be.

"Is Maverick okay?" I ask, and he frowns.

"Why wouldn't he be?"

"What Panda said about his dad… he wouldn't look at me after."

He glances over at Maverick before looking back at me. "He didn't say anything about that, but we were talking about everything else."

"He can't think I'd blame him for his dad's shit," I say softly. "Whether Panda was lying or not, I'd never blame Mav for that."

"You should tell him that." His voice is low and gravelly, sending a shiver down my spine. Pretty sure that jumping his bones *isn't* what I should be thinking about right now, but I'm wrapped up in him, in bed, and I'm only human.

I shake off the thought, focusing back on all of the other shit we have to deal with. "How is East?"

"Luc swung by after you fell asleep and let me know he's doing okay. He knows you're here though, so when it's not the middle of the night, we'll go see him. Then we can see about getting you discharged so we can go home."

"Your uncle Luc? He's in town? How long was I gone? What else did I miss?"

He winces and that just makes me suspicious. "Yeah, Uncle Luc. And you were gone for nearly two weeks, today is Thursday. As for what else you missed... I'll catch you up later."

I quirk a brow at him and purse my lips. "Why do I get the feeling I'm not going to like this?"

"Because you're not," he says, frowning a little. "Now how are you feeling?"

I let out a deep sigh. Just once I'd like the sand under my feet to stop shifting so I could get some balance. Apparently today is not that day. I take an assessment of my body, the aches and pains still very much apparent, but I'm okay. I'm here, back with them, and I survived.

"Am I sad about how everything ended? Yes, of course, and have I dealt with it all yet? Abso-fucking-lutely not. But it could've ended much worse."

Except... it's not really over yet. Whoever was working with Panda is still out there. I say as much to him, and the frown on his face deepens. "We'll figure it out. Don't change the subject. How are you feeling?"

The guy is like a dog with a bone, but I can't deny anymore that he cares for me. "I'm okay. I swear. It could've been much worse."

"You were stabbed, burned, and have multiple other injuries, Octavia. If he hadn't killed himself, I'd have killed him my damn self."

I cup his cheek with my hand and sigh. "I promise, I'm okay. I'll heal."

He watches me closely, as if looking for a lie. When he doesn't find it, he nods and pulls me back against his chest. "I'm going to wrap you in fucking bubblewrap or something."

I laugh softly. "You could try."

I feel his smirk against the top of my head.

"You two talk too much for this early in the morning," Finn grumbles, and I look over as he stretches while yawning from the chair he slept in. Maverick is still out cold. "Does anyone want coffee?"

"Yes," Lincoln and I say in sync, making Finn chuckle.

"Okay, I'll go get some," he says, looking down at his watch. "I'll grab some food too, then we should be able to go see East before getting the hell out of here. I assume he brought you up to speed?"

He says the last bit just to me and I nod. "He did. Mostly. Thank you. For everything."

Moving across the room until he's standing in front of me, he captures my lips with his while I'm still curled up in Lincoln. "Nothing to thank me for, V. You know I'll always come for you. We all will. I'll be back in a minute."

He turns to leave, and I lean back into Lincoln. I can't help but be surprised at how well they all seem to take sharing me. I can honestly say that sharing any of them would drive me to murder. "We should probably get up."

"In a minute," he says, tightening his hold on me while being mindful of my ribs. So I lie with him until Finn comes back with coffee and food, waking Mav as he turns the light on.

I eat my croissant quietly, sipping at the coffee while they talk quietly about something I'm not in the loop with, but I know they'll tell me later if I ask. We've come a long way since I got back to the Cove and I'm pretty sure they're past keeping stuff from me.

I really freaking hope so anyway.

I finish my breakfast and the doctor comes around to check on me. Once she takes my blood pressure and she's happy enough with it, I'm given the all clear, and we pile out of the room and head toward East's room. I clench my hands to stop them from trembling. I hate that he's here because of me. It occurs to me that Lincoln never did answer my questions since Smithy interrupted us, so I have little idea of what I'm going to find.

I move a little faster, walking ahead to the room number Linc gave me for East, and push the door open.

My heart about stops when I find him hooked up to a dozen or so machines with a giant gauze bandage down the center of his chest. He smiles at me, but I can't help but gaze back down at his chest.

"He was shot in the heart?" I question before East can say a word as I turn to face Lincoln, who winces again.

"He was, but he's okay. He's getting out of here today too."

I grumble under my breath about stupid boys and only giving half the fucking information, and turn back to East. The man in question is still smiling as I enter his room at last and head straight for the bed. I want to hug him, but he was shot in the fucking chest. I'm not going to hurt him any more by being an idiot.

"Are you okay?" I ask the stupid question because I can't help myself, and he barks out a laugh.

"I've been better, but I'll survive. Are *you* okay?"

"Meh, same." I shrug as I perch on the edge of his bed; the others stay outside giving us some privacy, shutting the door between us. Guilt slams me as I take stock of him. "I'm so sorry."

The words are choked as I speak them, but he takes my hand and squeezes it tight. "V, I'd die to keep you safe. I didn't die, and you have nothing to be sorry about. Besides, I took the bullet for my idiot brother. If anyone should be sorry, it's him for getting in the way of yet another gun." He laughs softly and I roll my eyes.

"Are you seriously making jokes right now?"

"I'm not joking." He shrugs and I shake my head. "They have a lot more power in the world than I do, but that is something I can do. And for you, there's no limit to what I'll do."

I lean forward and kiss him chastely, aware that I don't want to hurt him, but I can't *not* kiss him. Not when he says shit like that.

"I won't break, you know?" He grins as I pull back.

I laugh softly, shaking my head. "You look pretty breakable to me right now."

"This?" he says, waving to his chest. "This is nothing."

"You're an idiot."

"I'm your idiot though." He grins at me, eyes sparkling. He does at least look okay, and he seems perky enough. "Now, can we get the hell out of this place? I've been losing my mind trapped in here."

"Yeah, Linc said he was getting me discharged. I assume he meant you too. I need a bubble bath. A really long bubble bath."

"Want company?" he asks, wagging his brows as the door opens behind us.

"You, Mr. Saint, will not be having bubble baths or any other exertive activities for some weeks." I blush as the woman's stern voice reaches me, turning to see her standing in front of a smirking Lincoln. "We've already been through this. If you won't stick to your care plan, I will *not* be discharging you."

East's eyes go wide and Mav snickers behind Linc. "I'll do as I'm told," he huffs.

"Good, then I have no issues discharging you. We've liaised with the private rehab center your brother set you up with, so they're aware of your rehab schedule. If you have any pain or any of your incisions become infected, you need to come back here immediately. Am I making myself clear?"

He nods, and I fold my arms. "If he gets so much as a slight temperature, he'll be back."

The doctor nods, smiling. "Oh I like her. Hopefully, I won't see you again, Mr. Saint." She nods and turns, leaving the room.

"Is there anything else I don't know yet?" I ask, my glare bouncing between the four of them.

Finn scrubs the back of his neck. "Did you tell her about Indi yet?"

Lincoln groans as I screech, "What about Indi?"

"Guess not. My bad. I'm going to go get the car," Finn says, bouncing out of the room.

"I'll come with you!" Mav shouts and runs after him.

"What the fuck happened to Indi?"

———

After the run down on the drive home of everything I missed while I was with Panda, I swear to storm the fucking gate if Lincoln doesn't get Indi back here by the end of the goddamn day. Otherwise, Alexander Saint is going to answer to me and all of my fury. I'm giving him sixteen hours, and if Indi isn't in my house before the clock strikes midnight, I'll riot.

But for now, I ask Maverick to stay with me while Linc and Finn help get East settled. He's going to need more help than me, and Mav has barely looked at me since Panda announced that Edward killed my dad, let alone spoken to me.

I'm not about to let anything like that come between us.

"Oh, Miss Octavia, you're home!" Smithy greets us as the door closes behind us and he wraps me in a hug so tight my ribs practically creak.

"Smithy, need to breathe and you're going to pop one of my stitches," I push out and he drops me.

"Sorry, I was just so worried." He brushes his hands down my arms as if looking for injury. "Are you really okay?"

"I'm fine, Smithy. I promise. I just need some good food, a bubble bath, and a night of relaxation."

"Food I can do!" he says, almost flustered, before heading back toward the kitchen.

"Don't think I've forgotten about Matthew either!" I shout behind him. He just raises his hand as if to wave me off before disappearing into the kitchen.

I feel restless and I want to talk to Mav, so rather than head upstairs, I take his hand and lead him to the stairs down to the music room. Once we're sealed in the soundproof room, I sit on the piano stool and he sits on the small sofa by the door.

Fluttering my fingers across the smooth ivory, I trill out a couple of quick scale runs. I've missed this, but it isn't why I came down here. Without looking at him, I play a soft melody, pouring some of my pain and anger into it.

"Why won't you talk to me, Mav?" I ask quietly, continuing to play.

He doesn't respond. When I turn to face him his elbows are resting on his knees, hands in his hair, and he's bent forward staring at the floor.

"Mav?"

He glances up at me and the pain on his face breaks my heart. "How can you even look at me after what Evan told you? I'm a monster that comes from a long line of monsters. *That* is my legacy. We're *all* legacies and you deserve better than that."

I move to stand before him and crouch when he still won't look up at me. "I don't care what he said."

He still doesn't look at me and my heart breaks. I need him to know I don't blame him and whatever guilt he's feeling isn't his to feel.

If Edward did kill my father, then that's something he needs to pay for. Not Maverick. Just another line on my list of reasons that all of their dads need to jump off a fucking cliff.

"Look at me," I say, gripping his chin. "You are not your father, and you are not accountable for his sins either. Whether or not what Panda said is the truth, that doesn't fall on you and I will never hold you responsible, do you understand? I love you, Maverick Riley, and nothing and no one is going to change that."

He looks at me with glassy eyes. "No one has ever said that to me before."

I suck in a breath, startled. "Well, then other people are monsters. You are worthy of love, Mav, and I love you. From now until the stars fall."

"I love you too." He captures my lips with his and pulls me onto his lap so I'm straddling him on the sofa. He kisses me like I'm the oxygen he needs to survive.

He pulls back, and that cheeky glint is back in his eye. "I never fucked anyone on a piano before."

I let out a sharp laugh. "Not sure how easy that feat is, buddy. A baby grand isn't a sex toy."

"I do love a challenge." He wags his brows at me and I laugh again.

Before I know what's happening, there's a bang as the piano lid is closed and I'm in the air a moment then find myself sitting on the smooth top of the baby grand, legs spread wide enough to accommodate Mav's body mere seconds after he's pulled off my leggings and panties.

"Princess," he says, sucking in a breath as he sees some of the damage done.

"Don't. I'll heal," I assure him, tamping down the creeping self-consciousness. I refuse to let what Evan did to me interfere with my boys. I can own my battle scars and I know none of them will give a damn about them outside of wishing they could kill him themselves every time they see them.

He runs his hands up from my ankles, following with his lips, tracing every fading line and burn.

"Mav..." I trail off as he moves up my body.

"Yes, princess?"

"What are you doing?" I've never heard my voice sound so damn sexy. All breathy and raspy.

"I'm going to eat your pussy like it's my last meal." If I thought I was wet before, I'm now dripping and aching for him to honor his promise.

"Well, then, don't let me keep you from your dinner."

Propping myself up on my elbows, I watch as he slides his arms under my thighs and grabs my ass so he can access my pussy at the right angle.

Then he's there. His mouth is on me, his tongue lapping up every drop I give him. The sounds he's making are wicked and sinful, like he's forgotten all his manners at the table. I fucking love it. In fact, the sounds and the scent of my arousal are turning me on even more.

Throwing my head back, I let my hair fall to the baby grand as I close my eyes and focus on the feel of his lips. His tongue. His teeth.

With soft kisses and hard bites, Mav expertly works me to orgasm in a manner of moments.

"Fuck, Mav, yes!" My ass is bare and my juices are coating my thighs and now the piano underneath me.

My breaths are coming in faster and when he notices, he looks up at me through hooded eyes and the glint he's fixing me with is made of pure debauchery. He's enjoying this, watching me fall apart at the tip of his tongue.

"Hold on, baby." I don't have time to ask him what for before his teeth latch onto my clit and my orgasm just flies out of me with so much force I think I might lose consciousness for a moment.

My fingers grip onto the smooth wood as my body shakes and quivers from the overload of emotions and sensations.

Then he buries his entire face between my legs and coats my juices all over his mouth, nose, and chin before using his tongue to accompany my orgasm to the apex and back down.

I'm a panting mess, chest heaving and breaths coming in fast and ragged. By the smug look on his face, I'd say Mav is quite proud of himself.

"Time to fuck you, now, princess."

"Here?" I don't know if I even know my name right now, but I do know that fucking on this piano does not sound comfortable.

"Anywhere, but yeah, why not here?" Mav is capable of finding some way to shove his dick in my pussy no matter where we are, but I need a minimum level of comfort.

"I have a better idea." I grin, quickly pulling my panties and leggings back on and leading him up to my bedroom. I head into my closet and pull out the toy box Indi gave me for Christmas. "Want to play?"

I upend the box onto the bed and dozens of sex toys fall from it: restraints, toys, lube, anal beads, and several things I'm not sure I could find my way around if I were given a map. Indi really went the whole nine yards with this box. My heart races at the restraints that fall onto the bed among the vast variety of goodies, but I'm not about to let what happened spoil my fun. Not a chance.

"Oh, princess, you really do love me." He grins wildly as he picks up the restraints. "Trust me?"

I drop the box and move to stand before him, pulling off my hoodie and tank, letting them fall to the ground, leaving me in just my leggings and panties. "With my life."

He drinks me in with his eyes, pausing on my wounds, before savagely grasping my hips, closing the distance between us and kissing me like the beast I know and love.

We're all desperate hands and hungry mouths as we kiss with wild abandon. Picking me up and urging my legs to wrap around his hips, he takes me to the bed and gently lays me down next to the array of sex toys. His body follows mine before he slams his mouth back onto mine once more.

"You taste so fucking good."

His dick is huge behind his jeans, and the need for him runs through me harder and hotter than I ever remember feeling. He pulls back, sweeping most of the toys back into the box on the floor, and looks down at me with so much love, I feel more cherished than I ever have.

"You sure you're good with this? It's not too soon?" he asks, the soft padded cuffs hanging from his finger. My heart races, but I nod. No time like the present to get back on the horse. The bruises on my wrists are still healing and my ribs ache, but if nothing else, this whole ordeal has only reinforced just how short life is.

"Words, princess."

I nod again and say, "Yes, I'm okay. I trust you."

If someone would have told me a few months ago that I'd be here, with him, saying these words, I'd have laughed in their face, but a lot has changed in the last few months.

I raise my arms above my head, a drop of fear and anticipation rushing down my spine as he ties my wrists together, and to the bed frame. "If you need to stop, use your safe word."

"I know, but I won't. I'm okay." I refuse to let fear rule my life anymore. I've let myself be weak enough since they found me, enough is enough. There's too much out there that I have to deal with. In here, with him, with them, I'm not going to be afraid anymore.

He kisses me again, working his way down my body until he pulls my panties and leggings down, throwing them across the room. I shudder under his intense gaze and his eyes darken as he drinks me in. "You're fucking stunning, princess. Words can't do you justice."

I feel a blush creeping up my neck and cheeks as he devours every inch of me with his eyes.

Without looking away from me, he reaches back, pulling off his shirt and throwing it to the side. Biting his bottom lip, my anticipation soars as Mav unbuttons his jeans then pulls his zipper down, his cock springing free. He lets his jeans and boxers fall to the floor, stepping out of them before crawling onto the bed.

"If I'd have lost you..." he trails off and I wish I could touch him. Offer him some comfort.

"You didn't, and you never will."

His eyes burn as he locks his gaze on mine, looking as fierce as I've ever seen him. "Mine," he growls as he grabs the underside of my knees and pulls them up to my chest, his cock pushing inside me in one smooth move that has me arching my back like a wanton, sex-deprived vixen.

Possessing every part of me.

I gasp and Mav moves in to swallow my pleasure with an aggressive kiss that steals my breath. With his hands cradling my head, he thrusts in and out with abandon, making sure his every move rubs up against my clit. Wanting more, I wrap my legs around his waist, using my muscles to pull myself up on every push of his hips. I pull on my handcuffs out of habit, needing to touch him, to hold him, to show him how much he consumes me.

"Mav." I gasp out his name. Not really knowing why, just needing to hear it. Needing him to hear his name—filled with need—falling from my lips. Lips he's kissed and bruised.

"I love you." The words are something like a prayer and he stills, hovering above me, looking down at me like I'm not real.

"Say it again." His voice is little more than a whisper, as his shoulders strain where he holds himself above me.

"I love you, Maverick."

His mouth crashes back onto mine and he devours me without a care in the world. He bites my bottom lip until I bleed. He sucks on my tongue.

"I love you too, princess," he says as he thrusts into me with a vicious force that has my entire body hitching up toward my headboard, but Mav's hands are there to protect me. Always protecting me, like he's promised a thousand times.

He shows me all of him: his fierceness, his wounds, his weaknesses.

As he rubs up against my clit, I feel the first stirrings of another orgasm and I don't even try to fight it. I let it happen, let him consume me.

Mav's mouth moves to my neck and then my shoulder and just when I think I can't hold my climax back, Mav sinks his teeth into the meaty part of my collarbone and my back flies off the bed, pinned by him above me.

Fucking me relentlessly, Mav doesn't slow down as I ride the high of yet another orgasm, letting it rush through my bloodstream. He whispers words of devotion and protection as his orgasm takes over him and he spills inside of me.

Once we fall back down from the intense high, we're both left panting, taking in jagged breaths. Mav reaches for the key and unshackles me, rubbing and kissing my wrists where the already-purple bruising looks angry from the pressure I put on them when I lost control.

"Don't move," he tells me in a quiet voice.

I feel like a cooked noodle and couldn't move if a grizzly were chasing me down.

I watch, sighing at the sight of Mav's painted back and glorious ass walking to the bathroom. I hear the water running and then he's back with a washcloth. Slowly, he spreads my legs and places the warm cloth on my pussy, wiping it down gently. When he's finished caring for me, he wraps himself around me and brings the covers back up.

We're in our own little cocoon, his lips on the crown of my head when he whispers, "I love you, too, Octavia Royal."

TEN

OCTAVIA

S tretching out in bed, my body aches in the best kind of way as I yawn, thankful to be waking up in my own bed wrapped up in Maverick. It is considerably better than how I've woken up the last week and a half.

I check my phone and note how early it is, but the urge to run, to be free, to feel just how alive I am with that burn in my body, runs through me. I bring up my thread with Lincoln and drop him a message.

Me:
Want to go for a run?

I bite my lip, waiting for a response as I shimmy from the bed and head to the bathroom, trying not to wake Mav up. When I'm finished and there's still no response from Linc, I realize that I still haven't heard from Indi.

Son of a bitch.

I guess I'm not running today.

Today, I'm going to rain down some hell on Alexander Saint. He doesn't get to take my goddamn bestie; I don't give a fuck if it's all tied into the Kings. What is the point of having the power that comes from being associated with the Knights if I can't keep my goddamn friend out of this shit?

While I might not technically *be* a Knight, my guys are and Alexander should know fucking better. I might not have seen Lincoln or the others in the years I was gone from here, but I did see Alexander. He kept in touch with my dad after we left and he'd come visit sometimes.

Hell, I'm pretty sure I knew him better back then than Lincoln did. Though I had no idea about the whole gang, secret society shit. That must be part of why he stayed in touch with Dad.

I might despise everything that the Knights stand for—at least what I know of it—but am I going to use that shit to help Indi right now? You're damn straight I am.

I tiptoe out of my room and downstairs as quiet as I can to where Smithy put my dad's things. I know his journals have to be in here somewhere, so I start going through the boxes as quietly as I can.

I've avoided going through any of this since I came back, but if there's information in here that can help me today, I am absolutely plowing through it. Even if my bruised heart gets a little more battered.

I find what I'm looking for in the fourth box.

Jackpot.

I skim through the pages, looking for something, anything, that might help.

I frown a little as I come across a passage about the Knights and Rebels. It brings up memories I'd forgotten about and I remember some of the stuff my dad told me about the Rebels, stuff Alexander would talk about when he visited with us.

My dad might not have told me about the Knights, but sometimes, when he drank too much, he'd get chatty. Hopefully some of what he told me will come in handy today. I'll do what I have to do to get Indi back, but I hope it doesn't come to that.

I keep reading, shocked at how much my dad wrote down in here. There's not much about the Knights, but this is like a memoir of all of the other shady shit that has been going down in and around the Cove. There's stuff on the Rebels, the Kings, and other organizations I've never even heard of.

Alexander might only be a few months older than East, but there's more than a few skeletons in his closet and, apparently, my dad knew a good few of them.

As much as it hurts to realize how much my dad kept from me —hurts to hear his voice in my head as I read his words—I'm thankful that this treasure trove exists... and that I haven't told anyone about it. I grab all of the journals from the boxes, having only managed to get through a fraction of them in the hour I've been down here, and stash them in the vent in the music room. Pretty sure no one is going to look for them in there.

Me:
I assume you didn't hear back from Alexander. I'm getting dressed, and I'll be over in ten. We're getting her back. Today.

Linc:
I'm awake. Making coffee. See you soon.

I jump in the shower, washing off the remnants of the last however long and the evidence of my night with Mav, washing my hair properly, though I'm pretty sure it's a lost cause at this point.

I'm going to need to book an appointment with Gracie.

But that's a luxury for later.

For now, I need to pull on all of that rage that sits in the well inside of me. If Alexander Saint wants a battle, I'll give him one. Battered and bruised or not.

I still can't believe Lincoln's cousin is wrapped up in this bullshit. Do the Saints ever take the easy path? What's wrong with a nice, normal, quiet life?

I swear to God...

Once I'm showered, I find Maverick half awake, but still in bed. "Morning, princess," he mumbles sleepily. "Why are you up already?"

"Indi," is all I say and he yawns, nodding. I head to my dresser and dry my hair roughly, scraping it back into a messy ponytail before getting dressed. Once I'm wearing an outfit that makes me feel like a powerful bitch, I quickly do my face. By the time I'm done, Maverick has showered and redressed.

"I have fresh clothes over at Linc's. Finn's still there from yesterday. You good to go?"

"Yeah, just need shoes," I say, before ducking into my closet and grabbing a pair of boss-ass-bitch stilettos. Is my body in the best condition for this outing? Absolutely not. I'm going regardless. Indi would do the same for me. Ride or die.

I'm more shocked that Ryker hasn't said fuck it and broken her out himself. That's a question for Linc later.

I slip my shoes on and straighten my jacket before following Maverick downstairs. "What do you know about Alexander?"

"Not much," he says with a shrug. "He's run with the Rebels for a long time from what Linc told us. Worked his way up through the ranks, and now he runs the city."

I frown, wondering how much Linc knows of what my dad did. Surely if he knew, he'd have used what he knows? Or maybe he isn't as motivated as I am.

That or he just doesn't want to be an asshole to his cousin.

Either way, Alexander Saint is going to have a bad day if he doesn't hand Indi over willingly.

"Miss Octavia! Good, you're awake," Smithy says as I stride across the living room toward the kitchen, but he frowns when he looks at me properly. "Where, exactly, do you think you're going? You should be resting."

"I have something to take care of. Indi needs my help. I'll rest later."

He purses his lips, glancing over at Mav who shrugs. "Don't look at me, I'm just following her lead."

I roll my eyes, little traitor. He just doesn't want to lose his food privileges.

"I don't think you should be doing anything right now, Miss Octavia. I called the school and told them you wouldn't be back today. I told them you've been ill. I do wish you would stay home and rest."

I sigh, folding my arms over my chest. Arguing with Smithy isn't something I want to do, but he isn't going to stop me right now. "I appreciate that, but I'm helping Indi."

My tone brooks no argument and he shakes his head. "You're too headstrong, just like your father." I level him with a glare and he backs off a little. "Fine, fine. But on Sunday, I'd like us to have dinner with Matthew. Miss Indi is welcome to join if everything is okay with her."

"Thank you, Smithy." I walk over to him and kiss him on the cheek. "I'd love to meet Matthew finally. I'll be fine. Hopefully, I won't be gone all day, but I'll keep you in the loop, okay?"

"That will make me feel better, do you want something to eat before you leave?"

I shake my head, smiling softly. I feel sick even thinking about food. "No, but thank you. My stomach still isn't really feeling up to much, but I promise I'll eat later."

He gives me a quick one arm hug and mutters, "You best."

Once he releases me, I move back to Maverick, taking his hand and heading out the back and through the gate to the

Saints'. By the time we enter the kitchen, Lincoln and Finley are already sitting at the kitchen table, coffee in hand.

"I'll just go get changed," Mav says, kissing me quickly before jogging out of the room.

"How is East?" I ask as I pour myself a cup of coffee before joining them at the table.

"Sleeping," Linc says, draining the last of his cup. "He took his painkillers this morning, so I imagine he'll be out for most of the day. Mrs. Potts is keeping an eye on him while we head into the city."

I'm glad Mrs. Potts is here. It means I can focus on Indi without worrying about East. I'd have liked to have seen him this morning, but I'm not about to wake him up just to make myself feel better.

"We doing this?" Mav asks as he strides back into the room in fresh jeans and a long-sleeved black tee and boots. How do they all make such simple things look so goddamn hot?

Lincoln nods and stands while Finn takes my hand and squeezes it. "You sure you're up to this?"

"Wild horses couldn't stop me," I tell him, squeezing his hand back.

"Good," Linc says, grabbing his keys and phone, pulling a gun from behind him and handing it to me. "Then let's get this show on the road shall we?"

The drive into the city takes a few hours. Mav and Finn play some stupid game on a hand held console the entire journey, while I spend all my time thinking of nothing but Indi and how the fuck I'm going to make this happen. I still don't exactly have a plan, but I'm not leaving without Indi. And if I have to unearth some secrets, I will. It might piss Linc off, considering it's his cousin, but this is one of those times when the ends justify the means.

Linc's hand rests on my thigh, the same way it has the entire drive. "Do you know why Ryker hasn't just gone in guns blazing and taken her back?"

He shakes his head, the other two going quiet in the back of the Porsche. "I haven't talked to Ryker much since you've been gone, but Indi was taken the day after you were, so I've been a little occupied. I only know that whatever it is that the Rebels want from the Kings, it's not a quick and dry trade. So getting Alexander to give her up isn't going to be easy. I've already tried. Twice."

I look over at him, chewing the inside of my cheek. "I know. I appreciate it, but I can't just quit. There's no way Indi would quit on me, and I can't help but feel responsible. She was out there with you guys looking for me when she was taken." I don't tell him that I'm pretty sure I know what the Rebels want from the Kings, and why the Kings won't just comply.

I also keep the information about Alexander to myself. I don't want to use what I know unless I have to.

We drive the rest of the way in silence, just the songs playing on the radio filling the empty space. It's not long before we're pulling up to what looks like an abandoned warehouse.

"Don't let the appearance fool you," Linc says, taking in the skeptical look on my face. "There are a dozen apartments in there, as well as a warehouse space. Alexander basically made this place a fortress."

Awesome news. Just freaking delightful.

"So how do you propose we get in?" I ask, not wanting to use my hidden advantages just yet. A girl gets to have some secrets, especially with the treasure troves of them this bunch have.

He shuts off the engine and turns to look at me, smirking. "I thought this was your crusade?"

Mav barks out a laugh from the back seat, and I flip him the bird while I glare at Lincoln. "Fine, you stay here. I'll get this shit done myself."

I open the door and climb from the car, slamming the door shut. "V, come on. You know he's just being an asshole. Wait up."

Finn's voice makes me pause, and I turn to face them, brow cocked. "I don't *need* you to help me. I'll get my girl back my damn self."

"We know you don't need us." Lincoln sighs, scrubbing a hand down his face. Something flickers in his eyes that raises red flags, but it's gone as quickly as it appeared. "We are all very aware of that, so maybe just let us help you."

"I asked for your help. You're the one stuck in asshat mode." I turn back around and head toward the door on the side of the building, pounding my hand against it until the small viewing hatch in the door is opened. "I'm here to see Alexander."

"Sorry, lady, you're at the wrong place."

I pull the 9mm Lincoln gave me on the ride here and put the barrel through the hatch before he can slide it shut.

"Shit," Finn curses, and I hear them all move quickly behind me, preparing themselves for war.

"I don't think I am. Now let me repeat myself. My name is Octavia Royal, and I'm here to see Alexander Saint."

The sound of footsteps and shouts sound through the door, but I keep my gun trained on the guy behind the door.

"Do not make me ask again."

"Fuck you, bitch," the guy grunts.

I let off a shot beside his ear.

"That was your last warning," I growl before looking up at the camera by the door. "Get your ass down here, Saint."

My heart pounds in my chest; my bravado is little more than a show right now—I'm just winging it here.

There are more shouts and the sound of metal scraping on

metal before I hear Alex's voice. "Open the door, Benny. She'll shoot you in the nuts and not think twice."

Lincoln looks at me suspiciously, and I shrug. His cousin hasn't come up before now, how was I supposed to know Alex didn't mention that he and my father kept in touch, and by proxy, he'd kept in touch with me?

I holster my pistol as the door opens and a smiling Alex stares down at me. His floppy brown hair falls in his bright amber eyes. I forgot how freaking tall he is, and he definitely buffed up since I saw him last, but he's still the same Saint-looking, sarcastic asshole he's always been. "Baby Royal! It's been a minute."

He wraps me up in his arms and I roll my eyes. "Don't act like we're friends right now, Alex. You have my girl and I want her back."

"Why do I feel like we're missing something here?" Mav says, scratching the back of his head.

"You never did beat around the bush, baby Royal, but that is a request I gotta deny. I already told Lincoln. But don't let this be a wasted trip, come on in. I can show you your girl is in good shape and being treated like a queen."

I look at him skeptically, though I don't miss the glare Lincoln is shooting us both. Alex links his arm through mine and pulls me forward through a web of halls until we reach an open space.

"V?" Indi squeals, running over to me from where she was sitting in a chair under a blanket, squeezing me so tight my ribs ache. "You're okay, thank fucking Christ. What happened? Who had you?"

"Are *you* okay?" I ask, and she nods as she pulls back.

"I could be worse," she says, lifting her casted arm. I glare at Alex. "Pissed off at being here, but Alex isn't the worst, I guess." The guy in question barks out a laugh.

"You're starting to like me. Don't deny it, Indigo."

"What the fuck did you do to her?" I growl at Alex, and he holds his hands up in the air.

"Wasn't me, sweetcheeks. That was my guys. Once I knew she was your girl, I got her looked at and fixed up."

"He's telling the truth," Indi says, glaring at him, but there's something in her eyes...

Does she *like* him?

I shake my head, that is so not relevant right now. I turn back to face Alex, folding my arms across my chest. "What is it going to take to get you to let her go home with me?"

"Come on, Octavia," Alex groans. "Don't make me be a hard ass. You know I don't like it."

"Can one of you fill the rest of us in on just why it is you're so chill?" Maverick pipes up. I glance over at him, he looks about as happy as Lincoln does. Finn has his typical poker face on, but I don't miss the tightening of his jaw.

"Daddy Royal and I were tight while he was on tour. So baby Royal and I hung out a bit while you lot were running around with the Knights," Alex says shrugging, before dropping into one of the comfy-looking chairs across the room.

"I'm taking her home with me, Alex. I don't care what your deal is with the Kings. She's mine."

He leans forward, resting his elbows on his knees, hands clasped. "You don't really have much sway here, V."

I really didn't want to do this. I *tried* to be nice. "Don't make me talk about Colorado."

His eyebrows rise in shock as he blows out a breath. "How do you know about Colorado?"

"What the fuck happened in Colorado?" Lincoln asks, while the others stay quiet, watching with an intense fascination.

"Nothing," Alex says before cursing under his breath. He looks over at Indi and something passes between them. "If you want to go, then go. But, V, Colorado stays buried in the past, you understand?"

I nod. "I was happy to leave it buried. You're the one who told me I didn't have much sway."

"Yeah, well, I didn't realize you knew so much."

"Next time, don't underestimate me."

He shakes his head, before leaning back in his chair. "Well this was fun, but you guys should leave. I need to work out what else the Donovans covet enough to pay their debt."

"You're not going to hurt them, right?" Indi asks him, and he softens.

I have no idea what happened here between them during the last however long, but I get the feeling there is more to this story, too. Trying to block out the waves of rage coming from my guys, I stay focused on Indi and Alex.

He looks almost conflicted. "I'm not going to make promises I can't keep. But maybe talk some sense into Ryker and we can keep the peace."

The drive home from the city was pretty quiet other than Indi and I. I caught her up on what happened with Panda and she looked like she was going to cry on my behalf. The guys though... to say that my guys were pissed at me is an understatement. In fact, I've barely heard from them since we got back Friday afternoon.

A day and a half of almost radio silence since then. It sucks, but I get it. I've been pissy enough with them about secrets, and I wouldn't tell them Alex's secret. It isn't something that will help them, and the threat of it was enough to get Indi home. And as I reminded them, it's not like they tell me everything either.

We dropped her off with Ryker, under the promise that I got to see her today. I want to talk to her about what happened while she was gone, but also, I miss my bestie. I feel like we've both been wrapped up in our own chaos lately, that we haven't hung out properly in too long.

At least I got to spend the day with East yesterday, even if the others were MIA. Watching movies in bed with him was awesome, plus I got to make sure he was actually okay. He seemed a little distracted, but other than that, I think he's actually doing okay, all things considered.

I glance over at the clock.

Five thirty on a Sunday morning should be an illegal time to be awake. But here I am. Brain running at a million miles a minute.

I grab my phone and pull up my thread with the four of them.

Me:
Going for a run. Obviously the stalker thing is mostly over, so you don't have to come. Just telling you so no one freaks out at me later.

My phone buzzes almost instantly.

Lincoln:
You don't run alone. Not until we know who Evan was working with. Give me twenty, and I'll come with you.

I smile down at my phone. I guess the silent treatment is over.
Yay me.

Me:
Okay, I'll meet you at the gates in twenty.

Maverick:

You guys are insane. Go the fuck back to sleep.

East:

What he said.

Finley:

Enjoy your run. Crazies. Meet you after for breakfast?

Me:

Sounds good. East, can you come over, or are you still on bed rest?

East:

Pretty sure I can manage it across the yard to yours.

Mav:

I'll be there.

Me:

Perfect. See you all soon.

I throw the covers off and head to the bathroom to brush my teeth and get ready. It doesn't take me long, and I'm down in the kitchen doing my stretches in under ten minutes. Why it takes Lincoln so long is beyond me. I always thought it was easier for guys to get ready than girls.

"Good morning, Miss Octavia." I jump as Smithy appears, letting out a squeak.

"You move so quietly!" I gasp, and he chuckles.

"A man of mystery, that's me. What has you up so early?"

I shrug, grabbing a bottle of water from the fridge. "Couldn't sleep so thought I'd run. I didn't mean to wake you, sorry."

"You didn't, I'm usually up this early. Would you like me to sort you some breakfast for after your run?"

"You're the best. I actually invited the guys over for breakfast, so we can order in if you don't want to cook." The words were worth it for the look of horror on his face.

"I think not! I will arrange breakfast for you all. Order in... Pfft." He mutters to himself as he heads back down the hall to his quarters, and I check my watch. Time to head outside.

I find Lincoln already waiting for me and end up practically drooling. You'd think by now I'd be used to seeing him looking like that, but hot fucking damn. Sweats and a muscle top really are my kryptonite on Lincoln Saint.

"You finished eye fucking me?" He grins, stretching out.

"I'd rather actually fuck you," I mutter as I reach him.

His eyes darken and he gets in my space. "I'm pretty sure that could be arranged."

I suck in a breath, suddenly very fucking warm, and not feeling like running at all. There are much better ways to get sweaty.

Just as I open my mouth to speak, he steps back and puts in his AirPods. "Let's go."

"Tease," I grumble, and put in my own pods before taking off on our normal route. My body is still not where it was, but a few days of running and eating and I'm pretty sure I'll be okay.

We start off slower than usual, but it's not long until I hit my normal pace. I refuse to let myself be beaten. That might make me stupid, but I don't want to be defined by the shit I've gone through lately.

We run in silence the entire way, not making our usual pitstop because I don't feel like I need the break, and I know Lincoln only ever stops for me.

Once we get back to the house, he follows me inside rather than going back to his. We find Smithy, Mav, Finn, and East already in the kitchen, the smell of breakfast making my stomach growl. Linc slides onto the stool next to East while I drop onto the open seat next to Mav.

Everyone seems like they're back to normal. Apparently the silent treatment is officially over.

"Since we're all finally in one place, I have something to tell you guys," East says as Smithy finishes dishing out breakfast.

"What's up?" I ask, taking a bite of my eggs Benedict. Hellooooo hollandaise.

He looks a little nervous, and my stomach twists when he starts and stops speaking a couple times.

"What is it?" Lincoln asks, his concern obvious.

"I had a visitor while I was in the hospital. Chase Armstrong," he says, the name obviously meaning something to the others.

"Who is that?" I ask, and Linc is the one to answer.

"One of the Conclave." He turns back to East, fists clenched. "What did he want?"

"He came to tell me he helped you guys locate V," he says, pausing. Finn nods, as if confirming what he said. East lets out a deep breath and butterflies take flight in my stomach. "He also told me he's my father."

After the bombshell East dropped over breakfast, chaos pretty much ensued. It made me realize just how little I know about the Knights and their ranks. The four of them went back to the Saints' to deal with the repercussions of the news once East reassured me he was okay, just reeling.

If I didn't already have plans with Indi and Smithy today, I'd have made them all stay here and keep me in the loop, but apparently the fates like me chasing my tail.

Lincoln and I are overdue for a long talk though. I need to

know everything I can if I'm going to survive whatever it is that the Knights want from me.

I don't have time to focus on that as Indi bounds into my room like the ray of sparkling sunshine that she is. "Morning, friend," she sings as she drops onto my bed.

"You're awfully chipper today." I can't help but feel guilt as I take in the cast on her arm again.

She grins at me, blushing a little. "I'm home, I'm happy and healthy. I am loved. What's not to be chipper about?"

I quirk a brow at her. "You had a good homecoming then?"

She giggles, then covers her mouth with her hands, eyes wide. "You could say that. Ryker was very thankful to have me back." She blushes and I smirk. "Though he vowed to break Alex in multiple places when he saw my arm. He also said he owes you one, so tuck that away in your hat. He doesn't hand out favors all too often."

"He doesn't owe me a thing. It was my fault you were out there, that you were taken. How is your arm?" I ask, waving her off, but she shakes her head.

"It wasn't your fault. Alex explained some stuff to me, he'd have come for me another time if I hadn't been vulnerable then. But apparently being around you and the Knights, or with the Kings, makes me a little hard to kidnap usually. And my arm is fine, Ellis took me to an actual hospital, got it looked at; they said it seems to be healing as expected, but I'm going to need the cast on for another few weeks. At least Alex did that bit right I guess." She rolls her eyes and steals a pillow from behind me, hugging it against her chest. "And he wasn't all bad."

"I still want to dropkick the asshole who did that to you. But yeah, Alex is basically a human Labrador most of the time." I snort and she nods enthusiastically.

"Right! I said that exact same thing! He's a human puppy. It's kind of adorable. I don't get the whole terrifying thing everyone else seems to picture him as."

"I mean, you love Ryker. If you don't find him terrifying, pretty sure you're going to look past Alex's brand of scary," I shrug. I haven't seen that side of him, though I'm pretty sure Indi would see the best in a serial killer. "Plus, Alex is a softie under it all really."

"He really is," she says, sighing.

"What was that?"

Her eyes go wide. "What was what?"

"That cutesy little sigh." I quirk a brow at her and she looks down at her hands in her lap, wringing them out.

"He wasn't all bad. I know it makes me a terrible person to think so, all things considered. Considering the issues between him and Ryker... but," she shrugs, looking back up at me. "He was nice."

"Indigo Montoya, what exactly happened while you were with him?"

She lets out a deep sigh. "At first, I was just his prisoner. They broke my arm when they captured me but then Lincoln called and everything changed. He found out I was your friend and all of a sudden I was still his prisoner, but it was like he wanted to be my friend, too. So he brought in a doctor, had my arm put in this cast, and well... he looked after me." She pauses, looking up at me almost afraid.

"What did he do?" I ask, rage bubbling in my stomach. If he hurt her, I swear to Christ, I will burn down his goddamn warehouse and tell everyone all of his goddamn skeletons.

"He kissed me."

"He did fucking what?" I shout.

She chews her lip, and I only just manage to keep a lid on my shit. "He kissed me. I don't think he even meant to. We were messing around, no not like that, but just messing around because there was nothing else I could do, and it just happened. I felt awful about it, he apologized, said he didn't mean to. That he shouldn't have…"

"Did you tell Ryker or the others?"

She shakes her head, and my heart sinks for her a bit. "I don't want to make things worse and they were just so happy I was back, but there's a giant pit of guilt sloshing around inside of me and I feel awful."

"Did you kiss him back? Zero judgment either way, you know that. But he kissed you, you didn't instigate it."

She nods, looking back down at her hands. "I just kind of got lost in the moment. But then I remembered where I was, who he was, everything, and stopped it. Kept my distance. Nothing else happened. I know I should tell them, but they're a little possessive, and well, Alex isn't exactly their favorite person."

I nod, he's not exactly my favorite person right now either, the shit head.

"Do you like him?" I ask softly. There is zero judgment from me, no matter what she says, I just hate that she's hurting so badly.

"I don't think so?" It comes out as more of a question, and she chews on the inside of her lip again. My heart hurts for her.

"Okay, so you need to tell Ryker and the others, but I can be with you when you do. Secrets don't help anyone, especially ones like this. Did Alex tell you what he wants from the Kings?"

"He wants them to join the Rebels. Everyone knows that Diego isn't in the right place to run it anymore, and the Rebels want the territory. But Diego also owes Alex a fuck ton of money. I think that's why Ryker didn't come for me; he didn't have it."

I roll my eyes. "Alex shouldn't need money. He's a Saint."

"He is, and he isn't. Luc and he apparently don't speak much anymore, especially since he got tangled in the whole Rebel thing. He's not a Knight, so he doesn't benefit from the Saint money. At least that's what he told me. He also wouldn't let Lincoln pay him, because he's trying to prove a point. The money needs to come from Ryker and Ellis. It's a street, fear, stupid boy ego thing I think. Who the fuck knows? I'm just worried they're going to get hurt."

"We'll get to the bottom of this," I say, trying to reassure her when there's a knock at my door. It opens and Smithy steps into the room.

"Ladies, dinner will be ready in twenty minutes."

"Thank you for having me over, Smithy."

"Miss Indi, you are always welcome at our table." He smiles at her before turning to me. "Matthew is running a little late but he'll be here before dinner is served. Please be nice."

I mock outrage, clasping at my chest. "Me? I'm always nice."

Indi just laughs. "You are always protective. That doesn't always mean nice. And who the hell is Matthew?"

"I can be nice!" I defend, ignoring her question.

"Please, Miss Octavia. I am rather smitten with him, and you are my family. The two of you getting on would mean the world to me."

"Ohhhhhh." Indi waggles her eyebrows.

I roll my eyes at them both. "I will be nice as freaking pie."

"Thank you," Smithy says before leaving and closing the door behind him.

Indi smiles softly. "He seems nervous and happy. I hope Matthew is a good guy."

"Me too," I say sincerely. "Smithy deserves happiness. He's been alone for far too long. Come on, let's head down and get this party started."

"You can't grill him, you know." She smiles knowingly. "But Smithy didn't ask *me* to be nice."

"You'll lose your milkshake privileges if you start thinking like me too much," I cackle.

The look of horror on her face makes me snort-laugh.

"We didn't talk about you though. You were taken... by *Panda*. How are you holding up?"

I shrug. "Honestly, it's weird. It's like I'm numb to it. I'm sad and I'm angry... but it's like those emotions are removed from me a little. I mean, he told me Mav's dad murdered my dad, but I have no way to know if it's true, and even that just feels... like it all happened to someone else."

She frowns at me. "That doesn't seem healthy."

"Oh I know, and I'm sure when it all catches up to me, when I deal with it, I'm going to feel like I'm drowning. *If* it catches up to me."

"It will," she says, looking overly concerned. "Maybe you should speak to someone? A professional."

"I'm not sure anyone is equipped enough to deal with my shit." I laugh, trying to make light of it.

"V, I'm serious. I'm worried about you."

"I'm okay. But if it will make you feel better, I'm going to try and talk to Lincoln about it all. Or Finn. Maybe all of them; try to work out what's actually true and what's part of this web of lies. Pretty sure once I know for sure what's going on, I'll *feel* more."

"As long as you promise not to just shove it down and put a cork in it. Bottling your emotions up isn't healthy."

"I'll do my best," I say, honestly. "Come on, let's do this."

We head downstairs, but Indi seems to have lost some of her sparkle. "Are you sure you're up for this?"

"If you can survive nearly two weeks of what you did and do this, then I can do this. Alex didn't treat me badly, he just wouldn't let me leave or have any contact with the outside world. Hell, he wouldn't let me see or speak to anyone but him. So yes, I'm up for this. It's just the gross guilty feeling weighing on me."

I nod and take her hand, squeezing it. "We'll get it all worked out."

We head into the kitchen, and find Smithy with a tall man with salt and pepper hair. "Miss Octavia! Good you're here. I'd like to finally introduce you to Matthew." He turns to face Matthew, beaming. "Matthew, this is Octavia and her good friend, Indi."

Matthew smiles at us warmly, but something about him doesn't sit right. I don't know what it is, but my gut is screaming at me. "It is so good to finally meet you both."

He approaches, and takes my hand in his. "I'm glad you're feeling better, Octavia."

"Thank you," I say, painting a smile on my face. "It's nice to meet you too."

He draws me in for a hug, and I try not to stiffen up.

Then the smell hits me.

Peppermint, wood, and spice.

ELEVEN

OCTAVIA

Linc pulls into the parking lot, and I swear every single student at ECP is here, staring at us.

At me.

None of us have been at school for two weeks, and I have zero doubt that Blair has been reveling in our absence, lying about God only knows what. Knowing her, I'm probably such a slut that I've added Indi to my harem of lovers and we've all run away to an exotic island to get married.

Yep, that sounds like something she'd say.

"Are you ready for this?" Linc asks as he pulls into his spot beside Mav's bike.

No Finn yet.

I look over at him and nod as Mav climbs from his bike and opens the back door. "I'm not about to survive Panda just to be afraid of this place. The only thing I'm worried about is how badly my GPA is going to suffer from being away so much and being so distracted all the damn time."

Here's hoping that Smithy convinced my teachers I was sick enough that they don't have me try to do the work I missed and just give me a pass.

I'm not that lucky, but it would be nice.

At least tomorrow is the start of March, and there are only a few months of school left, only a month and a half until my birthday. If I can just graduate with my required GPA and stay alive long enough to reach 18 then maybe, just maybe, things will start looking up.

I haven't even had much time to worry about it lately with everything going on, but now that I'm here, back in the cold hard light of day—back to real life—it's just one more thing to weigh me down.

Mav jumps onto the back seat and leans forward, kissing my cheek. "Don't worry, princess. We got you. I mean, I don't, but Linc and Finn are boy geniuses. They'll help you with anything you need, but you're a smart cookie, I doubt you'll even need them."

I laugh softly, turning in my seat to face him. "I like this unrelenting positivity. Maybe some of it will rub off on me."

"I'll rub off on you," he jokes, wagging his eyebrows at me, and I can't help but laugh at him while Linc rolls his eyes.

"I'm sure you would," he mutters. "Where's Finn?"

"Getting coffee," Mav answers before leaning back. "He shouldn't be long."

Indi pulls into her space, waving at me from her Wrangler, so I jump out of the Porsche and head over to her. "Morning, Rainbow Sparkle. How you doing today?"

"Better, how are you? You were weird at dinner yesterday." She frowns as she grabs her bag and climbs out of the car.

"I'm okay, I just felt a bit off. I thought I hid it." I bite my lip, hoping I'd hidden it from Smithy and Matthew at least. I'm sure the smell was a coincidence. I've never met Matthew before, and he's never met me. Probably just some popular brand of cologne. That's the most logical explanation.

None of it makes any sense, and the bags under my eyes are a testament to how little sleep I got last night as I played it out in my head over and over again.

She shrugs, pulling on her backpack. "You probably did, I just know you too well."

"I'll be fine," I say, trying to wave it off. We head over to where Finley is waiting for us with the guys, a tray of coffee in one hand.

"Morning," I say, smiling at him. He hands Indi and I our coffees, and I kiss him chastely. "Thank you, and thank you for including her," I say softly as he tugs me against his side, hugging me.

"She's your person. Of course I'm going to include her." I smile up at him, tuning out Indi and Maverick's bickering until Lincoln's patience runs out.

"Will you two just fucking stop," he growls, and Indi flips Mav the bird.

"I will if asshat does."

Mav scoffs, opening his mouth to say something else, but I move from Finley to between him and Indi before he says something else and puts Linc in a foul mood for the rest of the day.

"Let's just call a timeout, shall we?" I grin, and Mav kisses me.

"I can think of a fun way to spend my time out in the naughty corner."

"You're so cheesy."

"Uhm, guys?" Indi says, stealing my attention. "Incoming."

I turn and find Blair and her bitch squad heading toward us, along with Raleigh, Jackson, and a few of the football team.

This is going to be fun.

"What do you want, Blair?" I sigh as she reaches us, Raleigh at her back. Those two fucking deserve each other.

"I'm not here for you, skank," she says, sneering at me before looking over at Lincoln.

"You don't speak to her like that, Blair. I warned you once

already," he says, cutting her off. "Anything you have to say to me, isn't something I want to hear."

"I'm pretty sure you want to know this," she says, smirking. "I ran into Georgia Fontaine over the weekend. We get our hair done at the same place."

I suck in a breath at the name. I hate that girl for zero reason and there is nothing I can do to change it.

"She told me how your father and hers are arranging to announce your engagement at the party your father is hosting on Friday."

Maverick's grip on my hip tightens, keeping me standing as Lincoln takes my hand and squeezes it.

"I guess she must be confused, because I'm not engaged to anyone."

She shrugs, glaring at me, like she knew that too. "I suppose it's possible, but there aren't many other Lincoln Saints in the Cove."

"Was there anything else you wanted, Blair? Or are you just here to stir shit?" Lincoln sighs, like she hasn't just crawled beneath my skin and set my blood on fire.

"Only to offer my best wishes to your brother. Apparently fucking Octavia is a deadly game these days."

Flicking her hair over her shoulder, she turns to walk away from us. She doesn't get very far before Indi darts forward, grabs her by the hair and yanks on it hard enough that Blair tips back on her heels and they both crumble to the ground. Screaming ensues as they attack each other and I move to intervene, but Finley stops me. "I got it."

Maverick holds me in place as I huff, trying to make sense of everything going on inside of my head right now, while Finley lifts a kicking and flailing Indi up off of my cousin who has bloody scratches down her face. Indi has a handful of Blair's hair, which she apparently ripped out, and I bite my lips together to stop from laughing.

Apparently my girl has fire.

"You're going to regret this, you depressive little whore," Blair shrieks at Indi, and Mav finally releases me as I step forward.

"Threaten her again, Blair. I fucking dare you. You might not be afraid of me, but you should be."

"The only thing scary about you is that you're a walking STD," she hisses, touching at the blood dripping down her face. "I'll ruin you both and laugh while I do it."

She storms off, her little band of sycophants trailing behind her, so I turn back to Indi. "Are you okay?"

"I'm fine," she sighs. "She just pisses me off. Walking around here like her shit doesn't stink. Apparently Dylan's bad habits are rubbing off on me."

"That was kind of fierce though." I laugh, trying not to let what Blair said get to me. At least not on the surface.

"It kinda was, huh?" She giggles.

"Come on, killer," Finley says, taking her arm. "Let's go get you sorted, and give those two a minute to talk, shall we?"

She looks at me and I nod, so she goes with Finn and Mav, leaving me alone with Lincoln.

"It's not true," he says, moving toward me, cupping my cheek with his hand. "I would have told you."

"I know you would, but what if your dad didn't mention it to you?" He grinds his teeth together at my words and drops his forehead to mine.

"My father is about to have a whole storm to deal with if he didn't. We need to talk privately about the Knights. About some things we discovered while you were gone." My stomach twists at his words, but I nod and move to wrap my arms around him, resting my head on his chest. "It's going to be okay, Octavia. I won't let them break you. Any of them."

"I know," I say, wondering just how bad the stuff he has to tell me is, but I know I don't need to voice that fear. Not to him.

"I won't let them break you either."

He holds me like I'm made of glass until the bell rings. "Come on, let me walk you to class," he says softly. "We'll talk later."

I pull back from him and he takes my hand, intertwining my fingers with his. Standing next to him like this, I feel like there isn't any battle we couldn't win.

I just hope we can weather the storm that's coming.

Today at school fucking sucked, so despite knowing Lincoln and I need to talk, I persuade him to hang out with me and East first. Which is exactly why we're all camped out on East's giant bed, Lincoln in sweats and a muscle top, me in his hoodie and my leggings, watching a cheesy action movie.

Pretty sure East is bored out of his mind, but he sits on the other side of me, and I'm wrapped around the two of them.

Lincoln's phone rings for the eleventy-billionth time since we hit play and he sighs. "I'm going to have to get this," he says, standing and leaving the room. East pauses the movie and looks down at me.

"How are you doing?"

I kiss his cheek softly and smile. "Pretty sure I should be asking you that."

"Well I asked first," he says, his eyes sparkling.

"I'm okay, just worried about him," I say, telling him what Blair said earlier in the day. Lincoln has been distracted ever since. Not that I blame him, but I wish he'd talk to me.

"Harrison is such a fucking asshole. Pretty sure if he didn't think Lincoln would leave, he'd have kicked me out of the house already." I frown at the thought.

"If he does, just come stay with me. I mean, you could just come stay with me anyway. You all could. If I thought it would help, I'd insist on it."

He laughs softly, shaking his head. "I'm sure you would, but unless they can get free of the Knights, there isn't anything that can help them."

"Is there a way to get them free?"

He shakes his head and my heart sinks. "I've been trying to think of a way for years. Ever since Harrison told me I wasn't his heir, that Lincoln would be inducted. I contemplated running away with him, trying to make it on our own, but he was so young, and they inducted him before I had a chance to do anything. The only way out of the Knights, as far as I can see, is death. The only person who is out, without it, is you."

Confusion rushes through me. I didn't think I was free? I mean, I know I haven't been inducted but... none of this makes sense. "Me? But I thought the Knights wanted me? That was the whole point of everything they did to me when I came back here."

"That's part of what I wanted to talk to you about," Lincoln says, as he steps further into the room. I hadn't heard him open the door.

"Sorry man," East says, wincing. "I thought she knew."

"It's fine. I was going to tell her tonight anyway," he says as he moves toward the bed. "Have you had your meds?"

East groans, shaking his head. "No, I wanted to be coherent since you guys were around and they just make me fucking sleep."

"East, you can't miss your meds, you only just got out of the hospital!" I scold, and he frowns. "I want you to get better. If anything else happens to you because of me..."

I trail off and he grabs my face in his hands, making me look at him. "This wasn't your fault." He kisses me, pouring every part of himself into it, and I sigh against him. He pulls back and glances over at Lincoln. "You guys should talk, but I'm here if either of you need a sounding board. Not being a Knight gives me a different perspective sometimes."

I clasp his hand as he releases my cheeks. "Thank you,"

"You don't ever have to thank me, V. I love you. I'd literally burn the world for you if you asked me to. Maybe even if you didn't."

I laugh softly, and Lincoln coughs out something that sounds like "suck up."

"Come on," Linc says, holding his hand out to me. "We should probably get this over with sooner rather than later." He turns to East and quirks a brow. "Take your damn pills. I'll check on you later."

I climb from the bed, kissing the inside of East's wrist as I do. "I love you too. I'll see you tomorrow?"

"I'll be here," he says with an easy smile.

I take Linc's hand and he takes me down the hall to his room. There is something soothing about the room. It could be that it smells like him, or it could just be that this is his inner sanctum and I know that having me in here means something to him.

I move to his bed and climb on top of it, hugging one of his pillows. I get the feeling I'm going to need the comfort for whatever he's about to tell me.

He paces in front of me, running his hand through his hair. "I'm not even sure where to start."

I reach out for him and he moves toward me, sitting on the bed to face me. "Just start from the beginning."

He nods, looking almost sad. "Just don't hate me." He looks so fucking vulnerable, my heart feels like it's going to break in two.

"I couldn't hate you if I tried. And trust me, I tried." I laugh, but it's forced and he doesn't smile.

He takes a deep breath, squeezes my hand, and looks me dead

in the eye. "When you were gone, Finley found something. It's how we convinced the Knights to help us find you."

"Okay," I say when he pauses, trying to remain calm as my heart races in my chest. He seems stressed enough having to tell me this, so I do my best not to let my emotions show to keep him from feeling any worse.

"We found the agreement your dad made when he left."

The words hang in the air and I almost don't dare to breathe.

"Your father never really got out. He just kind of stepped down. Stone was the Regent before he took you away from here. He made a deal with Harrison that you would be out free and clear. In return, he would give up his seat as Regent *and* his seat at the table of the Conclave. He would work for Harrison when needed, he would never truly be free, but you would be. And so would any children you were to have in the future."

He scrubs a hand down his face, but confusion clouds my thoughts. "I don't understand. That sounds like a good thing. I'm free?"

He shakes his head. "You *were* free. The contract stated that should any Knight approach or harm you, that you would take your birthright as Regent of the Conclave."

I feel like I can't breathe.

That can't be right.

"Why would my dad put that in there?" I clasp my throat, trying to suck in air.

"My guess is to keep the Conclave from coming after you. It's a pretty good deterrent. No one wants to give up that sort of power, and the Regent's word is law to the sect."

I feel like my entire world just got tipped upside down. "What does this mean now?"

He lets out a deep sigh and squeezes my hand. "I don't know. I've been trying to find that bit out, but unsurprisingly, Harrison is being tight-lipped. What I do know is the senior Conclave has been meeting way more often since I dropped that bomb in their lap."

"But if Harrison made the deal, surely he knew? So why invite me to the gala? Why come after me? Panda—*Evan*—said that he had Edward kill my dad, that they fucked with the will to make sure I came back here. Why would they do that if it meant risking me taking the Regency?"

"I'm working on finding out; it doesn't make sense to me either. Stone must have had something that was worth them risking it. That, or Harrison figured you'd never find out with him being dead. None of the other Conclave members knew about the deal he made, which means it got signed off by one of the Kings of the Prism—the Prism is the tier of Knights that sit above the Conclave. Which also means this goes way higher up than I ever imagined."

"This sounds dangerous," I say, biting my lip, trying not to let fear get the better of me.

"I won't let them hurt you, Octavia. Not while there is breath in my body. No one is ever going to hurt you again."

I kiss him softly and he groans as I pull back. "There's more you need to know."

I wait patiently for him to speak. He's always been someone who weighs his words carefully, and I'm not about to rush him.

"My father... he has made it very clear that he doesn't want me having anything to do with you. He was clear about it before we stormed the Conclave to get you back. He's been even clearer about it since then. He won't have my happiness ruining his plans." He pauses and I open my mouth to curse Harrison out, but he shakes his head. "We need to be smart about this. Harrison isn't an enemy we want, and with this whole Regency thing, keeping him on our side is vital. He's already suspicious. I told him we're nothing more than friends, that you're with Finley, and close with the other two, but that I am keeping my distance as instructed."

"I don't like this." I sigh, my heart sinking.

"Neither do I, but for now, we need to play his game. When we have more leverage, when we know what he wants from you… know more about what Stone did to get you free, then we'll have more wiggle room, but for now—"

"For now we need to pretend that we aren't a thing where your dad is concerned."

"Which means that outside of here, we have to be careful."

"You mean at school."

He rubs a hand down his face and nods. "I mean everywhere but here. I need you to be safe, Octavia, and if that means sneaking around, then that's what I'll do. Sacrificing for you isn't a sacrifice."

TWELVE

FINLEY

I sit in the boardroom, twiddling my fucking thumbs, trying not to let my brain seep from my ears in sheer boredom as Harrison drones on about something that I've paid exactly zero attention to. The junior Conclave members are all here, seated with their senior counterpart. Which means I'm wedged between my father and Edward Riley.

Joy of fucking joys.

The six other juniors look as bored as I do, except for Mitchell. Simping little lap dog is about as strong as a wet noodle. If his father had any other children, they'd be here instead. The disdain is obvious every time his father looks at him. But in his father's defense, Mitchell is a sniveling little weasel. I'd trust a venomous snake more than I'd trust him.

The empty chair beside Chase has never felt so ominous before, but the daggers that Harrison continues to glare at him now mean that that chair isn't likely to stay empty for long.

It's either that, or Chase's line will 'mysteriously' end and a new family will be lifted up in rank.

Though as long as it's not Raleigh, I won't get too murderous about it.

"—Octavia Royal."

The sound of her name has my attention back to Harrison, a snarl on my lips that I brush off as quick as it appeared.

"The girl has been recovered and is healing nicely according to Finley." Everyone's gazes swing to me, and I nod once to confirm.

"Obviously the terms of the contract her father made have come to light, so this is something we shall need to deal with. Once she is healed, I will handle it. As we have discovered, there were terms of the agreement that none of us were privy to." Harrison's lips thin and I glance over at Chase. He told East that he helped Stone, but I wonder if even he knew what Stone had agreed to in full. "I have checked the contract over myself and checked it over with the Prism. Only the Regent of the Prism was aware of its existence. It seems it was made with the highest member of the Knights—the somewhat-absent Archon. I know none of us have ever personally met our illustrious leader, but I have had the Prism Regent's assurance that he will check in with Archon to ensure the contract is as ironclad as it seems."

My ears prick up at the mention of the Archon. Stone must have had some sway if the Archon dealt with his deal personally. I didn't think anyone in this sect had ever met the Archon. He's the faceless, nameless leader at the top of the pyramid. I was beginning to think he was nothing more than a myth.

We're all aware that Harrison, as Regent, sits on one of the various Boards. That each board has a King which makes up the Prism who supposedly answers to the Archon, but still... never meeting said person makes them like a bedtime story rather than a reality.

"You mean to say that you will be stepping down for a stumbling girl?" Archer DuPont scoffs from his seat across the table. He's a hapless money bag, but his daughter—Artemis, who sits at his side staring a deathly glare into the side of his skull—is anything but. He might be useless, but her? She is dangerous.

Cold and calculating in a similar manner to Lincoln, she reminds me a lot of Blair, and I'm secretly glad that the Board rejected Blair's request to sit in the empty Royal seat. Blair and Artemis together would have been... just no.

"I will take her under my wing, and help her lead if that is what the Archon decrees," Harrison says proudly, but that shadow in his eye tells me it won't be quite so simple. I glance over at Lincoln, seated beside his father, the tic in his jaw bouncing. I guess he believes Harrison about as much as I do.

"What if she doesn't want to take the seat?" Chase challenges, and Maverick snickers on the other side of his father.

"The deal struck was broken, which means the same rule applies for her as for *all* bloodlines." Harrison's words are pointed, but Chase doesn't back down. I'm guessing knowing he has an heir that he wants to keep clear has his back up.

"Then I guess we should all meet with the girl and ensure that she is made aware of *everything*."

The tension in the room ratchets up, the threat dripping from Chase's words making everyone still, like the calm before the storm. Except Harrison just smiles at Chase. My blood runs cold at the sight of it and it's not even directed at me.

"I will ensure the girl is made aware of everything, but please, Armstrong, feel free to meet with the girl. She will be here with us all, bound by our oaths before long."

I look back over to Artemis, whose face is blank, but her clenched fists give her away. Something is going on with her, and while she's never met V, I'd put money on the fact that that isn't going to last much longer.

"If nobody else has any further questions, we can wrap this up. I have plans for the rest of my evening." Harrison stands as if to dismiss us all, when my father clears his throat.

"We should discuss Rico."

The room sucks in a breath, and it's like you could hear a pin drop. It's as if my father is taunting Harrison, and I don't know why.

"I will deal with Rico, Charles." Harrison glares at my father, and everyone else looks bewildered as to why the Regent of the sect in Cancun is being brought up. "Dismissed."

Harrison strides out of the room, leaving behind a low murmur as people start to make their way from the room. My father turns to me when the room is nearly empty.

His eyes dance with glee and a stone forms in the pit of my stomach. "Play your cards close to the chest, boy. With the Royal girl at your side, there are a myriad of possibilities at hand. Change is coming."

THIRTEEN

OCTAVIA

L inc has been treating me like I'm made of glass since our conversation on Monday. This softer side is definitely something I could get used to seeing every now and then, but I almost miss his assholeish ways. I don't want to be looked at like I'm breakable.

It's not who I am.

All it's doing is acting as a reminder of what happened to me, and what could still be waiting.

It could've been worse—so much worse—but I got myself free, and he got me out. We'll find a way around the other stuff. We haven't been able to get a straight answer about this fucking engagement bullshit either, and it has him on edge.

So when I woke up with him in my bed again this morning, I made a decision. If he won't take my words as proof that I'm okay, that we'll be okay, then I'm going to show him with my actions. We haven't taken that step yet, but I'm more than ready.

I pad back into my bedroom and find him half asleep, looking at me in that dazed, still possibly going to fall back to sleep, yet impossibly alert way he has. His shirt is wrapped around me, and when he notices that, his eyes go a little wider and he looks a little more coherent. "You look good with me on you."

I grin at the cheesy line. I love that I get this side of him that no one else sees. It's like we're in a bubble, and I know I'm safe here.

Sashaying over to the bed, I let the shirt drop from my shoulders, and his eyes narrow as he watches me intently. This might be my show, but I'm very aware that my tenuous control of the situation is likely to pass to him when I make my next moves.

The shirt pools at my feet and I stand bare in front of him before climbing onto the bed, slipping beneath the sheets. I move closer to him and capture his lips with mine, running my hands up his bare chest, tangling my fingers in the small patch of hair there. Moving slowly I push him onto his back and move to straddle him as his hands grip my hips.

There might be his thin pair of boxers between us, but it is more than a little apparent that he is on board for what I have in mind.

Maybe I should be more tentative since we haven't done this before, because of everything that's happened between us before now, but I'm tired of denying what he means to me. To him and to myself.

"Octavia," he murmurs as I pull back for breath, his gray eyes dark and stormy as he holds me in place with one hand, another moving to fist my hair. "If we do this, there is no turning back. We already crossed enough lines that I'm never letting go, but this… this means you're mine and there is nothing in this world or any other that will keep me from you. The stars may fall, and the sun may never rise, but you will still be mine."

His words make my heart race, and I nod my head as much as I can in his grasp. His eyes flash and I'm on my back in a heartbeat, his body hovering over me. He leans his forehead against mine, closing his eyes, and takes a breath as my heart pounds against my ribcage. "I've got you, always. Never forget that, Octavia."

He captures my lips again, and I get lost in the feel of him. Every sense heightened by the anticipation of what's to come.

Our tongues move as if in a dance we've been practicing our entire lives and I revel in the feel of his heat. A strong chest hovering above mine—breaths becoming more and more shallow—with arms caging me in while he kisses and licks every inch of me. He tastes like a new morning, like a new beginning, and I can't seem to get enough of him. With my feet planted firmly on the mattress, I push my hips up to meet his crotch but he's keeping his dick away from me on purpose.

My groan and whimper tell him everything he needs to know: I want it, now. He chuckles in my mouth and the lightheartedness of that sound is fuel to my burning fire.

"Linc, gimme!"

"Patience. I want you to beg for it." With that declaration, Linc ends our kiss with a bite of my bottom lip and pulls back, eyes darting all over my face like he's assessing my state of being.

"I'm fine. I keep telling you but you're too stubborn to get it."

"You're fine when I say you're fine." If it weren't for the glint in his steel gaze, I'd be offended by such a declaration. But he's kidding, trying to rile me up, and lucky for him, I'm more than just riled up. I'm near losing my mind with wanting him.

I think I've always wanted him, from the first time we spoke all those years ago. Linc and me? It's been a long time coming.

And hopefully, we'll both be literally coming sooner rather than later.

Wrapping my legs around his waist, I push my heels down on his ass and pull myself up to rub my pussy against his boxer-clad cock. Linc moans and the sound goes straight to my clit, making me shiver with need.

"Linc, please. God, I need you."

"There it is." With a dexterity only he could possess, Linc is completely naked in less time than it takes me to realize it. We're skin to skin—heat to heat—and the feel of him is nothing short of heavenly.

Then he's gone. Completely untangled from my hold, Linc travels down the length of my body, one leisurely kiss at a time. One bite and one suck at a time. His mouth latches onto my nipple—sucking it in almost to the point of pain—and his fingers search out my folds, finding them wet and ready for him. My back arches, aching for more of his touch, more of his mouth. Always more when it comes to him.

With his tongue flicking my hard nub until he tears a long moan from me, he looks up and winks right before his teeth sink down and my entire body springs off the bed.

"What the—" I'm gasping in air, my pussy desperate for more attention as he only rubs my pussy from the outside, leaving me begging for more of him, more of his touch.

"Shh, be good."

I sink my teeth into my lip and squeeze my eyes shut when I feel his hot, wet mouth travel down to my mound, giving it a soft, almost loving kiss. It's so gentle and different from the Linc that I've come to know. Except I'm not a fragile flower and I need more than just soft. I need him to consume me. To bring me to the edge then pull me back to reality.

"Linc, please. I need more. This whole sweet shit isn't going to fly with me."

The fire in his eyes could be from desire or it could be from anger. I'm not quite sure until he shows me exactly what he thinks of my idea.

"You're not the one in control here."

This is when I remember that Linc is not one to take instructions very well. Not from his dad, not from his brother, and apparently not from me either.

"But Linc…"

His teeth sink into my pussy lip before he licks a slow, torturous, path across my flesh. Down one side, up the other. It's like he's playing with my patience and loving every squirm and every whimper I give him.

"Linc, please…"

He doesn't relent. Doesn't even pretend to accelerate his moves to bring me to peak any faster. I'm beginning to think that he's purposefully playing with me like a cat plays with its mouse.

I'm quivering as his tongue circles my clit, around and around, until I can feel my juices spilling over from my overwhelming desire. My uncontrollable want of him.

"Please, Linc. I'm begging you. Please, please, please."

Grabbing me under my thighs, lightning quick, he pulls me into him just as he positions himself on his knees. My back is flat on the mattress and his full frame is towering over me like an ominous yet alluring presence.

"You want the full force of me, V? Are you sure you know what you're asking?" The rawness in his voice and the steel in his eyes make me wetter than I thought possible. His power, his control. His need to dominate turns me on in ways I didn't know were possible. Am I sure?

"Yes. Yes, to both."

"Don't say I didn't warn you."

Grabbing me by my ass cheeks, Linc pulls me up until my knees are over his shoulders and my pussy is level with his hungry mouth. He kisses me like he's a starved man as I try to hold myself as still as possible. At this point, the only part of me still on the bed are my shoulders and head. His tongue is deep inside my channel, licking my walls and biting my folds. His nose is against my mound as his lips suck on every inch of me. When he releases one of my ass cheeks, he slams two fingers inside me —his mouth latching onto my clit—and my entire body shakes with the force of it. I think I cry out but I can't be sure since my brain is only able to register the pleasure he's giving me right now.

Curling his fingers inside me, he presses against the one spot that has me immediately chasing an orgasm.

"Oh fuck!"

My hands are fisting the sheet as he relentlessly rubs against my g-spot before I lose all of my control. My body is no longer mine. It's all his. He's playing it like a fucking violin and I'm okay with it. I surrender completely.

Twisting his fingers inside me, he pulls them out—ignoring my protests like he doesn't give a fuck what I think—and without any preamble, he slides one, then the other, into my ass. He's careful at first, making sure he doesn't hurt me, but when his lips descend on my clit and sucks it in with the force of a hurricane, I lose myself in him. Lose myself as I come harder than I have before. I'm thrashing and crying out while Linc continues to pull the orgasm out of me with precise expertise.

As soon as I come down from my high, Lincoln pulls me down to his cock where he impales me, slowly, inch by inch, like his own personal fuck toy.

Holy fucking shit he feels so good. I am so fucking full and I'm definitely not going to complain about it. I'm not stupid.

His hands move to my ass cheeks as he throws his hips back and forth, fucking me like he's a god and I'm his most treasured possession. My body moves along the mattress as he bottoms out on every thrust; the sounds of slapping skin and wet pussy surround me.

He fucks me like he's desperate for me, like he needs to imprint himself on me, and there's no way for me to stop him even if I wanted to.

He fucks me like a savage until I'm almost at the edge, but stops just this side of Nirvana and I swear I want to throw something at him.

"What are you doing?" I don't even know if he can understand me. My voice is hoarse and my words are spilling together like I'm drunk on him.

"Whatever the fuck I want, V. You should know that about me by now."

In one practiced move, he has me on my stomach, on all fours, as he hitches my ass up just the way he wants it before he slams his hard, thick dick right back inside me. At the same time, he pushes two thick fingers inside my ass and goes back to fucking me with the force of a titan.

I have to clutch the sheets and use every muscle in my body to avoid moving up the bed, even though one of his big hands is holding onto my hip for leverage. In tandem, he fucks my pussy as his fingers bottom out to the last knuckle in my ass. One then the other and my orgasm begins to make itself known. It starts at the bundle of nerves in my clit then radiates throughout my body like electricity traveling through my bloodstream.

"I told you, Octavia. If we did this, you could never get rid of me. Ever. I'm about to come inside your pretty little wet cunt and there's nothing you can ever do to make me walk away. Nothing. You. Can. Do." He punctuates every word with a hard thrust and on the last one, I explode in a flurry of colors and feelings and complete incoherence.

As I try to calm my heart rate, Linc stops everything, takes in a deep, calming breath, and watches me with lust and love engraved in his steel gaze. Every one of his movements is calculated, like he's trying to dominate himself. He didn't come yet so I'm guessing he's testing the boundaries of his control.

It's when he reaches for the lube that everything clicks into place.

The anticipation runs through me and as excited I am to do this, I can't deny that the fear of the pain is real.

"Shh, baby, I'll be careful. Has anyone ever fucked your ass?"

I'm loving this caring side of Lincoln Saint just as much as I love the closed-off control freak.

With unwavering care, Linc slowly slides the crown of his head into my ass before I get the chance to answer him, massaging my ass cheeks as he goes, murmuring words of encouragement.

You're beautiful like this.

I love seeing my dick in your ass.

I've always loved you, Octavia.

Finally, he bottoms out, and when he does I let out a sigh of complete bliss. He doesn't move for a bit, just sits there, digging the pads of his fingers into my flesh until I push back, begging for more.

"Linc, please. I need…" He knows exactly what I need, and he gives it to me.

With one hand on my ass cheek, he reaches down with the other to tweak my clit as he pulls almost all the way out before pushing back in. I don't know how he has lasted this long without coming.

"Fuck, the sight of you taking my dick in your ass is more than I can handle, Octavia. I'm not gonna last." I love that I have that effect on him. I love that I am the one who can break him away from his control. It's heady as fuck.

Pinching my clit with one hand, he slaps my ass with the other as he begins to fuck me like I'm all he's ever wanted. Slow at first, easy and careful, making sure he's not ruining it for me. In and out, slap, slap, pinch, until he progressively loses the battle against his primal needs.

With one final thrust that sends me sliding against the headboard, Linc pulls out and the unmistakable sound of him jacking himself off reaches my ears.

He's marking me.

He's coming all over my ass.

I reach down to my clit, even though I know it's a long shot, and try to alleviate the need that I feel at the image of Linc violently stroking himself, about to come all over me.

The first jet of cum hits my sensitive skin, making it come to life like a dormant volcano exploding into the night sky, but when I rub out my clit, the pleasure it produces has me screaming into the mattress.

Linc roars out his orgasm and squeezes my ass as he comes over me. It's hot and it's heady and it makes my head spin, but holy fuck that was hot.

I think I may pass out from pleasure—I feel like Jell-O—but not before I hear the deep timbre of his voice, words dark and ominous yet only making me love him more.

"I'm all over you, Octavia," he declares, panting and deadly. "For-fucking-ever."

We both collapse onto the bed, him on top of me, his dick nestled between my ass cheeks, as he whispers in my ear.

"All mine."

FOURTEEN

OCTAVIA

S tarting my morning off with a bang—literally—put a definite pep in my step, even if I feel like I've been walking funny all day.

Not that I'm complaining.

Lincoln breaking down that final barrier between us... it's like that final wavering part of myself has found solid ground.

There might be a mass of chaos in my life, but my four guys are here to stay. They'd give anything for me and I'd do the same for them.

The morning at school has passed in a happy blur, so when I sit opposite Indi at the table in the cafeteria, I still have a giant smile on my face.

"I don't know what you had today, but can I have some?" she asks, looking exhausted as she shotguns a can of coke.

It's impossible to stop the laugh that breaks free. "No, no you can't. Pretty sure you and Lincoln wouldn't merge that well. Like, I love you, but no."

She pulls a face, sticking her tongue out. "Yeah no, not my type, but hell yes for you. It's about fucking time you two got down and dirty. Was he a monster dick? Don't answer that. I bet he was. All that big dick energy he has... just damn."

I laugh at her, shaking my head as I take a bite of my burger. "My lips are sealed."

"For now anyway." She giggles.

"What's so funny?" Maverick asks as he drops into the seat beside me. I start laughing uncontrollably. Indi joins in and we laugh till we cry.

"I swear it's not even funny," I say, trying to breathe and stop the laughter.

Mav just quirks his brow at me and steals one of my fries. "If you say so. Girls are weird."

"You love my brand of weird," I tease, and he pulls me into his lap, kissing my neck.

"Yes I do."

Indi shakes her head. "Who would've thought that you could turn Maverick Riley into a cheeseball."

I grin at her, their prodding back and forth is beyond funny.

"Only for her," Maverick says, shrugging. "I can show you my other side if you'd prefer?"

He grins, baring his teeth at her, and I roll my eyes as Linc and Finn join us at the table.

"Oh good, the boss is here," Indi snarks. "Put your leash back on."

"Oh look, they're friends again," Finley snorts as he sits. "I knew you beating Blair the other day would soften him to you."

"Has anything come of that?" I ask, worrying my lip.

Lincoln shakes his head. "I dealt with it. It'll be fine."

I blow him a kiss and the corners of his lips turn up. That might be the best I can get from him in this cesspit of a school, so I'll take it. At least there are only, like, four months left until we're out of this place.

We should probably start thinking about colleges, or at least have that conversation, but with everything else that's been going on, we haven't exactly had time to think about it.

Well *I* haven't.

I had so many plans when I came back last summer: a clear goal and the steps that would get me there.

Now?

Everything has changed.

I can't even say that I'm mad about it, but I definitely need to work some shit out.

"Just so you all know, the party Blair was going on about is happening. Tomorrow evening at the house." He looks directly at me and it's like the rest of the world ceases to exist. "I have spoken to Harrison and he assured me there is no engagement."

"Goddamn right there isn't," Indi huffs. I love her too much. "And if there was, I'm pretty sure between all of the resources at my disposal these days, I could help you make her disappear."

Huh. My little ray of sunshine got *dark.*

I laugh while Lincoln graces her with the rare approving smirk. She doesn't even notice and continues to chow down on her lunch.

"Oh that reminds me!" Indi pipes up. "I got us booked in with Gracie tomorrow. I figured we could use a hair day!"

"That's so perfect! My hair is a mess. Wearing it up all the time does not suit me. Does anyone have plans tonight?"

The boys all look between themselves, before Lincoln answers me. "We have a meeting."

My heart sinks. I almost forgot that they have those. I can't help but flick back to the conversation I had with East, about how they'll never be free, and my chest hurts. What if this whole Regency thing means I could get them free?

I tuck the thought away to ponder over later. "Oh, okay. It's cool."

"We can swing by after?" Finn offers.

I shake my head. "No, it's fine. I was going to say we should start talking about college, but it can wait."

"I'd come over, but Ryker is being a little... possessive right now."

I smile at her, hating how torn she looks, but also hating that this is where we're all at right now. Pulled in a dozen different directions. "Honestly it's fine, I can have a date with my piano. It's been a minute and I kind of miss it. Plus, I can go hang out with East. He's probably going insane."

"Okay," she says, giving me a tight smile.

"You're not wrong though," Linc adds. "He is going stir crazy. Just don't let him exert himself too much."

I smirk at him and shoot him an exaggerated salute. "Yes, sir."

The corners of his lips tip up and his eyes light at my words. Well... apparently he likes that. I'll tuck that away for future reference. Might just get me another morning like today, and well, I'm not about to say no to that.

I turn back to Indi who is grinning shamelessly at me. "What time is the appointment with Gracie?"

"I got her for ten a.m., so I can swing by and grab you if you like?"

"Sounds good."

Maverick kisses my neck softly, stealing my attention. "Eat." I look back at him and he's looking at me, concern pinching the corners of his eyes. "You haven't been eating the same since we got you back, and while I love you no matter what you look like, you need to eat."

I chew the inside of my cheek and pick up my burger. I hadn't noticed, but apparently he has. People—including himself—never give him enough credit. He always says he's not the guy with the plan, not the thinker, more the do-er... but he pays far more attention than anyone realizes.

The bell sounds and I plow down the last bites of the burger before chugging back my bottle of water. Finley stands, grabbing my bag, while Lincoln clears our trays and Mav takes my hand. People stare at us all as Finley kisses me despite Maverick holding my hand, and I couldn't give less fucks if I tried.

They don't have to understand us. We've walked through fire to get here and I'm not about to explain everything we are to small-minded assholes who mean nothing in the long run.

"We'll walk you to class," Linc says as he reappears. I smile at him, nodding as he holds out his hand to me. I falter, thinking back to our conversation. He seems to read my mind and his hand falls to his side, but Finley offers me his instead.

Apparently they all know about the bullshit.

Maverick slaps my ass and releases me as I step up and take Finn's hand. Indi beside me, Linc and Mav behind us. My dad always said that family isn't just about blood, that the family you choose is the best kind of family you can have, and I think I'm finally coming to realize just how right he was.

Blood might be thicker than water, but love is thicker than blood.

After a long day at school of mock exams and the sheer amount of work set for end-of-year assignments to get final grades, my brain aches. Plus the substitute in Gym is an actual beast. I don't remember having ever sweat so bad in a gym class, but this woman is absolutely slaying.

So when I let myself into the Saint house and head up to East's room, I am so excited at the idea of a chill night with him. I texted him after lunch to see if he wanted company tonight and he practically rhapsodized the idea. I guess being cooped up is driving him insane.

I knock on his door and push it open, finding him perched on the edge of his bed in nothing but sweats.

"Are you seriously working out?" I ask, undecided if I should be impressed or yelling at him.

He grins up at me as a bead of sweat runs down his chest. "Rehab is a bitch. Plus, this is nothing, but I refuse to waste away in this room. I have official rehab tomorrow, but my trainer emailed me over some stuff I can be doing at home."

"Should you really be doing this so soon after coming home?"

He nods, running a hand down his chest. "I went and saw the doc today, got the all clear on the incision. It's healed pretty nicely, though the scar is for life. I told her I was losing my mind and she said there wasn't any harm if I was feeling up to it. She also recommended actual therapy. Don't think I've laughed that hard in a while."

I look at the pink, puckered line on his chest, and my heart races with the fact that I could have lost him. We are so freaking lucky that he's still here with us.

"Don't look at me like that, V. I'm not going to break." He looks fierce as fuck as he stands, but I race across the room to stop him. He might say he's okay, but I am so not going to be responsible for him getting hurt again.

"Maybe you won't break, but that doesn't mean you can be Superman just yet either. Sit your ass back down. I thought we had a snuggle date." I grin up at him, trying to make light of the fact that I can feel him trembling beneath my touch. Apparently he already overexerted himself today.

He kisses my forehead before sitting back down on the bed. "Fine, fine."

I don't blame him for being frustrated, I would be if I was cooped up in here all day too, but I need him to look after himself, because I can't lose him.

I can't lose any of them.

I might not have wanted any ties when I came back to Echoes Cove, but a lot has changed since then. I don't even feel like the same person I was last summer.

Once I've helped him get comfortable, I climb over him and snuggle into his side.

"How was your day, anyway? Distract me with your tales of youth," he teases, and I smile at him, kissing his chest. I regale him with the dull nothingness of school, the drama that fills the halls, and when I tell him about Indi and Blair, he laughs so much he snorts and it's cute as fuck.

"It's about time Blair realizes she can't push everyone and not get some pushback," he says as he mindlessly plays with my hair.

"Yeah, but who would've thought Indi would be the one to throw down?"

"Oh I absolutely did. That girl loves you fiercely. She's a little spitfire." He chuckles and I nod. He isn't wrong.

A knock on the door steals my attention and Mrs. Potts appears. "Would you dears like some dinner?"

"That would be amazing, thank you," East says with a smile. "I don't suppose you'll let me have pizza?"

She rolls her eyes at him, and I clamp my lips together to stop from laughing. "You know too well that pizza is off the menu. You boys are incorrigible. How does some lean meat and veggies sound?"

He groans and this time I don't manage to stifle the soft giggle.

"Sounds delicious," I say to her and she grins.

"I knew I liked you, Octavia. I'll be back in a little while with some food for you." She closes the door as East trails his fingers down my ribcage.

"You shouldn't encourage her. It's all lean meats, no processed food... no fun food."

I sigh and move to straddle him so I can look him in the eye properly. "She's just making sure you heal properly."

"Healing is no fun."

"I didn't realize you were so whiny," I tease. "But I can think of some fun we can have."

The doctor said no sex... they didn't say anything about anything else. I lean in to kiss him softly, careful of the fact that he is still healing, but he's not having any of it.

Grabbing me by the back of the head, East curls his fingers into the strands of my hair with overwhelming passion, crashing his mouth to mine like he's a man starved.

Making sure I don't touch him anywhere that could hurt him, I hold myself up on one hand planted next to his head. His hips rise up as his tongue explores every inch of my mouth, my lips, dueling with my tongue.

"I want to make you feel good, East." My words are whispered against his panting mouth.

"You always make me feel good, V. Just being here is everything." He really is a Saint among sinners.

With a wicked glint in my eye, I smile against his lips before giving him a lingering last kiss.

"Where are you going?" His voice is hoarse and if I weren't a sinner I'd feel bad that I'm about to blow his mind while he's trying to heal.

"Making sure you remember I was here." Slowly, I lift one leg and kneel beside him as I push down the front of his sweats until his cock springs free. I'm surprised that he's already hard for me, and when I look back at him he's got a boyish grin on his beautiful face. "What can I say? You just being here makes me so fucking hard, V."

Licking my lips, I kiss the top of his dick, licking along the slit, and revel in the sound of his groan. It's like fuel to my already burning fire.

His hand moves to touch me but I swat it away.

"This is about you, East. It's not about me."

"Don't you know, Octavia? For me, it's always been about you. From the very beginning."

His words make me weak, and matched with the longing on his face, I cave. I slide a little closer to his hand to allow him better access to my skin. I lean in and place my mouth over the head of his cock, sucking softly and caressing him with my tongue.

I lower my mouth until my nose is at his crotch and I'm gagging on his dick. Tears fill my eyes as I take him down before pulling back and wrapping my fingers around his shaft, spreading my saliva with every stroke I give him.

East snakes his hand under my uniform skirt and latches onto my panties, trying to pull me close enough that he can touch me. I give into him because, of course I do, and angle my body just enough for him to be able to touch my wet, aching pussy. His groan as he sinks one finger inside of me, tells me he needed to feel me as much I needed to have him in my mouth.

Harder and harder, I suck him into my mouth, taking him deeper and deeper as I go. East rocks his hips up every time I bottom out, my throat opening up for his cock. The sounds I hear from him only make me want to give him more so I slide my hand down to his balls, rolling them in my hand, eliciting a long, drawn-out moan from him. Every time he reacts to my touch it makes me even wetter and I know he can feel it because he adds another finger, and fuck me, it feels too good.

I should be worried about his wounds but all I can think about is making him feel good, and if making me feel good helps with that, I'm not about to deny either of us that.

I bob my head on his cock faster as he finger fucks me with greater force than before. We're both panting as he tries to bring me to orgasm, and just like that he's taken control of the situation I thought I was commanding. I guess this is what they mean by topping from the bottom.

With my mouth focused only on the head of his cock, I jack him off as I suck and lick and kiss the entire head of him. East's movements become erratic, like he's barely holding back.

"Give it to me, V." I know what he wants and I can't refuse him. Just as he slides the pad of his finger across my clit, I rub myself out on his finger all the while concentrating on using my mouth to bring him to climax. Holding his balls in my hand, I glide down his shaft and let it go as far as it can until I feel his head at the back of my throat, gagging again and not caring about the sounds I'm making.

"Gonna come, V." His words are hoarse and the urgency in his voice is all I need to lose my self-control.

I can't cry out but my entire body moves with the force of the orgasm he gives me just as he spills down my throat, the tangy taste of him coating my tongue.

I swallow every drop—because spitters are quitters—and slowly lick every inch of him clean before I kiss the top of his softening cock and pull his sweats back into place.

Turning to face him, I feel a blush coloring my cheeks when I see the goofy grin that makes him look like the boy I used to know, way back when things were less complicated.

"Best visit ever." He brings his fingers to his mouth and licks them clean before he pops them out from between his lips and winks.

"Best snack ever," I retort. As I'm trying to get off the bed, he shakes his head, grabbing me and pulling me closer to him.

"Don't run away, V. Kiss me, first."

And I do. I kiss him like I love him. With abandon and purity.

A night with East was exactly what we both needed. The others joined us after their meeting, but we didn't speak about it. We just hung out like five friends, watching crappy movies and jabbing at the terrible action scenes.

I don't think I've felt that much like a teenager in months. Sometimes it's easy to forget that I'm only seventeen, that I'm supposed to be young and carefree, that life isn't meant to be this much of a mess. This much chaos.

We all ended up crashing at the Saints' overnight, one giant puppy pile on East's bed. It took some maneuvering but we made it work and I can honestly say I've never slept as soundly as I did. Even with the limited space. I woke up with each of them touching me in some way or another and I've never felt safer.

I'd be lying if I said I didn't wake up and think of how much fun we could've all had together, but it was not to be.

Not yet anyway.

Though doing the walk of shame through our yards this morning was more than a little funny. Especially when I noticed our gardener out there a little too late. At least I was dressed, I guess. Even if it was in my school shirt and a pair of Lincoln's sweats.

I looked fucking ridiculous, but it was cute that he offered them to me, even if it was just to walk back home.

The house is quiet since Smithy is spending the weekend with Matthew, so I pad through the house up to my room and take a quick shower, dressing in something comfortable before going down to make myself a bagel with cream cheese for breakfast. I know I can make that without breaking the kitchen, and after Maverick's comment yesterday, I'm trying to remember to eat.

The way Panda used food against me apparently fucked with me more than I had realized. I never thought anything could fuck with my love for food. Apparently I was wrong.

But I'm going to try harder, and that has to count for something. Even if I'm not going to talk it out with anyone. I'd rather work my feelings out with the piano than with another human.

Especially a human I don't know or trust.

Pretty sure any therapist I tried to explain my life to would call me a dramatic bitch that makes shit up since so much of this shit is freaking unbelievable.

Fuck it.

That's what music is for.

My phone buzzes on the counter as I eat my bagel, and Indi's name flashes on the screen.

Indi:

On my way, figured we can grab food and coffee on the way. Breakfast burritos for the win!

Is everyone trying to feed me? Have I really been that out of it? I look at the few bites of bagel I've eaten and wince. They might be right.

Me:

Sounds good, I am here for that burrito.

I wrap the bagel and pop it in the fridge, I can snack on it later. Plus, that burrito sounds too good. My stomach gurgles almost in response and I frown. Maybe I *have* been neglecting myself a little bit without meaning to.

Dashing upstairs, I change into something more suitable for

peopling and being outside. I finish pulling on my jeans as Indi buzzes at the gate. That was timing.

I rush down the stairs, pulling on a pair of boots as I shrug into my jacket, my hair in a messy bun on the top of my head. I'm sure the paparazzi would have a field day with how I look if they bothered to stalk me anymore.

Definitely not something I miss about my old life.

Having my life splayed across every tabloid on the planet isn't something I look back on with any kind of fondness.

I reset the alarm and lock up before jogging down the drive and bundling into Indi's waiting car. "Please tell me how you manage to look so put together and flustered all at once? Is there a secret I missed at orientation to being a girl?"

I laugh at her as I buckle in. "Shut up. Like you don't look fabulous as shit for a hair appointment."

She grins at me, sitting there in her leather-look leggings, black tank with skulls, and a long black cardigan. She's a freaking pixie. "Fair point. You ready to go?"

I pat myself down, making sure I have my phone, wallet, and keys, then nod. "As ready as I'm going to be."

"Awesome. Food, coffee, and hair. What else does a girl need?" She grins before pulling away from the curb.

"You sticking with your purple?" I ask casually as she drives, and she shakes her head.

"I'm thinking of going back to blue. I kind of miss it."

I grin at her, 'cause hell yes. "Do it, why the fuck not?"

"You going to let me talk you into adding some color into those luscious locks of yours?"

I bark out a laugh. "Not a chance. I just want to get my length back, maybe once it grows out we can talk about fun colors."

She sticks out her tongue as we pull into the Starbucks drive-thru. "Spoil sport. But fineeeee, I guess."

I cackle as she places our order before we head to the Mexican place. I feel gross still coming here, all things considered, but it's the only Mexican place in the Cove, and I'm not about to let Raleigh and his bullshit stop me from enjoying life.

I head in and grab breakfast for us both before ducking back out to the car. "Let's eat and drive. Gracie will kill me if we're late."

"I'm good with that." I nod before taking a bite of the spicy egg deliciousness.

How could I ever not love food when it tastes like this?

"You're feeling better?" she asks, side-eyeing me as I eat.

"I am." I smile. "I hadn't realized I wasn't eating properly. Mav poked me and apparently becoming aware of it was what I needed."

"Good. I didn't want to say anything while you've been recovering and dealing with all the things, but I was only going to give you another week, tops."

I laugh softly. "I love you too."

"Of course you do, I'm fabulous." She grins as she taps the steering wheel along to the music playing in the background. "How are you feeling about this party tonight?"

"Honestly?" I pause, taking a deep breath. "I've been trying not to think about it. Lincoln says his dad isn't marrying him off so I have to take him at his word. Harrison, that is. There's still so much up in the air about this Regency shit too, I have no idea what's going on, but I've been so focused on trying to get my ducks in a row that I haven't let myself focus on it too much. I know that's probably not the smart thing to do, but I figure the Knights will seek me out when they're ready. I want nothing to do with them, so I'm happy to avoid it all for forever and a day."

"I get that," she nods. "Just let me know if you need anything. I got your back, always."

"I know you do, but if I can keep you off their radar, you better believe I'm going to."

She shrugs as she pulls into the parking lot of the salon. "Don't keep me free and clear if it means you drown. Ride or die, remember? We can drown together."

I let out a deep breath as I stare at my reflection in the mirror. Gracie worked miracles with my hair, and I feel better from that alone. We did a whole round of beauty treatments, which made me feel better than I have in weeks, and the shopping trip after helped to remind me that my life isn't just kidnapping, secret societies, and all of the other bullshit I've been dealing with.

I have the best friend I could ask for, four guys who practically worship me, Smithy who rocks my world... I have a lot to be thankful for.

Though my dad hasn't been far from my mind most of the day. I can't help but think what he'd say about how I'm handling everything. If he'd disapprove. If he'd be proud. What words of wisdom he'd give me to help get me through it all.

I didn't know the part of him that was a Knight, so it's not something I'll ever have answers to, but I like to think he'd be proud of the woman I'm becoming. Of the way I'm handling shit... or at least trying to handle it.

That he'd tell me to keep my head held high as I walk into this viper pit tonight.

I've spent most of my day preparing for this stupid party, molding myself into the image of someone who isn't afraid; someone who has survived and come out fighting. Except I don't think I look like me right now.

Imposter syndrome is real.

My dark hair is slicked back, falling down my back in a deadly straight line. My eyes are done in an extreme smokey eye, my lips are pale, glossy. Giant drop earrings in each of my ears make my neck look longer, even wrapped in the gold snake chain that I picked out this afternoon to go with my dress. I even found black stilettos with gold snake clips to match.

It'll all pair perfectly with the little black dress—with a sweetheart neckline and a dipped hem so my ass isn't on show—that is currently hanging on the back of my closet door.

It's going to look amazing; it just feels very... not me, all of a sudden. I feel like I've spent so much time recently dressing up and playing pretend and I'm tired of it already.

But tonight I'm just going to have to suck it up. There's no way I'm leaving the others to deal with the Knights—plus most of the Cove's who's who—on their own. I might not like these things, but I'm not about to abandon my guys.

I grab my phone and shoot Indi a message.

Me:
Be thankful your guys don't have stupid functions like this.

Indi:
Oh I am, but you're going to rock it. Remember, they can smell your fear. You got this.

Me:
I've got something **drunk emoji**

Indi:

Do you need one of my famous pep talks?

I laugh softly at her message.

Me:
No, I'm good. I just really don't wanna.

Indi:
Get through as much as you have to, then sneak away with the four of them hot on your heels. I'm pretty positive none of them are going to complain.

Me:
That's a good idea. Let's just hope Harrison doesn't have other plans.

Indi:
If he tries to marry Lincoln off, we'll cut his brakes.

Me:
You're ruthless and I love it.

Indi:
Only for you. Don't tell Ryker. He still thinks I'm a ball of sunshine.

Me:
You are. You're just as dangerous as a ball of sunshine too.

Indi:
Go, have fun, try not to think about the piranhas circling. Let me know if you need backup… or a distraction.

I drop my phone back on the dresser and move to finish getting dressed.

Ready or not, here I come… I guess.

FIFTEEN

OCTAVIA

The Saint house is unrecognizable.

Considering I was just here this morning, it shouldn't look so different, and yet...

I walk up the driveway, which is absolutely *slammed* with cars, psyching myself up for this. Normally I'd just use the side gate, but considering that's hidden and this is an official party, we decided I should use the main entrance. The valet service at the gate looked more than a little horrified when I arrived by foot. For a moment I thought they were going to refuse me entry and did a mental happy dance. Alas, I am Octavia Royal, and his boss recognized me just before he was about to turn me away.

Teetering away on these stilettos as I weave my way toward the house, an icy drop of dread runs down my spine. The steps to the door are lit with fairy lights, the same ones that are woven around the branches of the trees and in the bushes that line the drive. The door opens before I can lift my hand to knock and I come face to face with Dylan.

Indi's Dylan.

In the Saint house.

Opening the door.

In a goddamn tuxedo.

"Ermmm?" is all I manage to say, because I'm pretty sure my brain is broken. He grins down at me and ushers me into the house.

"Looking good, V. I'd take your coat, but I'm pretty sure if I took any layers from you Indi would have my balls and your guys would be next in line."

I look down at the shawl covering my shoulders, held together by my hands that clutch both it and my purse. "Why are you here?"

"Indi wanted you to have some help in this snake hole, and well, the money was good," he says with a shrug. "Hustlers gotta hustle right?"

That twinkle in his eye makes me think there's more to it than that, but I let it go. I am learning that I don't always need to know every single detail. I am not Lincoln Saint, and I don't want to run the world.

I hand Dylan my shawl, considering the temperature in the house I don't think I'm going to need it. "Thanks. Just how insane is the guest list?"

"Not great," he says, pursing his lips. "Most of the Cove's elite are here. The LaFontaines included. Indi's request for me to refuse them entry wasn't exactly easy to uphold."

"It's fine," I say, waving him off, mentally high-fiving my friend. "She doesn't mean anything in the long run, just Daddy Saint waving his dick around like it's made of fairy dust."

He bursts out laughing as he hangs my shawl in the closet. "You and Indi really are too alike sometimes."

"She's the best," I say, looking around with a tight smile. "Don't suppose you want to hide me in that closet too?"

"Nah," he says with a lazy smile. "You've got more backbone than that. I doubt you've ever hidden from a fight in your life."

Doesn't matter that he's right. That closet seems far more welcoming than the rest of this party.

"I guess. Any sightings of my guys?"

"East hasn't come down yet, but the others are out back. I think that's where most of this shindig is happening."

"Thanks," I say with a tight smile. "Better go face the music, I guess."

I head through the house, swiping a glass of bubbles from one of the many roaming servers and throwing it back. Some might call it Dutch courage, but for me it's just a way to tamp down the urge to run.

I don't head toward the smaller kitchen that I usually find the guys in. I have zero doubt Harrison has that part of this floor shut off tonight. God forbid anyone sees the homely parts of this mausoleum of a house. I leave the foyer into the giant living room that leads to the wall of glass at the back. The wall is open, letting people spill down the steps and out into the yard. If you can really call back here a yard. It was definitely created for entertaining. I don't usually pay it any mind, but it seems Harrison had someone in to spruce it up a bit.

Whoever it was apparently has my penchant for fairy lights. They're everywhere and it's beautiful.

"Octavia, there you are." I wince at the sound of Harrison's voice. I should've grabbed more than one glass. I force a smile on my face and turn to face him. He's waving me over to him so I head in that direction, my gaze sweeping the space for my guys, but not finding any of them. "Welcome, it's good to finally see you. I'm sorry I haven't been around much since your return. My condolences about your father."

"Thank you." Suspicion courses through me. What game is he playing? Because doting and caring isn't a façade I'm buying. We spoke at the gala and he was nothing more than a giant asshole. To me and to East.

"Ah, Miss Royal, I haven't had the pleasure. William LaFontaine." The man standing beside Harrison holds his hand out to me, so I shake it because my dad didn't raise me to be rude. Plus, this guy hasn't done anything to me.

I don't think.

"Lovely to meet you," I say with a saccharine smile. "Are you new to the Cove?"

He looks almost flattered by my question, and I don't know whether to be grossed out or not. "We don't live here currently, but I am considering the move from the big city. I understand you recently returned after traveling the world. How would you say it compares to the city?"

My smile tightens as Harrison glares at me. "There's no place quite like home."

"A beautiful sentiment, and too often true," William says with a big smile. My gaze bounces across the room when I see them.

Lincoln with Georgia wrapped around him, her lips at his ear while he smiles like he's never been happier.

He's just putting on a show.

At least that's what I try to tell my stupid heart that hurts like it might just break, because I don't know if I've ever seen him look *that* happy before.

Why didn't he warn me he would be here with her? Or that she would be here at all.

I guess I should've known, especially when I saw Harrison with William, but it still didn't click. Stupid me I guess.

Doesn't stop the pain I feel at her hand on his chest, her hold on his arm, caressing him like his lover.

"Ah, here's the couple of the night," Harrison says, grinning down at me. I want to smack that smug-ass smirk right off of his face. Or stab him with my snake stiletto.

Either option might make me feel a little better.

He calls them over, and Linc's eyes go wide momentarily

when he sees me before the smile snaps back into place as he brings Georgia over.

"Georgia, Lincoln, how are the happy couple tonight?" William asks, shaking Lincoln's hand when they reach us. "Georgia, have you met Miss Royal yet?"

"I've not had the pleasure," she says, smirking at me, as she gives me one of those, I'm-better-than-you finger waves.

Seeing her, I instantly understand why her and Blair would've gotten along so well: they're cut from the same cloth.

"I'm sure the pleasure is all mine." The words sound like honey as they fall from my lips.

As if summoned like the devil herself, Blair appears with Raleigh beside Linc and Georgia.

If there is a god out there, please just strike me down dead now.

"I see you finally met my cousin, G," Blair says, that resting bitch face of hers cracking with a smile like she's one-upped me.

"If you'll please excuse me," I say with a smile, extracting myself from this bitchy pit. Lincoln is obviously a better swimmer than I am, because I feel like I'm drowning surrounded by these people right now.

Where the fuck are Finley and Maverick, and why the hell didn't anyone tell me about this bullshit parade?

I head to the downstairs bathroom, glad to find it empty, and lock the door before sitting on the closed toilet lid. Fuck wading through this shit without someone on my side. I can usually handle my shit, put on my public figure face, and pull on all my inner peace bullshit... but after everything that's happened the last few weeks, my quota for dealing with this hell alone is at its limit. I pull my phone from my clutch and open up the group text I have with the guys.

Me:

Other than Linc, who is apparently busy, where the fuck are the rest of you?

I sound more than a little salty, but I don't have it in me to pretend otherwise right now. Logically, I know it's all a game. Emotionally though... emotionally I'm so fucked right now that my heart is very much not listening to my head. Panda's words are still too loud in there.

I close my eyes and rest my forehead on my hands, taking a deep breath. There was me thinking I was a strong independent woman, but apparently dealing with the shock of seeing Lincoln and Georgia together is more than I can take right now. Especially with Harrison watching me with hawk-like intensity. I know that Lincoln said Harrison had told him to break all ties with me, and that he's aware Lincoln is the one who found me, but beyond that, I'm not sure how much he knows. I just know we're not meant to be anything more than acquaintances.

I'm pretty sure after Lincoln busting into the Conclave and demanding they help find me that Harrison isn't fooled, but I don't want to be the reason Lincoln suffers any more than he already has.

"Open the door, pretty girl."

I let out a deep sigh at Finley's voice and reach over to unlock the door. He slinks in, relocking it once he's inside, and crouches in front of me. "How you doing?"

"Oh me? I'm peachy keen, jelly bean," I deadpan, and he smirks at me.

"Glad to see your sense of humor is still intact. We only found out when Georgia arrived that she was even coming. I've been dealing with my dad, who arrived at the same time as William, and Mav is helping East. We didn't have time to warn you what was going on. I'm sorry."

"He's going to announce their engagement isn't he?" I say softly, and the pain in Finley's eyes is the final stab to the heart.

I fucking hate the Knights, what they stand for, everything. How dare he make Lincoln into his whore for his own personal gain.

"You can do this, it's just for show. You're stronger than hiding in this bathroom. You don't need any of us at your side to ride out this storm, but we'll all be there, even if it feels like you're alone. We're never far from you."

I take a deep breath and nod. He's right. I am strong enough to deal with this. To carry it all. I guess I just needed reminding.

Taking his hand, we stand together and he pulls me into his arms. "Ready to face the sharks?"

"As ready as I'm going to be."

He tucks a lock of hair behind my ear, cupping my cheek, and gazes down at me, his bright blue eyes seeing into the depths of my soul. "Remember, this is all just a show. We know the truth, and we're stronger for it."

I nod. "Let's do this."

He reaches for the door but I stop him. "Wait, where is East? Is he actually coming to this insanity?"

He nods, grimacing. "Harrison insisted. Chase is here too, so East will be with someone we can trust. You just focus on me and playing our parts. Maybe we'll learn some of what we need to and make it out of all of this in one piece."

"Okay," I say softly and open the door, slinking out with his hand in mine as we rejoin the crowd. I steal another two glasses from a waiter as we head out to the yard, offering Finley one, but chugging them both back when he declines.

Blair spots us as we reach the outskirts of the party and heads toward us.

"Incoming," I mutter, and Finley squeezes my hand.

She practically hangs off of Raleigh and my stomach twists.

Did he rape her? Or does she know about his proclivities and just not care?

Not the time, Octavia... she doesn't need your bleeding heart.

"Octavia, I see you're hiding away. I guess I would too if my world was about to crumble like yours is."

I roll my eyes at her. "Blair, what do you want? I don't have the time or patience for you and your bullshit riddles."

"I mean, oh cousin dearest," she says with a deadly smile, "that Raleigh and his family are about to be inducted. And I, well..." she trails off and holds up her hand, showing off the giant fucking diamond on her finger.

I bark out a laugh. "You have got to be kidding me?"

Looking over at Finley, he looks as shocked as I feel about the news.

"Who confirmed your induction?" Finn asks Raleigh, an eyebrow quirked.

"Your father," he says with a grin. "I might not be on the Conclave yet, but I hear that some family lines are running out and a seat might just open up."

My stomach twists.

The Armstrongs.

East said his father didn't want to continue his line, that he didn't have children because he didn't want to continue the madness.

There is no way Raleigh could end up in that seat.

"Well I guess you better hope I don't claim my birthright then, huh? " I hiss, and he frowns at me before looking down at Blair. "Oh she didn't tell you? Funny that the queen snake might hide things from you. Be careful who you get into bed with, Raleigh, because she is a black widow in the making."

I walk away from them with Finley at my side. We re-enter the house and he takes my elbow, pulling me toward the main function room, but tucks me into a corner. "Hot as that was, it might not have been a great idea. We don't know how this Regency thing is going to play out."

"Yeah, but they don't know that," I say with a shrug, and he laughs softly.

The sound of a clinking glass draws my attention, so we move to the foyer and find Harrison, William, Lincoln, and Georgia standing on the stairs above us all. Lincoln looks thunderous, but when he catches my gaze I smile at him, trying to pretend that this is all okay. He doesn't need me feeling like shit to add to his plate right now. He doesn't smile back, he doesn't do *anything* as Georgia takes his hand and it's impossible to miss the rock sitting on her finger.

I try not to let it affect me, and Finn squeezes my hand as I look away. I spot my aunt and uncle on the other side of the room, standing with Blair, Raleigh, and his family—all smiles.

"Thank you all for joining us here tonight. It's been a wonderful evening so far. We'd like to share some news and make this night even more special." He pauses like he's building anticipation and I think I'm going to be sick.

"I would like to announce—" He's interrupted by the front doors crashing open and armed FBI agents flooding the room.

"What is the meaning of this?" Harrison roars, storming across the room, coming face-to-face with an agent who waves a piece of paper in his face.

"We're here with a warrant for Nathaniel Royal's arrest," the officer announces as my uncle is torn from my screaming aunt and placed in cuffs.

What the actual fuck is happening right now?

The party ended swiftly with Nate's arrest and my mind has been spinning since. Finley ushered me back to my place as soon as the FBI agents were done, and pretty much everyone else left at the same time. Way to bring down the mood of a party. Not that I'm complaining; my stomach hasn't stopped rolling since I saw the four of them standing on the steps.

I'm not sure how we stop this.

The Knights are too powerful. They control too much.

I don't even care about myself, I just want my guys to be free to live however they want to.

Finley left me here, with the alarm set, to head back to the madness over at the Saints', with the promise to return with everyone as soon as he could. I hate that I can't help more, that I can't be there for Lincoln—or any of them—right now.

I head upstairs and peel this stupid dress off, scrubbing the makeup from my face, and pull my hair into a messy bun on the top of my head before slipping into Lincoln's hoodie and a pair of leggings with some thick socks.

This charade is over. We need a plan. An *actual* plan, rather than just running in circles and hoping we'll find a path out of the maze that is this society shit. The only thing I can think of is my dad's journals, so I grab my phone and go down to the music room. The alarm is set, no one is getting in the house without me realizing, so I know I can read the journals in peace without worrying about being interrupted.

There have to be some answers in there.

I can't imagine my dad would have left me this helpless against something he wanted me to be free and safe from. It might be putting a lot of trust in him, especially considering he isn't here and he wasn't exactly the most stable at the end, but he was always my dad. He always tried to protect me, even in his darkest moments.

And now there's the rumor that he didn't kill himself. If I let myself believe what Panda said—even if it was fueled by madness —then I have to think he was going to tell me something. His journals might not hold all the answers, but there has to be *something*.

I don't even give myself time to think about why Nate could've been arrested—the possibilities are endless and I'm sure I'll find out eventually. Besides, my family made me very aware that we were not family, that I wasn't their problem, and so, heartless as it may seem, I just don't care enough to worry about it.

I have bigger fish to fry.

Starting with Harrison Saint.

Once I've pulled the journals from the vent, I pore over the pages until my eyes sting. There's so much here, but so little of it is useful information. At least not that I can discern. It's almost like my dad had his own language some of the time and it is frustrating as fuck that I don't understand it.

I guess I really didn't know him as well as I thought.

My phone buzzes and I see Indi's name on the screen, along with the time.

Wow, it got late.

I frown, realizing how long I've been down here and that I still haven't heard from the guys. Finley said they'd come over once the storm died down, but I guess things must have gone off.

I have to trust that they'll tell me when I see them, that me being there would make whatever it is worse, so I swipe my screen and check the message from Indi.

Indi:
I heard you had an insane night. Are you okay?

I pause, a little confused, then remember Dylan was working the party.

Me:
Something like that. I'm fine, just put back in my ivory tower until the world stops burning.

Indi:
That might be a while. **link**

I click the link, beyond curious, and it opens up a local news page

ROYAL SCANDAL
ARRESTED FOR EMBEZZLEMENT AND FRAUD, IS THE ROYAL REIGN REALLY OVER?

Well fuck.

I skim the rest of the article, reading through theories about my uncle's fall from grace, trying to work out fact from fiction. I guess this could explain the grab he and Aunt Vi made for my money when I got back here. If they really were in a hole, it might have saved them.

Is this what Blair has been chirping on about since I got back? Is this why she hates me?

If it is, why wouldn't they just *say* something, rather than treat me like the scum of their lives?

Shaking my head, I close out the article and put my dad's journals away. It's late and I need to sleep. I haven't learned one damn thing tonight, well, nothing that helps us anyway. Once they're secure, I pad back upstairs, double checking all the doors as I move through the house.

I open my balcony doors, disabling the alarm on them, thankful for the cool air that filters into the room, before climbing into bed. My mind whirrs with the possibilities of what could be happening next door, but the night is dark and silent, so there are no clues there either.

Closing my eyes, I try to shut my brain down and let everything go so I can actually sleep; which is no small feat, but I'm going to be useless to everyone if I don't get some shut eye.

It takes far too long to shut off, but once I'm asleep, my dreams are plagued with visions of my dad, his hands covered in blood. Visions of my mom dead at the bottom of the staircase, lying in a pool of blood.

"Octavia." The calling of my name pulls me from the nightmares, and as my eyes flutter open to the dark of night, I find Lincoln, crouching at the side of my bed, looking as broken as I feel.

"Hi," I whisper into the darkness, the corners of his lips turning upwards. "Are you staying?"

"Can I?" he asks softly.

I smile and lift the sheets. "Always."

He gets undressed and slips beneath the covers, resting his hand on my hip. "We should talk."

Leaning forward, I kiss his lips softly. "We can talk tomorrow."

"Are you sure?" he asks, his thumb tracing across the curve of my hip. I nod and close my eyes as he pulls me onto his chest. "I love you, Octavia. Please never forget that."

"I love you too."

SIXTEEN

OCTAVIA

I wake up with Lincoln wrapped around me, and for just a moment, that one between sleep and truly waking, I forget all of the chaos that surrounds us. For just a moment, I am truly happy lying here in his arms.

I cling to those seconds, squeezing all the joy I can from them before reality comes crashing down, and it hits me that Lincoln is engaged.

Engaged to someone who isn't me.

It may not be his choice, and he may not love her, but that doesn't make it any less real. Especially not when I saw the ring on her finger.

"What's wrong?" His sleepy voice breaks through the shadows in my mind, and I turn to face him. His storm-cloud eyes look tired, older than his eighteen years.

I guess a life like his will do that to a person.

"I'm fine," I lie. There's no point in making him feel worse about a situation that is already out of his hands. For a person like Lincoln, who requires control, I can only imagine how this shit with his dad is already making him spin out. "Are you okay?"

He closes his eyes and lets out a deep sigh before leaning

forward and kissing my forehead. "I am now, but we should still talk. There's a lot you don't know, and I should be the one to fill in some of the gaps."

I smirk at his choice of words and he rolls his eyes at me, so I shrug. "Hey you're the one picking the words. Not my fault my brain takes me to far off places."

"If we didn't have to talk, I'd show you just how many more gaps I can fill at once," he winks.

Lincoln Saint *winked.* Be still my beating heart.

I laugh softly, shaking my head. "You're terrible."

"I am, but you love it."

I smile at him, running my hand through his hair. "I do. Love you, I mean. We might fight and disagree... a lot. But I do love you."

He twines his fingers through my hair and kisses me with so much passion it makes my toes curl. By the time he pulls back, I'm practically panting. "To be continued. Get your sexy ass out of bed, we need to talk."

He climbs out of bed and pulls on his boxers and jeans. I happily drool over his taut back and peachy ass until he turns back around to face me.

I pout playfully and it's totally worth it to hear his bark of laughter. "Octavia Royal, you are a brat. And if you're not careful, I'll make you pay for it."

I wag my brows at him. "That's kind of the point."

He leans down on the bed and I think he's about to give in, but then he opens his mouth and his low gravelly voice sends a shiver down my spine. "Oh, you'll pay, baby. Just later... when you're least expecting it."

He winks again and kisses my cheek before standing, leaving me wondering who the hell has taken over Lincoln Saint's body. Not that I'm complaining, I am totally on board for this side of him, but I'm definitely pouting for real now... and also excited for whenever later is.

He pulls his t-shirt from the floor and slips it over his head. "I'm going to run and grab a change of clothes, but I'll be back in ten. I'll get some coffee brewing on my way out."

I groan, slumping back down into my pillow as he disappears from the room. As much as I know we need to talk, that I need to know what's going on, I'd much rather have had some fun with him first.

Sometimes his level-headedness is a pain in my ass.

Begrudgingly I climb from the bed and put my hair into a messy bun before jumping into the shower. A brisk wake up is exactly what I need. The cool water shocks me into alert mode and I finish up quickly.

I pull on a long sweater dress and slip on a pair of leggings and some cute socks before heading downstairs where the smell of freshly brewed coffee awaits me.

Heaven.

I pour myself a very large mug and slide onto one of the stools at the island before taking a sip.

Ahh, sweet nectar.

I connect my phone to the speakers and put some *Lindsey Stirling* on softly in the background. There's nothing quite like the sound of strings in the morning to hype you up for the day. Goosebumps take over my entire body as I zone out to the enchanting music and lose track of time as I give myself over to the sounds.

I open my eyes as the strings draw to a close and find Lincoln observing me from the doorway. "You are truly breathtaking."

I blush at his words, especially because I know I can look like a total idiot when I get lost in music like that. "What can I say? Music is my higher power."

"Is that what you want to do? After school and college, I

mean? Music?" I bite my lip as I realize we've never talked about what we might want for the future. We've spent so much time since I've been back fighting just to *have* a future that we haven't taken the time to talk about what we might want from it.

I nod. "I always wanted to be involved in music. Not like my dad was, but have my own studio. Give artists the freedom to explore who they want to be with the support of a label rather than bog people down with the restrictions most other labels have."

"That sounds like something you'd be good at."

I smile as he grabs a mug of coffee and sits opposite me. "What do you want from the future?"

"My future is already planned out," he says, the light falling from his eyes. "I don't get a say in what I want. It's never mattered."

"Of course it matters."

He shakes his head. "I'll never be free from them, so it doesn't."

"What if you were free?" I ask quietly. "What would you want then?"

He sits quietly in thought before smiling. "Honestly, all I ever wanted was a simple life where I could help people rather than hurt them the way the Knights do. But I've never thought about it much because I know it's an impossible dream. I've never been one to let myself hold on to impossibilities."

I frown, hating that he seems so resigned to his fate.

There has to be a way to get him free.

To get them all free.

Maybe if this Regency thing is real, I can set them free. Even if I don't get to be free with them, they've suffered enough already.

"Octavia." His voice pulls me from my thoughts, his brow furrowed. "We need to talk about last night."

I shrug, not really wanting to, but avoidance has never really been my style. "What part? The whole you're-engaged-when-you-said-you-weren't? Or the part where my uncle was arrested?"

He looks at me, his mouth set in a grim line. "Both."

I let out a sigh and finish my coffee before speaking. "Blair as much as told us about the engagement. We should've known better than to take your father at his word. Self gain at the expense of others is entirely his speed. All I care about is how we stop it."

"I don't know," he says sadly. "But I'm not going through with it. I told him as much. I will play his game and keep up the façade for now, but I will not marry that snake. As for your uncle? There is a lot more to that story."

"Well, I figured he wasn't arrested for being a nice person. I already know he *isn't* nice. What do you know?"

"More than I probably should." He grins, as his phone buzzes on the counter at the same time as mine. "The others are here."

I nod, seeing the messages pop up on my screen.

Our conversation pauses while we wait for them and I refill our mugs. I take my seat again as the front door opens and the three of them filter into the kitchen. East walks gingerly across the room before easing onto the stool beside me, and I kiss his cheek before Mav slips behind me, wrapping his arms around my waist and kissing my neck. "Morning, princess."

"Morning." I smile up at him, kissing him softly before he takes a seat next to Linc. Finn, who is already sitting beside East, gives me a smile that makes my heart flutter in my chest.

"Where were we?" Linc asks, and I roll my eyes.

"Nate."

Maverick groans and jumps up. "I need a drink for these sorts of conversations."

"All I have right now is water or coffee."

"Coffee it is." He moves to the coffee pot, Finn and East chiming in and asking for a cup too.

"You filled her in on the Georgia situation?" Finn asks, looking at Linc with a raised eyebrow.

Linc's jaw clenches and he nods stiffly. "I did."

"Good, just making sure everything's been covered." Gah, that man. I love that he refuses to keep me in the dark anymore. He's fought Lincoln every time when it comes to telling me things I need to know. At least since he decided I should know about the Knights when Lincoln didn't agree.

It makes my heart swell to know he has my back, even against Linc.

"As I was saying," Lincoln sighs. "Nate was arrested for embezzlement and fraud."

I suck in a breath, eyes wide as that settles in. "Holy shit, so it's true then?"

"Yeah. He's been in a hole for a while, since before Stone died, but you know as well as anyone just how much they didn't get along. Stone wouldn't help him, so the Knights wouldn't either. I discovered last night that Nate was a Knight once upon a time, before Stone married your mother. Stone was always the heir, but as every family is meant to have two votes, Nate stepped into the role when your grandfather passed the mantle. Except Nate fucked up and made a lot of enemies. So he was pushed out of the role when your parents married and your father became likely to produce a legacy."

"I don't understand what this has to do with me?"

"Well, before you came back, we tried to bargain for Nate and Blair to take the Royal seats at the table. Obviously that was declined, though no one told us why. Partly to keep you clear, but partly because Blair came to me for help when she discovered the trouble Nate was in."

Things start to click into place in my mind—things that Blair has said, done—it all starts to make sense.

"You said the deal with her was done. Is this the deal you meant? Helping her out of this mess?"

He nods, taking a sip of his coffee. "There was only so much I could help with once the Knights declined her, but I figured if we could get you out they wouldn't have any choice but to accept her and Nate. But once it became clear that wasn't going to happen, and she stopped keeping her end of the deal, I called it a day."

"What was her end of the deal?" I ask, trying to sate my curiosity.

"At first, help us get you gone. As you can imagine, she was on board with that. But I also needed her to get me some information on her father's fuck-ups. She never did, and then she stopped doing what I asked," Lincoln says, shrugging.

"So how did the FBI get involved?"

Maverick laughs. "That might've been me."

"What did you do?"

He shrugs as he sits back down. "I was sick of her being a bitch, of everything the QB was doing, and them teaming up. So I might've sent some information to a friend of mine."

I pinch the bridge of my nose and let out a sigh. "How bad is this going to get?"

My gaze bounces between all of them and Lincoln shrugs. "We don't know yet, but Harrison is fuming that they raided the party last night."

"Harrison has multiple sticks up his ass currently, one more isn't going to make much of a difference," East snorts. "He'll get over it."

He's interrupted by the buzzer for the gate going off and I check the feed on my phone to see Aunt Vi standing there, pushing the button.

"What in the..." I trail off, showing the four of them the screen.

"Do you want us to stay while you talk to her, or do you want to ignore her?" Finn asks.

This can't be good. "You might as well stay, it'll save me telling you all about it later. Just stay in here, and let me deal with her though."

"I won't make promises I can't keep, princess."

Maverick grins and I roll my eyes as I push the button to open the gate. "This should be fun."

I head to the door and open it, finding my aunt standing there looking like she's bitten into a lemon. "Well are you going to invite me in or leave me standing out here like a commoner, Octavia?"

I bark out a laugh and fold my arms across my chest. "Why on earth should I invite you into my home willingly when you never did the same for me? When there was always a price to pay for your tolerance of my mere existence?"

"You always were dramatic. Just like your father." She rolls her eyes at me, standing there, waiting. I clench my jaw, trying not to snap at her, because she is still family even if I'd happily yeet her off the mezzanine.

"You're making it really easy for me to leave you out here in the cold, ya know?" I quirk a brow at her, and she lets out a high-pitched huff. A laugh escapes me at just how put out she looks.

Her jaw clenches, but she smiles tightly at me. "Will you please allow me in, Octavia?"

I pause a moment, offering her the same level of grace she once offered me before letting her into my home. I close the door behind her then stand, waiting for her to speak. There's no way I'm letting her any further in without knowing what she wants.

"Why are you here?"

She looks around the space, pursing her lips, disdain dripping from her. She seems to think better of saying anything and lets out a sigh. "I need your help."

I bark out a laugh. "You're kidding, right?"

She glares at me, like I'm the one in the wrong right now. "We helped you."

"No you didn't," I snap. "You manipulated me into staying with you, giving you money, and now I apparently know why."

"Well if you know why, then you should help regardless. You're family."

I shake my head. The gall of it all. "We are family, but you get treated the way you treat people. You didn't help me. You weren't even kind to me. My father had died and you treated me like a discarded, dirty burden. Get out of my house and don't ever ask me for help again. You won't get it."

She opens her mouth to say something when Lincoln's voice echoes around the foyer. "She told you to leave. I suggest you listen to her."

My aunt looks like she's going to stomp her foot and throw a tantrum. Must be where Blair gets it from. "You Knights are all the same. Your time will come to fall, and when you do, I shall sit and laugh."

He stands there, hands in his pockets, looking at her like she's the most insignificant creature to exist. I *almost* feel bad for her. "If you still exist, should that happen, you are welcome to. But I wouldn't be so sure of it. A threat to the Knights is usually dealt with swiftly."

Her mouth opens and closes, and I clamp my lips together to stop from laughing then open the door. "You can go now."

"But—" she starts, and I shake my head, cutting her off.

I wave to the door, more than prepared to force her out if I have to. "Karma is a bitch. I'm sure the two of you will be fast friends."

She storms from the house and I watch as she leaves the property. Closing the gate behind her, I let out a sigh, a twinge in my chest as I shut the front door.

"Did I do the right thing?" I ask of nobody in particular. Turning, I find the four of them looking at me like they'd ride into Hell beside me if I asked them to.

Finley steps toward me, taking me into his arms, and I rest my head against his chest. "We will back you, whatever you decide to do."

I sag against him, questioning myself, when I feel someone at my back. "You did the right thing, princess. And if anyone dares to say otherwise, they'll face us."

"Thank you," I say quietly, thankful to have them all on my side.

Lincoln and East move so that I'm surrounded by them. I look between them, and Lincoln grips my chin. "We face the rest of what is to come together. Win or lose. Live or die. Together or not at all."

After a stormy weekend, I'm almost glad to be going back to school. For a hint of the mundane, if life at ECP can ever be called that. After a morning of exam prep, and getting the details of our final assignments, my brain is basically Swiss cheese.

Not helped when Miss Celine announces that our final for the year will consist of performing for the school.

I think I'd rather fail.

Stupid fucking 4.0 GPA requirement.

I leave Music and head toward my locker where Indi is waiting for me. "What's up, buttercup?"

I grin at her as I put my stuff in my locker. "Just the thought of performing in front of the whole damn school, no biggie."

"I get to hear you sing again?" she asks, eyes lit up. "You might hate it, and I hate that for you, but I can't be mad about it. You're amazing."

I blush at the compliment and wave her off. "Hardly. You know I'm not exactly a fan of it. But 4.0."

"Yeah, I know. Stupid clause. But, you'll slay it. You always do. Now let's go eat because it's pasta day and I am *starving.*" She rubs her stomach to emphasize her hunger and I laugh. "Did you hear about your aunt and Blair?"

I shake my head. "I don't think so. What happened now?"

"Well, rumor has it, all their assets have been frozen, and they've been kicked out of the house." She loops her arm through mine and pulls me toward the cafeteria. "I also heard that Raleigh dropped her. It's a bad day to be Blair Royal."

"Is she even at school today?" I ask, because I haven't seen her and that's unusual.

"Yeah she's here. Though, she's wandering like a lost lamb. The bitch squad have apparently abandoned her too."

My jaw about hits the floor. Nothing quite like loyalty in the hard times. Fucking hell.

Am I seriously feeling sorry for her?

Me and my stupid bleeding heart.

"She deserves nothing else. She's literally shit on everyone to get ahead. It's about time karma bit her in the ass." My bestie sounds fierce as fuck, and I remember that Blair put her through a year of hell before I even got here. Any pity I might have had flits away. She can shit on me and I'll take it, but do *not* fuck with my friends.

"No truer words have ever been said. Fuck the haters and rise above."

She snickers. "Yeah, maybe, but I'm probably going to sit and watch her downfall with popcorn. I can be a petty bitch when I want to."

"Can't we all?" I laugh.

We grab our food, the chicken and spinach cream pasta has me salivating as we sit at our usual table. I finish catching her up on the craziness of the weekend and everything that happened at the Saints' on Saturday night.

"I still can't believe Lincoln is engaged to her. Are you okay?"

I shrug, taking a bite of my pasta. "As okay as you would be if Ryker was engaged to someone because his dad told him he had to be."

"Fair point," she says, looking like she's about to pop off. "Speaking of Lincoln, where are your guys?"

"I have absolutely no idea." I sigh, pulling my phone from my pocket. I drop a message into our group chat asking where they are but get no response.

"Weird," she says, pursing her lips.

Cackling from the bitch squad's table catches my attention, so I look up and see Blair enter the room, trying to ignore the people she used to call her friends as they point and laugh at her.

So much for long live the queen.

Mikayla sure looks comfy with Blair's sycophants crooning to her.

Blair keeps her head held high as she joins the line to get food, but when she's shunned by even the lowest on the totem pole of the school hierarchy, I see her wobble. It's only a moment but it's there.

She grabs her food and glances around the room, locking eyes with me just long enough for me to see the hate and rage she still has for me.

Oh, goodie.

She starts to walk our way, but someone trips her before she can reach us and she eats the floor, her tray flying upward and dumping most of her lunch on her head and back as it comes crashing down.

"You should be more careful where you walk, gutter rat," Mikayla cackles, the room erupting in laughter. Blair pushes up to her knees, and while I feel bad for her, I can't help but think that if it was anyone else, she'd be the one in Mikayla's shoes.

I don't think even going through this will change the way she is.

"Be careful sitting up there on your throne, Mikayla. Secrets only stay secrets if everyone keeps their mouth shut," Blair snaps at her before turning and storming from the room while most people point and laugh.

"I wonder what that means," Indi says, turning back to her food.

I frown, my appetite gone. "It means that war is coming and we better take cover."

Lincoln, Maverick, and Finley appear not long after and slide into the empty chairs at our table. "What did we miss?" Maverick asks before smacking a kiss on my cheek.

"Blair getting what she deserves," Indi grumbles. "Can't even enjoy it, stupid nice person that I am."

I smile at her, glad I'm not alone. "Same. Where were you three? Lunch is nearly over."

"Dealing with politics," Lincoln grumbles.

"What he means," Finn adds, "is that Harrison called and told Lincoln he has a date on Friday."

"You do?" I ask, brows raised.

"This stupid deal of his is pissing me off. But yes. I'm supposed to take Georgia out for dinner to celebrate our engagement," he growls. I hate the sound of the words out loud, but I shove it down and try to remind myself it's all a game.

Finley looks at me with a smile. "Which means, pretty girl, you and I are going on a date too."

"We are?" I ask, shocked. "Why?"

"Well, someone needs to have his back while he's out there in the shark tank, and Mav has an errand to run."

I glance at Maverick who doesn't give anything away, but that makes me worry as much as anything.

"Don't worry about me, princess. It's nothing major. Nothing I haven't done a dozen times before."

"That's hardly reassuring," I deadpan as the bell rings. "This conversation isn't over."

"Course it is," he says, stealing the garlic bread from my plate. "But I look forward to fighting it out with you later."

***

"Are you ready for today?" Indi asks as she pulls into the drive-thru to grab our morning coffee on this sunshiney Wednesday.

Why isn't it the weekend yet?

Though, the weekend comes with its own freaking issues.

Stupid Georgia.

Stupid date.

I let out a deep breath, shaking my head. "I am never ready for the masses of ECP, but with all of the extra press this arrest has been getting, the paparazzi are stalking me again and I'm beyond ready to be done with all of it."

"Yeah it totally sucks about the blow back you're getting. But I kind of meant our presentation in English." She laughs before the robotic voice blares through the speaker.

I lean my head back against the rest, groaning. I don't want to say I forgot about the presentation, but I also can't say that I'm prepared.

"Fuck."

She laughs softly as she pulls forward in the line. "It'll be fine. You've totally got this."

"Here's hoping that my winging it skills are on point today," I groan. "Is it awful that I'm thinking about taking a gap year next year? Just to have a year off and try and settle some of the chaos that is my life?"

"Not even a little," she says, shaking her head. "I thought about doing the same, going traveling, experiencing more of what the world has to offer before I knuckle down and get on with the rest of my life."

"I say we do it. Everyone should travel if they have the option. There is nothing like seeing the world and experiencing everything you can before getting bogged down in plans for the future."

She sighs as we pull up to the window. "Now just to get Ryker, Ellis, Dylan, and my parents on board. Can't be that hard, right?"

I can't help but laugh at the exasperation on her face. "Take the boys with you. Pretty sure they'd like to see the world too."

"God, could you imagine?" She shakes her head, pausing to grab our drinks before handing them over to me as she pulls away from the window, heading toward school.

I put hers in the cup holder before taking a sip of my peppermint mocha and grin. "Actually, I kind of could. I think it would be brilliant. Maybe let's try and persuade them to do a group trip over summer first? Or Spring Break? That could be fun."

"That, my friend, is an excellent plan. And then after Spring Break, we are totally making plans for your birthday."

I roll my eyes as we pull into the school parking lot, finding Lincoln and Maverick waiting for us. "We don't need to do anything for my birthday. I'm happy with tacos and movies."

"After the fuss you made about *my* birthday, you can fuck off. I love you, but no." She grins as she puts the car in park and Maverick bounds over to my door and opens it.

"Morning, princess." He grins, basically scooping me into his arms and out of the car. I squeal as he lifts me, and Lincoln takes my drink before Maverick spins me in a circle.

"Why are you in such a good mood?" I ask, laughing. "And please put me down."

"My dad is going away for three months at the end of next month, my mom is going with him, though fuck knows *why*, but that means my summer is basically free. What isn't good about that?"

He kisses me playfully before putting me on my feet. "That is good news."

Lincoln hands me my drink back and I look around for Finn but don't see his car. "Where's Finley?"

"He's got a project today," Lincoln says, a slight shake of his head telling me that we can't talk about it here.

"Okay," I say as I grab my phone and drop the guy in question a text instead.

Me:
Hey, where are you? Is everything okay?

Finn:
Morning, beautiful. Everything's fine. I've just been looking into who Panda was working with, and hitting dead ends. So I'm spending the day going through everything he had at both houses to see what I can find.

Me:
Do you want help?

Finn:
Not a chance, beautiful. You have your GPA to worry about. I've got this.

Me:
If you're sure.

Finn:
You doubting my skills, pretty girl?

Me:
shocked face I would never.

Finn:
Ha! Lies. I'll shout if I find anything or have any questions. How's that?

Me:
Perfect. I still think I'd rather skip school.

Finn:

Don't tell Maverick. He'll whisk you away before you can say boo.

Me:
It's tempting.

Finn:
You got this, V. Go face the masses with your crown on. I'll see you later?

Me:
Okay. Also, since when did you get so good at pep talks?

Finn:
Wink emoji

I tuck my phone back away, leaning into Maverick, hating the distance I need to keep from Lincoln in public until this bullshit with Georgia is over. We walk into school; whispers still follow us but it's easy enough to drown them out.

Indi pauses, staring down the hall, and I stop beside her. "What?"

I follow her line of sight and see Blair, crying, at my locker.

"Did hell freeze over?" Indi hisses. "Why the fuck is she

waiting for you? For us? And fucking crying? I didn't know she could cry."

"Fuck knows, but I guess we're about to find out," I say as Lincoln's calculating gaze takes in my cousin.

We walk toward her, and she wipes away her tears when she sees us. "Lincoln, I need your help."

Maverick laughs loudly, drawing attention, and I mentally groan.

"Why should I help you, Blair?" Lincoln asks, folding his arms across his chest. I get a little distracted by just how good he looks right now, then turn back to my cousin.

"You have no reason to. None. I'm a bitch, I'm fully aware of it. But I don't have anyone else to ask."

Her voice wobbles and my heart softens. Why am I such a soft touch?

"What do you need, Blair?" I ask.

She looks at me, hatred shining in her eyes. "I don't need anything from you."

"Blair," Lincoln warns, and she flushes.

"Sorry. I just... we need somewhere to stay. They took the house, they took everything until after my dad's trial. My grandparents won't help us, saying they don't want anything to do with Dad's fallout. It's all such a mess. I don't have it in me to try and pretend to be nice."

"At least she's honest," Indi sighs.

I bite my lip, wondering if I shouldn't have been so harsh to my aunt.

"Octavia?" Lincoln says my name, as if making it my decision, so I nod. No one deserves to pay for the actions of others like this. Not even my black-hearted cousin and aunt. "Fine, you can stay in the cottage. It's small, but it's warm. It's on the outskirts of the Cove, so it's close enough for school."

"Thank you," she says to him, even though her smile doesn't

quite meet her eyes as she turns to me. She nods, wiping at her tear-stained face before holding her head up high and walking away from us through the masses that call her names and jeer at her.

None of it seems to faze her.

I'll give her one thing: no one wears a mask of indifference quite like Blair Royal.

I just can't help but wonder if it'll do her more harm than good.

SEVENTEEN

OCTAVIA

I run my hands down my little black dress, trying to settle my nerves. The thought of watching Georgia paw all over Lincoln tonight doesn't exactly fill me with joy, but he wants us there, so I'm not about to tell him no.

Plus it's a night I get to spend alone with Finn, and it feels like it's been forever since we did that.

The low neckline makes my girls look extra bouncy, and the curls of my hair fall nicely down my back. I've gone for a subdued, natural look for the evening, because the whole idea is not to have any attention on us. Plus, Millers is a super high class place, and I'm pretty sure we only got a table because of the Knights.

Apparently the waitlist is like eight months long. Freaking ridiculous.

My phone buzzes on my dresser and Finley's name lights up the screen.

Finn:
I'll be there in five.

Me:
Sounds good. I'm ready when you are.

I grab my clutch, sliding my phone, keys, and wallet into it and pick up my stilettos before padding down the stairs.

"You look beautiful, Miss Octavia," Smithy gushes as I reach the foyer. He's got his weekend bag packed and his long coat on already.

"Thank you, Smithy. Looking forward to your weekend with Matthew?" My stomach flips at the thought of him. I refuse to believe that Smithy's slice of happy is part of the cause of my misery.

I'm pretty sure that whatever cologne he was wearing is a generic one, which is why I haven't mentioned it to anyone. Unless Finley tells me he's found proof that it's Matthew that was working with Panda, I'm not going to put any weight behind the thought.

"Yes, we're heading to my sister's for the weekend."

"Oh, he's meeting the family, this is a big step." I smile at him as I slip into my heels.

"He already met my family," he says, moving toward me. "And I can't thank you enough for making him feel welcome in our home."

"He makes you happy, Smithy. As long as he keeps doing that, he will be welcome here."

Smithy drops his bag and hugs me tightly. "Thank you, Miss Octavia. I hope you enjoy your dinner date with Master Knight. You have my number if you need anything."

"I do, but I won't use it," I say, squeezing him back. "And hey, it's Spring Break since school got out today; if you extend your trip, I can totally fend for myself."

"So it is!" he exclaims as he pulls back. "I might just keep that in mind."

"Just let me know if you do, or if you need the jet," I say as the buzzer sounds, letting us know Finley is here.

"You're too generous, Miss Octavia. Now have fun. I'll keep in touch and let you know my plans."

"Love you, Smithy."

"I love you too, Miss Octavia."

I wave to him as I leave the house, knowing he'll lock it up securely before he leaves. I sashay down the drive, putting an extra sway in my hips when I see Finn's grin from where he's leaning against the car.

"If Lincoln didn't ask for backup tonight, we wouldn't be going anywhere," he growls, pushing from the car and taking me into his arms. "You look good enough to eat."

I laugh softly. "Pretty sure that's not as filling as where we're going."

"Oh, pretty girl, pretty sure I could fill you up," he winks, and I laugh at him again.

"That was terrible."

"It was, but it made you laugh, so my work here is done."

I kiss him softly. "Thank you, I needed the laugh considering where we're heading."

"You sure you're up for this?"

"Watching my boyfriend being basically molested by the girl he's been forced to get engaged to? Oh yeah, I'm all for it."

He frowns at me, quiet for a minute. "You don't have to come. I can go alone."

"Not a chance. We haven't hung out, just us, for too long. I just need to remind myself that he doesn't *want* to be there."

He cups my cheek, looking down into my eyes. "You have

nothing to be jealous about. I guarantee he's going to be the jealous one tonight."

I smile up at him. "Let's get this show on the road, shall we? Don't want to be late, and we need to get there before they do."

"Your carriage awaits." He bows, and I laugh again, moving as he opens the door for me.

"I forgot how freaking low this car is."

He grins at me as he rounds the car, climbing in and setting off to the city at a speed that makes my heart race. He grips my thigh between shifting gears, making my blood heat. We don't speak much on the drive; nerves flutter in my stomach about keeping a lid on my crazy while I watch Lincoln with Georgia tonight, and Finn... well, he's not exactly the talkative type.

I try to distract myself with the songs on the radio, and when we pull up to the valet parking in front of the restaurant, I let out a deep breath.

"Ready?"

I smile over at him and nod. "Let's do this."

He climbs from the car as the valet opens my door. Finn's there a second later, offering me a hand to help me out of the seat, and walks me inside the restaurant. The maître d' smiles widely at us as the door closes behind us. "Mr. Knight, it's a pleasure to see you again. Miss Royal, lovely to have you with us. Please, follow me, your table is ready."

I quirk a brow at Finn who shrugs. Apparently the staff do their research on the clientele. Though I suppose if this is a Knight business, of course they know who Finn is. This 'date' will also help the story Lincoln floated of me being with Finley.

The maître d' pulls out the chair for me and tucks me under the table as Finley sits opposite me. "Would you like something to drink?" he asks as he places a menu before each of us.

"Just water, please," Finley says, and I ask for the same before looking at the menu.

"What the fuck is a mung bean?" I ask incredulously, and he laughs softly across from me.

"Not a fucking clue, but apparently this place loves them."

He isn't wrong. What even is this place?

At least they have steak. Can't go wrong with steak.

Finn stiffens in front of me as he looks over my shoulder and reaches over to take my hand. "Don't look now, she'll see you, but Lincoln saw us already, too."

My back stiffens and I swear I can feel the heat of Linc's gaze even though I keep my eyes on Finley.

A server drops off our water and I focus back on the menu, trying not to look around at where they're sitting.

"I spy with my little eye," Finley says, and I look up to find him smirking at me. "A politician dining with an escort."

My eyes go wide and I look over in the direction he nods.

"This place is discreet about pretty much everything," he adds while I laugh softly.

"How do you know she's an escort?" I ask and instantly regret it.

The laughter in his eyes dims a little. "My father."

"Sorry."

"Don't be," he says, shaking his head. "Did you decide if you're having the mung bean soup, or the tortilla chips with mung bean dip?"

I laugh softly at him. "I need to pop to the bathroom, but I'm thinking the charcuterie board to start and steak for the main course?"

"I was thinking the same." He grins. "I'll order if they come by while you're gone."

He kisses the inside of my wrist before releasing my hand as I stand and work my way across the dimly lit restaurant to the bathroom.

Thankfully, it's empty, and I lean against the door of the stall for a minute just to catch my breath.

I can do this.

Fuck knows I've done worse.

Though tonight is like self-inflicted torture. Even if hanging with Finley is fun.

"Octavia."

I startle at the sound of Lincoln's voice, followed by the sound of the main door to the bathroom locking.

"You shouldn't be in here," I hiss as I open the door and find him standing there, hands in pockets, looking like he gives exactly zero fucks.

"Yeah well," he shrugs. "Want to play a game?"

"A game? Aren't we already playing enough games tonight?"

His eyes sparkle. "Not like this one."

He pulls a hand from his pocket and opens it.

"Is that a vibrating egg?" I squeak.

"Want to play?"

He can't be serious... can he?

"What's the game?" I ask, curious.

"I keep the remote, and you have to try not to come until you leave."

I smirk at him, tempted. "Pretty sure I shouldn't be your focus tonight."

"Fuck her," he growls. "The only person I want to focus on is you. She's snakey enough to not really require my attention. She talks enough for us both. Now do you want to play or not?"

I bite my lip, torn between what I should do and what I want to do.

"Fuck it," I say, holding out my hand.

He shakes his head and kneels, lifting one foot over his shoulder, kissing the inside of my thigh, biting down before moving toward the apex of my thighs. He runs a finger from my clit to my slit and grins up at me. "You're already so wet."

"What can I say? I like games."

He pushes the egg inside of me, kissing my pussy before putting my leg back down and standing up to tower over me. He shows me the small black remote and pushes a button.

Holy shit.

I grip his arms as the vibration rocks through me, a moan slipping from my lips. "I told you I'd make you pay." He winks and kisses me hard and quick before disappearing from the bathroom.

I might regret the decision to play, but I'm not about to back down.

I just have to work out how to let Finn in on the game.

By the time I get back to the table, there's a glass of red wine at my setting and Finley is sipping a glass of whiskey. I raise a brow as I slip into my seat, acutely aware of the egg inside of me. "How did this happen?"

"Lincoln sent them over on his way to the bathroom." He smirks. "I hear we're playing a game."

Heat spills across my cheeks as I nod.

"I do love games." His eyes sparkle. "Especially tag team ones. Now then, where were we?"

We fall through the door of the house laughing. Tonight was definitely not what I expected it to be. I feel bad that Lincoln looked so miserable all night, but I'm pretty sure the drink I spilled over his date was the highlight of his evening. Though I did lose our game, much to his and Finn's delight. Coming as I ate my chocolate torte for dessert was definitely an experience. As was Finley removing the egg in the back of the Uber that brought us home. He had a few drinks, so we decided that was the best plan. We can pick up his car tomorrow.

I kick off my stilettos and shut off the alarm, feeling Finn's heat against my back before he softly presses his lips against the curve of my neck.

I gasp as a shiver runs down my spine, when his hands flutter down my ribs. Panic hits me that Smithy might find us, but then I remember he's spending the weekend with Matthew and relax under Finn's touch.

He spins me around to face him and presses me up against the wall. "I need you, V."

His words are more of a growl than anything as he kisses me, trailing down my neck, and across my chest until he reaches the sweetheart neckline of my dress. A thought sparks in my mind and I grin. I've already been at *their* mercy tonight.

Now it's my turn.

"Upstairs," I whisper and he lifts me from my feet, taking off up the stairs at a run. Apparently the whiskey after dinner has him looser than usual, and that works entirely in my favor. He places me on my feet at the end of the bed, turning me from him and unzips my dress, caressing my back with his lips as he drags the zipper down.

"Do you trust me?" I ask, barely more than a whisper, and he stills. I turn to face him, resting my hands on his chest, before moving to unbutton his shirt. He sucks in a breath as my fingers whisper against his bare chest.

"You know I do." His breath becomes ragged as I move my hands down his chest to the belt of his slacks. I unbuckle him and push them and his boxers down before dropping to my knees in front of him, palming his dick.

When I look up at him, his gaze is on me with an intensity that makes my skin prickle with lust and need. Without taking my eyes off him, I bring the head of his cock to my lips and kiss the top. Engulfing it in my mouth, I suck it like a lollipop, licking it on all sides before darting my tongue in the slit. Finn sucks a breath in through his teeth like he's in pain, but I know better. There's something incredibly sexy about watching the one you love give you pleasure. The visual is part of the erotic fantasy.

One of Finn's hands comes to the top of my head as he tries to take control, but I stop my movements, let go of his cock, and pop a brow at his action.

"No one said you could touch me, Finn. This is my game. Just enjoy the ride." It's Finn's turn to cock a brow, surprised by my audacity. He's always in control and I get it, but tonight? Tonight, I want to be the one working him over. I want him to be able to just let it all go as I make him come.

I didn't think it would work, but I'm thrilled when I feel his hand release my hair and watch as he balls his fists at his sides, eyes like a hawk, watching me with unmistakable desire.

My fingers tighten around his shaft as I bring his cock back into my mouth, licking the underside and circling the head before I pop it back into my mouth, sucking him off as a thrill runs through me, knowing I can bring him to his knees like this.

"Fuck," I hear him mutter, his lips parted and his nostrils flaring. It's fucking hot to see his reaction, this raw need in every one of his muscles. It all just spurs me on.

Speeding up my hand motions, I move closer to him, needing his body heat closer as I place both of my hands on his ass cheeks as leverage as I sink my mouth onto his dick, choking on his girth and not caring that my eyes are watering.

Finn reaches up and with a tender touch and a loving smile on his lips, he uses the pad of his thumb to wipe away a tear from my cheek.

It makes the romantic in me swoon and also makes the slut in me hornier than ever.

"V, I don't want to come in your mouth, baby. Please." Looking back up at him, I give his dick one more suck, using my tongue to swipe at his precum before, once more, kissing the top of his cock and sitting on my haunches as I smile up at Finn like the good girl he loves.

"Fuck, when you look at me like that, I want to—" I cut him off before he gets too carried away. I'm not done playing with my tenuous grasp on control yet.

"Still my turn, Finn. On the bed." He hesitates, his mind warring between his need for control and his desire to meet and exceed my every desire.

"Octavia." One word. It's a warning but also a plea. He's asking me to not take advantage. He's begging me not to take it too far, and I won't.

After a few seconds, I release a breath of relief when Finn steps out of his pants, shucking his shirt, and makes his way to the bed. He's lying down with his arms folded behind his head, his big body on display making my mouth water and brain melt for a second before I spring into action. His posture screams control so I feel I need to bring him down a notch.

Finn watches me intently as I make my way to my secret drawer of toys and come back out with a silk scarf. At first, he's confused and I can see his mind working a mile a second. I know the exact moment he realizes what I'm about to do. His entire body tenses, his eyes narrowing into slits as he stares at the scarf, and I fear I may have gone too far.

"I promise, I will never go too far. If you need to break free, you'll be able to." I wait for him to make a decision and little by little, as his body sinks back down onto the mattress, I send a silent thank you to the universe for giving me a chance.

With my dress completely unzipped, I let it fall off my shoulders and let my bare feet carry me back to the bed, crawling on top of him until I'm straddling his chest.

"Give me your wrists." He only hesitates for a fraction of a second before he presents me with his upturned hands. I place a kiss on the inside of one wrist, then the other, before I place the scarf on them and make two revolutions before bringing them up above his head and to the headboard. I tie the scarf around the wood, making a knot loose enough that he can free himself if things get too intense for him.

I have to respect his limits all the while trying to push them.

"Now what, V? I'm at your mercy. What are you going to do with me?" His voice is pure sex. Dark and honeyed with a hint of danger that makes me so wet I'm sure I'm going to find a wet spot on his chest beneath me.

"Anything I want."

His grin is wolfish, like he's on board but also knows that anything he's not okay with is going to stop and I'm going to pay the price in multiple orgasms. Which, honestly, I'm totally okay with.

I lean in and kiss his forehead, his eyelids, one cheek, then the other. By the time I reach his mouth, he's seeking out my lips, pulling on his restraints trying to get to me.

"Hmm, you're so impatient." I'm trying to use my sexy vixen voice, but it all comes out in a shaky breath because he may be impatient, but I'm not exactly the poster child for patience, either.

What a pair we make.

I kiss him with every fiber of my being, making sure he knows that all of this is a safe space and I would never do anything that isn't built on love and respect.

He gives as good as he gets, our tongues dancing around each other, lips frantic with our kisses. Panting, I back away just enough that he can't reach me before I go back in and kiss his chin, earning a groan from him.

I guess he likes kissing me.

I kiss his neck, slowly making my way back down his chest

before I reach the flat disk of his nipple and tease it with my tongue, before doing the same thing to the other.

Backing up, I feel his thick girth sliding between my pussy lips so I move, intentionally coating his shaft with my juices. Back and forth, back and forth, until he's growling at me to just fuck already.

"Tsk, tsk, Finn. No topping from the bottom. I seem to remember that you don't like it when I get sassy with you." I can't deny that I'm loving this.

"Not the same, V." No, I suppose it's not, and yet...

Placing both of my hands on his chest, I let my hair fall all around us as I sink onto his cock, slowly and torturously. As soon as I bottom out, we both sigh in relief.

"Fuck, that feels incredible."

I agree, it's been too long and I needed this.

Lifting myself up, I stop just before the head of his cock slides out then push myself back down on him. Once, twice, I do this to get him at the edge of his sanity before I bring my entire body on top of his and kiss his neck as the rest of my body rubs against him, fucking him oh so slowly. I can hear him losing his everloving mind, panting his controlled breaths. I'm pretty sure he's trying to keep his hands bound, trying to show me how much he trusts me, letting me do whatever the fuck I want with his body.

Nibbling his neck, I start getting lost in my own game, actually needing him to touch me, to dig the pads of his fingers into my flesh while I fuck him until we both lose our minds.

We're both coated in sweat but I know I'm about to lose at my own game. As much as I love the control, I also love when his big hands are all over me.

From below me, Finn thrusts his hips up, making sure he goes as deep as possible, making sure I'm getting the friction I need on my clit. Making sure I feel the utter power of him. Inside and out.

With a quick flick of my wrist, I undo the tie and within

seconds, he has me on my back, fucking me into the mattress, his mouth attacking me with desperation and need. I'm his and he's mine. And this moment, as tender as it began, is now a mass of clenching fingers and entwined legs. A series of moans and groans with hurried kisses and painless bites.

"Fuck, everything about you, V." His words don't make sense, but what is missing in his speech is said by his body. He's hurried, chasing our joint orgasm because he won't come without me. Never has, never will.

My back arches, my head is thrown back, my eyes closed tight as the fireworks of blues and yellows and pinks and reds explode behind my lids. I think I scream but I'm not quite sure because all I hear is Finn's roar as his climax takes over his entire body. He's shaking and jackhammering inside me as I coat his cock with my juices. It's only when I come back down from that moment that I realize my nails had dug into the skin of his back.

Eyes wide, I search out his gaze, hoping I didn't go too far, or betray his trust, but he just smirks at me.

"Beautiful, digging your nails into my back while you come all over my dick is more than okay."

EIGHTEEN

OCTAVIA

Maverick arrived in the middle of the night and crawled into bed with Finn and I, so when I wake up sandwiched between them, it takes me a moment to become coherent and remember where we are.

The soft sunlight filters in through my windows, and I try to shimmy down the length of the bed so as not to disturb either of them. It's hard not to laugh at myself as I wriggle like a nutcase until I slink onto the floor, grabbing my robe before heading to the bathroom down the hall. No point in going through that effort if I'm just going to wake them up by using the bathroom.

I pad downstairs once I'm done and set up the coffee pot, staring out as the sun climbs into the sky. I should definitely still be asleep, but apparently my body has other ideas.

Once the pot finishes, I pour a mug and head out into the back yard, sitting on one of the patio chairs, enjoying the early morning sun. I close my eyes and bask in the warm rays, the quiet of the morning so peaceful it's as if the world is standing still.

"Fancy seeing you here so early."

I squeak as I startle, opening my eyes and finding the Saint brothers watching me, almost identical smiles on their faces. It's hard to come to terms with the fact that they have different fathers when they look so alike. I guess they have more of Fiona in them than they realized.

"Why are you both here? What's wrong?" I ask, standing as they approach.

Linc stays beside East, watching him like a hawk as he moves toward me. "Nothing's wrong. I have rehab shortly, Linc is taking me, but I wanted to see you before we go. And he might not say it, but he wanted to see you too."

I smile softly as East reaches me and pulls me into his arms. I close my eyes and sigh as I wrap my arms around him, holding as tight as I dare. "How are you feeling?"

"I could be worse," he murmurs into my hair. "How are *you* feeling?"

I smile against his chest. "I could be worse, too."

"Breakfast?" I ask as I pull back.

East's eyes crinkle at the edges as he looks down at me. "Not if you're cooking."

"Meanie," I tease, laughing a little. "Finley and Maverick are in bed; we all know Finley is the whizz in the kitchen with you out of action. I'll volunteer him as tribute."

"Sounds good. I'm going to go grab a cup of coffee," he says, cupping my cheek and kissing me softly before he leaves me alone with Lincoln.

"Hi," I say with a small wave, feeling almost awkward. Which is a tad ridiculous, but with his date last night hanging between us, even with our game, I'm not sure where to start this morning. Do I ask him if he kissed her? Do I let myself wallow in the misery and jealousy of not knowing?

What are the rules here?

"Morning," he says, his voice low and growly. "Did you have a good evening?"

"It was positively stimulating," I quip. "Did you?"

His eyes narrow, his gaze raking over my very thin robe before he stalks toward me. "I've never been more jealous of Finley in my life."

His low words send goosebumps skittering across my skin as he closes the distance between us, and I can't tell if the heat on my skin is from him or the sun.

"Pretty sure you were still the guy in charge," I say, looking up into his storm-cloud eyes. They seem darker this morning, as if burdened even more than usual. "Was everything okay after we left?"

"You mean after you accidentally knocked into that server and Georgia wore the tray of drinks? Was probably a highlight of the evening." He smirks, before sighing. "Yes, everything was okay after you left."

I bite down on my lower lip, chewing it to stop the questions spilling from my lips. He uses the pad of his thumb to pull my lip from my teeth and leans down to nip it himself. "What do you want to know, Octavia? I'm not going to have secrets between us where she is involved."

His gaze is so intense, I think I might burn up from the inside out. How does he always know the right thing to say? I battle with myself about asking, hating that I sound like *that* girl. Especially when I literally just kissed East in front of him.

"Did you kiss her?"

The corners of his lips tilt upwards, and I clutch at his t-shirt. "I didn't kiss her, and I have zero intention of letting her touch me in any way that is avoidable."

While I feel better that he didn't kiss her, the rest of his sentence doesn't exactly fill me with joy. Avoidable isn't always going to mean no.

He leans down and kisses me softly. "All I could think about the entire night was you. You plague my every waking thought, and my dreams, Octavia. If it was my choice, I would see no one but you for the rest of my existence and be happy."

He kisses me again and I tangle my fingers in the back of his hair, letting his arms take my weight as he holds me flush to him.

"If you're done, Shakespeare, coffee is ready," Maverick's teasing tone breaks our moment before he laughs and I hear the door close.

"He is lucky I love him like a brother," Lincoln grumbles into my neck before releasing me. "Come on, we should go in. I need to catch up with him about last night too. When did he come here?"

"About two in the morning. He grabbed a shower then crawled into bed with Finn and me. Where was he last night?"

"Come on," he says, linking my fingers with his. "We're going to cover it over breakfast anyway."

I nod and let him lead me inside, grabbing my coffee mug from the patio table, finding Mav and East sitting at the counter while Finley is at the stove. "Oh God, that smells so good."

I move over to Finn, putting my mug on the counter before kissing him between the shoulder blades as he flips the sausage on the griddle.

"Morning, beautiful." His voice is still full of sleep, but he looks over his shoulder, smiling down at me. "I figured you'd be hungry after last night."

His eyes twinkle with mischief and I love it. "I'm always hungry," I tease, running my fingertips down his ribs. "But you already know that."

He growls lowly and a shiver of excitement runs through me, making my toes curl. I'm glad he's coming around to my touch, especially when I get to tease him. It's fun prodding them all sometimes.

I kiss his back again before refilling my mug and sitting at the counter. The three of them are already muttering away about something sports related so I tune out and just enjoy this moment of peace. It feels like it's been a hot minute since we were all together and there was nothing urgent hanging above us.

It feels like the first time we've all been together, and in once piece since before I was taken... before East was shot.

I shake off the thought, tuning back into the moment with my guys, and just enjoy the fact that we're all here, alive and somewhat healthy.

Finley dishes up breakfast, kissing my cheek as he sets a plate in front of me before taking the seat next to mine. He looks over at Mav, who is teasing Lincoln about God only knows what, before speaking. "What happened last night?"

They all fall silent, and the light in Mav's eyes dims a little. "What do you mean?"

"I mean, you don't typically crawl into bed with V after a job... so what went wrong?" Finn's voice is soft, but firm at the same time. It'd be hard to miss how much he cares for Mav, even with the forceful tone.

He's worried.

Should I be worried?

"Job went okay. That bit was fine," he says, letting out a deep sigh. "It was after, when Harrison cornered me, and told me he wants to see V at the next meeting. That's when shit went sideways."

"He wants what?" I gulp, my appetite disappearing.

Lincoln frowns, but it's East who speaks. "Why would he ask you rather than Lincoln?"

"Because he didn't want to distract me from Georgia," Lincoln says, his jaw clenched.

"What does this mean?" I ask, trying not to sound as on edge as I feel with my heart like a jackhammer against my ribs.

"It means," Lincoln says slowly, "that they've decided to honor the contract."

After a tense Saturday of worrying about what Maverick told us over breakfast, then spending yesterday doing some self-defense training with him and Finley in the cage—after Smithy let me know he's taken my advice and is extending his trip—I've decided to try and not worry about it. What will be will be and all that.

It's also like telling water not to be wet, but I'm trying.

Which is exactly why I'm sipping mocktails around my pool with Indi, trying to enjoy the first day of spring break as we soak up some of the early year sun.

"Do you guys have many plans for the week off?" Indi asks before taking a sip of her mango and passionfruit concoction.

"Nothing that I know of yet. To be honest, I'm looking forward to some down time."

She nods. "I get that. I managed to get Ryker to agree to some time away, so we're going for a long weekend from Thursday. Heading back east for a few days. Showing them New York City and some of my old favorite places. I hate that we couldn't all do a group thing, but with my guys still being pissed about the Alex thing…"

She trails off and I wave her off. "Honestly it's fine, and that sounds like fun!" I'm happy for her, truly. She also deserves a break. As if senior year isn't enough of a stressor without everything else we've dealt with on top of it. "I can't wait till summer, we really do need to do a girls trip."

"You know I'm totally on board for that." She grins, and I start making mental plans.

"Just tell me your wishlist, we'll work it out."

She nods, putting her glass back down, and pulls her sunglasses down her nose, peering at me over them. "You going to tell me what's got you so stressed?"

I let out a deep sigh. I thought I'd managed to cover it pretty well, but I should've known better, she reads me like a book every freaking time. "The Conclave wants to see me."

"What the what now?" she exclaims, sitting up.

I run her through everything Lincoln told me about the deal my dad made to get him and me out, and how Panda trying to free me essentially just tied me to them instead.

"That is so fucked up." She runs a hand through her glossy locks and bites her lip. "I realize the answer is probably no, but is there anything I can do?"

I smile at her and shake my head. "No, I'm not even sure what they want. Even if Lincoln thinks they are honoring the contract, I don't see Harrison Saint handing the keys to his kingdom over to me, do you?"

"Not really." She shrugs. "Have you heard anything more about your uncle?"

"Honestly, I haven't really been digging for information. They're family in biology only. He made his bed, and he can lie in it. I know Lincoln is putting Blair and Vi up at the cottage, but I only said yes because I hate the thought of them paying for Nate's major error in judgment."

"They don't deserve any of it. Though I'd do the same. We're too nice."

I smile softly. "I'd rather be too nice than be like most of the other people around here. My conscience is clear at least. I can't say there's no red in my ledger, but I also don't struggle to sleep because I fucked someone over."

"Amen to that," she says, raising her glass. "Do you have anything planned for tomorrow?"

"I don't think so. Smithy said he won't be back until Sunday, and the guys haven't mentioned anything."

"Good." She grins at me, and I almost regret not having plans. She looks positively wicked. "Ryker is giving me my first tattoo and I thought you might want to come."

"Ryker does tattoos?"

She nods, smiling softly. "He's done almost all of Ellis and Dylan's. A few of his own too. He's so freaking talented. He could have his own shop if he let himself see life outside of the Kings."

"Does Ryker know you're inviting me?" I ask, brow quirked.

She smirks. "I like to keep him on his toes. Plus I found these adorable bestie tattoos for us."

I let out a laugh. I've always wanted a tattoo, it's just not something I've ever taken the initiative to set up. Jenna always told me that she was hooked after her first, and I don't need that sort of addiction in my life.

"Sure, why not? I have a design I've always wanted, too."

She lets out a whoop. "Yeah, our bestie design won't be the first one to grace my skin, Ryker wants to paint on me first, but I'm excited! I can't wait to see your guys' faces when you tell them you let Ryker ink you."

I groan at the prospect. "Yeah, I'm probably going to give them a heads up. It won't stop me doing it, but it'll save them from bitching about secrets afterward."

I pick up my phone and pull up the group thread.

Me:

Heads up. I'm getting a tattoo with Indi tomorrow. By Ryker. No you don't get to have input, this is just me telling you.

Maverick:

As if he's the one getting to ink you. I'm coming. If anyone gets to grace your skin with pain, it's me.

I show Indi the screen and she giggles. "Saw that coming. Tell assface he's welcome to come."

Me:
Indi says you're welcome to come, but have you ever even tattooed someone else?

Maverick:
I haven't, but we can both be virgins again. I do like being your first *wink emoji*

East:
Have fun, just be careful. Can't wait to see it.

Finley:
I'm allowed to not want Ryker to see your tits right? *laugh emoji*

I let out a laugh, shaking my head. I mean, I always wanted under my boobs done, that doesn't count, right?

Me:
No tit tattoos happening. You're good.

Lincoln stays suspiciously quiet, but I think he's with Harrison so I don't fixate on it.

"Ryker says it's chill for Maverick to come. He'll even give him a rundown if you do want him to ink you first."

"Sounds good," I say, and reiterate it to Maverick.

Maverick:
Tell me when and I'll be there.

"Well, apparently we have a date." I laugh and she grins.

"Hell yeah we do. This is what I saw for us." She shows me her phone and the two arrow images, similar, but not identical.

They're beautiful.

"Ryker said he can do them easy enough, and they're small enough that we can put them almost anywhere. He also said if you send me a picture of your other design, he can set it up."

"Maybe we should start small, especially if Maverick wants to come and join in too."

"Sounds good. Just let me know, he's so freaking good. Pretty sure if he and Maverick got on better, they'd spend all their time together talking ink. Both of them are covered."

"Mav's is mostly his top half," I say, smiling softly.

"Yeah, Ryker is like, covered. It's fun to trace the lines though." She blushes and takes a sip of her drink. "Anyway, back to more serious talk because I don't want to be gooey and distracted. How is East doing?"

We spend the morning catching up, just hanging out like two teenagers should be able to, and I love the mundaneness of it all.

Most people want to be anything but ordinary. Me? I'd do a lot for a chance at normal.

Indi heads home when her mom calls about their dinner date, so we make a date for early tomorrow morning at Ryker's for our ink adventure.

Once she's gone, I get dressed in a pair of cutoffs and a hoodie, plonking myself down on the sofa, attempting to watch TV but failing when my mind constantly wanders.

Maybe this meeting with the Conclave won't be so bad. Maybe they'll just release me and honor my dad's wishes.

If only dreams and wishes were more than air and dust.

They were after me before the Panda thing, which means they knowingly broke the contract, and if I had to bet on it, I'd say they were just hoping I was blissfully ignorant.

My stomach churns at the thought of what it is they could possibly want from me. What would possibly make them risk the terms of my dad's agreement? I wasn't joking earlier, there is no way Harrison wants to hand over his place as Regent, so risking it must mean that whatever they want is huge.

I bite my lip, running over the possibilities, knowing that it's unlikely I'm going to work it out.

All I can do is hope that whatever it is doesn't come at a cost I'm not willing to pay.

After spending most of the day spiraling, a text from Bentley—the PI I hired to look into Mom—was out of the blue, but welcome. I'm definitely not pacing in my foyer while I wait for him to arrive.

Nope.

Definitely not.

I jump when the buzzer interrupts my thoughts and find

Bentley looking through the camera at the gate. I buzz him in and open the front door.

Not even impatient.

"Miss Royal, it's good to see you," Bentley says politely as he climbs the steps to the house. His casual look is the same as he had when I saw him last time, with his black hair looking like he's mussed his hands through it all day, and his dark, almond-shaped eyes warm as he smiles at me. "Shall we?"

I nod, trying to shut up the butterflies that are hurricaning in my stomach, and step back to let him into the house. His smile might've been to try and help set me at ease, but there's no chance of that happening right now. I lead him through to the kitchen, feeling super awkward. "Drink?"

"Coffee would be great." He smiles warmly before pulling a folder out of the bag in his hand. I pour us both a mug, handing him his, grabbing the sugar and creamer should he want them and putting them on the island before sitting at the counter. "Shall I begin?"

"Sure, why not? That's what I'm paying you for, right?" I laugh nervously. It's not that I'd forgotten about the task I gave him, I've just had a lot of other stuff occupying my mind. My mom hasn't exactly been a major blip on my radar for years. She left us and never looked back. As far as I know anyway. If it wasn't for everything happening with the Knights, I probably never would have searched for her.

But what Panda said about her niggles in the back of my mind, though I'm not sure how trustworthy he truly was at that stage.

"So, I found quite a bit," he starts, opening the folder, and laying out a ton of photos and documents. "In the early years after her separation from your father, she left a frivolous trail. There was no party too exclusive, no shop too expensive."

He hands me credit card records, photos, and clippings from

newspapers and magazines.

How have I never seen any of these photos?

Something to focus on later.

"But then, around your thirteenth birthday, she seems to have fallen off the face of the earth. I can see where she started trying to wipe her digital print, which isn't easy these days, but if you're good with technology, it's not impossible." He pauses, watching me closely. "But then it all just goes dark. No more parties. No more shopping. No fancy vacations. She fell off the grid entirely, and I have yet to find even a whisper of where she went after that."

I gulp, bringing my coffee cup to my lips even though I don't take a sip. The movement is almost automatic.

"Now I can keep searching, and I'm happy to, but I've spent the last two weeks digging into where she could have gone, and I've come up empty. Unless you have any more details, I'm not sure what luck I'm going to have. I wouldn't want to waste your time or your money."

"I appreciate that," I say quietly. "There's no record of her death either, I assume?"

He shakes his head. "No, nothing at all."

I blow out a deep breath, running a hand through my hair. "Okay, thank you. I don't think continuing to search is going to be of any use if you've already tried and come up empty. You don't seem like the sort of man who chases his tail."

He grins at me and I catch a glimpse of ruthlessness. "I'm not, but I'm also not one to give up so easy either."

I nod, he doesn't seem the type to just quit. "Thank you, I appreciate all of your help."

"If you need anything else at all, you have my number." I stand and shake his offered hand before walking him out.

Once I'm alone, I take everything he brought to me and lay it out over the coffee table, poring over it to see if I can see anything that he hadn't. Any faces that might raise suspicion. Either to confirm or deny what Panda implied.

But there is nothing. I don't recognize any of these people.

I barely recognize my mother.

Letting out a sigh, I put everything back in the folder Bentley brought to me and tuck it away. Maybe she *is* dead, maybe Edward killed her and my dad, just like Panda said, but I still have zero proof of anything.

Giving up I pull out my phone and send a message to Lincoln. Maybe he can get some answers I can't. Or maybe Harrison will tell him the truth of what happened to my father.

I would just like to put my nightmares to rest, even if the truth isn't what I want to hear.

Because when it comes down to choosing whether your dad killing himself or being murdered is a better outcome, life is already all kinds of fucked up.

"Are you nervous? I'm nervous. We have nothing to be nervous about right?" Indi's mindless babble as we head to Ryker's in the Wrangler does nothing but make me smile.

"I mean, if assface back there can get a tattoo, I can. Right?"

"Don't you start with me, Pixie Spice." Mav grins and I pinch the bridge of my nose. These two in a small enclosed space might not be the best, even if it is funny watching them bicker like an old married couple.

"Don't call me Pixie Spice, dick for brains."

He grins at me in the rearview. "It's good dick though."

I don't bother containing my snicker.

"So good she laughs about it," Indi snarks with an eye roll before winking at me. I love how far she's come. From cowering to him, to enjoying sniping at him. "We're here."

She pulls the car to the curb and shuts off the engine, bouncing from the car when Ryker appears in the doorway of the house.

"Princess," Maverick says, touching the top of my arm, making me pause. "You sure you're good with this?"

He makes my heart burst, I swear to God.

"I'm good. I won't let what happened hold me back. Plus you're here too. I know you've got me if I need a minute."

He watches me intently before nodding and climbing from the car. I follow suit, taking his hand as I close the door to the Wrangler and head toward where Indi is waiting with Ryker. Dylan appears behind them, all smiles. "Glad to see you two joining the party today."

I wave at him with a soft smile, Mav heading inside with him and Ryker, while Indi holds back, waiting for me. "Ready?"

I grin at her. "Are you?" She pulls me into the house and we head down into the basement, following the guys. Mav looks back, as if making sure I'm still here, as he talks up a storm with Dylan.

"I'm a little nervous, but yes. I asked Dylan to be here, to help keep the peace. Ellis will call Ryker on his shit, but that usually turns into a whole twin thing. Whereas Dylan has zero issues with your guys."

"That's some diplomacy skills at work, my friend."

Ryker pops his head out of one of the three doors that lead to smaller rooms in the basement, gaze searching for Indi. "You ready?"

She takes a deep breath and nods. We head into the well-lit room which looks like a mini tattoo studio.

"Huh, this looks..." I trail off as she grins at me.

"Painting on skin isn't something I fuck around with," Ryker grunts. "It's too easy to get infected or fuck shit up. So this place is all coded and set up the same way any professional shop is. This is just easier, and more fun for me."

The wicked smile that graces his lips practically drips with sin as his eyes dance with mischief.

"Who's going first?"

Indi pops her ass into the chair and wiggles around until she's sitting in it properly. "Me."

"I redrew your arrows, because I'm not putting someone else's design on your skin," he tells her, and she rolls her eyes at him.

"Well, let me see it then," she teases, and he pulls a sketchbook from the counter behind him, handing it to her. She waves me over, and Mav follows closely behind.

This room is not made for this many people.

"That's so good!" I exclaim, trying not to sound as shocked as I feel. I know Indi said that he was talented, but shit. Something so simple, yet so beautiful.

Rather than one arrow, it's two crossed over, an infinity symbol at the crossing, sitting on top of a pink to blue watercolor puddle.

"I figured you could change the colors if you wanted, but this was what I saw in my head."

She grins at me before turning back to him. "I love it. So freaking much. Thank you."

"Okay, well then, let's get started." he says, picking up the tattoo gun on the tray beside the table. "You good with those colors?"

"Yep!" she says, popping her p. "V?"

I nod, leaning back onto Maverick as he wraps his arms around my waist. "I might lose the pink, go more for a green, but otherwise I'm good."

"Where you putting it, princess?"

I chew on my lip, leaning toward the side of my wrist or back of my neck. "What do you think, Indi? Wrist? Neck?"

"I'm thinking foot, though I like the wrist idea. Side of?"

"Ooooo, Pixie Spice is brave," Maverick teases and she flips him the bird.

I shake my head, and focus back on my girl. "Side of the wrist is where I was thinking."

"Decision made then."

Ryker nods. "Okay, well I'm free-handing your other design. We still doing your hip?"

She nods and I take Mav's hand as Ryker glares at us while she unbuttons her jeans. "Come on, let's wait outside."

"You don't have to," Indi says, her gaze flitting back to Ryker's glare.

"It's good." I squeeze her hand. "I'll be just outside."

"You can stay," Mav whispers in my ear. "I'll go play Xbox with Dylan for a bit. Just holler at me before you get in that chair." He kisses my cheek before leaving the room, closing the door behind him.

Ryker nods at me before the buzz of the gun starts up and Indi takes my hand. She hisses as the needles touch her skin, her grip squeezing the life out of my hand.

I watch Ryker work, mesmerized as he draws on her skin. Indi clamps her jaw together, and I think this might be the longest I've been around her with her not talking unless she's asleep.

Once he's finished the first piece, he shows it to her and tears fill her eyes.

It's stunning.

An anchor, lying beside a compass. More watercolor blues behind it, and the words, *'Let your past be your compass, but never your anchor.'*

I get the feeling there is more to that than I know, but I squeeze her hand back, a giant grin on my face. I feel a little better about Ryker's skills having seen it, and my nerves disappear.

"Ready for part two?" he asks her softly.

"Can we pause for a minute? Let Mav do V's first one or something?"

He watches her closely, as if searching for something hidden in her words. "Sure thing."

I open the door and find Mav and Dylan in a heated COD war, grinning as they shoot shit at each other.

"You still want to mark my skin?" I ask, and Dylan lets out a whoop as Maverick gets distracted. He rolls his eyes as he drops the controller, but still grins as he swaggers toward me.

"Princess, I always want to mark your skin." His eyes heat as he reaches me, kissing me until my toes curl.

"Come on, love birds," Dylan teases. "Ink first, fuckery when you're not here."

Indi pads out of the room, her hip wrapped.

"How you feeling, Pix?" Mav asks and she shakes her head, trying not to smile.

"I'm fine, go get your girl ready." She sits gingerly next to Dylan who wraps an arm around her shoulders.

Mav takes my hand and pulls me back into the room with Ryker, who's wiping down the chair.

"You sure you want to let him ink you?" Ryker asks as I take a seat, looking at Maverick skeptically. "It's not as easy as it looks, and it's easy to fuck up."

Mav laughs. "Oh I know. I'm just going to do a tiny line image. You can fancy it up. But I know you get it. Would you have let anyone else tattoo Indi first?"

Ryker's eyes darken. "Fair point."

Maverick shows him the design we picked together, and I tune them out as Ryker walks Maverick through all his shit, way more professional about it than I would've imagined. I guess when something is your art, your passion, you take it seriously. It's no different than my dad and his music. It seems easy from the outside, but the hours, the blood, sweat, and tears, those are the things that people don't see. It's more than just something you do, it's like a living, breathing part of you.

"Ready, princess?" Maverick asks, looking confident as ever.

"I think so."

Ryker prints out the design, and I lift my top, revealing my ribs. "You two sure are gluttons for punishment. Both going for two of the most painful spots for your first time. You sure you want it on your ribs?"

"I'm sure," I say with a firm nod. "The other side still has my stitches, but this side is all good."

He nods and places the paper against my skin, rubbing it over until the purple pen lies on my skin. The birds span across from just under my boob and around my ribs upwards with the words '*Not all those who wander are lost.*'

"Tolkien is a master of words," Ryker says as he pulls away. "Don't attempt the script. Just start with a bird, I'll deal with the rest."

Mav nods and sits on the stool beside the chair, tattoo gun in one hand, the other splayed across my ribs. He looks so intent on getting it right that I relax a little. The buzz starts up and I close my eyes, sucking in a breath as the sting across my ribs starts.

It's a weird kind of pain. Almost not like pain at all.

Maverick hands the gun over to Ryker after a few minutes, moving to the other side of the chair and taking my hand, all while watching Ryker work.

I lose track of time, and when the buzzing stops, I let out a deep breath, admiring the artwork on my skin. "It's beautiful, thank you."

Indi bursts in the door, like she's been not-so-patiently waiting, and grins when she sees my ribs.

"Stunning," she says as she bounces over toward Ryker. "Ready for round two?"

I grin at her, shaking my head. "Why not."

NINETEEN

OCTAVIA

"What do you mean you booked us a trip?" I blink at Lincoln across his kitchen table, trying to process everything. "We can't travel; East is still healing."

"I'm staying home," East says softly. "I have rehab and shit to get through, but it's Spring Break, and you all deserve a break."

"We can't go without you."

He takes my hand and kisses the inside of my wrist. "Yes you can. I want you to."

I purse my lips, guilt tugging at my heart, but the idea of a mini break does sound good.

"I mean, it's already booked, we leave this afternoon. You just need to pack," Lincoln says, shrugging as he takes a sip of his coffee. "Surprise?"

I bark out a laugh. "Of course." I sigh and look back over at East. "Are you sure you don't mind being left behind? It feels wrong going without you."

"We've got forever. A few days away isn't going to change that."

"You see," Linc says, "it's agreed. Now go pack."

I quirk a brow at him. "When has ordering me to do anything ever worked for you?"

"I can think of a few times," he says lowly, and a blush spills across my chest.

Asshole.

"Fine. Fine. I need to let Smithy know." I stand, pulling my phone from my pocket as I do. "I might need to go shopping."

"Anything you don't have, we can get when we're there. It's Mexico, not the middle of nowhere," Lincoln says, rolling his eyes at me. "Four nights doesn't require a shopping trip."

East grins at him. "It might."

"Okay, I can totally do this." I paint a smile on my face. I'm awesome at giving gifts, but receiving them... yeah I suck at that.

I kiss them both goodbye and start running through everything I'm going to need in my head. I fire a message off to Smithy to tell him what's happening, sending a similar one to Indi so she doesn't think I've just fallen off the face of the earth.

When I'm home, I drag a small suitcase out of the spare room closet and stare at it.

Can I really go away right now? We have zero answers about who Panda was working with. We don't know what the Knights want from me, and the meeting with them is still hanging over my head. We still don't know if what Panda said about Edward is true... and I didn't get any real answers about my mom.

Wow... when I put it like that, we haven't really achieved much. I know we've had a lot going on, and I'm recovering, all while trying to actually graduate high school, but goddamn we kind of suck at the moment.

I wonder if Linc has put it all together like that.

Who am I kidding? Of course he has. It's blatantly driving him insane, but he's also dealing with his father and the Georgia thing.

Maybe we really do need this break. Just a moment to push

pause on the crazy of our lives and come back refreshed so we can actually get shit done.

Letting out a deep breath I drop onto the bed.

Is this really a good idea? Should we go away with everything hanging in the air like this?

"You up there, princess?" Maverick's voice echoes in the foyer, bringing a smile to my lips.

"Yeah, up here," I call out, my smile widening at the sound of his footsteps racing up the stairs.

He bursts into the room, full Superman pose, and I burst out laughing. "Psyched for our trip?"

"Feeling a little guilty about it. Wondering if it's a good time to go away with everything. But other than that... yes?"

His smile drops a bit and he moves to crawl onto the bed, pulling me back against him. "We deserve the break, V. *You* deserve the break. Yes, there's a lot going on, but this is the story of our lives. There is *always* a lot going on."

I snuggle into his chest. "I guess you're right. It just feels weird. I haven't even had my stitches out yet. East is in recovery. Should we be leaving him alone?"

"East will be fine, he's a big boy. Plus Chase has put a layer of protection over him Knight-wise, so he should be good. We'll only be gone a few days." His murmurs make me feel a little better. "Plus, the idea of you on a beach in a bikini for four days is my version of a living wet dream."

"You're incorrigible." I laugh, shaking my head.

"I am, but I'm also supposed to take you to see the doc before we fly, so get a shimmy on with your packing. Personally I'm happy for you to spend the entire trip naked, but I'm pretty sure you aren't going to approve of my plan."

"Definitely not." I scoot out of his arms and throw a few days' worth of stuff in the suitcase, along with an array of bikinis and anything else I might need, because a girl needs options. It doesn't take long to get packed once my decision is made. "I think I'm done."

"Awesome. Let's get you to the doc so Lincoln doesn't tear me a new one, then we'll meet him and Finn on the runway."

"How are we getting there?" I ask. Probably should've done that already.

He grins at me and I can't help but laugh at the devilish look on his face. "Linc spoke to Smithy... we're going in your jet."

"Works for me. I don't mind commercial, but life is so much easier flying private." I shrug. I get why he asked Smithy, he wanted it to be a surprise and we might as well use it. It's already paid for. "Okay, I'm good. Let's go to the doctors and get my ribs checked, shall we?"

"Your chariot awaits." He grins, waving me out of the room, my suitcase in his hand. I lift up on the balls of my feet and kiss his cheek.

Maybe this break is exactly what we need. I, for one, am going to use these four days to indulge in my three favorite F's.

Food.

Fun.

Fuckery.

I let out a sigh. Four days with three of my guys sounds like bliss when I let go of the rest of my baggage.

Here's hoping for smooth sailing.

The plane taxis onto the runway, a bumpier landing than I'd like, but vacation mode is fully in place, so I can't find it in me to care too much. The doctor took out my stitches, so I'm left with a faint line on my ribs, my other injuries are healing nicely, and she seemed happy with everything.

So I'm going to try and take advantage of these few days away from reality. Fuck knows I need the brain break. Leaving East at home sucked, but he wasn't cleared to fly, even though I asked at my appointment.

I swallow down the guilt and smile as Maverick grabs my bag. "Ready, princess?"

I look up at him, taking his outstretched hand. "Hell yes I am. Bring on the relaxation."

They usher me off of the plane and into the waiting car.

"You really thought of everything, didn't you?"

Lincoln smirks at me knowingly. "Did you even doubt me?"

Finley tucks me into his side and once everyone's inside, we pull off through the city. It takes about an hour to reach the resort, but the giant buildings make me feel like a kid again. I've traveled to a lot of places, but I don't know the last time I just went on vacation like this.

We climb from the car, and Lincoln heads inside to check us in while the greeter brings us watermelon smoothies that make me want to dance on the spot. The heat is beautiful and the sun feels so good on my skin. I tilt my head back and close my eyes, just soaking up the rays.

"How you doing?" Finley asks quietly as he wraps his arms around me from behind. Resting my head back on his shoulder, I suck in a deep breath of the fresh air and smile. "Don't just tell me you're fine. These last few weeks have been insane. It hasn't even been a month since you were taken, and we've all been acting like everything is fine, just kept rolling with the punches. But I'm worried about you."

"I'm okay," I tell him honestly. "There's a lot to process, and I should probably journal or something just to get some of it out of my head, but I'm okay. I'm not sure if that means I haven't processed everything fully, or if I'm just repressing shit, but for right now, I just want to be here with you guys and enjoy these few days of bliss."

He kisses my neck, sending a shiver down my spine. "Okay but if you need to talk, I'm here. And if you don't want to speak to any of us, I know a good therapist."

Shock sparks in me, but I'm not about to judge him for talking to someone. "A Knight therapist?"

"She is a Knight, but not like the others. She's aware of the organization, but isn't a part of it. Doctor Patient confidentiality goes a long way."

"I'll think about it, thank you."

Lincoln appears, keycard in hand, looking almost relaxed. "Ready?"

I grin and nod as a golf-cart-style transport appears, the guy taking our bags before we climb in. There are only three other seats, so Maverick pulls me onto his lap, grinning at me as he does. I squeal as it takes off, Maverick laughing at me but tightening his grip anyway. We zoom through the giant resort, weaving through the villas and apartments, our driver pointing out various different pools and restaurants dotted around the place.

We pull up in front of a beach villa and the driver grabs our bags. Lincoln tips him before he zooms off, leaving us with our own little slice of paradise.

"Unpack and then beach?" Mav suggests, and I nod.

I am so ready for a little piece of peace.

This hotel room is *everything.* I mean, I have stayed in some very nice places all over the world, but it's like all of my favorite things about traveling have been put in one very sunny location. It helps that everything here is catered to full-scale relaxation, and I feel like we all need this in our lives.

Especially right now.

I still can't get over the fact that the four of them got together and planned this trip for me. I'm sad that East couldn't come, but I fully intend on spending a ton of time with him when we're home to thank him for his part in this.

I shut off the shower and wrap one of the big fluffy towels around me. There is something about a powerful shower after a day on the beach that is just revitalizing. I pad into the bedroom and find the three of them lounging in the room, waiting for me, in various states of undress. Even in Mexico, Finn hides his chest, and it hurts my heart. I hope one day, I can show him that his scars don't define him. That he doesn't have to hide. Until then, I'll just continue to respect his boundaries.

"Shower's free if you guys want it."

Maverick just laughs at me, shaking his head. "Princess, it took less time for each of us to shower in the other bathroom, than it took for you to shower in this one."

"Oh." I grin as a blush spills across my chest. "I'm not even sorry."

"We know." Lincoln smiles as I pad over to the dressing table. They go back to their conversation while I blow out my hair. It's impossible not to feel their heated stares on my skin. When I'm done, I realize they're all watching me silently, so I turn to face them, biting my lip.

Finn tilts his head, leaning forward in his seat, hands clasped. "Want to play?"

My eyes go wide at the three words.

I can't say I haven't thought about playing with all of them, especially after the fun on Maverick's birthday, but it's not something I've pushed. Each of them have their own... quirks. I'm not about to make them play together if they don't want to.

But I'm also not about to say no if it *is* something they're up for.

Standing, I untie my towel and let it fall to the ground. I own my body, curves and scars included, and catch each of their gazes. "Do *you* want to play?"

Lincoln's gaze fixes on the scar that runs across my ribs for a minute before looking back up at me. Everything in his eyes is exactly why I know I don't need to hide from them.

Not anymore.

"You are... there are few words to describe you aptly."

My entire body is on high alert—alive with those words—and judging by the various looks on their faces, mine is a visible reaction.

Lincoln is the first to stand, his lithe body unfurling like a panther, his gaze fixed on his prey.

That's me.

I'm the prey and the feeling of being hunted is, in this instance, exciting, exhilarating.

Finn and Maverick are next, flanking their fearless leader like the trio of danger that they are.

I bite my lower lip, playing coy and enjoying the flare in their eyes as all three pairs zero in on my lips.

I don't dare move because I know this is Lincoln's game. He always calls the shots, the moves, the positions.

Lincoln is the alpha of all alphas.

Finn secures their prey.

Maverick plays with it.

Together, their only focus is to make me come. Repeatedly.

"Get on the couch, Octavia. Legs spread so we can look at you." Lincoln's words are leveled—clear—and as if he's just set a chess game in motion, the others get into position. Finn and Mav take one step forward while Lincoln moves away to give me a wide berth—like he's afraid of touching me—following me only with his calculating eyes.

When I reach the couch, I turn, sit, then instantly spread my legs so my pussy is in clear view for all of them.

Hungry eyes stare back at me, hard dicks clearly outlined behind their clothes.

Linc looks over to the guys and without a word, they both come and kneel on either side of me, following his silent command.

Mav's the first to move, wrapping one hand around my wrist and bringing my palm to his cock, rubbing it—harder than I ever would—thrusting his hips into my hold.

Finn mimics Mav's moves after taking my wrist to his lips first —kissing it reverently—before bringing my hand to his impossibly hard dick. I turn to look at one then the other before my gaze lands on Lincoln as he takes one last step closer and drops to his knees, his hands on the inside of my thighs.

I watch in rapt attention as Lincoln licks his thumb then his forefinger, before bringing both to my nipple and tweaking hard enough to make me flinch, but the pain feels so good.

"Fuck," Mav groans, his voice little more than a rumble.

"You should see how wet she is." Lincoln's eyes snap to mine, and he leans in and swipes his tongue through my slit before he lands on my clit and circles it agonizingly slowly.

I'm mesmerized but his steel gaze traps me in his snare. Telling me without a single word that I'm his.

That I'm theirs.

Mav and Finn rub their cocks on my hands, using the fabric of their clothes for friction, and before I understand what's happening, Mav hands my wrist to Finn who places it with my other, trapped together in one unbreakable hold.

In a heartbeat, Mav's lips are on mine, kissing me with an intensity that takes my breath away and just as quickly as he attacks, he's gone.

Finn does the same, swiping his tongue across my mouth— quickly delving inside—before he jumps over the back of the couch and stands behind me, my arms up and above my head.

The position makes my tits push out, my back arch, and my head lean heavily against the headrest.

I'm completely exposed. My thighs are held down, my cunt is being devoured, my arms are trapped above me, and my nipples are primed for the taking.

I practically drool as Maverick and Finn start to undress. Lincoln keeps my legs spread as he leans back and unbuttons his jeans just enough to free his cock through the V of the open zipper.

"How many times have you dreamed of this, Octavia?"

I don't have time to answer Linc's question, because Mav has my throat in a chokehold—fingers pressing down just below my ears with his thumb and middle finger.

"Her pulse is like a freight train. I'm guessing a whole fucking lot." My eyes dart to Mav, blinking to answer him. To tell him that, yes, I regularly dream of having them all at my mercy. That even when I'm not the one calling the shots, I'm still in charge.

Finn bends over my shoulder and takes my free nipple in his mouth, flicking the hard bud with his tongue, fast and erotic. It tears a moan from my lips earning me a chuckle from Linc.

"Fuck, I need to come or else I'm never going to last." Mav leans into my mouth, whispering on my lips. "Time to suck my cock, V. Nice and deep, the way you like it." I whimper at Mav's words, a sound that tells him I really do want to have it in my mouth.

"Such a good girl." Fuck, I love it when Linc calls me that.

My eagerness earns me a finger in my pussy, pushed in nice and deep. Twisting and scissoring like he's preparing me for something. For his cock?

God, I hope so. I'm so fucking ready to get fucked, right now.

Mav licks the seam of my mouth before trapping my bottom lip between his teeth and biting hard enough to hurt.

Then he's gone.

I've got one finger pushing and retreating, turning and twisting inside my pussy while Finn continues to lave my nipples. One, then the other. Electricity runs through my veins. As if my nerve endings are on fire.

"Fuck her mouth, Mav."

I lick my lips and open up for him as requested, anticipation running through me that this is actually going to happen.

Finn grabs me by my upper arms and turns me so I'm lying down on the couch. Linc follows me, finger fucking me without losing a beat.

Contrary to what I'm anticipating, Finn doesn't place my head on a cushion, he lets it hang off the armrest—hair hanging freely toward the floor—face up, mouth still open and ready.

Finn brings my arms to my stomach, his order loud and clear when he squeezes my wrists together. "Don't move."

"Jesus fucking Christ, look at her." Mav is right there at the side of my face, his dick caressing my cheek before he places the head of his cock at my lips and runs it around like he's painting them.

Then he pushes inside. Slowly, until my nose is against his groin, the hair tickling my nose and depriving me of my breath as he grabs my hair and fucks my face for a second too long.

"Give me your tears, V. Fucking give them to me."

Lincoln adds another finger to my pussy, fucking me harder and harder as Mav places his hand on my throat—massaging the column—like he's trying to feel his cock.

Finn steps away and Mav practically straddles my face from behind, his balls heavy on the bridge of my nose, like he wants to fuck my throat, and I love that I make him crazy with need.

Before coming back, Finn takes a belt from somewhere in the room. When he straddles my chest, he takes my hands and uses it to secure them at my forearms, tight enough to give me a bite of pain. My hips leap from the couch, pushing Lincoln deeper into me, harder, in and out.

Finn takes both of my tits in his hands and as he creates a tunnel with them, he places his dick in the valley, lubricating my skin with his precum.

With Linc finger fucking my pussy, Finn fucking my tits, and Mav in my mouth, I'm losing my grasp on reality—my orgasm rising from the depths of my soul.

"The view is fucking fantastic." I hear Mav's words but the adrenaline is rushing through my ears so his voice sounds far away. The only clear sound is me gagging on his cock and loving every second of it. My impending orgasm is so close I can practically taste it along with Mav's precum.

Digging my nails into my palms, I try to fight it off, try to make it last longer, but it's no use.

"She's about to lose it. Pull out, Mav."

He just grins, instead of pulling out, and just fucks me harder, deeper, rather than following orders. He relishes in the saliva that pools at my mouth, the tears falling down and across my temples. He's like a beast, choking me just enough to make the edges of my vision go black but not enough that I lose complete consciousness.

Just when I think I'm going to bite down for air, Mav pulls out and jacks himself off on my lips as I scream out my climax. Ribbons of his cum are jetting across my mouth, my tongue, my cheeks. I'm gasping and trying my best to breathe when Maverick reaches down and possessively spreads his cum over my skin, my chin, my throat as Finn fucks me harder and harder until he, too, loses all control.

Grunting with every jet of cum that hits my tits, my nipples, my cleavage, Finn looks me straight in the eyes as he releases all over me.

"Nice. Took the edge off. Now I can concentrate on you." Mav leans in and kisses my mouth, undoubtedly tasting himself on me but he's Maverick fucking Riley, he doesn't have any fucks to give.

Except, maybe to me. He would give me all of his fucks.

"Enough." Lincoln's voice is deep, like he's using all of his strength to keep himself under tight control. He hasn't come yet. Only using his fingers, he was essential to my orgasm and now... well, now, I think he's going to unleash himself on me.

Fuck, I can't wait.

He disappears and returns with a washcloth, helping me to clean up before dropping a chaste kiss on my lips. "Such a good girl. Ready for some more?"

I nod and he stands, taking the washcloth back to the bathroom.

The three of us are still panting as Finn picks me up and carries me to the bed where Lincoln is shedding the last of his clothing. He and Mav are both naked whereas Finn is still wearing his fucking shirt.

I'm drunk on my orgasm and my mouth opens without any regard to the words that are about to escape.

"I love your scars, Finn. Give them to me."

Finn just leans in and kisses me like I'm giving him life.

Releasing my mouth, Finn places me in the center of the bed like I'm fragile glass.

Maverick is already there with a cheeky smile, kissing me like I'm his queen and he's just a servant, while Finn unbuckles the belt and releases my bound arms. I shake them off but I know better than to think I'm free to touch and do whatever I want. It's not their style.

"Thank you," I manage to whisper, and the mischievous grin Mav throws back to me almost scares me.

"Don't thank me yet, princess."

Oh fuck.

Lincoln kneels on the bed, slowly making his way between my

open legs and without any preamble, he pushes his incredibly hard and thick cock inside me as he folds his elbows at the sides of my head, effectively caging me in and holding all his weight on his arms.

Finn and Mav are watching us from either side of the bed, but our position is like a private bubble and here, just the two of us, I can see the side of Lincoln that he only gifts to me. His eyes soften just a fraction as he looks down on me, a small smile etched at the corners of his sensual mouth.

"Octavia Royal, you'll be the death of me but I'll walk willingly into the depths of Hell for a second with you." I don't have time to respond before his mouth is on mine.

Our kiss walks the edge of violence.

He's not just loving me, he's owning me. Fucking my mouth while his dick is a slow piston in and out of my pussy.

Suddenly, I'm turned around, finding myself lying on top of Lincoln. His grin tells me his chess game is going exactly as he planned.

With his hands on my hips, he accelerates his moves, fucking me from below and never losing his rhythm.

That's when I hear the sound of metal on metal. Reluctantly, my gaze lifts and I see them. Finley and Maverick have secured cuffs to the headboard, long chains attached to another set of cuffs for—I'm guessing—my wrists. Thank fuck they look soft with their wool interior and leather straps on the outside.

"Give them your hands, Octavia." Lincoln's order is low and undeniable. His authority isn't something he's practiced. It's a birthright and it fucking turns me on to no end. All the while his dick is leisurely pumping in and out of me, like its only job is to get me worked up.

Once my wrists are secured by soft wool and unyielding metal, I watch as Finn kneels at my side and Mav kneels behind me.

I don't know what's going to happen but I'm sure whatever it is, I'm going to love every second. I trust them enough to know that they won't do anything I won't enjoy.

Finn brings his hand to my cheek and caresses me softly, his lips spreading into a smile that steals my breath. "You're stunning like this: bound and the center of our attention. Always."

My eyes burn with unshed tears at his words.

Fuck, he's amazing.

They all are in their unique way.

My romantic moment is interrupted by my gasp as I feel Mav's tongue licking a hot path up one of my ass cheeks before he bites it, growling like a lust-filled animal. It's erotic and intimidating.

Linc fucks me steadily, a constant rhythm that slowly makes my body hum with vibrant energy. He's building the anticipation and as I turn my gaze back to his steely eyes, I feel centered. I feel secure in the fact that no matter what, he's got me.

Then Mav's mouth is at my ass with a quick swipe before I feel the cold dollop of lube that hits my puckered hole. He rubs it around, pushing a finger inside, and the fullness I feel between Linc's dick and Mav's finger makes me gasp. I instinctively pull at my restraints. I want to reach out and touch them, hold them. Something.

Anything.

Instead, Linc's hand is at my nape—fingers tightening in my hair—calming me, grounding me as Mav adds a second finger.

"Fuck. Oh God."

Finn runs one hand down my spine, up and down, soothing me with his warm touch.

"After tonight, you'll truly be ours," Finn whispers in my ear, and I physically feel my juices coat Linc's dick. He feels it too, judging by the wide grin I get from him.

"You like that, don't you?"

"Yes." It's just one word, but it's a breathy mess of lust.

"Are you ready, princess?" I hear from behind me as Mav

scissors his fingers inside my ass. Linc pulls out then pushes in half-way and just when I think I can't get any fuller, Mav presses the head of his cock where his fingers were a moment before. I'm surprised by the stretch. I mean, I knew this would happen but I didn't think it would feel... full. My eyes go wide as my body tenses.

"Shh, baby, relax. Let him in. There's a good girl." Below me, Linc coaxes me to calm down, wills me to listen to him.

"Fuuuuuuck, there it is." Mav slides in the head of his cock and I scream out, pulling on my restraints but not because I want to stop. The bite of pain is there, the fullness, the impossible stretch of my ass and pussy to accommodate them.

But once Mav is in, I only need one thing.

"Fuck me, please. I need to feel... you. Move." I'm gasping, trying to talk with ragged breaths in and out.

"Your command, princess." I don't get the last of the phrase, I lost myself to the feel of them both, reveling in that line between pleasure and pain. Just when I think it can't get any better, Finn kneels at my side and my eyes go straight to his cock where his hand is slowly stroking up and down, almost violently.

The pain subsides, the pleasure taking its place when Finn turns my head and kisses me like life is about to get complicated.

Lincoln reaches up and unlocks the cuffs. I place both hands on his chest, following his instructions as he pushes my head to where Finn's dick is eagerly waiting for me to suck it.

"You are fucking beautiful, Octavia Royal. I love watching you come undone."

I gasp around Finley's cock as both Linc and Mav push deep inside me at the same time. I don't think I'll ever get used to the stretch, the feeling that I may rip in half, but at the same time, the pleasure is so high that I can't imagine stopping either.

"Suck his dick, Octavia. Concentrate on Finn while we focus on you."

"Fuck yeah, this is by far my favorite position." I barely hear Maverick behind me as I sink my mouth onto Finn until my nose is pressed against him, breathing becoming more difficult.

Once I get into the rhythm, I let the pleasure take over my body.

"Come on, V. Suck it. Let me feel your throat swallow me whole." Fuck, I love it when they talk dirty.

"Oh yeah, she's fucking soaked. I can feel her all over my dick."

The more they talk, the more I feel my orgasm creeping up on me.

Linc, who is half-way leaning against the headboard, releases the nape of my hair only for Finn to wrap his fist in it and push my head further down, forcing his cock deeper into my throat. I'm choking, saliva dripping from my mouth as Linc and Mav speed up their movements, alternating their thrusts.

Mav's hand snakes around my waist and the second his fingers circle my clit, I'm done.

I can't scream but my entire body begins to shake, my skin is coated with fire as I dig my nails into Linc's chest.

"Jesus fucking Christ, she's going to squeeze the life out of my cock. Fuck, fuck, fuck!" Mav's chants are like a lifeline as my orgasm threatens to make me pass out.

"You feel amazing, Octavia. Coming all over my cock. Take what you need, beautiful." And I do. I milk them all with my spasms, squeezing both their dicks until I hear Mav roar out his second orgasm.

Linc follows, his fingers so tightly planted in my hips that I know I'll have bruises there later.

"Fuuuuck!" Linc's body rears up, his head pressed against the headboard, and he's never been so fucking gorgeous as when he loses all control.

I don't know how I'm able to continue sucking off Finn but I keep it up until he finally loses himself in my mouth.

Finn throws his head back and grunts his orgasm out, his fingers tightening on my head until he pulls me off of him.

Reverently, he wipes my swollen lips with his thumb and leans in to kiss me, a whispered thank you on his breath.

Pulling out, Mav's heavy breaths echo around the room as he saunters over to the bathroom. When he comes back, Linc has pulled out and the evidence of our orgasms seeps out of my pussy.

A warm cloth on my pussy first, Mav wipes me clean then brings it up to my ass before he kisses my ass cheek again, and I can almost feel his grin.

Fifteen minutes later, we're all four lying on the bed. Half my body is draped over Lincoln, one leg touching Finley with my hand is resting on Mav's chest.

I fall asleep like that.

Cocooned by these boys-turned-men.

Mine.

All mine.

TWENTY

EAST

T here is nothing quite like being left behind to make a guy mope about like a sap. The fact I helped Linc decide where to go, that I encouraged them to go, doesn't make it suck any less. But being shot will mean missing out on shit.

At least I'm still alive.

At least *she* is still alive.

I have plenty to be thankful for, but staring at the ceiling in my room, in this tomb of a house, isn't something I'm feeling exactly rainbows and unicorns about. It might've been over a month since I was shot, and I feel like I've come leaps and bounds, but my doctor is still cautiously optimistic. I'm healing faster than expected, but I'm not healed.

I grind my teeth together, hating feeling so useless, so I climb from the bed and start some of the exercises my rehab nurse gave me.

It doesn't take long until sweat is rolling down my spine, and I curse myself out for being so weak. I hate feeling as shackled as I so obviously am right now.

I pull off my tank, using it to wipe my face before flinging it in the corner. My stomach growls at me for missing breakfast and lunch, so as much as I need to shower, I decide to venture out into the battlefield of a house to eat. I just hope Harrison isn't here.

The coast is clear as I reach the kitchen, reheating some of the taco pasta Mrs. Potts left in here for me. I check my phone for the umpteenth time, smiling at the picture from V of her on her sun lounger in nothing but a bright red bikini.

Nope, not jealous of those three assholes at all.

The microwave beeps, letting me know my reheated pasta is done, but when footsteps sound down the hall and heading in this direction, my appetite disappears. Harrison sneers at me when he finds me in here, and I take a deep breath, preparing myself for the onslaught I know is coming.

It always does.

"Still here, leech? I'm surprised you didn't run to your coward daddy with your tail between your legs."

Not as bad as I expected. He's either tired, or losing his touch. Little does he know, I've been talking with Chase plenty. It's been weird as fuck getting to know him, and I still don't trust him fully, but he's done nothing but try to help us since he found out that he's my father.

Still feels weird even thinking it.

I roll my eyes as I carefully fold my arms across my chest. He eyes the pink line that runs down it like he wants to cut me back open. I wouldn't put it past this asshole to shove me, just to see if he can put a hole back in my chest. "I told you a long time ago, I won't be leaving without Lincoln."

He laughs at me, like I'm insignificant and absurd. "He will never leave."

"Then I guess you're stuck with me, aren't you?"

His eyes shine, like he has something heinous ready to throw at me, when the doorbell sounds. I hear voices as Mrs. Potts answers the door, and less than a minute later, I spot Chase striding down the hall toward us.

Well, fuck.

"Chase," Harrison snarls. "I don't remember inviting you to my home."

"Good thing I'm not here to see you then." He looks away from Harrison—who bristles at the casual dismissal—to me. "How are you doing?"

I smile at him and Harrison narrows his eyes at me. "I'm healing," I say with a shrug. "Everything okay?"

Being in a room with both of them is awkward as fuck. Mostly because Harrison is looking at me like he'd rather I was bleeding out at his feet than breathing, and we both know he could do it, too. Except now I'm technically an heir and there are rules.

If he wanted me dead, he should've done it long before now.

"Everything is fine, just wanted to check in on you since I know the others are away." He glances at Harrison, who is distracted by his phone ringing.

"Rico?" he says as he strides from the room and takes the tension with him.

Chase eyes him as he leaves, but once he's out of earshot, I relax, grab my pasta, and move to sit at the table with Chase following. "Why are you really here?"

"Exactly what I said. I can't imagine being cooped up here with just that stick up the ass for company is any fun."

I take a bite of the steaming, creamy, spicy pasta and shrug. "I've dealt with it my entire life; I'm used to it."

He frowns at my words, but I'm not going to mind them. He might not have known about me, but I'm not about to change my entire life just because I know who he is now.

"You don't have to—"

I cut him off with a shake of my head. "I will not, under any circumstances, leave Lincoln to deal with that monster alone."

"Understood."

Annndddd now it's awkward again.

"I started looking into the things we spoke about last week," he says quietly. I glance over his shoulder. Harrison isn't anywhere to be seen, but that doesn't mean shit. I'm convinced the walls in here have ears.

I drop my fork, because I want that information, just not here. "Want to go out and grab some food?"

He smiles, looking a little shocked. "I'd like that a lot."

"I'll be two seconds." I dump my pasta in the trash, putting the bowl and fork in the dishwasher, and head upstairs to change out of my sweats.

"You two deserve each other. Cowards, the pair of you." Harrison's vitriol catches me off guard as I open my door.

I sigh, so done with dealing with his bullshit. "Then just fuck off and leave us be I guess. I'm sure nothing would make you happier than never speaking to me again, Harrison."

"You do not speak to me like that in my house," he roars, and I shrug.

I narrow my eyes at him, wondering how far I can push him. "Let Lincoln leave and I'll be out of your hair."

He grins at me. "You'll be out soon enough either way, don't worry."

Without another word he turns on his heels and strides down the hall, turning the corner that leads to his office. I take a deep breath and try to push back the rising anger, remembering Chase is downstairs waiting.

If he has the information I need, then Harrison might not have the power he thinks he does for too much longer.

Change is coming, and I can't wait to watch his downfall.

TWENTY-ONE

OCTAVIA

Two days of sheer bliss is all it's taken for me to be able to pretend that this is my new reality. Lying beside the pool shouldn't feel so good. I can do it at home. But what I don't have at home is the three of them walking around, carefree, in just swim shorts, making me drool. The swim-up bar in the pool is a godsend, and somehow we seem to have eight pools—*eight*!—to ourselves.

Definitely *not* complaining.

"You need more lotion, princess?" Mav smirks at me as he steps up beside me, when four men in Hawaiian shirts walk toward us. Maverick stiffens as Lincoln pulls himself from the water and Finley sits up on the lounger beside me, watching their approach with a scowl, moving his body to shield me from view.

The hairs on the back of my neck stand up as the tension increases tenfold around me.

"Why are you here?" Lincoln asks, his voice low and lethal.

"Rico told us where you were staying. Your father offered your... skill set. We're having some problems."

He quirks a brow, looking cold and dangerous, even dripping wet. "No."

I peer over Finley's shoulder as the easy smile falls from the man's face. "It wasn't a request."

"I don't know what to tell you," Lincoln says, shrugging. "My father made an offer he can't uphold. I suggest taking up your issue with him. I'm on vacation. I am not his lapdog."

The second guy steps forward, but the one who spoke stops him. "I am sure we will be seeing you again very soon, Mr. Saint."

They turn and leave, and once they're out of sight Maverick launches a table into the pool. "What the fuck is wrong with your father!"

I sit there, wide-eyed, hating that whatever relaxation we were finally feeling just walked away with whoever that was.

Lincoln grabs a towel and drops down beside me.

"Is that our vacation over?" I ask. They're all so tense. Finley turns to face us, his mouth set in a grim line.

Finley says, "Yes," at the same time Lincoln says, "No."

"Uhm?"

"We're not leaving early because Harrison is an asshole," Lincoln says, placing a hand on my thigh.

"What if they come back?" I ask, my gaze bouncing between the three of them.

"Then we'll handle it," Mav says, moving to stand behind me, rubbing my shoulders.

"Are you sure that's a good idea?" Finn questions, and I hate to side with any of them over the other, but I'm firmly in line with him right now.

"No." Lincoln frowns before turning to me. "If you'd rather we left, we can. I just wanted to do something nice for you, but Harrison is a cunt."

"He is, but I'm not sure I feel all that safe after that. It hadn't occurred to me that they would reach us here. Stupid naïvety I guess." I bite down on my lip, hating how this has all played out, our little slice of paradise marred by shadows.

"The Knights are everywhere, and they can reach you anywhere. There is *no* hiding from them," Finley says quietly. "But we arranged with the Conclave that we wouldn't be called upon this week. It's why they agreed to wait until next week for your meeting. This is bullshit."

"How likely is it that they'll come back?"

"They shouldn't. Rico is more likely to lose his shit at Harrison than send them back here. He's always been pretty reasonable. He likes my father about as much as I do. He was a friend of your dad's."

I blink at Lincoln. It still amazes me that these three know a whole side of my dad that I had no idea existed. I try not to get emotional about all of it, but my bubble has officially burst.

"Maybe we should just help them so we don't have to worry about them coming back? What did he mean *your skill set,* anyway?"

Any traces of warmth drop from Linc's face at my question.

"You don't have to tell me," I say quietly, half wishing I could take the question back. Anytime we end up speaking about what it is they do for the Knights, it's like being plunged into an icy pool.

"There are some parts of me—of us—that we'd rather you never knew existed." He sighs. "But life doesn't work that way."

"She already knows mine," Mav says, shrugging. "My penchant for knives and blood isn't something I've hidden from her, and she barely even blinked. Give her more credit for accepting the monsters that live inside of us."

"You don't have to tell me," I say again. "But you also don't have to hide yourselves from me. I love you. Each of you. Demons and all."

Lincoln's phone rings on the table between mine and Finn's loungers, and he glares as he grabs it and answers. "What?"

He goes quiet, his face turning more thundery with each second he remains silent.

It feels like a lifetime passes as his jaw clenches and his eyes darken. "Fuck you, too," he mutters as he ends the call.

"What was that?" I ask hesitantly, shivering despite the scorching sun.

"That," he growls, "was orders. It seems you're being roped in early."

"She's coming with? Fuck no," Finn says, turning pale.

Lincoln grips his phone so hard, I worry it might crack. "We don't have a choice. Let's head back and get dressed. A car will grab us in an hour."

My stomach churns, and I get a little dizzy. "I thought you said you had an approved reprieve?"

Lincoln stands, turning to look down at me. "Apparently the Regent changed his mind. Long live the King."

The car ride has been silent and bumpy. A million thoughts whirr through my mind, but every time I consider opening my mouth, I look at the three of them and reconsider. Lincoln has barely said a word since the call came in, and despite Maverick playfully joining me in the shower, he didn't say a word about any of this either.

They've all officially gone to a place inside of them that I don't have access to. Everyone with trauma has that safe space, and these three have more trauma than anyone else I've ever met. Except for maybe Panda.

I shudder just thinking about the possibilities of it. What they went through.

Though I can't help but wonder just how aware of some of it I'm about to become. While I know *why* Lincoln bows to

Harrison's hold, I can't help but wonder if Harrison would actually release the video of Lincoln killing someone. Surely, it would be just as bad for him as it would be for Lincoln.

I keep that thought to myself for now, but it's something to think on. Really, I need to learn more about how the Knights work. I need to pin Lincoln down, or someone, and get answers so I know how to navigate this sinister path I'm on.

I make a mental note to clear a day once I'm home to finish going through my dad's journals, too. I'm not sure what insight they'll give me, but there has to be something.

The car slows, pulling to a stop at a set of gates, the stone wall they're attached to stretches as far as I can see.

"Rico's home away from home," Lincoln says quietly in my ear. "A Knight holding."

The gates open painfully slowly, but once they're open we start moving again. It's a very tense, quiet few minutes as we drive up the cactus-lined drive before we pull up to a huge villa. The white walls and terrace roofing look like something out of a travel brochure.

Except this isn't a place for dreams or paradise.

I get the feeling this is just the shiny front for a place of pain.

The car door opens and the two guys from earlier smirk down at me, offering me a hand, which I take as I climb from the car.

"I see you came around," he says as Lincoln climbs out behind me. "The boss will be pleased. Not so sure about the guy waiting for you though."

"Let's just get this over with, shall we?"

He takes my hand and pulls me into his side as Maverick and Finley walk behind us and we head into the giant villa. The sounds of my footsteps echo in the high-ceilinged room, which is strangely cold.

"Ah, Lincoln, so good of you to come." A man's voice filters down from the mezzanine above us. Rico, I assume. He looks like the cartel bosses you see in films. Tan skin, dark hair slicked back, white pants, white shirt. "I see you brought friends. The more the merrier."

His smile seems warm, genuine almost, as he descends the stairs.

"Oh my," he says as he moves closer, beelining straight for me. Lincoln stiffens at my side as he cups my face in his hands. "Octavia Royal, as I live and breathe, is that really you?"

"Who are you?"

He almost looks taken aback. "You don't remember your Uncle Rico? I suppose the last time I saw you, you were very young."

He takes a step backward. "Martin, take our friends to see our guest. *Si respiran mal, maten a la niña*."

Nothing like being able to understand the people around me. Of course Spanish is one of the languages that I'm more than a little rusty with. The man who spoke as we came in steps forward. "*Si jefe*."

"*Asaca estés cabrones de aqui! Y ponlé in ojo a ellos guys*."

The other guy points a gun at me, and I suck in a breath as Maverick looks like he's about to throw down. "If you'll please go with Martin, he will get you some refreshments."

Mav takes a step forward, but Lincoln barks his name as Finn clamps a hand on his shoulder. Mav's brown eyes are wild as he snarls at Rico, but follows as Martin ushers the two of them into another room to the left of us. "What is going on?"

"Just making sure no one gets any stupid ideas, little Royal." Rico smiles, his eyes darken and his smile turns sinister. "Want to make sure we get what we paid for after all. Now, if you will just follow Jorge."

I look up at Lincoln, whose jaw is clenched so tightly I think his teeth might snap. It would seem Harrison has truly fucked us. "She doesn't need to be there for this."

Rico's eyes sparkle as he laughs at Lincoln's words. "Of course she does. Can't love a monster without seeing its true form."

My heart races in my chest and I grip Lincoln's hand tighter. It doesn't matter what I see, it won't change a thing. Martin moves ahead of us, motioning for us to follow in the opposite direction of where they took Mav and Finn. I glance back, Rico's slimy smirk burned into my brain.

What the fuck is wrong with everyone in this organization? How was my father friends with this guy? I still can't quite correlate the man I knew my father to be with the man who would've been a part of all of this. It's like he was two entirely different beings.

I follow behind Linc as we're taken out back and across a courtyard before we enter what looks like stables. Except, once we're inside it just looks like a torture chamber, confirmed by the guy hanging from one of the beams, his wrists wrapped in chains and a burlap sack over his head.

What in the fuck have we been dragged into?

"What is it you want to know?" Lincoln asks Martin, who smirks at him as he waves his gun at the hanging man.

"There is a rat, he knows who it is. We want a name."

Lincoln nods and rolls up the sleeves of his shirt. "You'll get it. If you'll give us some space, I do my work better without guns in my face. Or hers."

"Not a chance."

Lincoln stiffens, and my eyes go wide. "It wasn't a request. You want the name, you fuck off."

Martin's eyes narrow as he stares at us both and Lincoln maneuvers himself so that he's standing in front of me. While I'm thankful, I also really don't want him to get hurt. I put my hand on the center of his back, feeling him stiffen under my touch.

"Raise that gun in my face again and you'll be wishing you hadn't," Lincoln growls as Martin moves to lift his arm again. He looks a little afraid, and I can't help but wonder exactly what Lincoln has done to instill such fear in these people. To the point that they'd separate the three of them.

"*Chinga te, princessa*," the man growls before turning and leaving the room.

Lincoln stares after him until the door is closed , then relaxes a little. "Octavia, I don't want you to see this either."

He keeps his back to me, his head hung. "I'm not going anywhere. I'm not afraid of you or anything you're capable of, Lincoln. I love you, even the darker parts."

A shudder runs down his spine and I wrap my arms around him from behind. He relaxes further under my touch, covering my linked fingers with his hands.

"Let's get this over with, shall we?"

I pull back from him and move back toward the wall. I'm pretty sure the guy with the gun is just outside the door, so I can't go anywhere anyway, but I'm not about to leave him alone in this. He might not want me here, but I also know he'd rather know where I am.

Leaning against the wall I watch as Lincoln lowers the chains, letting the man sit on the floor, before removing the sack from his head. He leans forward and murmurs something in the man's ear, and the man bursts into tears.

"Please, sir, no. Take pity. I have two daughters and a beautiful wife. I don't know what it is that they want. I tried to tell them." His broken English is hard to understand through his sobs, but I make out enough to get the gist of what he's trying to say. Lincoln offers him a bottle of water, letting him drink as much as he wants before stepping back.

My heart races as Lincoln heads to the table lined with instruments of pain. He picks up a thin blade, no wider than my pinkie nail, and heads back to the man.

"I'm going to ask once more..." Lincoln sighs, swiping the

blade on the back of his jeans before pulling on the chains until the man is standing again, his toes just barely reaching the ground. "If you tell me now, we can save you from any more pain. If you don't... it's between your life and hers. I'm going to pick hers."

"Please, sir. No. I don't know anything!" The man screams, and Lincoln shakes his head.

"Don't say I didn't warn you." I don't see what Lincoln does as he stands in front of the man, but the screams that come from the man grow louder, more high-pitched. I don't flinch or look away.

I told him I wouldn't think any different of him, and I meant it. Seeing this side of him doesn't scare me. It probably should, and that likely says more about me than it does about him.

"Name," Lincoln barks as the screams quiet to whimpers. When the man doesn't speak, Lincoln moves forward again; the screams that follow echo around the room.

I lose track of time as the screams turn to sobs. Small flashbacks of my time with Panda flash in my mind as the interrogation continues, but I know Lincoln wouldn't be here if he had a choice. That's the difference.

When the blood letting doesn't work, he uses a towel over the guy's face, pouring the bottles of water over it until he chokes, and even uses the car battery in the corner.

"Thierry," the man whimpers as Lincoln moves back toward him with the jumper cables. "Thierry Montessary."

Lincoln watches him closely before nodding and disconnecting the cables. He uses the sink to wash his hands and arms before coming over to where I'm standing. He doesn't look me in the eye when he speaks. "We can leave now."

He moves to the door and pounds on it. Seconds later, it opens.

"Thierry Montessary," Lincoln says to Martin, who nods and waves us out of the room before taking us back to the main house where Rico is lounging on a couch smoking a cigar. God, it fucking stinks.

"Done already?" Rico says, clapping his hands together as he stands to greet us. "I knew you were the man for the job. Bring his friends out and take them back to their hotel. I'll send my regards to your father."

Lincoln nods and storms out of the main door where we originally entered as Martin disappears to get the other two.

Well... this isn't awkward at all.

"Are you okay?" Maverick asks as he stalks toward me.

"Where is Linc?" Finn asks, searching the room.

I walk toward them, sinking into Mav's open arms. "I'm okay, and he's outside."

Finley watches me closely, but nods before heading outside.

"Come on, princess. Let's go," Mav says, keeping his arm around me as we leave the villa.

Rico's laugh sounds softly behind us as we leave, a shiver runs down my spine as he speaks. "I'll be seeing you again soon, Miss Royal."

The car drops us back off at our little beach cottage, but the sparkle and shine of the place is gone. This was meant to be our slice of paradise. Instead, it turned into just another thing the Knights took from us. The drive back was silent, and Lincoln still hasn't looked at me. He stomped inside the minute the car stopped, face like thunder, before the rest of us had even climbed from the car.

"You should go and speak to him, beautiful. We'll head down to the beach and give you guys a minute," Finley says softly, kissing me before grabbing Mav and dragging him toward the beach. My stomach flips. Facing Lincoln isn't the problem. The problem is making him see that I don't see him any different.

I know what he said to that man was true. It was between my life and his, and he picks me time and again.

I just wish he'd clue in to the fact that I'll pick him too.

No matter what.

I head into the cottage and hear the shower running. I bite my lip before deciding on a plan of action. Kicking off my shoes, I pad into the bathroom and find Lincoln furiously scrubbing at his skin. Any blood was cleaned off back at that villa, but it's like he's trying to scrub the whole thing away. Instead, he's just scrubbing himself raw.

My heart breaks for him, seeing him this fucked up over it all. Especially since I get the feeling that it wouldn't have been this bad if I hadn't been there.

"Lincoln," I start, but he either doesn't hear me or he's ignoring me.

Knowing him, it's the latter, but I'm not about to let him get away with it. Not this time.

I strip out of my clothing, shivering against the chill in the room before stepping toward the shower and opening the giant glass door.

"Lincoln Saint. You don't get to ignore me or hide from me. Not now."

His eyes bounce up, his gaze meeting mine, and my heart cracks at how broken he looks. "I don't want you to see me right now, Octavia. *Please.*"

Usually, that please would make me rethink everything. It would make me do whatever he asks. But not today.

"I'm not going anywhere, Linc. I see you, and nothing has changed. I see all of you." I step toward him and place my hands on his chest; a shudder runs through him at the touch. Leaning up on tiptoe, I kiss him softly, trying to show him how much I mean what I say.

It takes a second, but he softens and his arms wrap around me, pulling me flush to him as the hot spray of water washes over us both.

"You have no idea what I'm capable of." His voice is cold as ice. "But I can show you."

He grips my wrists hard enough to bruise. "I'll show you just how much of a monster I am."

I blink back the shock as the temperature between us goes from hot to freezing in the breath of one simple sentence.

"Linc?"

"Shut your fucking mouth, Octavia. For once in your life, just fucking listen." I rear back like he's just slapped me, and suddenly I'm back to the beginning of the year when he treated me like shit on the bottom of his shoe.

"What are you—" I don't have time to finish my thought, Linc transfers both of my wrists to just one hand and with his other, he grips my throat so hard I can almost feel the imminent bruising.

It hurts.

But not as much as his cold, icy stare. The void in his voice. The cruel twist of his lips.

He thinks he'll push me away if he shows me the monster inside him. He thinks I'll run away—cower—at his cruel treatment of me.

It's going to take a fuck load more than his pathetic theatrics to make me run away. Bring it fucking on, Lincoln Saint. I can take it.

The cold, hard tile of the shower slams against my back as Linc pushes me into the wall and levels his glacial glare on me.

I don't even flinch.

"You think you know everything. You think you understand

everything. You know fuck all, Octavia. The Lincoln you think you love is a lie. You want to know me? Here the fuck I am."

The smile that spreads across my lips only serves to piss him off more and within seconds, I'm turned and slammed against the tile wall, Linc at my back, kicking apart my legs and positioning himself behind me.

"You want the monster to fuck you, Octavia? You want to know what it's like to have all of me? Well," he brings his mouth to my ear and his dick aligns along my pussy as he finishes his thought, "don't say I didn't fucking warn you."

Without another warning, his cock is slammed inside me. No preamble, no coaxing. No loving strokes.

Letting go of my throat, he grabs onto my now wet and tangled hair and pulls. Hard. Hard enough to make me whimper. Tears spring to my eyes from the bite of pain. I wish I could say that I'm scared—that would be a normal reaction—but I'll never be afraid of him. And he needs to realize it.

Pulling as hard as he can without snapping my neck, Linc keeps his mouth at my ear, grunting like a fucking animal every time he bottoms out.

Fucking me like I'm nothing more than a whore he can use and then throw away.

So I do what I always do. I push back.

"Harder."

My voice is drowned out by the sound of the shower, the water beating down on the tile floor, so I try again, louder this time.

"Harder." I know he hears me this time, his tensing body a clear giveaway.

"You want harder? You want me to break you, little girl?"

Silly man. He thinks I don't know what he's doing.

"That's what I said. What's wrong? Is this all you've got?"

He roars before pummeling my pussy. My entire body slaps

against the wet tile every time his dick slams inside me, over and over and over again.

We are reduced to nothing more than grunts and curses, the silence saying so much more than words ever could.

By punishing me, by hurting me, he's punishing and hurting himself.

Except, he can't hurt me. I want this. I want it all. Every single thing he has to offer, because I won't ever get enough of him.

"Don't be a pussy, Lincoln. Fuck me like you mean it. Give it all to me."

Linc roars out his frustration and anger. His hand tightens in my hair, pulling me away from the wall seconds before he releases my wrists, forcing me to brace myself or else fall flat on my face.

Practically at a ninety-degree angle, Linc doesn't miss a beat, fucking me like a ragdoll, fucking me like he doesn't give a shit about me.

Like he's only doing it to wet his dick

Like he's ready to throw me away.

Like he hates me.

Fuck that.

"Harder."

I go to rub my clit out but he's quick to slap my hand away.

"This isn't about you, Octavia. You don't get to come."

Asshole.

My head hits the wall twice before Linc pulls out of my pussy and throws me down on the floor, his dick aimed at my face. Water washes down all over me and I can barely keep my eyes open but I realize what he's doing just as I feel the first jet of his cum on my cheek.

Fucker thinks this will debase me? Degrade me?

Kneeling like a good girl, I open my mouth and greedily try to lick up any of the cum that drips onto my lips and chin.

His stare is cold and unforgiving, but I know he's in there somewhere.

It's only when he turns the water off and steps out of the shower, leaving me there alone, that I realize the extent of his self-sabotage.

Idiot man.

He can't get rid of me that easily.

While our time away wasn't what we'd hoped it would be, I can't help but feel closer to Lincoln than I was when we left, even with everything that happened after I saw that side of him. He hasn't apologized, but I don't need him to. I told him I love him, dark parts and all, and I meant it. At least we did get a bit of a break... even if it wasn't as peaceful as we'd have liked.

Lincoln pulls the Porsche into his driveway, stopping by the garage. "Do you want to come in?"

I grin at him and nod. "Yes. I want to see East, too. It's been strange being away from him, even if it was only a few days."

He nods, putting his hand on my thigh as I unbuckle. "Octavia... what happened in Mexico..."

"It's already done and dealt with. We're good."

He smiles tightly at me. "I know, but maybe, let's just not mention it to East just yet. I don't want him to freak out. His heart... I know he's making progress in therapy, but it's only been six weeks. He still has a way to go. I don't want anything to delay his progress."

"I won't lie to him, but I won't offer the information either," I say grimly, not exactly happy he's putting me in this situation, but at the same time, I get it. He watches me closely before nodding and releasing me. I shake it off and climb from the car, excited to go and see East when the front door opens and Harrison stands in the doorway.

"Go home, Octavia. Lincoln and I have some things to discuss."

I look over at Lincoln, fully prepared to stand my ground and tell Harrison to fuck off, but Linc rubs a hand down his face before nodding at me. "It's okay, we'll call you later."

I guess with the whole, we're-not-supposed-to-be-in-a-relationship thing, and everything that happened in Mexico, we should've been expecting this, but fuck.

I grab my bag from Linc's trunk and start making my way down the drive. An icy drop of dread runs down my spine, and I can feel the heat of their eyes on me when I hear Harrison's voice. "I'll be seeing you soon, Miss Royal. Make sure not to be late."

TWENTY-TWO

LINCOLN

These last few days didn't exactly go to plan, and the message from Harrison on my phone before we boarded the plane home isn't exactly filling me with joy either. I tap my fingers on the steering wheel, counting it out to try and calm myself down as I pull up beside the garage. I look over at the girl who I've come to realize owns me entirely, but who I know I don't get to keep.

Harrison has made that all too clear, so until I can figure out a way extract myself from the claws he has in me, I'm fucked.

Regardless, I'm going to enjoy every fucking second with her that I can. At least for now, I can enjoy this moment with her. "Do you want to come in?"

She smiles at me and the tight knot in my chest loosens a little. Ever since she saw my monster, she's accepted all of the poison I've spat at her and still looks at me like that. I don't understand it, any of it, but I'll accept it like the selfish bastard I am. "Yes. I want to see East, too. It's been strange being away from him, even if it was only a few days."

I put my hand on her thigh, unable to keep myself from touching her. I think I'm starting to lose myself a little, but losing myself in her is basically all I've ever wanted. Though I already know what I'm about to ask of her is going to piss her off. Not that that means I won't ask it. I don't have a choice. "Octavia... what happened in Mexico..."

"It's already done and dealt with. We're good."

She thinks I mean what happened after, but I don't. Rico was not part of the plan when I took her away, and East is going to freak the fuck out when he finds out. I just want to know his heart is going to be okay before we tell him something that's going to stress him out. The smile on my face is tight before I let out a deep breath. "I know, but maybe, let's just not mention it to East just yet. I don't want him to freak out. His heart... I know he's making progress in therapy, but it's only been six weeks. He still has a way to go. I don't want anything to delay his progress."

"I won't lie to him, but I won't offer the information either." Yep, there's the fire I expected. I watch her closely, because I can't look at her without wanting to see all of her. Except this time I can see as the anger dances in her eyes before the reluctant acknowledgement that she knows I'm right settles on her.

She climbs from the car, my cold heart beating like a traitor as I watch her ass shimmy out. I know her smiles are for East, not for me. Especially right now, but I'm going to drink them in regardless.

I run a hand down my face, wondering exactly when I became such a sappy asshole, but since it's only her that will ever truly know it, I don't mind so much.

Climbing from the car, I slam the door shut when Harrison's voice fills the space. I clench my jaw at his arrival. Of course he couldn't give me just another day.

He stands in the doorway, glaring at the girl who owns my heart. I told him she's with Finn, but I'm positive he doesn't believe me.

"Go home, Octavia. Lincoln and I have some things to

discuss."

She looks over at me, that fire in her eyes that's enough to make my heart beat, but this isn't something I want her mixed up in if I can help it. I rub a hand down my face, wishing that Harrison would just drop dead on the spot, but knowing how unsatisfying that would be after all of my fantasies of ending him.

I nod at her and sigh. "It's okay, we'll call you later."

She looks pissed, but I'm hoping she understands. She might be okay with my monster, but if Harrison ever had reason to put his hands on her... I clench my jaw just at the thought. No fucking chance in Hell.

She grabs her bag from my trunk and walks away from us. I refuse to follow her movements, because while Harrison might not believe that I'm not with her, I don't want to give him anything to use against me if I can help it. I grab my own bag when his voice rings out around us. "I'll be seeing you soon, Miss Royal. Make sure not to be late."

Asshole.

I shoulder my bag and move toward him. "You wanted to speak to me?"

He puts his hands in his pockets and stares at me like he's trying to read my thoughts. He fucking wishes he had that power. Paranoid asshole that he is.

He turns and walks into the house, and I grit my teeth at his expectation that I'll just follow. Except I do because I have very little choice about much of anything. I follow him up to his study. East pops his head out of his door, smiling, but I shake my head in response and his smile drops. He notices me following Harrison, then looks as pissed as I feel, but closes the door and retreats.

I need to find out what happened here while I was gone. But first, I need to get Harrison off my back. Even if the reprieve is temporary.

Walking into his office, I close the door behind me, dropping my bag beside it as he stands on the other side of his desk.

I fucking hate this room. Memories assault me every time I step foot in here, no matter how much I want them to stay buried. I might not wear scars on my skin like Mav or Finn, but that's only because mine are buried deeper. Harrison made sure of it.

"You disappointed me." He clicks his tongue as he waves to the chair in front of his desk, the silent command ringing between us.

My feet feel like lead as I pick them up to make my way across the room. I fucking hate it in here, and he knows it. I take a few deep breaths, trying to stave off the weakness that rolls through me, the panic and dread that sits on my chest like an unwelcome visitor.

"You disappointed me in Mexico, Lincoln." His gaze is unwavering as he watches me, and I try not to buckle beneath the weight of it.

I clench my jaw, trying to keep my shit in check as I answer him. "I was promised a reprieve. It was agreed upon by the Conclave."

"Well I changed my fucking mind," he roars, throwing the glass in his hand across the room. The smash as it shatters against the wall makes my jaw tic, but I try to stay calm. He wants a reaction from me, and while I can't do much against him—for now anyway—this I can control.

"Apparently. I did what Rico asked, so I don't see what the problem is." I lean back in the chair, slipping into that cold, aloof mask, trying to cover the writhing panic that this room evokes. I'm not the same kid I was back then. I have no reason to fear this fucking room.

He glares at me, his hands shaking with his rage. Apparently he's drunk too much today. Usually he's better at keeping a lid on his shit. "You and the Royal need to be over."

"I'm not with the Royal."

He takes a deep breath, realizing that I'm not going to lose control like he has, and I watch as that cold mask slips over his skin, too. He takes a seat opposite me and watches me silently.

This is when you should be afraid of Harrison Saint. The loud, ballsy bullshit isn't anything terrifying. But the quiet calm... that's when he's dangerous.

"You will stop seeing the Royal and focus on Georgia or I will have her throat slit and make you watch as she bleeds out on the ground. I don't care what agreements her pathetic father made, if she continues to be a problem, she will be dealt with."

I remain as still as I can, despite my heart feeling like it's going to beat out of my chest. I grip the arms of the chair, and he smiles.

I'll slit his fucking throat and laugh as he bleeds.

"I told you, there is nothing between me and her." The words come out clipped, and his grin grows.

"Then there won't be a problem with you finally securing your engagement with Georgia, will there? And I'm sure you'll have no objections to sharing a room with her after the party I'm throwing next week. Where your engagement *will* be officially announced. If one more Royal gets in my way, I will watch them all burn."

"The Royals won't be a problem. I already told you I won't fuck the girl, but I'll play the rest of your game."

His eyes darken as he leans forward on the desk. "You will do whatever you have to, even if that means fucking her. Because if she doesn't believe the engagement is real, she will tell me, and your precious fucking bitch will reap the consequences."

He pauses, making sure I understand everything he isn't saying, then dismisses me like I'm nothing to him.

I stand and leave, knowing that all it would take is one phone call to fuck with his plans, but I won't risk Octavia like that.

Except that she's probably going to hate me for what I have to do to keep her safe anyway. But I'd rather she was breathing and hate me than love me and wind up dead.

TWENTY-THREE

OCTAVIA

S liding into my dad's Range Rover, I hook up my phone and let out a deep breath. The first day back to school after break always sucks, but knowing that my guys are going to be MIA today as a result of whatever the fuck happened with Harrison after he dismissed me yesterday makes it suck even harder.

But, for a change, I'm picking my girl up for coffee and breakfast before school. After Finley inspected my car at ass o'clock this morning while Lincoln and I went on our morning run. Apparently they're still not taking any chances. Not that I can be mad about it.

My phone buzzes as I start the engine and I smile when I see Smithy's name.

Smithy:
Good Morning, Miss Octavia. We shall be flying home this evening, so I will likely make it back to the house sometime tomorrow. I hope you had a wonderful break. Make sure to eat breakfast, and have a good day at school.

Me:

Morning! Totally fine, take your time and enjoy yourself **heart emoji** Heading for breakfast now. See, I can adult!

Smithy:
Yes, if you say so. **raised eyebrow emoji** See you soon.

I laugh as I place my phone back on its holder, putting on my morning playlist before pulling out of the drive. The trip to Indi's doesn't take very long, and I drop her a message to let her know I'm outside.

She emerges from the house, practically skipping toward the car and I can't help but grin at her. She is an enigma wrapped in a conundrum. She's such a bad early morning person, but get her ready for the day and she has so much pep, it makes you sick.

She bounces into the car, her blue fishtail braid swinging free, and hugs me like she hasn't seen me in four months, not four days.

"Morning!" she practically sings as she squeezes me. "How was Mexico?"

"It was good. Maybe a little too... exciting at times, but good."

"Oh no. What did those assholes do now?" She frowns as she pulls her seatbelt on, and I pull away from the curb.

"Not them. The Knights. It's nothing, but they won't be at school today."

"I did wonder why I got you back for the morning. I'm not sad about it, but is everything okay?"

I shrug as I stop at the light, waiting for the green. "I have no idea. I think so. Lincoln didn't give much away this morning—shock, horror—but I like to think if it was really bad, then he'd tell me."

"How is he doing? Juggling the whole Georgia thing?"

"Honestly, he doesn't say much about her. Which I guess is a good sign, but I don't really know. He doesn't want to upset me by talking about her, so he doesn't say much. I know he's ready for the charade to be over and that's about it."

"I don't blame him, poor guy." She frowns as she taps away on her screen. "But I'm glad you had a decent break, even if it did come with a little excitement. Now back to the drama of ECP. You heard anything from Blair?"

I bark out a laugh as we pull into the Starbucks drive-thru. "Never in a million years is the answer to that question going to be a yes. Why, what did you hear?"

"That your uncle is in deep shit. Like, royally fucked. Oh, look, I'm punny." She giggles before dropping the smile and getting all stern again. "But for reals, I think it's going to get bad. We might get another paparazzi swarm here."

I groan as we pull up to the mic. "Just what I need. You want your usual?"

"Course." She grins.

I order our usual drinks before pulling around to the next window, wondering how the fuck I'm going to deal with another influx of paparazzi if it happens. With everything that's going on with the Knights, the last thing I need is people watching my every move and trying to capture it on camera. I've just finally gotten used to not having to hide everything I do.

What a pile of ass.

I grab our drinks and toasted sandwiches, handing them to Indi before I head toward the school. "Have they announced official charges yet?"

"Not that I've read. I've been following it online as much as I can. They're playing it close to the vest, but I think they are going to be out a lot of money when all the details come out. There is going to be a lot of hate thrown in his direction. Blair and Vivianne might not be able to stay in the Cove if it gets too bad."

"What a shame," I deadpan, rolling my eyes. "Like I feel for them, but also, they can get fucked."

We pull into the parking lot and I park in Lincoln's usual spot. It's weird not seeing their cars here. "Let's do this shall we?"

"At least Ms. Summers won't be too crazy this morning. We handed in our assignment already. Pretty sure it's just going to be exam prep between now and the end of the year," she says cheerily as she hands me my drink before climbing from the car. I follow suit, grabbing my bag from behind her chair and making sure to double check that I've locked the doors. I don't exactly have a great track record with cars, so I'm trying to make sure I look after Dad's car. Even if it is technically mine now, I guess.

We head inside, dropping our stuff off at our lockers before heading to the library, slipping into our usual early morning study spot. I munch on my toasted sandwich while I read through my Business textbook, trying to make sure I'm up to date with the reading before today's class.

We're sitting quietly, reading and prepping for the day, when a shadow descends over the table. I sigh when I look up and find Blair staring down at us. "What do you want, Blair?"

She still looks haughty as fuck, looking down her nose at me like I'm beneath her. If she wants my help, she needs to sort out her resting bitch face.

"All of our assets have been frozen, and we need to sort Dad's legal fees." Her face twists, like I just stabbed her. "Mom asked if you would help us. We're trying to make it go away quietly, and to do that we need a Knight lawyer."

"What exactly do you want me to do, Blair?"

She sighs dramatically, like I'm the one asking her for a favor. Jesus fucking Christ, this girl needs to get a grip. "I need you to speak to Chase Armstrong. He's a lawyer, the best in town. He's a Conclave member. We need him."

Indi's eyes go wide at the mention of East's dad. Pretty sure *that* isn't public news yet, so I shake my head subtly. "I'll see what I can do."

She nods, looking like she's sucked on a lemon. "Thank you."

She doesn't say another word before turning on her heel and storming away, head held high like she's still the queen bee around here. I have a feeling even with everything going on, she's going to come out on top.

"Do you think she knows?" Indi asks quietly.

I shake my head. "I don't know how she could. No one outside of you, me, Harrison, and the guys knows. Pretty sure they haven't even mentioned it to the Conclave. Harrison wouldn't like that sort of embarrassment," I say rolling my eyes. "I'll speak to the others about it when I see them next."

The bell rings and we're packing our stuff up when she asks, "Are you going to speak to Chase?"

"I said I would," I say with a shrug. "I doubt it'll make much of a difference, but it can't hurt right? Plus, if it can be kept quiet-ish, and I avoid my house being swarmed again, then I'm all for it."

I let out a deep sigh as I pick up my books and drop my trash in the can beside the table. Here's hoping this goes the way I want it to. I am not feeling any more chaos in my life than already exists.

Today is kicking my ass.

If I thought school without the guys was bad yesterday, it's nothing compared to today. Mikayla and the bitch squad have ramped up their torture of the freshmen threefold, and I've about had enough of it. I don't want to be queen, and Blair might have been an asshole, but even she seemed to have some limits.

Mikayla is ruthless and needs kicking down a peg or two. It's only lunchtime, and I've already seen more girls crying in the last two days than I have in my entire year here so far. I leave class and head toward my locker so I can meet Indi, and another girl runs past me toward the bathroom, tears staining her cheeks.

I find a vibrating Indi, clenching her fists at my locker.

"What's wrong?" I ask, wide-eyed. It takes a lot to make my sunshine friend this angry. I pop my stuff in my locker and give her my full attention.

"Mikayla," she growls. "She went full tyrant in our last class, then terrorized a group of freshmen that were waiting in the hall afterward. She needs to be stopped. I'd take Blair over this bitch."

"Funny, I was just thinking the same thing. I'm just not sure how." I frown, wishing I had a better idea. Bringing down empires is definitely more Blair's thing. She's by far the more cold and calculating one of us. Sometimes I wish I had a bit more of that in me, but cold and calculating just isn't who I am.

Angry and vengeful? Sometimes, yes.

But I definitely didn't get the traits from the family tree that would handle this situation best.

I look up and spot Blair walking past us, and figure fuck it. "Blair, hold up."

She pauses, turning to look at us, eyebrow raised. "What?"

"How does getting your crown back and knocking Mikayla down a few steps sound?" The enemy of my enemy and all that.

She heads toward us, obviously interested, but more than a little wary. "Why would you help me?"

"I'm not helping you. I'm helping the freshmen. You might be a bitch, but she's a tyrant." I shrug as she barks out a laugh. "Do you want to help or not?"

"I'm in, what did you have in mind?" she asks, folding her arms over her chest.

I grin wide. This mini truce might just work, and I can feel good about having done something positive with my time here. Even if it's not *that* great. "Well you see... that's where you come in."

"What does that mean?"

"It means," Indi says sarcastically, "that we need your evil genius brain."

Blair walks with us to the cafeteria as Indi explains what we want from her. "Sounds good, I've already got an idea but let me sit on it and we'll talk tomorrow. Now if you'll excuse me, I'd rather not walk in there with you both."

She flicks her blonde hair over her shoulder and heads inside, leaving me slack-jawed.

"That girl has got some fucking nerve," Indi growls under her breath.

I laugh, shaking my head. "I think I'd be more shocked if she did anything else. Come on, let's head inside. The guys will be here soon and I'd rather eat something before Mav arrives and tries to steal half my lunch."

She grins at me, all thoughts of Blair gone. "I get the feeling he'd rather eat something else."

I laugh at her as we head toward the line. "You're as bad as he is."

We walk in, finding the guy in question already in line. He turns as we enter and grins at me. When we reach him, he pulls me into his side and smacks a kiss on my cheek. The big dork.

"You're in a good mood," Indi snarks at him, and I clamp my lips together.

"What's wrong, Pixie Spice? You not getting enough good D? You should really speak to those Kings, shouldn't hold out on a girl." I elbow him in the side, rewarded with an *ooph* and a smile from Indi.

She skips past him and picks up a tray. "Keep talking about my kitty cat and see how much Ryker likes it." She winks before grabbing her food.

"I'd rather focus on *your* pussy," he growls into my ear, and heat spills across my chest. "Sleepover tonight?"

"I'm going to see East after school, but sure, why not?" I grin and he slaps my ass.

"That's my girl. Now, let's get some grub. You're going to need the energy for later."

Lincoln pulls into his garage, turning off the car before he looks over at me. He has barely spoken to me since Harrison dismissed me on Sunday, and I've had about enough of it.

"Are you going to tell me what happened?" My words come out snappier than I wanted, but I'm sick of the silent treatment. Going backward isn't what I want. We've played this game before, I'll be fucked if we go back.

"There's nothing to tell. Harrison doesn't want me spending time with you. He wants me to focus on Georgia. My *fiancée*. This isn't news," he snaps right back before climbing from the car and slamming the door.

"Why are you being such a dickhead?" I yell at him as I climb from the car. He spins on the spot and his eyes dance with fire before he narrows them at me.

"This is just who I am, Octavia. Take it or fucking leave it. I'm not changing. Not for you. Not for anyone."

I stand there, speechless, as he storms away from me.

What the fuck is going on with him? There has to be more to it than he's telling me. He doesn't usually just snap at me like that.

I'm obviously not going to find out what it is right now, not when he's in whatever mood it is that he's in, so I paint a smile on my face and head into the house tentatively.

I find East in the hall, about to head upstairs.

"Hey, you."

"Hey, yourself. Come to keep the bedridden company?" He grins so I know he isn't as forlorn as his words make him out to be, so I slip over to him and he kisses me like I'm oxygen and he's struggling to breathe.

When I pull back to find air, he grins down at me. He looks happy. "How was your appointment today?"

"It was really good. Doc said my age and health are on my side. Incision is still looking good, bloodwork was good, no signs of infection. Sternum and muscle healing is basically done, likely thanks to my age. Things are looking real good. Apparently I'm very lucky."

"Really? That's freaking amazing news!" I hug him gently and my heart soars that he's doing so well. The severity of his injuries have been weighing on me a lot. It was my fault he got shot. My fault he nearly died—that he technically *did* die.

"Yeah I'm not sad about it, and my day is even better now you're here."

I laugh softly at him. "You're such a cheeseball. So do you even need to still be cooped up in your room?"

"No, not really, but Harrison is on the warpath, so I'm staying out of his way. Plus, I was hoping you'd swing by tonight, too. Because I got some other good news today. Since I'm basically all healed up..."

Quirking a brow at him, I wait for him to continue.

"Oh no, sweetheart. I'm going to show you rather than tell you. It's more fun that way."

"Where are we going?" I laugh as he takes my hand. This playful side of him is fun, I've kind of missed it among all of the crazy we've been juggling.

"Show, not tell, remember." He grins, wagging his brows at me.

"Then by all means, show away."

He tugs me up the stairs, pulling me into his bedroom and closes the door behind us before pinning me against the door. "Fuck, I missed you."

His words are breathy before he kisses me like a starving man and I'm his favorite meal. I tangle my hands in his hair as he presses against me, his dick very much making itself known.

"I thought you weren't allowed to exert yourself," I pant as he pulls away. He just grins.

"Good news, remember?"

"Oh," I say, eyes wide. "Are you sure?"

He grins at me, devilishly. "Doc said yes, I'm not about to question it."

My smile matches his as I run my nails down his chest, careful of the scar I know is beneath his t-shirt. "Who are we to question medical advice?"

"My thoughts exactly." He smirks before kissing me again.

We are all tongues and lips and lost breaths as he cages my face in the palm of his hands like I'm the one who's fragile.

It doesn't matter though, because the way he holds me so reverently makes me feel like I'm everything. Like I'm his whole world.

One of his thighs pushes between my legs, just below my skirt that I can feel riding up my thighs. Reaching down, I unbutton my blazer and throw it blindly to the side, hoping it doesn't break anything. Without missing a beat, I kick off my shoes, my concentration still very much on East and his talented mouth.

The harder he kisses me, the more his hands roam, the more turned on I get. I don't have to touch myself to know my panties are getting soaked with how much I need him.

"Touch me, V. Don't hold back." In the back of my mind, I know I shouldn't get carried away, I know I need to be mindful of his injury, even if he says he's okay, but at his words my fingers curl around the fabric of his shirt until I'm fisting it with an urgency that we can both feel.

"That's it. Fuck me, you're so wet."

My pussy on his thigh, I ride him—chasing my pleasure—as his mouth slams back onto mine.

I don't know how long he kisses me but I relish every second of it. Sometimes, a kiss is just a kiss. But sometimes? It's a fucking volcano. Explosive, hot, destructive.

Letting go of my face, East runs his hands down my arms until he reaches the hem of my shirt before unbuttoning and ripping it off then throwing it into the depths of the room, pausing our kiss for the briefest of seconds.

Our tongues are once again fighting for control, caressing until we have to break apart for breath.

East rests his forehead on mine and, with his eyes closed, he stays there for a few seconds, his chest heaving.

"Are you okay?" I ask, alarmed that maybe he's not up to this yet.

"I'm good, V. Just trying to decide what to do to you first." When he opens his eyes, his gaze is full of heat, a spark of something that makes my heart rate skyrocket. If I thought I was wet before, I'm fucking soaked now.

He kisses me once more, abrupt and hurried, then pulls away again, his teeth trapping my bottom lip as he slowly releases it.

When his gaze travels to my chest, the swell of my breasts peeking out from beneath my bra, I rely on the door to keep me upright. East is attentive and loving, but I can't forget that he's a Saint at heart and his dominant side is never far from the surface.

Hands at the cups of my bra, East glances up at me, a mischievous glint telling me he's about to do something that might piss me off.

The sound of ripping fabric confirms that, yes, he's going to get an earful but... not now. Right now, I just can't bring myself to give a shit.

"That's better," he says right before his mouth is on my nipple, sucking and pulling until I'm a mess of hormones running wild in my blood.

Too soon, his mouth is gone. When I open my eyes, he's on his knees pulling my skirt and panties off before placing his mouth on my pussy, licking up every drop that I give him.

My head bangs against the door as my hips push into his mouth. I need more, so I plant my hand on his head and without questioning my actions, I hold him steady as I basically try to fuck his face, searching out the friction on my clit and chasing my orgasm.

Until his mouth is gone.

My lids fly open. My eyes, wild with lust, search him out and when I find him, he's sitting on his haunches watching me.

"Who's in charge, V?"

What?

I must voice my question aloud because he asks again.

"Who's in fucking charge, V?"

"You?"

"Is that a question?"

"No?"

Taking my hand, he places it on his head then warns, "I fuck your pussy, V. I'm in charge." Without actually saying the words, I understand that me taking control of the situation is not in the cards.

I suppose after what happened, he deserves to feel a little control in his life.

I get it. That's why I let him call the shots. Also, because it's fucking hot.

With his mouth back on my pussy, East works his magic and no more than a minute later, I'm coming all over his tongue and chin and it's the hottest fucking thing in the world. My entire body shakes with the aftermath of the orgasm, my legs barely able to keep me upright.

When East pulls back, he looks straight into my eyes—wiping his mouth with the back of his hand—and smiles like a man crazed.

"I love eating your pussy."

Once he stands, I don't have time to catch my breath as I'm thrown over his shoulder in a fireman's hold. East carries me across the room and carefully places me on the bed while he stays on the side, watching me.

"You might be okay, but you probably shouldn't be carrying me," I say, frowning up at him, unable to stop the worry that floods me.

"Don't freak out, V. Everything is fine."

East reaches back and pulls the collar of his shirt up and over his head, flinging it to the side before he pushes his gray sweats down and simply steps out of them before he joins me in bed.

I gasp at the sight of his scar but I try to remember that if the doc said it's good, who the fuck am I to argue?

When East joins me in the bed, he pulls the covers up above our heads as we come together, face-to-face—chest to chest—with our legs intertwined and my pussy riding his thigh.

Then he brings our mouths into another heated kiss where I can taste myself on his lips. It should probably be weird how erotic that is, but I'm not about to question it.

Positioning us just perfectly so, East takes the back of my thigh and hikes it up his waist as his cock finds itself inside me in one smooth, invigorating slide. We're both breathless again. The fullness of him, the intimate position in our man-made cocoon of sheets and covers, makes it feel like the outside world doesn't exist. The only important thing is him and me.

His hips piston back and forth, my clit searching out the friction of his groin as he takes his time fucking me, almost painfully slowly. Deliberately.

I can feel every delicious inch of him as he glides out, the sounds of my wet pussy and our accelerating breaths all we can hear.

We don't talk, our bodies are speaking loudly and clearly. We aren't fucking, really. He's making long and intense love to me, and that slow burn is working its magic on me. But he's not immune to it, either.

East shifts just a little so that he's at a better angle, giving me access to his back with my nails. This way, he can thrust harder, fuck me deeper, and with every slam inside me, my nails dig deeper, my groans grow longer. My grunts a little louder.

"I need you to come all over my dick, V. Give it all to me."

With his mouth at my neck, my hands on his back, his finger searches out my clit and the moment he circles it just once, I'm coming like I haven't climaxed in a lifetime.

I gulp down air as the tsunami that is my orgasm grips me in my lower belly before traveling up my chest and into my throat, turning into a desperate scream.

East groans, his own climax fueled by mine.

Seconds later, we are both trying to come down from the intensity of our lovemaking when he kisses my lips once more and repeats his words from earlier.

"Fuck, I missed you."

TWENTY-FOUR

OCTAVIA

After my evening with East, and Maverick staying over last night, I feel like a hussy. A very satisfied hussy, but a hussy nonetheless. Which makes my run with Lincoln even more frustrating. He met me at my gate, like he does every morning, but I feel like we've gone backward about four months. He's barely spoken to me, and when he has, I wouldn't call it talking so much as I'd call it snapping.

I wish he'd just let me in. That he'd share whatever the hell is eating at him. But I've tried to ask him half a dozen times what's wrong and nearly lost my head, so I don't see that happening any time soon.

He runs two paces in front of me, the same way we've been doing since everything happened with Panda, but today, he takes a different turn after we pass the pier.

"Where are we going?"

He doesn't answer and I want to throw my fucking sneaker at the back of his head, but rather than let him win and see how pissed I am, I push through his punishing pace so I can keep up with him. There's no way I'm giving him the satisfaction. Especially not when he's in this mood.

We head up the hill, and I swear my lungs feel like they're going to explode between his pace and this fucking incline.

"Lincoln!" I half shout, half huff, because fuck.

He doesn't pause, he just keeps going. Whatever demons are riding him that he's trying to exorcize this morning must be insane, because even in asshole mode, he never ignored me.

Not since I learned the truth of everything.

Not like this.

I call his name again, and he finally slows. Glancing back, he finds me in the middle of the road, bent in two, sucking in air.

"What are you doing?" he barks, while running in place. "We don't have time to slow. You need to be faster. If you're not in pristine shape, you're going to get yourself killed."

And then it dawns on me.

The demon riding him is me.

My meeting with the Conclave.

Lincoln Saint is *afraid* and it's driving him insane.

I stand up straight and walk toward him. "Is that what's wrong? The last few days? Is that what this has all been about?"

He stops all movement, staring at me before tugging on his hair. "Everything I've ever tried to do is about keeping you alive. Keeping you safe. And now the Conclave wants to meet with you, but Harrison won't tell me a goddamn thing about you. He wants me focused on Georgia and sealing his deal. You should not be on my radar as far as he's concerned, but he doesn't see that you are *everything*."

I place my hand on his chest, his racing heart pounds beneath it as he looks at me with wild eyes.

"It seems like people have been coming for me my entire life, Lincoln. I've survived this long. We just need to play their game, find out what it is they want, and then we can make a plan."

"You don't understand. The contract Stone made... that potentially jeopardizes everything Harrison holds dear. If he sees you as a threat to his seat—his power—he'll kill you without a second thought if he thinks he can get away with it. The only thing keeping him from it right now is the fact that everyone knows about the deal. It would be obvious it was him. There might not be a ton of rules in the Knights, but killing other members, especially Conclave members…"

He trails off and it occurs to me that if that's the line, then it's possible they've already crossed it. If Panda is to be believed anyway.

"Is that why no one knows if Edward killed my dad? Because it's against the rules to kill another Conclave member?"

"Yes and no." He sighs. "Technically, Stone wasn't a member of the Conclave anymore. The seat was just empty. The reason I can't get a straight answer about your dad is because *if* that's what happened, it's likely it was just between Harrison and Edward, and neither of them is going to say a goddamn thing."

"That makes sense," I muse. "When am I supposed to be meeting with the Conclave? I haven't heard anything. I assume I'm going to be summoned?"

He nods, pulling us out of the road to stand on the pavement. "Yes, you'll be summoned, but again, I don't know when and it's driving me fucking insane. I can't keep you safe if I don't know the plan, and that's probably Harrison's fucking idea."

His phone buzzes and his mouth twists. "Finn has news about who was working with Evan."

My eyes go wide. It's not like I'd forgotten about it, but I was beginning to think we'd never know since P killed himself. "What did he say?"

"Nothing but that. It's safer not to say anything in a message."

Well I mean, duh, Octavia.

"Okay," I say, trying not to be disappointed. I know Finley won't keep me on tenterhooks for too long. That's Lincoln's game.

"So the Conclave?" I ask as we start jogging up the hill.

He glances over at me, frowning again. "I'll try and get some information from Chase, but considering his known stance on everything, I'm not sure how much use he'll be either."

Shit. "I need to speak to Chase anyway, so maybe I could ask him."

"What the fuck do you need to speak to him about?"

We reach the crest of the hill and I could almost do a happy dance realizing the rest of the way home is downhill. "Blair came to speak to me. Nate needs a lawyer and funds for said lawyer. She asked me if I'd speak to him."

"Does she know about him and East?"

"I doubt it, but who knows? This place is full of the worst kept secrets. She didn't make out like she knew, so I'm assuming not." He stays quiet for the rest of the run home and doesn't say another word until I key in the code on my gate.

"Leave Chase to me. I'll speak to him for Blair too. The less you have to do with the Knights, the better."

He turns and stalks off up his drive without another word, leaving me staring at his back as he walks away from me. Just when I thought he was slipping out of asshole mode, he whips it straight back out.

One day I'll understand Lincoln Saint, but today is not that day.

I end up not having any time to speak to Finley about what he learned about Panda's accomplice, because my morning turned into a whirlwind of Indi having a meltdown over Alexander showing up in the Cove last night and being spotted by the Kings.

So when Blair accosts me at my locker, I know my day likely isn't going to get any better. "Did you speak to Chase yet?"

"No, Blair. I haven't spoken to Chase yet. Lincoln is going to speak to him, since he actually knows him." I close the door to my locker and turn to face her.

She rolls her eyes at me and it takes all of my strength of will not to just slap the condescending look off her face. "You'll never survive their world if you let them do everything for you."

I let out a sigh and fold my arms across my chest. "If I want your advice, Blair, I'll ask for it. Was there anything else?"

"I have an idea of how to bring Mikayla down, but you're not going to like it."

"Of course I'm not, you came up with it. But that was the whole idea. What's the plan?"

She grins, and I swear my blood turns to ice. "It involves Raleigh."

"Blair—" I start but she cuts me off.

"I know, he's a monster. But he's a monster I have on a leash, even if everyone thinks I don't."

I quirk a brow and lean against my locker. "I'm listening."

She tells me her diabolical plan as we walk toward the library where I said I'd meet Indi to study over lunch.

"You're twisted, you know that?"

"Thanks," she grins. "So I won't ask if you approve, but are you okay to do your part?"

I bite the inside of my cheek, just as a girl appears from the bathroom, still crying, clutching her blazer to her chest, her shirt in ribbons.

"I'm in," is all I say before I approach the girl.

"Do you need a shirt?" I ask her, and she looks up at me, wide-eyed. Like she's afraid of me.

"N...n...no," she stammers, eyes darting around us like she thinks it's an ambush.

I open the bathroom door and wave her in. "In."

She scampers back into the bathroom, and I call in after her. "I'll just be two minutes."

I haul ass into the library, finding Indi at our usual table. "Do you have a spare shirt?"

"I always have spares. Why what happened?" she asks, looking me over, confused.

"Girl in the bathroom down the hall, shirt in shreds."

She frowns harder. "I swear to God, we need to deal with Mikayla. If I wasn't so opposed to just outright killing people…"

"I mean, fair, she's the devil incarnate."

"I never thought I'd miss Blair being the Queen Bitch. You wait here, I'll grab the shirt and help the girl. You're a little more intimidating than I am."

My jaw drops and she laughs as she bounces away from me. While I'm glad she's helping the girl, I hate the thought that the girl was scared of me.

I'm not intimidating.

I'm the nice Royal.

Or so I thought.

Shit.

I chew on it, while I unpack my stuff onto the table. It's only a few minutes before she flounces back in, all smiles. "All sorted, and Florence is all smiles again. She's a sophomore, never had any issues, even tried out for the cheer squad and did okay. But apparently she looked at Mikayla wrong today."

She drops into her seat opposite me and opens her text book.

"I'm not intimidating… am I?"

She bursts out laughing, literally holding her stomach as she cries with laughter. "V, I love and adore you. I know you're like, the nicest human, but yeah, you come off as intimidating. And having those three at your side most of the time doesn't help. You're the girl who overcame and rose above. If anyone was going to be able to take the throne from Blair, it would've been you, but you don't want it, so it fell to the she-devil."

I shake my head, that's so twisted.

"You have a very humble way of viewing who you are, and those around you, but from the outside, yeah you're still Octavia Royal, The Nation's Princess." She shrugs and pulls a soda from her bag.

"I guess I thought everyone just kinda forgot about all of that. I'm just me."

The doors to the library swing open, and the three dark knights in question enter like the three horsemen of the apocalypse—which feels oddly fitting for them.

Halloween idea next year!

Mav rubs his hand on the top of Indi's hair before dropping to the chair next to her. She punches his arm and ends up shaking out her hand like it hurt.

We really need to teach that girl to fight properly.

Lincoln takes the seat between Indi and I and Finn sits on my other side. They both seem tense as fuck and my stomach knots.

What the fuck did Finley find in his search?

"Just tell me, I can't take any more tension today. A girl my age should not live through this sort of stress." I sigh, looking at Finn.

"Wait, what did I miss?" Indi asks, looking around the table.

"Finley found a lead on who was helping Evan when he took Octavia. He's been tracing the Dranas lead, and with Luc's help, we finally got some answers." Lincoln's voice is solemn and my heart pounds against my chest.

"Will someone please just tell me what the hell you think you've found?"

Finley looks down at the desk before looking back up at me and the pain in his eyes breaks me. I almost don't want to know. The words nearly fall out of my mouth, but I shove the weaker parts of me down and stay strong, even when I don't want to.

"I found out the name of the person who booked the team with Dranas. V, I…"

He trails off, looking at Lincoln, like he doesn't want to have to tell me. So I drag my gaze to Lincoln, who looks like he wants to tell me about as much as he'd like to cut off his right hand. But he nods at Finn and turns to me anyway. "The name of the person who booked the team was James Smith."

"How many more stores do you want to hit?" I groan as Indi drags me into another boutique. We've been shopping for an hour and I'm dragging already. Today's Professional Development Day means we have a free Friday, which gave us chance to shop for the stupid Knight ball Finley dropped on me late last night.

He's still looking into the Dranas thing, because I flat out *refuse* to believe Smithy had anything to do with it. I don't care if the money trail magically lines up, that shit can be faked. Also, who would be stupid enough to book something like that in their own name.

And I don't care that Lincoln said it would be genius to do exactly that, *because* no one would believe it.

It's so stupid. I can barely focus on a fun day with Indi because I'm tripping over everything else going on.

"Earth to V," Indi says, shaking me to get my attention.

"Sorry, I spaced."

"Oh, I noticed. You okay?"

I shake my head. "Not really. There's too much going on. It's hard to work out which way is up sometimes. I can't help but wonder what it would be like to be a normal seventeen-year-old. Just focused on boys and college and thinking that was literally the end of the world."

She frowns at me, tugging me deeper into the store, away from the ears of the three girls behind the counter. "Do you want me to come tonight?"

"I love you, but fuck no. I don't want you in their crosshairs. Plus there is no way Ryker is going to *not* kill me if I lead you into that viper's nest."

She snorts. "That's true, but he also doesn't rule my life. If you want me there, I'm so there."

I chew the inside of my cheek. It would be awesome to have her with me, she'd be the perfect wing woman, but I also never want her in danger ever again because of me.

"Thank you. Let me talk to Lincoln and Finley, make sure there's no reason to not bring you—anything that could get you killed. But let's get you a dress just in case."

"Hell fucking yes. Let's do this!"

I drop a message in the group chat, asking the question, then put my phone away to continue with our penis-free day.

We spend the next hour trying on dozens of dresses, having a full-on 90's *Clueless* fashion show between us in the changing rooms, snapping way more selfies than any person needs, but it's so much fun that I forget about the chaos of my life for a blip of time and actually enjoy myself.

"Did you decide on a dress?" Indi asks as she comes out of the changing room, redressed with a dress back over her arm.

"Yeah, I like the sapphire one."

"Ooh! I love that. And it'll look amazing next to my red one." She winks. "I'm going to get Gracie to do my hair tomorrow, I'm thinking new extensions, all black, crazy long and curled. It'll look amazing with this dress."

"You always look amazing. Do you think Gracie can squeeze me in too?"

"I have zero doubt that she can." She grins at me as we head to the counter. "Do we need shoes?"

"Of course we need shoes." I grin at her. It's fun being able to treat her. I feel like we haven't done enough of this lately and it fucking sucks. I'm hoping this impending doom of a meeting with the Knights will straighten shit out so I can at least start to plan my life out again. I'm past thinking I can just escape it. I know too much to be stupid enough to think that.

But rather than drown under the wave, I'm going to follow the current and try to push back to the surface.

That has to be the better idea, right?

Indi grabs a pair of kitten heels, which I add to the counter, deciding on wearing a pair I already have because my Choos are comfy as fuck. I check out our stuff and we make our way back to the car. My phone buzzes in my pocket and I see Sir Grumpalot's name on the screen.

Lincoln:
No reason why not.

To the point as ever. I wish he'd pull his head out of his ass. I know he has a lot on his mind, we all do, but using me as his emotional punching bag is a shitty thing to do.

"Looks like we're good to go to this thing together," I tell her as we slide into the Range Rover.

"Woop. I'll tell the boys the plan once I'm there. You okay taking my dress back to your place? I figured Gracie can come there, do our hair, and we can just get ready without making the extra stops. It'll be like Homecoming, just better."

"Sounds good," I say, nodding. Smithy went out of town with Matthew this morning and while I'm so happy he's happy, I miss the old guy. Hopefully when life calms down, I'll get to spend some more time with him, too.

Another reason there is no way he was the one working with Panda. He's too busy with his new beau to be meddling in the chaos of my life.

I pull away from the curb, focusing back on the road, when

Indi puts *Girls Need Girls* by Sophia Scott on the playlist. "This song, right here. I'm declaring this our song."

I laugh as I listen along to the lyrics. "Hell yeah it is. This is our *jam!*"

I lie back on my sofa with a groan. Between running, shopping, and just this week in general, I need a spa day. I love Indi, but she shops like a freaking beast. But at least we have outfits for tomorrow.

It was just a morning of shopping, but I'm beat, and I am *not* looking forward to this Knight party. Not even a little. Being the show pony at a Knight event isn't on my fun time list, but since my presence was requested by Harrison, I'm hoping I get some answers about what it is they want from me.

That this isn't just another dick measuring contest like last time.

Though Lincoln and Finley don't seem as optimistic as I'm trying to be about it all.

My phone buzzes in my pocket, pulling me from the thoughts that have stopped me sleeping properly the last few nights, and I smile when I see the guys' names on my screen. I pull up the group chat thread and try not to laugh.

Maverick:
Princess... what ya doinnnnn?

Finley:
You're such a sap, Mav. But yeah, what are you doing?

Lincoln:
What they mean is, come over here.

Oh look, he seems to have put asshole mode on the back burner. Well kind of.

East:
What my brother means, is please **eye roll**

Lincoln:
She knew what I meant.

Maverick:
Stop being an asshole otherwise she won't come and play.

Me:
Play? What are we playing?

Maverick:
Wags brows come and find out.

I give in and laugh, because he's ridiculous, but curiosity is definitely going to kill this cat.

Me:
As long as I get a foot rub out of this, I'm down. I am so not ready for tomorrow night.

I stand up and stretch, glad I'm still feeling kinda cute in my denim skirt and bralette. I tie the plaid shirt in a knot at my stomach and slip my Converse back on before heading next door.

Lincoln:
We're in the basement.

Different. I slip in the back door and head down to the

basement. The sounds of *Closer* by Nine Inch Nails blast through the speakers, the bass vibrating through my body as I skip down the stairs. I pause when I reach the bottom of the steps, Finley and Maverick are in the boxing ring while Lincoln runs on a treadmill and East lounges on one of the benches.

"You assholes think this is playing?" I fold my arms over my chest, because this wasn't the sort of play I had in mind. Though watching the four of them get sweaty isn't exactly my idea of a bad time either.

Maverick grins at me from the ring. "What's up, princess? Don't want to get sweaty?"

I bark out a laugh and head toward the ring. "More self-defense today?"

"No, we thought there were more fun ways to get sweaty with you. Did you bring a swimsuit?"

"No one said I needed one."

"You don't. Swimsuits aren't required in my hot tub," Lincoln adds from where he runs on the treadmill.

I swear I'm getting whiplash from his emotional back and forth. When the others are around, he's this version, but the second we're truly alone, he turns back into asshole mode.

I don't say anything because I don't want to provoke the asshole side of him, and the nympho side of me is down for being around all of them sans clothing. Maybe this is how I'll reach him. I peel off my shirt and kick off my shoes, practically skipping toward the door where I know the hot tub and pool are down here. "Last one in loses."

"What do we lose, princess?" Mav jumps over the ropes, his muscles tensing with the effort, and it makes my mouth water. Finn, just shakes his head at Mav's antics—bending enough to exit the ring like a normal person.

"You don't get your dick sucked, asshole," Linc calls out from the treadmill, slowing his run to a walk and then a stop before he turns off the machine completely.

Looking over my shoulder as I reach the door to the hot tub, I see East hot on my heels.

Mav is right behind him and Finn is following with his long strides that make it seem like he's bored.

But I know better.

He's focused. Totally different thing. Focused, I'll enjoy.

At the tub, I push my skirt down and kick it to the nearest wooden bench and turn to see East right there, inches from me.

"I never get tired of seeing your naked body, V." Threading his fingers through my hair, he curls them around the strands and brings our mouths together in a kiss so passionate I feel my juices pooling onto my panties. We're all lips and tongues and teeth, my hands grabbing onto his forearms as he grips his free hand to my hip and obliterates the offensive space between our bodies.

My hips automatically search out some kind of friction when I feel the heat at my back. It's Mav. His scent is unmistakable. While East is devouring my mouth, Mav brings a finger around and circles my clit through my panties, using the lace to add a pinch of rough to the experience.

I barely register the sound of water when East pulls back, taking my bottom lip with his teeth—his eyes glinting with fire—and Mav places an open-mouthed kiss on my shoulder before he's gone.

"Come on, babe. Let's get in." East's words are whispered against my mouth and just as he finishes his last word, Linc walks through the double doors and every atom in the room charges with an electricity only he can conjure.

Suddenly, the space is filled with barely sustained anticipation. We're ready; it's time to be the center of these men's lives.

Time to see if they really are ready to share.

All of them.

"Get in the tub, East." Without even a hint of a scowl, the big brother obeys the younger one. It's still fascinating to me how Linc takes control of any room he enters.

Without so much as a glance at East, Linc walks up to me and palms my jaw—his fingers squeezing hard enough to make my mouth pop open.

"Today, we own you, Octavia."

I nod, as much as I can in this position, before Lincoln's mouth is on mine, his tongue demanding entrance and not waiting for permission. He explores every last inch, licking and biting, sucking and caressing, as his other hand traces down my body.

Apparently he's still in asshole mode, but pretty sure I can get on board with this version of asshole.

Linc's finger pushes my panties inside me until he's breached the lace. Nothing stands between my pussy and the pad of his finger. Pulling at the hole he's just created, he brings me closer, widening the hole as he does.

"Fuck, that's hot," I hear Finn say from the tub, Mav agreeing with his signature grunt.

Linc's hold on my jaw tightens just enough for me to feel the difference, his lips pulling away until he speaks into my mouth.

"Get in the tub and sit on East's lap." I go to move, but Linc stops me with his finger still fucking me through my panties.

"But Octavia? Your first and last orgasms belong to me, so don't you dare come before I allow it." He smiles at my body's reaction to his words. It's no secret that his controlling qualities in the bedroom turn me the fuck on. I'm not too proud to admit it and there's no way I could hide it even if I was.

"Go." Simultaneously letting my jaw and pussy go, I shimmy out of my destroyed lingerie, reaching back and lifting my bralette over my head before stepping into the hot water and heading straight to East.

Flanking him, Mav and Finn have eyes only for me. Linc is right behind me but instead of sitting next to one of the guys, he plants himself across from us—arms resting along the back of the wood, legs spread and chin high. He looks like a king and acts like a god, and we are his subjects to rule over.

East reaches out, turning me around before pulling me onto his lap where his heavy, very hard, cock rests against the crack of my ass. I'm facing Linc, because of course I am. He's got a front row view of us and is in the perfect position to orchestrate our every move.

"Use your fingers, East. Get her cunt nice and ready for us." Linc's words are harsh, which only makes my heart race faster.

My eyes are solely on Linc, watching him watch me is addictive as fuck.

Linc's words come back to me and I whimper as East pushes two fingers inside me without preamble. He just thrusts them in up to the second knuckle and curls them just enough to earn him a gasp.

I can't come.

It seemed so easy to obey before the reality of it was here. The second Lincoln notices my wide eyes, a slow, primal grin spreads across his beautiful lips, and in that moment I see the devil inside of him that I love.

The one that gets off on this control. Knowing he's wielding his power over me. Over all of us.

From across the tub, his eyes are like molten steel, taking in each movement from East. Each reaction from me. He can't possibly see what he's doing—it's all under water—but his imagination is likely as potent as the reality.

"Tell me how she feels."

"Like home." East's words hit me in the chest, making my

head lean back onto his shoulder where I feel his mouth come down to my neck, nuzzling, licking, kissing me like I'm his favorite toy and taking care of me is his life's mission.

That's when I feel two mouths on my nipples and without even looking, I reach out to grab Mav and Finn's cocks but I'm stopped before I can reach what I want.

"Octavia." Lincoln's voice is sharp, and I want to challenge him in spite of it, consequences be damned, but then Mav bites down on my nipple and all thoughts of stopping this disappear. I'll listen for now, but later, he's going to deal with it.

I'm a greedy bitch and I want them all.

That's when I feel him at my mouth, whispering like danger.

"Octavia." His tone could cut glass.

"I'm sorry." I breathe out trying not to sound too petulant. "I'm just so..." Lincoln grabs my hair, pulls back and forces me to look into his steely gaze.

"Tell me." Searching my face, Linc looks over my features before he leans in and licks an erotic path across the seam of my lips.

"Tell me," he repeats, his tone softer, more controlled.

"I want to please you. All of you."

"Oh, Octavia. Don't you know? Every part of you pleases us." I can't help the smile that spreads across my mouth until he pulls my head back, sharply.

"But this is my kingdom, my rules. My fucking call, Octavia."

"Okay," I tell him, pouting despite my pussy getting fucked even harder by East as I feel my juices coating his fingers with every word that comes out of Linc's sullen mouth. As if none of this is happening, Finn and Mav just keep licking and sucking on my tits. Jesus, I can't believe I'm trying to have a conversation with Linc all the while getting delightfully handled by the other three.

Linc goes back to his perch, his seat right across the water from us, and resumes his voyeuristic position.

East continues his magic touches, alternating between sliding his fingers in and out and flicking my clit for what feels like an eternity. My body rises quickly to its first orgasm and no matter how hard I try, having two mouths exploring my body and two or three fingers fucking it is really hard to ignore.

"Hold on, Octavia." I try to think of anything but the feel of tongues and fingers all over my skin, inside and out. I try to think about the homework I should have done. About the fucking shootings and hospitals and sects that are trying to ruin us all.

I try really fucking hard not to come but they are seriously pushing all of my buttons.

"Come sit on my face, Octavia." Oh God. He's being crude on purpose. Linc knows his dirty talk is like a flame to a moth.

Asshole.

East takes his fingers out of me, turning my face to the side so he can kiss me like he needs it to breathe.

Every nerve ending is on fire as I walk across the space between us and I'm on the edge of losing my fucking sanity when I see the devious grin on Linc's face. I refuse to give him the satisfaction of punishing me for coming before I'm allowed.

"Ha! See? I can control myself, too." The words fall from my mouth and as I clamp my mouth with my hand, Lincoln's smile turns devilish. Like my outburst is the best thing he's ever heard.

"Is that so?"

Fuck, fuck, fuck.

My mouth gets me into way too much trouble sometimes.

"Mav, Finn. You hungry?" Linc doesn't even look at them as he speaks, his eyes are solely on me, taking in my small gasp, the widening of my eyes, the tensing in my shoulders.

There's no fucking way I can keep myself from coming if both of them are eating me out.

This is fucking torture. A sweet torture, but still…

"You wouldn't!"

"Oh baby, not only would I, but I was hoping."

Asshole switch is fully in the on mode.

In the moments that follow, I find myself lifted until I'm sitting on the ledge of the tub, my feet planted firmly on the wooden seat, legs spread, pussy open and on show for all four of them.

"Fuck, she's beautiful." Mav's words hit my ears a millisecond before I feel his tongue part my lips and his mouth sucking on my clit. Then he's gone and Finn takes his place, his tongue fucking my pussy as he searches out my juices and drinks them up.

Back and forth, they take turns eating my pussy, making me squirm, taking pleasure in watching me lose my ever-loving mind.

As I'm leaning back on my elbows, I let my head fall back and stare at the ceiling, wanting to think about anything other than the fact that their mouths will be the death of me.

My hips search out their touch, wanting more and less all at the same time. The battle between body and mind is a raging war, and I'm not sure it's one I'm going to win.

It's while I'm trying really hard not to come all over their faces that I feel the heat on either side of me.

Drunk on them, I turn to one side then the other and through my lust-filled gaze, I see my favorite brothers looking at me like it's Christmas and I'm the fucking feast laid out for them.

East kisses me, deep and soulful, then he retreats leaving me to Linc who—contrary to the oldest Saint—kisses me like he's invading the enemy territory on his way to save the love of his life.

Both kisses are passionate in their own way and I love that they are so different.

I've got four mouths on me and if I die right now, I'd be okay with that.

"My turn." As Linc's words echo throughout the room, everyone stops moving and I feel cold, but not for long.

Looking down the length of my body, Lincoln makes himself comfortable between my legs, kissing one nipple then the other before giving me that smile of his that's just for me.

"Such a good girl. And good girls get rewarded."

My heart flutters and I fill with warmth at his words.

My head falls back once more just as Linc brings his mouth to my pussy and eats me out like a savage. Alternating strokes with his tongue and his fingers, he uses his entire body to fuck me with his face. East, Mav, and Finn take turns sucking on my mouth and nipples and neck. Anywhere they can touch me, they do. It's when I hear Linc say, "Give it to me, Octavia," that my entire body abandons the fight and lets go completely.

I hold my breath, my entire body convulsing, my gasps swallowed by East as he continues kissing me.

I don't know how long my orgasm lasts but I can feel it surge through my veins, the blood rushing, my lungs working overtime.

All the while, Linc continues to eat me out, taking every single drop that I give him.

First and last. Those are his.

As the fog starts to dissipate from the intensity of my orgasm, I open my eyes—my breathing labored—and see a look pass between Linc and Mav, who is running the back of his fingers over the smooth plane of my stomach.

I miss his touch immediately but when it's replaced by Finn's mouth and the kisses he rains down on my skin I feel better.

"Catch." I blink and my gaze goes to Linc just as he catches a packet of something.

They all see my questioning look and Finn whispers across my skin.

"Lube."

Images of all of them inside me at once run through my head and I almost panic.

But then two fingers slide into my pussy, scissoring and preparing me for... what?

"Relax, beautiful. We'd never ask for more than you can give." I trust them but my imagination is pretty fucking healthy and dirty as fuck, so I'm not sure they've considered all of the possibilities I have.

Though looking at the way they watch me, maybe they have.

Still, I nod, not wanting this to end.

East's fingers are gone and seconds later, Linc's dick is inside me thrusting once, twice, a couple more times and then he's out.

"You're so fucking wet, Octavia. We're going to have so much fun tonight." His words would be ominous if I didn't know him better.

Next thing I know, Finn is carrying me—my arms wrapped around his neck—and I spy the other three over his shoulder, whispering in hushed tones with calculating looks all over their faces. It's when I turn back to see where we're going that Finn whispers in my ear. "Say the word and everything stops. Same rules as always."

"Never." My word is final and I can't imagine a reason why I would ever stop what is about to happen.

In the corner of the space, between the hot tub and the sauna, they've set up a quaint little space with a huge mattress and pillows all over. It's all black, red, and white. It's so fucking romantic with all the candles and shit that I almost laugh at the contrast. There's nothing romantic about getting gangbanged by the four men you love equally.

Fuck, maybe there is.

Finn gently places me on the mattress and grabs his cock like he just needs to relieve the pressure or else he'll lose his mind. I like the idea of me causing him to lose it.

Soon, I'm the center of four pairs of eyes all showing different levels of lust and need.

"East, you lie down. We'll be doing all the work tonight. You can just enjoy the ride." Lincoln smirks at his own words. I guess I'm the ride East is about to get. Joining me on the bed, East lavishes me with his warm kisses before he taps me on the hip—silently telling me to get on top of him.

I don't make him wait. Straddling his hips, I brace myself against the wall and let my hair fall in a curtain of black strands over his chest.

"Fuck, her ass…" Mav, ever the modern-day Shakespeare.

Finn positions himself behind me just as I align myself up and over East's dick. We both breathe in through our teeth, making similar sounds as I reach the hilt. He's so deep like this, filling me so perfectly.

Our gazes meet and all I see is love through his long lashes. He's reverent, always has been, but I can see he hates that he's not one hundred percent healed. It doesn't matter though. We'll have other opportunities.

Looking over my shoulder, I watch as Finn coats his cock with the lube, stroking himself like he's trying to calm himself first.

"Finn, I think our girl wants to stroke it for you."

I really fucking do.

And since we never do things simple, I'm greeted with two dicks—one for each hand—as East lets me fuck him slowly, deeply.

Finn and Mav are so fucking hard it's like handling steel.

"Hold her back, East." I have no idea what that means until Linc grabs my chin from behind and pulls my head back until I'm facing the ceiling, my throat taut with the effort.

Standing, Linc steps close and places his balls on my lips. "Suck." I open my mouth and use my tongue to lick his ball sack up and down, then around one then the other.

"Fuck, that's hot." Mav is getting even harder at the sight of me sucking on Linc's balls while I jack them off, all the while getting fucked harder by East.

Linc places both of his hands on the nape of my neck, arching my back as far as possible until his dick is sliding inside my mouth. Hearing Linc grunt as he pushes down my throat hits me like an aphrodisiac.

"Fuck, I don't know what you just did, but she's soaking my cock right now." I hear East's words, but I'm too focused on Linc's dick sliding down my throat to pay it any attention. I've even stopped stroking Finn and Mav so they each cover my hand and help me, squeezing my fingers as tightly as they need.

I gag on Linc, tears following with the pull of gravity and running into my hairline while he softly coos words of encouragement. He tells me that I'm perfect. That I'm beautiful swallowing up his entire length. That I'm a queen for giving them so much.

Too soon, Linc glides his dick back out of my mouth and gently straightens me back up. I'm light-headed, the blood having gone to my head, my vision glassy and blurry. When I can see again, it's East's face that greets me. He slides his hands in the strands of my hair and pulls me in, resting his forehead against mine and murmuring.

"So fucking beautiful." His breathing is labored; he's stopped thrusting up into me, like he's trying to catch his breath and avoid losing his load inside me.

While I'm sharing this intimate moment with East, Finn and Mav let go and my hands fall on the wall behind East. I get a soft kiss from Finn on my shoulder while Mav sinks his teeth on the fleshy part of my collarbone.

Fuck, those two are so similar for two men who are complete opposites.

"On all fours, Octavia."

My heart thumps in my chest. This is it. And yet, I have no idea what they are planning.

My body hums with anticipation and no matter what they have planned, I'm ready. So fucking ready.

East pulls out of my pussy as I reposition myself on all fours, my upper body resting on my forearms. He brings himself up to a sitting position, my face now between his legs and his dick still hard and angry looking.

"This may hurt, baby, but just say the word and we'll stop." Finn's words as he slides beneath me, swiping his tongue across my pussy as he passes by, make me suck in a breath, but I'm not stopping. No fucking way. I want this too much. I've been dreaming about this.

He stops when his eyes are level with mine, East's cock looming between our faces, and his gaze on me is filled with heat so intense I'm afraid he'll set me on fire. Mav draws my attention with a slap to my ass and I tear my gaze from Finn's to look over my shoulder. He swings a leg over Finn's knees, straddling him and positioning himself behind me, then he winks at me like he's got the best plan in the world before he pushes his thick cock inside me in one long, hard thrust. I gasp and brace myself. East and Finn hold me steady by the nape of my neck and my hips, their fingers digging in.

It's only once Mav slides in and out of me a couple times that the cool silk of the lube coats my pussy allowing him to glide easily in and out.

Finn slides one huge hand from my hip to my lower back and uses the other to slowly guide the head of his cock to my already-full pussy.

"Shh, you're okay, babe. It's going to sting a little and it might burn a little but you'll get all the pleasure after," East is cooing, his thumb caressing the side of my neck in a soothing rhythm.

Then he's in. The bulbous part of his head rips a cry from me but as quickly as it burns it's gone and the fullness is amazing.

Both Finn and Mav are inside me.

I look up at East and his smile is infectious.

"That's a good girl," Linc tells me, suddenly at my side, kneeling and stroking himself as he watches me getting fucked by his two best friends.

Reaching out with his free hand, he pinches the closest nipple to him and Mav groans, telling him it's making me wetter and wetter which only encourages Linc to continue.

Then East pushes my head down and his cock is pushing into my mouth, achingly slow.

I don't know how they do it. How they orchestrate the dance of it without losing the synchronicity of it all.

I'm sucking a dick while two others are fucking my pussy and my nipple is getting a good fucking work out.

Linc bends down and whispers.

"My turn."

I swear to fuck, those words almost make me come but I hold back.

Linc is gone and the faint sound of lube is back.

The cool gel of it hits the crack of my ass.

One finger slides in and I swear I see stars.

Did I think I couldn't get any fuller?

Fuck, was I wrong.

Two fingers. Two cocks. Holy shit.

Panting around East's cock, I try to keep my rhythm but really, East is coordinating it all. My mind cannot comprehend what is happening.

Linc scissors his fingers in, turning, thrusting, curling and widening my hole.

"Lean back, Mav." His fingers are gone and I feel the angle of the two cocks inside of me shift, drawing a moan from somewhere deep inside of me that has East hissing and his cock twitching in my throat.

I feel the makeshift bed jostle, and a moment later Linc has lined himself up with my ass, my entire world falling into place with a crystal clarity I've never experienced.

They are everything. I'm the center and they are the slaves to my orgasm.

I moan around East's cock again as Linc slowly pushes inside my ass and for a brief moment I think it might be too much. For a brief moment, I think I might tap out.

But the moment passes and there is only ecstasy left behind.

"Fucking hell. Yeah, that's it, V. Fuck yeah." East is pushing my head further and further down as I get thoroughly fucked from behind.

It's too much.

It's everything.

And I love every single moment of it.

I'm the first to come when Mav reaches around and stimulates my clit faster and faster until everything explodes behind my lids.

This prompts East, who pushes my head down until I'm choking and swallowing his cum. I don't care that I'm a mess. I lick up everything that's escaped my mouth while behind me, Mav roars his own climax and Finn follows right behind him. They both pull out and once they're gone, Linc fucks me like his entire life depends on this one, final orgasm.

Skin slapping skin, nails sinking into the flesh of my ass cheeks as Linc fucks my ass with fierce abandon.

It's when I hear the guttural cry he releases that I look over my shoulder, watching in rapt attention as he throws his head back and holds my body close to his as he empties himself out inside me.

Seconds pass as he lets everything go and when he does, his

eyes search me out and in that one moment—when our gazes lock—I know everything he's feeling. Because I feel it too.

Once Linc pulls out, I drop down on top of Finn, and I've never felt more deliciously used than I do right now.

East, Finn, and Mav shuffle me to the center of the makeshift bed while Lincoln walks off, naked, to the bathroom and comes back with four warm cloths and for the next fifteen minutes, I'm cared for, coddled and loved until I pass out from the most incredible evening of my life.

TWENTY-FIVE

OCTAVIA

This night is not going how I expected it to. Starting with Lincoln not arriving with Maverick and Finley to pick us up. East is sitting tonight out. Advice from Chase apparently, and I'm not opposed to it. If he can stay free and clear of the Knights and all of their bullshit, then awesome. I've been second-guessing bringing Indi with me all freaking day.

But Maverick's reassurance that he wouldn't leave her side made me feel a little better since Finn and I have to play the happy couple tonight.

The Lincoln thing is driving me nuts. I haven't heard from him all day. His father called him this morning and we haven't seen him since. Finley showed me the message he got from him, telling him he wouldn't be coming with us tonight, but that was literally all it said.

Goddamn Saint is frustrating as fuck.

I just want to know what the fuck is going on with him

As the town car pulls up to the same Saint mansion that we'd gone to for the charity ball, Indi lets out a low whistle. "Wow, these guys sure do love their swanky manors, huh?"

I laugh softly as Finley smiles at her.

"Better get used to it tonight, Pixie Spice. This place is full of pretentious bozos in fancy, shiny shit to try and hide who they really are. All of this is just a shiny exterior so no one looks too hard for the truth."

"I just meant it looks nice," she says, rolling her eyes.

I shake my head and lean forward. "You two need to play nice tonight. It'll only take one of these assholes to hear you arguing to decide that they want to use it against us."

Finn lifts my hand and kisses the inside of my wrist. "Relax, pretty girl. We aren't going to let anything happen to her. Or to you. This is just another ridiculous event for the bigwigs from the city and the Knights to show everyone how rich they are. I doubt they'll even try to speak to you tonight, but you not attending would have been a snub—especially since Chase helped us find you—and that is the last thing we want."

The car rolls to a stop and the valet opens the door. The boys climb out first, then help Indi and I out. The steps are lined with spiral-cut trees decorated in twinkle lights, and people of all ages are ascending them into the mansion.

Music plays softly, servers walk around in their black shirt and tie uniforms, far less obscure than the ones they wore the last time I was here.

This all looks almost, dare I say, normal.

"I don't know what you were so worried about," Indi murmurs as she slides up beside me as we enter the main room. "This just looks like a stuffy party."

Maybe she and Finn are right. Tonight is nothing more than a party for the rich and pretentious.

"Let's get a drink, shall we?" Mav says, clapping his hands together before holding out his arm, which Indi takes, even if she does pull a face at him as she does.

Finn grips my hand tighter and leans in closer, "How long till you think they end up killing each other?"

"I give it about twenty minutes. We probably shouldn't leave them alone too much."

"You're probably right," he murmurs, the warmth of his breath sending a shiver down my spine. "If I didn't tell you how stunning you look tonight, I should definitely be fired as one of your boyfriends." He pulls back and smiles down at me, before glancing around the room.

A tall, waif-like blonde approaches us, resting bitch face in place.

"Fuck," Finley mutters and entwines my fingers with his.

She stops in front of us, her gaze roaming over me, as if sizing me up.

Finley smiles tightly at her as he pulls me closer into his side. "Artemis, I'm surprised you bothered to come."

She looks a little older than us, but I don't recognise her. If she's here though, and she knows Finn, she must have something to do with the Knights.

"I thought I'd come and meet the infamous Octavia Royal, considering all of the fuss that's been made about her lately."

I quirk a brow at her as her heated gaze sweeps over me again, and her mouth tugs up in the corners. "I guess I can see why you've been tripping over yourself."

Finley chuckles as he kisses my hair. "Octavia, this is Artemis DuPoint. She sits on the Conclave, too."

"Nice to meet you," I say, offering her my hand, even though it feels awkward as shit.

She takes my hand and kisses it, making Finn laugh hard. "Pleasure was mine. I'll be seeing you."

She winks at me before walking away, and I just gawp after her wondering what just happened.

"I think she likes you," he teases before kissing me softly. He pulls back, gaze darting around the room when his smile drops. I follow his line of sight and I see why.

Descending the staircase is Georgia, her red hair piled up on her head and her creamy skin highlighted by the scarlet dress that's basically painted onto her. Her arm is looped through Lincoln's, whose smile is so bright it almost hurts my eyes.

It's just for show.

I repeat the line in my head like a mantra. *I know his real smile, that one he has just for me.*

"Come on, pretty girl. Let's get a drink," Finley says softly, stealing my attention from the two of them. I smile up at him, swallowing down the rising jealousy. I have no reason to be jealous.

I know who he really is. I know he loves me.

He already told me he wouldn't touch her, I just have to remember that.

Finn takes my hand and leads me to the bar, where Indi and Maverick are bickering over cocktails.

"Appletinis are not a girl's drink," Maverick growls. "They taste fucking delightful."

"If you say so." Indi laughs before turning to face me.

I know the instant she sees Georgia and Lincoln over my shoulder, because traces of amusement leave her face and her eyes shine with anger. "Imma claw that bitch's eyes out."

"Calm down, Kujo. Lincoln knows how to play the game. Too well. He's about as willing to be with her as any of us would be," Maverick murmurs to her, placing his hand on her shoulder to make sure she stays in place.

"It's fine," I say, waving it off.

Fake it till we make it, right?

I don't even turn around to look at them, even though I feel eyes on my back. It'd be a lot easier to swallow if Lincoln hadn't been a giant asshole lately. But this is obviously what had him so stressed.

Indi sucks in a breath, her eyes widening as she looks behind me. I already know what's happening before I look.

I step closer to Finn, who puts his arm around my waist and pulls me even closer. "You've got this. Just rise above."

"Octavia, it's so lovely to see you again!" Georgia's lilting voice makes me want to wince, but instead I paint a smile on my face and look over to the redhead hanging off of Lincoln's arm, catching a glimpse of Maverick moving Indi closer to him. I'm not sure if it's to protect him or to make sure he can stop her lunging at the bitch beside me.

"Georgia, you too. How have you been?"

She laughs, and it's so twinkly and ladylike, I want to punch her in the throat just to stop it.

"Oh, I'm great. I hear you had a bit of a rough time lately. Poor Lincoln told me about your rehab in Mexico. I hope everything is okay now." Her smile is wicked, her eyes glinting like she knows something I don't. I know rehab from the kidnapping was what Lincoln explained to Harrison, but I get the feeling Georgia knows more than she's letting on.

I glance at Lincoln who just looks indifferent. He barely even acknowledges me. It stings, but I just keep reminding myself this is the game.

"I need to go powder my nose, sweetheart," she says, leaning over and kissing Lincoln's cheek. "I'll be back. Octavia, join me?"

"Of course," I say, softly shaking my head at Indi before extracting myself from Finley. Lincoln's eyes go wide, a hint of panic filling them before he controls his reaction.

Weird.

I follow Georgia across the room and back up the stairs she just came down. "There's a private bathroom up on the mezzanine, though I imagine you already know that."

I just nod, not saying a word as I follow. I only agreed to this little jaunt to find out what it is that she wants. Maybe she's not as

343

bad or as conniving as I think. Maybe she doesn't want this engagement any more than Lincoln does. Maybe I should've asked him, but he won't speak about her to me.

We head into the bathroom, and she moves straight to the mirror, opening the clutch that hangs from her wrist. "I'm surprised you let him go so easily, you know."

"I'm sorry?" I keep my confusion from my face as best as I can.

"Lincoln. I'm not an idiot, Octavia, and Blair filled me in on the little whore ring you had going on. But knowing you let Lincoln go so he could be truly happy... it surprises me. Especially with a cock like that. Can't have been easy to give up."

I swallow the writhing jealousy—because how the fuck does she know about his dick—and smile at her in the mirror as I reapply my lip gloss.

"I have Finley, that's all I need." I shrug, hoping my nonchalance is believable.

She puts her lipstick away, the same shade on her lips as her dress, and turns to face me. "Well, I mean, I can understand that. He definitely isn't hard on the eyes. But that thing Lincoln does with his tongue... I'm not sure I could give that up."

"I didn't realize you two were so close."

"We weren't until you got back from your trip. I was as surprised as you are, but when he came to me, who am I to say no to the man I'm going to marry? I was a little resistant to the marriage at first, but after sampling his dick, and knowing his net worth... who am I to fight it when he seems to want it, want *me*, so much? I have to say, those dimples on his back are just adorable though. The freckles that almost make up the Big Dipper just above them, too. Who would've thought a man like Lincoln would have such adorable features underneath that steely exterior."

My blood runs cold at her words.

How the fuck does she know any of that?

"Well, I don't need to tell you, you know all of this. You ready to head back?"

I force a smile, hoping it reaches my eyes. "Sure, let's go party shall we?"

"Let's."

I pull the pins from my hair, trying not to hulk out. How I managed to contain myself all evening and night with the two of them all night is beyond me. Iron strength of fucking will is all I can figure.

"Are you going to tell me what happened?" Indi asks as she appears from my bathroom in her pj's. She flops onto the bed, staring at me as I try to calm myself.

"Georgia was just enjoying telling me intimate details of Lincoln's body and expressing how much she enjoys his tongue and dick. That's all."

Her jaw drops, and she blinks at me, as if computing, then screeches, "I'm sorry, fucking what?"

"It has to be a lie, right?" I say as I step out of the sapphire gown, not caring about the garment as I try to contain the whirlwind inside of me. "He wouldn't fuck her. And he wouldn't hide it from me if he did."

She sits, quietly raging on the bed, her fists clenched. "What did she say, exactly?"

Much as I really don't want to revisit the conversation, I tell her everything and by the time I'm done, she's practically vibrating. "I assume the dimples and dipper are real?"

I nod as I pull on my pj's and put my hair in a messy bun on top of my head. "They are."

"Could she have known the details from Blair?"

I shrug. "It's possible, but Lincoln hasn't fucked Blair. It doesn't mean she didn't find out from someone else, but Lincoln doesn't exactly whore himself out."

"Yeah, I'm not sure he's even fucked anyone but you at ECP," she says, twisting her lips. "That doesn't mean he hasn't though."

I drop back onto the bed, throwing myself backward so I can stare at the ceiling.

"It's not fair for me to be this jealous, right? I have all four of them. How can I justifiably stop him fucking someone else and not be a hypocrite?"

"Oh, hell no. One, they said they only wanted you, that they were happy to share, and you told them outright you wouldn't share them. They agreed to that shit, so you can absolutely be angry and jealous. Two, we don't know for certain he fucked her. You need to find that out before you do anything."

"You're right. I should just ask him." I get up and grab my phone, dialing his number before putting it against my ear.

It goes straight to voicemail.

Awesome.

"Try again, he was probably peeing or something," Indi encourages. I hate to be *that* girl, but I hit his number again anyway.

The line rings, and rings. Just when I'm about to give up, it answers and I hear her voice. "Hello?"

"Georgia," I say, trying not to growl at her answering his phone. "I just needed to ask Lincoln a question, is he there?"

"Oh of course, silly me. Sorry, we have the same phone, I didn't even notice I grabbed his. Let me grab him, he was just heading for a shower."

I clench my fists as she calls out his name, while Indi sits silently, watching me intently.

The sound of running water filters through the speaker and the sound of muffled voices reaches my ear before he speaks. "Hello?"

"Lincoln," I say, trying to remain calm. "I had some questions for you, but I see you're busy."

"What do you want, Octavia?" he snaps, and I feel my eyes fill with tears.

"Did you fuck her?"

"Octavia," he starts, sighing. I can almost picture him running his hand through his hair with frustration.

"Yes or no, Lincoln. It's a simple question."

"Nothing's ever that simple."

"Is that how she knew about the Big Dipper on your back?"

"Octavia, let me explain." He sounds angry that I even asked the question, but he doesn't deny it.

"That wasn't a no. Have a good night, Lincoln." I drop the call and fall to the ground as sobs rack my body.

"I'm going to sever his dick from his body," Indi growls as she rushes across the room and wraps me in her arms.

I can't speak. I can't do anything but cry as my heart aches in my chest.

I really thought we could survive all of this. His dad, Georgia, all of it.

But apparently I was wrong.

More fool me.

After spending the night tossing and turning in bed, Indi made me come and hang out with her and the Kings today. I left my phone at home after letting East know where I was going—she has hers if I really need to speak to anyone, but I don't see that happening any time soon.

We've been in the basement at Ryker's all morning while Dylan and Ellis play Xbox and Ryker... well he does whatever it is he does to keep his empire running.

Indi has been locked with him in his office for the last half hour, and I'm glad she's so happy, but being here, as a part of her happy bubble, is just making me see how fucked mine is.

"What's wrong, Princess Peaches?" Dylan asks as Ellis disappears into Ryker's office. "Indi wouldn't tell us anything, just said you had a shitty night and needed to chill."

"Would it be too dramatic of me to just say everything?" I sigh and he bursts out laughing.

"Honestly, probably not, knowing some of the shit you've been dealing with. Is there anything we can do?"

"Put out a hit on Harrison? Help me bring down the empire of the Knights? Storm the castle with me and help me save the princes? Maybe put out a hit on the redheaded snake sucking the life from me too?"

He raises his eyebrows and just blinks at me. "I mean, we probably could, but..."

I shake my head and bark out a dry, humorless laugh, "But why would you? It's fine. I'm just being a dramatic little bitch. Just need to lick my wounds then act like nothing's wrong. Story of my life."

"Want to go shoot shit? That always makes me feel better."

I start to shake my head and stop. "Ya know what, fuck it. Let's go shoot shit."

"That's my girl! I knew I liked you!"

"Should we tell them where we're headed?" I say, nodding toward the door.

He grins and walks over, banging on it with the side of his fist so loud I jump even though I knew he was going to do it. Indi squeals and Ryker swings open the door, eyes wild.

"V and I are going shooting. Thought we should let you fuckers know." He tries not to laugh as Ryker lunges at him and they end up wrestling on the floor. I lift my feet from the ground up onto the sofa with me, not sure whether to laugh or cry as they beat the crap out of each other, but since Indi appears in the doorway and just groans, I go with laughter.

"Ellis, will you help?"

Ellis appears, takes in the two titans rolling around the room, and shakes his head. "Not a chance I'm getting in there."

"Wuss," she teases him, sticking her tongue out at him. She takes a deep breath and shouts, "If the two of you don't stop, I'm not sucking *any* dick for two weeks."

She blushes when I laugh, but the ruckus on the ground stops almost immediately.

"Aww, but short stack, you suck dick so good." Dylan's groaning makes me laugh harder and Ryker pushes the big guy off of him as he climbs to his feet.

"No need to mope, asshole. We stopped. You're lucky she made us stop too."

"I could've taken you." Dylan grins back at him.

"Boys," Indi warns, and they both grin at her. "Now then, who are we shooting?"

"And that, short stack, is why you're my favorite." Dylan whoops and picks her up, tipping her over his shoulder. "We're shooting things, not people."

"Dammit, I thought for sure we were going to deal with that hopped up rich bitch," Indi groans. "Now put me down, ya giant."

I can't help but giggle as he slaps her ass before planting her on the sofa beside me. "You feeling okay?" she asks softly.

I nod, "Yeah, Dylan is a great distraction, and shooting should be fun."

"It's a shame we're not killing the redhead. I'd happily watch her bleed."

I shrug, pulling the sleeves of my hoodie down over my hands. "Maybe another day. Or maybe Lincoln truly is happy and I've been lying to myself. Or maybe he didn't fuck her and it's all one big misunderstanding. But he isn't talking to me, so I don't know what else to do but keep marching on."

She side hugs me as the boys get their shit together. "Come on, let's go shoot some shit, maybe sledge hammer some stuff, get out all the rage. You'll love it. Then after, Smithy should be home, so we can go back to your place, milkshake up, and snuggle on the sofa with a horror movie."

"You, Indigo Montoya, might just be my one true love."

She giggles at me. "Same, just don't tell *them* that. They might sulk." She nods over to the guys who are watching us both closely.

"Come on, boys," she says, slapping her hands against her thighs before standing up. "Let's go break stuff."

TWENTY-SIX

LINCOLN

THREE DAYS AGO

L istening to my brother with my girl is a fucked-up thing. It's not like I intended on it, but she isn't exactly quiet. A grin tugs at my lips at the thought of her crying out beneath me. Soon enough, I'll have her to myself again.

First, I have to get through the rest of this week and the party on Saturday. If I can survive that, then I can start planning a way to make Georgia think she was the one to decide against this farce of an engagement. I clench my fists just thinking about the corner Harrison has me backed into.

I've been trying to fight off my demons all night, and despite the hell I put my body through tonight, nothing, not even my exhaustion can keep them away.

Even in my sleep they haunt me.

Octavia might say she's understanding of what I'm having to do, but if I saw her with anyone who wasn't part of our group, I'd burn down the fucking world, so I know there is no way in hell she's actually handling it as well as she's trying to pretend she is.

Or maybe she's less of a jealous asshole than I am.

I turn on the shower in my bathroom and hit play on my

playlist so the room fills with music that matches my mood. When *Bring Me The Horizon* screams through the speakers, I strip out of my workout gear while I wait for the water to heat.

Stepping beneath the scalding water does nothing to distract me from the bullshit I've got to try and work my way through, but it does at least help loosen some of the tension in my shoulders. I lose myself to the music and the beat of the water as it assaults my skin.

I lean my head forward, resting my forehead against the cold tile, the clash in temperature sending a shiver down my spine.

The thought of Octavia writhing beneath my brother down the hall plays in my mind, and while it shouldn't be hot to think of her with the others, it is. Especially when I know there are some noises she makes that are just for me.

The caveman inside of me likes that a lot.

I freeze at the feel of fingertips on my spine. "Happy to see me, I see."

My jaw clenches at the sound of her voice. "Why are you in my shower, Georgia?"

I don't turn to face her, because Harrison's words ring out in my head, my hard on officially disappearing.

"Your dad gave me a key to this place. I thought I'd come surprise you, show you just how good we can be together. I know all about the other girl, but I can make you forget all about her."

She presses her chest to my back and a growl escapes me.

She seems to mistake it for encouragement and traces her fingers around my ribs to my chest. "I knew you'd forget her when you felt me pressed against you."

I have never felt more violated in my entire fucking life—and that's no small feat—and I remain still, trying to work out how to get her the fuck out of my shower without putting Octavia at risk. If Harrison gave her a key, I'm sure he encouraged all of this, and I'm also sure that she'll run back to him if I flat out reject her.

CHAPTER TWENTY-SIX

I'm going to be fucking sick.

She palms my limp dick and giggles. "I'm sure I can change his mind about me too."

"Let go of my dick, Georgia." I clench my fists, but she squeezes rather than letting go with another laugh.

Fuck this.

I grab her wrist, squeezing hard enough that she gets the message, and she releases me. I spin, keeping my hold on her wrist, and face her. I keep my eyes on hers, not bothered about whatever her body looks like, because she's not Octavia.

"Harrison may have invited you into my house, but I sure as fuck didn't invite you into my shower. I don't know who the fuck you think you are, but when it comes to my dick, I make the rules."

Her nostrils flare as I push her back against the tile, keeping a distance between us.

"I know you want me, Lincoln." She glances down at my dick and smiles maliciously. "You can try to fight it, but you won't win."

Her eyes glint as I let go of her, hating the feel of her skin against mine, and storm from the shower, wrapping a towel around my waist before leaving the room.

Fuck this shit. Fuck it all to hell.

I wonder if I can get Octavia out of the country and out of my father's reach. I'm positive she'll fight me on leaving—she fights me on everything—but maybe if I try to explain it to her...

Georgia strides into my room, still fully naked, dripping onto my carpet. She stalks toward me and fingers my towel where I've knotted it. "I'm fairly certain you don't want your father to know you're rejecting me. I'll let it pass for now, but make no mistake, Lincoln. I get what I want. Always."

She picks up a slip of black material I hadn't noticed by my door and pulls the dress over her head until she's covered. "I'll see you on Friday, fiancé."

Waving her fingers at me, she leaves the room with a smile, closing the door behind her.

What the fuck am I going to do?

TWENTY-SEVEN

OCTAVIA

I t's been two weeks since that stupid Knight party and Lincoln has barely looked at me, let alone spoken to me. Finn and Mav haven't talked to him either, and East said he's about as much fun to live with as a bear with a thorn in its paw.

But no one can get any answers from him about what the actual fuck is going on with him because he won't speak to anyone.

Frustrated and devastated doesn't even begin to cover how I feel.

But more than anything, I'm just sad and angry.

What's worse? I haven't heard from Harrison either, so I still have this bullshit with the Knights hanging over my head. I don't want to think that it's all wrapped up in the Lincoln stuff, but at this point, I have no idea what to think anymore.

I roll over in bed, grabbing my phone from the nightstand.

Eleven at night on a Friday and here I am, living the rockstar life of pining over a boy.

I pull up my private thread with him. His last message stares at me from weeks ago...

Tears prick my eyes. Nope, doesn't hurt at all.

Me:

Are you ever going to explain?

My thumb hovers over send for a few seconds before I hit it and stare at the screen like a crazy person. I know I should be content. I have the other three, and it's not like I love them less, or I love him more... I just don't understand.

The message shows as delivered.

Then read.

And then nothing.

I bury my face in the pillow and let out a scream so as not to alert Smithy. The one weekend he doesn't stay at Matthew's and I have a minor breakdown. Though it could be the sheer volume of tears, ice cream, and murder shows I've worked through the last two weeks that made him stay home this weekend.

It's the first night I've been alone since that night. Between Indi and the guys, someone has been here, but I told everyone I was okay. That I wanted a night alone.

I really don't want to be *that* girl.

But here I am, staring at my phone like a crazy person.

Three dots appear on the screen, and I hate myself for the way my heart skips a beat.

I practically hold my breath waiting for the message, but they just disappear.

Of course they fucking do. I pull up an audiobook, hoping that the sound of voices will lull me to sleep, but then my phone buzzes and I drop it, slapping myself in the face.

Might just be the highlight of my night.

Fuck my life.

I pick up my phone and see his name on the screen.

Lincoln:
You seem to have already decided you know everything. What's
left to explain?

Fuck my life. Why is he such a pain in the ass?

Me:
You didn't deny it.

Lincoln:
I didn't think I'd have to.

I bite my lip, guilt slamming through me. Is this all my fault? Did
I overreact?

Me:
She knew things, Linc. Things she shouldn't know unless she's
been naked with you.

Lincoln:

You want the truth?

Me:
Always.

Lincoln:
I was naked with her.

Lincoln:
But I didn't fuck her.

Lincoln:
I also didn't choose to be naked with her. She accosted me in the shower. So I guess that's how she knew whatever she told you.

Lincoln:
But it fucking sucks that you don't trust me... trust us... enough to already know that I wouldn't touch her. I told you I wouldn't. And you still believed her.

A lump fills my throat.

He's right.

I fucked this up. I didn't trust him. I did believe her.

God, I'm such a fucking idiot.

Anger simmers under the surface at what she did, and I add her to my list of people that are going to burn when I find a way. How fucking dare she do that to him?

Me:
I'm sorry.

Lincoln:
You have nothing to be sorry for. When you called, I was with her. I was in a shower and I didn't explain. Harrison forced me to share the suite with her that night and she was right there. I didn't know what to do. What to say. I didn't come to you after. But Harrison... It doesn't matter what the excuses are. None of this is your fault.

Me:
I'm still sorry.

Me:
I miss you.

Lincoln:
I miss you too.

I drop my phone onto my chest and just stare at the ceiling. This might've explained some stuff, but there still feels like there's this giant chasm between us. I don't know how we get back from this. Will there even be an us while Harrison rules over him? While the *acting* Regent of the fucking Conclave insists that Georgia is in his life?

If I looked better in orange, I'd be tempted just to take her out purely for what she did to Lincoln. Pretty sure that Harrison would make sure I was locked up for it though, and he'd throw away the damn key.

I toss and turn in bed, waiting for sleep to take me, but it doesn't come. When I check my phone again, it's two a.m.

Awesome.

A rustling outside my balcony door has me sitting up in bed, reaching for the gun Maverick insisted I keep in the drawer beside my bed. But when I see Lincoln open the balcony door, I stop, my heart hammering in my chest.

Why is he here?

And why do I feel so awkward that he is.

"You know you don't have to keep coming in that way, right?" I quirk a brow as Lincoln crosses my room toward my bed. This push and pull between us is getting to a point where we either need to fix things, or I need to put more distance between us until we can sort out the web of lies we're trapped in. I hate this limbo.

He clenches his jaw and shrugs as he slips out of his jacket. He drops his phone and God knows what else onto the bedside table, stripping down to his boxers before climbing into bed and lying down beside me in silence.

I open my mouth to speak but nothing comes out, so I close it again, wishing things weren't like this with us.

I know I'm probably overreacting, that this isn't his fault, but my stupid heart can't make sense of it all. All I have is pain and jealousy, no matter how unreasonable it is.

He rolls over to face me and lets out a deep sigh before pulling his phone from the bedside table. He taps the screen a few times before turning back to me and slipping an AirPod I hadn't noticed him grab into my ear. "I never thought I'd be the one you couldn't talk to. That we'd be here. That I wouldn't have the right words to fix this. So I'm hoping that this will say what I can't."

He goes quiet as the track starts playing in my ear. I close my eyes and listen to the lyrics, breaking a little inside—in the best way—over the fact that he chose to reach me with the one medium he knows speaks to the deepest, darkest parts of me.

So, can we close the space between us now?
It's the distance we don't need.
You're everything I love about the things I hate in me.

"What song is this?" My voice is croaky as waves of emotion wash over me. He shows me the screen as the song starts to play again.

Favorite Place by All Time Low.

My heart shatters in my chest, but not in the painful way I've been dealing with lately. I break in a way that I think I might be able to rebuild from. With him.

With all of them.

I just need a way to free them. To free us all.

I make a promise to myself that as soon as there is a way, I'll save them. All of them. No matter the cost.

As I roll over, the song still playing, he curls around me from behind, and that's how I fall asleep.

───────

I wake up to the feel of Linc's lips fluttering down my neck, the press of his dick against my ass. I can't say that I haven't missed this.

Missed him.

I know I should be over what happened, that it's all for show, but that doesn't make my heart hurt any less. Not when I know I'm going to have to keep seeing him with her. That there's nothing I can do to stop it.

We said we'd do everything together.

But this... he didn't tell me. Didn't warn me. Again.

And then I fell for her lies.

We both fucked up. Time and time again.

"Linc." His name is breathy as it falls from my lips, a shiver running down my body as his teeth graze against my shoulder.

"Linc, stop." He freezes at my words, pulling back from me as I turn to face him. I know I already asked him last night, but I need to see his face when he answers. "Did you fuck her?"

I hate how vulnerable I feel right now. How pathetic I feel.

How much I want to believe him no matter what Georgia said, but I know he won't be able to lie to me. Not to my face.

He grips my chin, a fire in his eyes. "I already told you I didn't. I swear to you, I've never touched her. She was there when you called, so I couldn't exactly explain. She knows Harrison has me by the balls... and the threats he made. Octavia, I will never risk you. Never. She knew what she was doing. She's a fucking snake."

He lets out a sigh, shaking his head. "All I can tell you is my truth. Do you really not believe me?"

I look into his eyes and I know he isn't lying. Some might call it me wanting to believe him, being naïve, others might recognize it as blind faith. But I know him, and despite my stupid warring emotions, deep down, I know he wouldn't do that to me.

"I believe you," I say softly. "Doesn't make any of it hurt any less, but I believe you."

"I'm sorry it hurt you, Octavia. Truly. I'd do anything to take that pain from you." The sincerity in his eyes weakens my heart a little, so I lean forward and kiss him softly.

He pulls me against his chest and buries his hands in my hair, holding me so tight it feels like he might never let go. "I missed you so fucking bad," he breathes.

He kisses me again, setting my entire world on fire.

"I'm going to make sure you never forget it."

Our legs intertwined, our mouths sealed, and our tongues searching, we make out like the teenagers we are. Rubbing against each other, Linc's hand tightens even more at the nape of my neck, my hair trapped between his fingers. That little bite of pain keeps me alert and needy, just the way he likes me.

"Clothes off." I stop everything, my lips pressed against his and look up into his intense gray eyes.

"You're the one groveling. You should be the one undressing me." I laugh, making sure to add a little sass to my voice because there's nothing sexier than Lincoln trying his best to rein in his frustration. And nothing frustrates him more than me mouthing off.

Payback is hell.

"Octavia. I will grovel with my dick inside your cunt. And I will make sure you come so many times you forget all of this. But," he pulls back on my hair and traps my bottom lip with his teeth, biting down hard enough for the sting to get my attention before releasing it and pinning me with a serious glare. "I still call the shots. Always."

I shrug like it's no big deal, but I wouldn't have it any other way. Still, playing with him is so much fun.

"Fine." I make a whole show of it and don't miss the arched brow he gives me, like he's about to show me where my attitude is going to get me.

Which is nowhere.

Absolutely nowhere.

I scramble up and in a flash, I'm completely naked and beyond ready to have his hands all over me.

"Good girl. Now, undress me." I have to seriously check myself to make sure I don't roll my eyes at his order. I mean, he could have taken off his own boxers and saved us some time, but of course he wants me to do it.

Linc rolls onto his back and arches that fucking brow at me again, and I'm equal parts annoyed and turned on by his brass attitude.

Grovel, my ass. He's loving this.

I bite my lip as I get on my hands and knees, shaking my ass as I straddle his chest—backwards, because fuck him. I can follow orders and have my fun all at the same time. The growl that rumbles out of him as I run my hands down his hips and slide my fingers under the hem of his boxers, pushing myself down his body with them in tow, tells me that I might actually get away with it. I throw them off to the side once they're off and smile over my shoulder at him, finding his Cheshire grin well in place as I sit up on my haunches and turn to position myself between his legs.

"Now what?" I ask, certain he already has a plan.

"Now, Octavia, you lie down on your back and let me worship every inch of you before I fuck you within an inch of your life." I grin like he's just told me it's Christmas morning and all my gifts are under the tree.

Eagerly, I jump up and position myself in the dead center of the bed as Linc vacates his space. As soon as I'm laid out for him, he covers my body with his and starts at my lips. Kissing and biting, sucking on my tongue and lips, Linc spends a long time paying attention to my mouth before he moves to my chin and my neck.

He holds himself up on his forearms, hands cradling my head as he leaves open-mouthed kisses on my neck. When he spends a little too much time on one spot, I smile knowing he's leaving a mark. Fucking barbarian.

Sliding down the length of my body, he reaches one nipple, laving it with his tongue before moving to the other and showing it the same attention.

My back arches, my chest chasing his mouth, wanting more, needing him to give me a little pain with my pleasure. So, of course, I tell him.

"Linc, please, m—"

"Do not fucking finish that phrase, Octavia, or I will stop right the fuck now and go back to my place."

He's lying through his teeth.

Right?

He has to be.

I mean, he wouldn't dare leave me like this.

Would he?

That's the thing with Lincoln Saint. He's capable of pretty much anything to prove a point and I'm not ready for this to stop.

Snapping my mouth shut, I let him go at his pace and reel in my frustration for the greater good.

"Good girl." He winks at me. Winks. Like he's won. Spoiler alert—having an orgasm means I win.

Once he finishes teasing my tits, he trails a hot path of kisses down my stomach, and when he reaches my pussy, he kisses my clit then rises up on his knees.

"On all fours. Now."

I don't even hesitate. I position myself on my forearms, my ass nice and high for him, unable to hide just how much I want him.

"Fuck, you're so goddamn gorgeous like this. All ready and shaking with need for my fucking cock. Mine." He places both of his big hands on my ass cheeks and pulls me into him as he nudges the entrance of my pussy with the head of his cock. I feel it there, just waiting and teasing. Sliding up and down my slit like he's teasing himself—teasing me—before giving me what he knows I want.

I'm about to sink onto him when I realize what he's doing. He's testing me. He wants to see how long I'll last before I act out.

Asshole.

As tempted as I am, I clench my fists and resist the urge.

Looking over my shoulder, I give him my best innocent look and bat my lashes at him—my only act of rebellion.

Linc smiles and it's a mixture of pride and danger right before he pulls my hips back into him and slams inside me to the hilt.

I grunt as he groans out his pleasure and freezes. His head hangs back, the pleasure of being squeezed by my pussy written all over his face.

Fuck, he's beautiful.

He slowly glides in and out of my pussy, thrusting in and out a couple of times, before he reaches up and wraps the strands of my hair around his palm, pulling me back up to kneeling, my back flush against his chest.

His mouth comes to my ear as he whispers, "Do you feel that?"

I nod because the fullness of him in this position robs me of words.

"You are mine, as much as I am yours, Octavia. Don't *ever* fucking forget that."

Letting go of my hair, he slides his hand to my throat—his

thumb and middle fingers on my pulse points—squeezing until my head falls back on his shoulder as he fucks me.

He's in total and complete control as he times his thrusts perfectly. Evenly. Dragging out every fucking moment and driving me insane.

I love when he gets like this. When he uses that calculating side of himself in the best of ways.

When his free hand finds its way to my clit, and he pushes up with his cock as he circles with his finger, I about lose my mind. I moan as the combined stimulation awakens every nerve ending in my body.

With every snap of his hips, he grunts in my ear like he can't stop himself.

His control is slipping, little by little.

It's my favorite part of us. Feeling the moment his walls come crumbling down, and for a moment, he's a mere mortal like the rest of us.

"Fuck, Octavia. Come all over my cock, beautiful." And I do. I let it all go because I want to and because he needs me to.

Reaching back, I dig my nails into the back of his neck as my breathing is constricted by his tightening hold on my throat. It's such a fucking high, the intensity of my orgasm is overwhelming.

"That's it, give it to me." Linc doesn't relent, he fucks me like he's losing his mind. Fucks me like he's not ever giving me up.

I try to scream, but it's in vain—his hold is too strong.

That's when he turns my head, lets go of my throat, and crushes his mouth to mine, swallowing my cries as he comes deep inside me.

I've never felt more possessed in my entire life and I fucking love it.

Lincoln left before breakfast, with some excuse I was too boneless to hear coherently, so I've been lounging around for most of the morning. Smithy went to the Farmer's Market with Matthew, so I decide to do something productive.

I'm going to read some more of my dad's journals and finally try to work out some of the insanity around me. Now that everything else is tucked away, things are a little less manic in my mind and I can actually focus.

I shower and get dressed, thinking that dressing like I'm going somewhere will make me more productive, before making my way back downstairs.

Just as I head toward the basement, the buzzer for the gate goes off, stopping me in my tracks. I head to the control box and see a black car sitting outside the gate.

"Hello?"

I wait for a response. The window rolls down, but I don't recognize the man looking at the camera. "Car for Miss Royal. I was sent by Harrison to collect you for your meeting."

Wait, that's now?

Why the fuck did nobody tell me?

What if this is a trick?

"I'm sorry, I wasn't aware of a meeting today," I say back into the mic. Seconds later, my phone buzzes in my pocket.

It's an unknown number, but I answer it anyway—because, weird timing.

"Miss Royal, get in the car," Harrison all but barks down the line. "Do not keep me waiting.'

The line disconnects, and I clench the fist not holding my phone.

Tripped up asshole.

I let out a deep breath, trying to calm myself and push the buzzer again. "I'll be a few minutes."

Without waiting for a response, I rush back upstairs, grabbing a black blazer to shrug over my band tee, and grab a pair of bad bitch heels to make me feel a little better. Paired with my skinny jeans, I look the part of heiress.

Now I just need to believe I can play the part of Queen. Anything less and Harrison Saint will eat me alive.

I pull up my phone and drop a message into the group chat. I assume they already know, but better safe than sorry.

Me:
I've been summoned by Harrison. If I don't see you there, I'll let you know what happens.

Finley:
Had no idea. Keep your phone on, I'll track you. If we don't hear from you in an hour, we're coming for you.

I smile at the phone as I lock up the house and walk down the drive to the waiting car, sending Smithy a message to let him know where I've gone, too.

Can't be too cautious when it comes to Harrison.

The driver climbs from the car and opens the door to the back for me, closing it once I'm settled on the cream leather seats.

It feels like the drive lasts forever, but that could just be my nerves. I stare up at what looks like an office building—a really fucking tall office building. The car pulls to a stop by the front doors and the doorman opens the car with a smile. "Miss Royal, we've been expecting you. If you'll follow me please."

"Uhm, sure?" I climb from the car, trying to look more

confident and put together than I feel, and follow him into the building.

No one pays any attention as we walk through the lobby to the bank of elevators. He pulls a card from his pocket and waves it over the black box on the wall before pushing the button. "Private elevator," he says, like that explains everything.

It only takes a few seconds until it *bings* and the doors open. We enter the car and make the ride up to the forty-fifth floor— which I only know because of the single lit button inside with the number forty-five on it—in silence.

The car *bings* again before the doors slide open. "Have a nice evening, Miss Royal. Mr. Saint is waiting for you."

I step tentatively out of the elevator, looking back as the doors close behind me.

Nope, this doesn't seem ominous at all. Taking a deep breath, I try to calm myself, to build some walls to hide all of my inadequacies that are very much on show before entering the small lobby up here.

My heels click on the marble floor, echoing in the quiet space.

"Good of you to finally join me." Harrison's voice catches me off guard as he appears in a shadowed doorway to the right. "I don't have all night."

He disappears inside the room, so I make my way down the hall, hoping I'm not walking to my death.

I enter the room, closing the door behind me, shocked to discover it's just the two of us.

My phone buzzes in my pocket, but I ignore it. I get the feeling Harrison isn't the type to be ignored because I have a text.

"How can I help you?" I ask as I slide into the chair in front of the desk he's put himself behind. He steeples his fingers, resting his chin on them as he examines me.

"We need to discuss the contract I made with your father."

I nod once, crossing one leg over the other as I lean back in the chair. "What is there to discuss? I was approached by the Knights, on *several* occasions, before I was kidnapped and tortured by one. I'm pretty sure the terms of the contract are clear as to the next steps."

God, I sound way more ballsy than I feel. And if the tic in his jaw is anything to go by, he's pissed. But considering everything he's done since my arrival in Echoes Cove, the shit he's done to Lincoln his entire life, I'm taking the small win.

His nostrils flare as he folds his arms across his chest. "So you wish to take your seat as Regent?"

"I didn't realize there was a choice."

"There is always a choice, Miss Royal." He grins, and my stomach flip flops. "If you can acquire for me the thing I approached you for when you first arrived in the Cove, I'm sure I could arrange to uphold the freedom your father bartered for."

"What is it that you want?"

I hold my breath as he watches me silently, assessing me. It makes me feel fucking dirty the way he watches me so intently.

"Your father was a very powerful man, with access to a lot of information, and a lot of friends in high places. Some in very low places as well. It would seem that as a backup plan, a failsafe as it were, he collected information. On me, our sect, on the Knights as a whole. Information that would be... damning, should it fall into the wrong hands. I want that information, Miss Royal. I want every trace of it returned to me, so that it can be kept... *safe*."

My heart hammers in my chest. "Is that why you had him killed? You hoped Edward would find the information after killing him?"

He smiles, it's so cold that a shiver runs down my spine. "My, my. You are astute, aren't you? I wonder which of your little lap dogs worked it out and told you."

My heart stops at his confirmation.

He killed my dad.

He'd probably have killed me if he could get the information without me.

My mind races, when a single thought screams in my mind.

"What if I have a different deal I want to make?"

He leans back, eyebrow raised, hands clasped in his lap. "And what sort of deal is that?"

"The information, but not just for my freedom. For Lincoln's. For Finley's. For Maverick's. Forever. There is no arranged marriage, no whoring out of your son. All ties are cut, but they are still afforded the same protections I am."

"No deal. I will not lose all four of you."

I shake my head and grit my teeth. Clenching my hands against the arms of the chair so he doesn't see them shake as I push myself to standing. "Then no deal. And now I know the information exists. When I find it, do not think I won't use it."

"Sit down, Miss Royal!" His voice booms around the room, turning my blood to ice in my veins. "The information for their freedom then. But not yours. I wonder, will you sacrifice for them, the way they have for you?"

"If I agree to this, I want their trust funds released instantly. With zero strings. No way for you to take back what is granted."

"You're stronger than I thought you'd be. If we bring you back into the fold, if I agree to your terms, you understand you will become my heir for Regent. You cannot take the seat until your eighteenth birthday."

I nod. "I understand."

He picks up the phone and makes a call, putting it on loudspeaker so I can hear as he speaks to Edward and Charles. As he tells them the deal. They're beyond pissed, but they do not argue.

Next he calls his lawyer, and I wait as he releases the trusts for all three boys. He signs the document emailed to him while we wait on the line, and his lawyer confirms it is done.

"It was nice doing business with you, Miss Royal. You have two weeks to find me the documents your father had or I will pull those three back in so fast their heads will spin, and none of you will ever find another way out."

"I won't fail," I say through gritted teeth. There is no way I'm going to let them down.

He stands, offering me his hand. "Then I accept your deal, Miss Royal."

My legs shake as I rise to my feet. I take his hand, an icy drop of dread running down my spine.

I just sold my soul to the devil, and I'd do it all over again in a heartbeat.

TWENTY-EIGHT

MAVERICK

My knuckles split as I hit the bag again and again. I don't feel the pain. All I feel is the trickle of wet down my fingers and that the bag gets a little slippery. Everyone says not to hit these things with bare knuckles, but how else do you prepare yourself for a real fight?

Real life is a lot more painful. There aren't gloves or wraps to protect you. All you have is yourself and your ability to block out the pain for longer than your opponent.

I've had a lot of practice at blocking out pain. I almost thought I'd become immune to it. Living my life in a numb state.

I thought I had no weaknesses left.

Until Octavia Royal blew back into my life.

I was a fool to think I had conquered pain and fear. Because now I realize that I was just living a half life. A life where I had just become used to the pain because that's all I had left.

But now that she's back, she's buried herself under my skin, and for the first time I can remember, I'm afraid.

Truly afraid.

Because if my dad did kill hers, I think I might lose her. And without her, the only future I have is either turning into my dad or being buried.

I almost don't want to know the truth, it's why I haven't looked at it too hard, but I can't keep hiding from it. The guilt is eating me alive. She might say she doesn't blame me for the actions of my father, but there is no way that she'll look at me the same if it's true.

If I was her, I wouldn't be able to look at me at all. I'm basically his mirror image. I hate it about myself, but there is fuck all I can do about it.

I stop hitting the bag when the slick becomes too much to land a decent hit and lean back against the wall. All day I've tried to distract myself from the fact that I'm here. I've tried to spend as little time at home as I could since my dad nearly killed me, but leaving my mom here alone with him permanently just isn't an option.

If we could be rid of him, life would be much simpler.

I leave my gym and grab a quick shower to wash off the blood and sweat. Mom asked me to be home today and I can't say no to her. She might be just as bad as he is, but she's still my mom. I've never been able to hate her the way I do him. Maybe that makes me weak, Dad sure thinks it does, but it's not something I can change.

I pad downstairs and grab a bowl of cereal, glad for the quiet in the house. It's rarely quiet. They're usually either screaming at each other or my dad is in the basement so my mom blasts music to drown *that* mess out. It doesn't matter that the basement is soundproofed, it's impossible to ignore what happens down there.

Most of the time I'm just thankful it's not my mom or Octavia down there. I'm aware that it makes me a terrible person to ignore it, but I've suffered too much to die at the hands of my father.

I have too much to live for now.

Unless he did kill Stone. If that's the case... well, I don't know what happens then.

Octavia is a better person than I am, a thousand times over, she probably wouldn't hold it against me. But I'd hold it against myself.

She's already too good for me, but I'm too selfish to let that be a reason to give her up... but this, I don't think I'd ever recover if it's true.

I finish eating, and rinse out my bowl, putting it on the draining rack by the sink when I hear my dad on the phone. He sounds pissed.

He walks into the kitchen, eyes dancing with rage as he slams his phone down on the counter. "You."

The single word makes my blood run cold. "What did I do now?"

I try to sound unaffected, bored almost, but his sadistic grin tells me I failed. I grab a bottle of water from the fridge, turning my back to him, which I know is stupid, but I hate that he makes me feel like a scared little boy.

I am not as weak as he'd like to believe.

I hear his footsteps as he strides across the kitchen, and shout when he grabs my hair in his fist, dragging me out of the room toward the basement door.

"Stupid fucking children! None of you know what you've gotten yourselves into. It's time for you to learn."

"What the fuck are you talking about?" I shout as the door slams closed behind me, my hands gripping his, trying to release his hold as he drags me down the steps.

The click of the light switch is all I hear before the pitch black room flickers as the overhead lights come on, bathing the room in an awful yellow light. He throws me to the ground, the crunch of my knees hitting the concrete echoes in the space. I groan at the pain, though it's only a shadow of the pain I've endured at his hands, before I look around the room.

I think I'm going to be sick.

The walls are lined with cages. Some of them occupied, some of them empty. I don't let myself linger on them as I take in the metal table in the middle of the room, lined with more instruments of torture and blood letting than I think I've ever seen in one space.

"What the fuck?"

Edward grins down at me, moving toward the table in the middle of the room. He pulls a gun and points it at my head. "You were a waste of fucking spunk, kid. I should've done this a long time ago."

A whimper behind him steals my attention and I glance over his shoulder.

No.

I look back at him, eyes wide. "I wondered how long till you spotted her. My prized pet. I nearly had the whole collection—her in my cage, his blood on my knife—and the princess would've joined her mom, but then you fucking idiots got in my way. You *keep* getting in the way. I've had enough."

"Emily?"

"Oh she won't answer you, kid, she wants to be here. That Royal knows who her master is. Pity you didn't learn the same lesson."

It takes a second for it all to fall into place in my head. He has her mom, he killed her dad, and he wants her down here too.

Blood rushes through my ears, the roaring all I can hear as I let out a guttural cry, pushing up from the ground, pulling a knife from the table and charging at him.

I knock him backwards, and he laughs as I slash at his forearms.

"Only you would be stupid enough to bring a knife to a gun fight, kid."

I roar again, attacking him with everything I've got, trying to wrestle the gun away from him. The knife clatters on the ground when it falls from my hand, distraction enough for my dad to get the upper hand.

He knocks me to the ground, but I end up pulling him down with me. The pop of the gun going off between our bodies is deafening as we hit the ground, pain tearing through me.

I'm sorry, Octavia.

ACKNOWLEDGMENTS

I swear writing this part of the book is harder than writing the rest of the book.

First, thank you to my besties, my sprint team, my cheerleaders. This series would absolutely not have made the light of day if it wasn't for you guys.

David, you sparkly unicorn you, thank you for everything, including the hilarious laughs when you should 100% be asleep! Thank you for loving these guys, and calling me out when it's needed. For making the words shine and well, for being my social butterfly bitch aha.

Eva, thank you for always being there when I need to gripe, and for well, all the things. If I listed it all I'd be here all damn day ahaha.

To my alpha & beta teams, you guys are freaking rockstars. Lisa, Zoe, Megan, Kiera, Jeni, Liberty, Kyla, Sam, Jessi & Nicole. Thank you for your priceless feedback, and for loving these characters as much as I do.

Thank you to Sarah and Sam for making sure the words shine by the time I'm done fucking around with them, and for letting me corrupt you aha.

Finally, to you the reader, thank you. For taking a chance on an author you've probably never heard of. For picking up a new book. For running the gauntlet with us. Just thank you.

Book 4 won't be long, so I guess I better go dive back into the book cave.

Peace out
xoxo

ABOUT THE AUTHOR

Lily is a writer, dreamer, fur mom and serial killer, crime documentary addict.

She loves to write dark, reverse harem romance and characters who will shatter your heart. Characters who enjoy stomping on the pieces and then laugh before putting you back together again. And she definitely doesn't enjoy readers tears. Nope. Not even a little.

Visit her online:
www.lilywildhart.com

For exclusive content, freebies and giveaways every month.
www.lilywildhart.com/subscribe

ALSO BY LILY WILDHART

THE KNIGHTS OF ECHOES COVE

(Dark, Bully, High School Reverse Harem Romance)

Tormented Royal

Lost Royal

Caged Royal

Forever Royal

**

THE SAINTS OF SERENITY FALLS

(Dark, Bully, Step Brother, College Reverse Harem Romance)

Burn - Pre-Order Now